the ROAD KING Chronicles

the ROAD KING
Chronicles
BLUE RIDGE RUN

HARRY HARRIGAN

CHAPTER 1

NOTHING CLEARS THE crap out of your head like riding a clean line through a tight curve. Doesn't matter if you're ripping up the pavement on a sportbike or chilling on a vintage Vespa. A well-ridden corner just makes you smile.

Unless you're stuck behind a slowpoke, like the old painter's van trundling blithely along ahead of me. I stalked the centerline, searching for a place to pass. When the road finally straightened out, I leaned the bike over and hit the gas.

That's when the girl kicked the rear window. Her foot left a smear on the glass, and it looked like blood to me.

I was riding south on Route 81, winding along the Carolina side of the Georgia-South Carolina border as it follows the Savannah River toward the coast. The chilly rains that had soaked the whole Mid-Atlantic for much of April had finally dribbled away and May was cooperating with perfect riding weather: sunny, but cool enough to zip on a jacket; warm enough to leave the chaps rolled up in the saddlebag.

Last night's impromptu farewell party at Camp Merrill in Dahlonega hadn't broken up until a couple of hours before reveille, so I'd left later than planned but I still had plenty of time to get home, change into my uniform one last time and report to Colonel Forwin at Hunter-Stewart by 1630 hrs. That's 4:30 in the afternoon for civilians and nearly-civilians like me. Today was my last day in the U.S. Army – after twenty-three years, two months and six days, according to the official record keepers – and the colonel insisted that no master sergeant in his command could retire without some sort of ceremony. And then there's the party my friends have set up at the G-String tonight. That is likely to be epic.

If it were up to me, I'd skip the hoorah. Mail me the paperwork and I'll spend the whole day riding instead. In fact, I would rather have kept going north from Dahlonega and headed for the Rolling Thunder tribute ride for Veterans and POWs in Washington, D.C. on Sunday. I've been looking forward to a lot of time in the saddle after I retire. I've had this idea of a "ride-about" percolating in my head ever since 2005, when I'd spent six months in Australia as liaison to the 1st Commando Regiment in Sydney prior to deploying with them to Iraq. My ride-about would be like the Australian Aboriginal "walk-about," except on a motorcycle. No map, no schedule, no destination and most especially no damn phone. Just ride. Stay off the highways. Navigate by the sun and stars, by the weather and intuition. Explore until I feel the urge to make my way back home. Motorcycling nirvana. All it takes is time, money and a motorcycle.

I'm lucky to have all three. The bankroll comes courtesy of an inheritance from my mother's side of the family and twenty years worth of saving every dollar I could squeeze out of my pay. After today I'll have the time – no wife, no kids, no job – and I finally have my old Road King sorted out. It's always been a favorite of mine – a bike as quintessentially American as the 1911 Colt .45 pistol or the 1894 Winchester rifle – but a few improvements on Harley-Davidson's original product were needed to bring out its true potential. Bigger pistons and more aggressive cams, stiffer forks and a set of sticky Pirelli skins on 18-inch Renegade wheels, six piston brake calipers with stainless steel lines and a Mustang seat to keep my butt happy. And I gave it the motorcycle fat farm treatment, stripping off about fifty pounds of metal flab the bike was carrying in lights, roll bars and decorations. The makeover included paint, too. Celtic design gold leaf pin-striping accented with silver shimmers on a new paint job so black and glossy it looks as deep as the ocean on a moonless night. OK, maybe that's more than just a few improvements, but now the bike is worthy of its name.

The painter's van I was passing was just an ordinary work van, its white paint faded to chalk and the rear bumper crimped on the right side from some long ago parking mishap. Two battered and paint-speckled aluminum extension ladders were bungeed to its sturdy roof rack. A red, white and blue magnetic sign, plastered slightly askew on the right side back door, advertised house painting by Trident Home Services, licensed and insured. A Birmingham address on the sign, Alabama plates on the van. A fair hike from these parts, but you take work where you can get it, right?

As I cleared the back of the van, I noticed the model name, *SAVANA*, out of the corner of my eye. It was printed on the left rear door with one of those little silver plastic badges the automakers love. I was headed home to Savannah, so the coincidental closeness of the name caught my attention. It was nothing really – the inconsequential, corner-of-your-eye kind of thing that sticks in your brain for a microsecond and then is gone and forgotten.

But that was also the precise moment someone's bloody bare foot bumped the window.

The back windows of the van were tinted dark enough that normally you'd have to press your face against the glass and cup your hands around your eyes in order to see inside. If I hadn't been looking in the right direction, I wouldn't have seen a thing. I did see it though, and it stuck in my brain as I rocketed past. I played it back a couple of times like a video loop, and each time I came to the same troubling conclusion: the owner of the foot was most likely female and she was definitely in distress.

I eased off the throttle and checked my rear view mirrors. The van had faded half a football field back, but I could see that both front seats were occupied. Hard to tell from this distance, but it looked like two men, both young and white. Not unusual by itself, but if two guys are riding in both front seats – normally the only two seats in a utility van – what the hell is happening in the back?

The road meandered through an undeveloped stretch of Sumter National Forest for the next four or five miles, with no signs of life other than one lonely gaggle of seedy trailer homes and a couple of hunter's blinds along the edge of a field. A log truck piled high with naked pine boles rattled by in the opposite direction, but otherwise the road was deserted. I lowered my speed to a more moderate pace, but the van still receded. Eventually it dropped completely out of sight. Another three miles down the road I pulled onto the cracked concrete drive of a defunct gas station on the outskirts of the next small town. I eased in behind the old pumps and waited for the van to catch up.

After ten minutes, it still hadn't gone by. I ran over the route in my head. Between here and the point where I had first encountered the van, only two roads intersected Route 81. Both were dirt roads; both marked off limits except to authorized vehicles, presumably forest service personnel.

I sat there a few more minutes, listening to the tick, tick of the Road King's v-twin cooling in the morning breeze. I checked my watch – plenty of time to get home, change and ride over to Hunter-Stewart. Anyway, what happens if you're late for your own retirement? They throw you out? I thumbed the starter button, kicked the gear lever down into first, let the clutch out and pointed the Harley back the way I'd come.

I slowed at the first dirt road, but one look told me the van hadn't turned there. The road was smooth red clay, dry as a bone. It looked like a tennis court awaiting a title match. Any vehicle passing down that road would have stirred up an orange dust storm, and I couldn't see any lingering cloud of it in the air.

The second road, another two miles north along 81, looked much more likely. This one was a gravel-lined fire road that cut straight back into the woods and then curved northwest and out of sight. I turned onto the gravel and rode gingerly along for almost a mile before I found an opening in the trees where I could tuck the bike off the road. With a flat rock wedged under the side stand to prevent the heavy Harley from toppling over on the soft dirt, I stripped off my helmet, gloves and jacket and left them on the seat. Wishing I was armed with more than the little Spyderco folding knife I keep clipped to my belt, I headed through the trees, keeping well back from the road.

About a quarter mile from where I'd left the Harley, I stopped short of a sandy clearing near a reservoir created by a dam on one of the tributaries linked to the Savannah River. A sign near the water warned that swimming in the reservoir is prohibited. Judging by the scattered, sun-bleached Budweiser cans and a circle of stones around a pile of ash, that sign didn't keep the kids from partying here occasionally. The white van had been driven around the old fire pit and was parked on a patch of firm sand at the end of the gravel, facing out along the road.

I eased around to the right, where the trees offered concealment almost down to the water, and crouched behind the broken stump of an old pine. I stopped maybe thirty feet from the van, which sat facing away from me with the rear doors open. Sunlight ricocheted through the windshield and into the van, illuminating my view of the interior. It contained none of the paint and brushes you would expect a painting service to require; none of the metal shelves filled with rollers and buckets, none of the air compressors and extension cords.

Instead, I saw the bottoms of two pairs of feet. One pair, bare and toes-up, kicked ineffectually in the air. Pale buttocks pumped above the other pair of feet, which were clad in black-soled running shoes. Hastily dropped blue jeans were still bunched around the ankles that lurched back and forth on the grimy, gray-striped mattress lining the van's floor.

A male voice said, "Yeah, baby, yeah! You know what I like!"

The bare feet kicked futilely again and I heard a spitting noise from inside the van. The sharp crack of a swift slap was followed by an anguished and weary sounding groan. Keeping low, I moved further around, toward the right side of the van.

Two other men, presumably the two I had seen in the front seats earlier, were standing by the open side doors. Each man held two thick pointed sticks sharpened at one end, like stakes for a circus tent. They tapped the sticks together, creating a rhythm for their buddy, and called out encouragements.

"Yo, Peter! She got you with that goober, boy!"

"Give it to her, Petey! Who the man? Who the man?"

I was moving before I thought about it, two decades of intense Ranger training and three combat tours kicking in automatically. Coming quiet and quick from their left, I was nearly on them before the cheerleading duo saw me. I booted the closest one behind the knees and swept him onto his back. He was still rebounding from his sudden impact with the ground when I tromped my left heel down hard on his throat, locked my knee and pivoted to face the second man.

That's when the situation went south.

I thought the guy I'd already taken out was the more dangerous of the two. He was tall and rangy, with flat slabs of muscle under a tight black T-shirt and heavy boots that looked they had been made for the sole purpose of kicking the shit out of people. But the second guy – a pudgy, soft-looking kid with a blond crew cut and a trucker's gut – dropped his sticks and snatched a revolver out of his pants with the reflexes of a rattlesnake.

If he'd pulled the trigger as soon as the barrel pointed my way, he would have killed me. In the lifetime it took him to extend his arm, I ducked under the weapon and body-slammed him into the van. I pinned him with my shoulders and hammered his rib cage with my fists. Left-right, left-right, left-right; solid jabs with enough impact to jar my forearms all the way to the elbow. He exhaled an explosive little "ooff!" with each punch, but the punishment didn't seem to discourage him. He jerked the trigger and the pistol boomed next to my head. The muzzle blast scorched my forehead and set off a deafening ringing in my left ear. I wedged him hard against the van, but he managed to work the pistol down until the barrel was nearly between us. I clamped both hands on it and pushed up.

Maybe twenty seconds had passed since my first kick, but

we were both panting like defensive linemen after a double set of wind sprints. I had him off balance against the van, but his left hand was free and he punched me three times in the side of the head. Bam! Bam! Bam! Hard shots that exploded fireworks in my eyes. He grunted in satisfaction and worked the gun down another dangerous inch. I cupped my right hand over the top of the pistol and clamped my fingers around the cylinder. With enough hand strength, I could lock it in place and keep him from firing.

His breath rasped in my face, wet and sour as old beer. His small eyes, nearly hidden in the folds of his grimace, gleamed with an alarming determination. He hit me on the temple again, shooting off more sparklers in my right eye, and gaining another half inch. I tucked my forearms in close to my chest and locked my wrists.

He stopped punching. He hooked his left hand on the back of my neck and pulled us even closer. The warm barrel of the pistol touched my ear like an electric prod. He bunched his shoulders and heaved. The gun slid further down my neck. The front sight raked across my jaw and jammed into the soft tissue underneath. His grimace turned to a grin. I suddenly realized he was enjoying this.

I felt the cylinder of the revolver turn in my grip.

"Hey, hey," he said. "Here she comes!"

I squeezed with everything I had. The cylinder rotated another fraction and the hammer cocked back a notch.

A sad, disbelieving voice in my head whispered that I was going to die now. Right here in the South Carolina countryside on a glorious spring day, less than a hundred miles from home at the hand of a chubby cretin with a big gun.

A harder, calmer voice near the back of my brain said, "Fuck that."

I screwed both feet into the sand and shoved with adrenaline-fueled desperation.

Boom!

The gun fired, loud and shocking as a lightning strike. Both of us had a death grip on it, but the recoil nearly jerked it out of our hands. The bullet missed my chin by a fraction, tore upwards through his neck and exited out the back of his head. With the lethal impact only a big hollow point magnum can impart, it ripped open the back of his skull in a horrific explosion of tissue and bone. It sucked the meanness out of his eyes and sprayed his brains in a bloody, dripping mess on the side of the van.

In the sudden silence I became acutely aware of my own heart thump-thumping on. My chest worked like a bellows, whooshing that sweet southern air in and out of my lungs. My face tingled where this second muzzle blast burned the skin on the point of my chin and along my right cheek. It felt cold as ice, but I knew the needles of pain would come in a minute or so.

I straightened up, took a step back. His limp hand let me have the gun without protest. He toppled sideways, smearing a greasy red arc of blood and brain across the white paint.

I spun, found the third guy at the rear of the van. He had crawled out and was bent over, hands shaking while he tried to get his pants untangled enough to pull them up. It didn't help that he was standing on the end of his belt, a thick black job with a red and white Confederate flag buckle the size of a dinner plate. When I cocked the revolver, he looked up.

"Please, Mister," he said. "Oh please, don't kill me."

His face was screwed up like a pathetic child. Tears streamed from his eyes. A clear glob of syrupy snot dangled from one nostril. He raised both hands. A heavy class ring with a red stone on his right hand had been twisted around to face his palm. It fit his finger tight enough that I figured he had turned it deliberately to inflict more pain when he slapped the girl. A thick gold Rolex glittered on his left wrist. His trousers had dropped into a heap around his ankles when he had raised his hands.

"Shut up, weenie boy," I said, stepping behind him quickly. I grabbed the fingers of his right hand in my left, levered his wrist into a come-along hold and exerted enough pressure to drop him to his knees.

"Pleeeaase!" he squealed, his voice rising to a shrill falsetto. I kept the pressure steady.

I risked a quick glance at the first man, the one I'd stomped in the throat. He was motionless; flat on his back, mouth wide open, his face a cold graveyard blue, eyes bulging, slack fingers uselessly prying at his crushed larynx. As stone dead as his brainless friend. I let the hammer down gently on the pistol, shoved it into my waistband and turned my full attention to pants-down-boy.

"Get up!" I said, delivering a fresh shot of sharp pain to his hand through the come-along. He yelped once like a pathetic puppy and struggled to his feet again. I dragged him across the sand and pine needles to the side door of the van. The trousers around his ankles forced him into the shuffling gait of a prison inmate wearing leg irons. Looking into the van, I saw a woman lying on the mattress. She was tied spread eagle, hands stretched out tight over her head.

I gave my captive another taste of pain to ensure his cooperation while I slipped the knife off my belt. I opened it one-handed and cut the ropes holding her left hand. She groaned and her arm dropped to her side. I had this guy under control for now, but I didn't want to risk letting him get away when I reached inside to cut her other limbs loose. I flipped the knife around so I had it by the blade and held it out. With only a slight hesitation, she took it from my hand and freed herself.

I backed away with weenie boy to give her room. For better control, I changed my grip, twisting both of his arms high up behind his back and holding him up on his toes in front of me. The girl worked her way feet-first out of the van and stood up.

She was completely naked.

Bronze skin, gleaming with sweat. Dark hair, matted and nearly black. Cut short, but not pixie cute. First guess, I'd have said five six, maybe five seven. Broad shoulders, long legs, small-ish breasts. Mid to late twenties, although given the present circumstances I could have been way off. Serious runner slim, abs you only get from dedicated stomach crunches.

Her upper lip had a puffy knot crusted with dried blood. Along the left side, the bottom of her jaw was swollen sausage tight. A cluster of angry crescent bruises that looked suspiciously like bite marks marred the smooth skin high up on her left thigh. The rough ropes had abraded red bracelets into her wrists and ankles, but she ignored the blood that seeped from these wounds onto her hands and feet.

She raised her head and fixed her eyes on my prisoner. They were dark brown with flecks of gold in the irises and pupils as black as the inside of a coffin. Any man who thinks women cannot be warriors has not seen a look like that. It stopped the wind in the trees and muted the noisy cries of the ravens wheeling in the sky. I swear it frosted the sweat on my neck.

With a shock, I realized I had seen her before. Six or seven months ago. Dressed, of course. I hadn't spoken to her, but I'd seen her over at Hunter Army Airfield, wearing a Nomex flight suit. A friend told me later that she was an Apache gunship pilot from one of the 3rd Infantry Division's Aviation Brigades. He wasn't sure exactly which unit, but he'd heard she'd done two combat tours and was getting out soon. I remembered the name tag on her uniform read Captain Ridge.

She held my knife out, waist high. Sliced the air. Left, then right. She waited. After a long, stupid second it dawned on me – she wanted me to hold him while she cut his dick off. Fine with me. Exactly what the asshole deserved. I jacked his arms up between his shoulder blades until he yelped, pulled him close to keep him steady. Then I nodded to the girl.

She rushed him, but the blade came up, not down. She slashed at the side of his neck and sawed away with such savage ferocity she almost cut his head off. She nearly caught my cheek with the blade before I tucked my chin to the right, out of the path of the knife. Bright gouts of blood gushed out of him, painting her face a dripping mask of red. She didn't step back, didn't flinch. She just wiped her eyes clear with the back of her other hand. She blinked once, then watched intently as he pumped his life out in rapidly diminishing spurts. Those dark eyes blazed briefly, the flecks in them glowing like molten gold.

He sagged and I had to brace myself to hold him up. When he was gone she reached down, hacked some more with the knife and stepped back with his cock in her hand. She heaved the bloody, flaccid flesh toward the river. It landed in the water with a plop. The biggest crow I'd ever seen, a jet black bird the size of a vulture, swooped down and nimbly snatched the morsel from the water. Two smaller birds tried to steal it, but he shook them off and flew out of sight with his prize.

I dropped the body in the sand and took the knife from her.

"Come on," I said, guiding her down to the little beach. "Let's wash up."

Amazingly, I wasn't covered in blood. All the gory splatter had been directed away from me. I walked into the water fully clothed anyway, and she walked with me. It was cold enough to raise goose bumps on her arms, but she didn't complain. The lake bottom sloped gradually, a mix of sand, pebbles and tiny white shells that was easy to walk on. When we were waist deep, she took a deep breath and ducked under. I kept one hand on her arm, partly to steady her, partly to make sure she came back up. She surfaced twice to breathe, less bloody each time. When she was as clean as she was going to get without soap, I started to strip off my shirt for her.

"No," she said. "My clothes… in van."

I offered my hand for support again, but she managed the walk back to the van on her own. While she retrieved her clothes and dressed, I sloshed over to a stump, sat down, and drained my boots. The disadvantage of fully waterproof boots, like my Alpenstars, is that when you pour a gallon into each from the top, it stays in. I tugged the soggy boots back on over soggy socks, then I searched the bodies.

All three had wallets in their back pockets. I had to shake my head at their arrogance. Or stupidity. Or both, since the two conditions are so often mutually supportive.

The pudgy-but-snake-quick kid with the pistol was named Drew Worthington. His Alabama license gave a Huntsville address. I took his revolver out of my waistband and looked it over. A polished nickel Colt Python with a four inch barrel. Nice pistol, but shiny is for wheels, not weapons. I carefully wiped my prints off it with the tail of his shirt and stuck it back in his pants. I had to lift a saddlebag of fat around his waist to get the barrel behind his belt and I marveled again at how damned fast he had pulled it on me.

The second guy, the one whose windpipe I'd crushed, was Jonathan Billings. Another citizen the good people of Huntsville would be horrified to know had lived among them. Skin-tight jeans and a form-fitting Under Armor T-shirt showed off the chiseled physique of a body builder. If he was still alive, I'm sure he'd have to be mortified by how quickly he went down, but that's how things usually went in a fight. Hesitate and you die.

The freshly neutered one was called Peter Nelson. The smiling photo on his driver's license gave no inkling that someday he'd be a corpse with a slashed throat and a dick-less crotch. Like his partners, Peter hailed from Huntsville.

Standing there with their wallets in my hand, I suddenly realized that these three were the so-called Roaster Rapists. The case had been in the news on and off over the last year. Some moron writing for one of the supermarket tabloids had tagged them the Roaster Rapists because they staked their victims to the ground and burned them into cinders.

Four horribly burned bodies had been found, two in Tennessee, one in Georgia and one in Mississippi. Some kind of homemade napalm had been used, gasoline mixed with oil and magnesium powder to intensify the fire. The theory – in this era of too much television CSI – was that the rapists were using the fires to destroy any microscopic or DNA evidence they had left on the bodies. Whatever they were doing, it had worked. And they were smart enough to stay away from home, to move around. The FBI had been brought in, and all they could add after their analysis of the crimes was that at least two men were involved, possibly as many as four. Twelve months later, they still had zip.

The woman I had rescued was dressed now. Blue jeans, black boots, long sleeve pastel yellow cotton shirt. She zipped on a pale gray jacket. I recognized it as a riding jacket, one of the short-waisted Cordura models from Joe Rocket with flexible armor in the elbows and shoulders. Her wet hair was still plastered to her head, like a slick black helmet.

She said, "Thank you, uh…"

"Roman," I said, "Roman Keane. My friends call me RK."

"I'm Rose Ridge," she said. She paused, then she added, "Winter Rose." Her eyes widened and she said, "I haven't used that name in years."

"Suits you, though," I said. "Cherokee?"

She nodded.

I had been thinking Mediterranean, but when she said her name it finally dawned on me that her ancestry was much closer to home. The reservation of the Eastern Band of Cherokee was not far from here, nestled up against the Great Smoky Mountains National Park in North Carolina.

I touched the padded shoulder of her jacket. "You were riding when they grabbed you?"

She looked down at her clothes in surprise, like they were artifacts from some long ago, long forgotten life.

She raised her head again and I thought she might cry for the first time. She hugged herself, though, and kept a tenuous grip on her composure.

"On my Ninja," she said.

Obviously talking hurt her mouth, but she took a breath and went on. "Rode the Dragon with some friends."

"I know it," I said.

The Tail of the Dragon is an eleven mile stretch of one curve after another along Route 129 in Tennessee, just north of the North Carolina border. I've ridden it twice, once at a leisurely pace on the Road King and once with more velocity on a Suzuki Bandit. It's a favorite with the sportbike riders, but it's great fun on any motorcycle and nothing will make you understand counter steering better than three hundred and eleven back-to-back turns.

"I came back alone," she said. "Yesterday… late yesterday. I saw them in a gas station south of Toccoa. They left before me… faked an accident down the road, near a little turn off with a picnic table. Like an idiot, I stopped."

"Anybody would have," I said.

She nodded, but judging by the misery still reflected in her eyes, she didn't believe it.

"That one," she said, pointing at the big muscled guy whose throat I had stomped flat, "hit me on the jaw. It felt like my head exploded."

She fingered the swollen line of her jaw and grimaced. She squeezed her eyes shut and rubbed them with the heels of her hands, then pressed her palms to her forehead and took a deep breath. When she opened her eyes again, she looked down instead of at me. Determined not to cry, I thought.

"I couldn't believe how much it hurt," she said.

I nodded again, sympathetically. It's not like TV, where the hero gets slugged in the face and jumps up with a big wide grin. A hard punch can do as much damage as a baseball bat.

"I tried to… to fight back," she said, "but I… I could hardly lift my hands. Two of them shoved me into the van. I think the other one rolled my bike into the woods."

"I have some friends who can look for it," I said. "First, let's get you a doctor." I gestured at the van. "If you can stand to ride in this thing again – front seat this time – I'll take you to the nearest hospital."

She raised her head and shook it violently, then immediately raised both hands to her temples. Clearly the head shake thing had not been a good idea.

"No," she said when the pain subsided enough to let her talk. "No doctors. No police."

She pierced me with the Valkyrie eyes she had used before. She waved a hand around the clearing, taking in the van and the bodies.

"I am not going to re-live this again and again," she said, "for every cop, every lawyer and every reporter who thinks he has to know every morbid, juicy detail."

In spite of her swollen lip, she managed to tack an impressive and steadily increasing degree of disdain on the words *cop*, *lawyer* and *reporter*.

"Your prints and DNA are all over that van," I pointed out. "On those bodies, too. They'll identify you sooner or later."

She gave me the eyes again. This time fear peeked out from among the gold flecks. The tears she'd been holding back finally welled up, spilling over her long lashes and down her cheeks.

"Help me again, Roman Keane," she said. "Please?"

Damn. I surveyed the scene, pivoting slowly through a full circle. The sun was nearly overhead, casting a hard, bright light down on the clearing. It looked like a mini-battlefield. Three dead bodies. Big stains in the sand where two of them had shed so much blood.

I glanced up the access road. Still empty. We were alone except for the buzzing flies already attracted to the carnage.

Maybe I could use the shovel that was strapped to the roof

rack with the ladders to spread fresh sand over the bloody spots, but then there was the van. The bloody splatter and arc left by the first guy looked like a grisly red shooting star on the white paint. No hiding that mural from hell unless I had a fire hose and a bucket of hot, soapy water.

I spotted the wooden stakes on the ground. A thought scratched tentatively at the back door of my brain. I checked the inside of the van. I found a flat black full face helmet between the seats that must be Winter Rose's. They had apparently shoved her, helmet and all, into the van when they took her. Beneath the helmet was a white plastic pail. It was one of the five gallon jobs, the kind they use for bulk paint. I set the helmet aside, lifted the pail out and pried the lid off. A pungent petroleum smell floated out. As I pounded the lid back in place with the heel of my hand, a plan tumbled into place in my head. We'd use fire to erase ourselves from this whole mess. If this flammable concoction worked for them, it could work for us. But we had to move quickly.

I shoved the pail to the side and grabbed the nearest corpse by the shoulders.

"Give me a hand," I said, dragging him to the open side door of the van. "Help me get them inside."

We hoisted them in like sacks of dirty laundry, rolling and shoving each one over to make room for the next. Then I shoveled sand like a madman, throwing as much as I could over the biggest of the dark stains. When it was well covered, I put Winter Rose to work moving the circle of rocks from the old fire pit into place over the stain I'd just covered with fresh sand. By the time I was finished with the other stains, she had re-located the entire circle.

"Perfect," I said.

Using the shovel, I carefully scooped the ashes and charred wood from the old fire circle to the new one, further disguising the bloody area. If my plan worked, nobody was going to be looking too closely at this area anyway. I threw the shovel into the van on top of the bodies and swung the doors shut. I made one last circuit to check that no obvious signs of the struggle remained. I helped Winter Rose into the passenger seat and climbed behind the wheel.

I reached for the ignition and mentally kicked myself. The keys! For an instant I thought I'd have to dig through dead pockets for them, but I found them wedged behind the visor. I started the van and drove slowly out the gravel road, stopping just beyond my Road King.

"Here's where the plan gets tricky," I said. "On the main road about two miles south of here, another dirt road leads into the woods. I'm going to drive the van in there and douse it inside and out with the jellied gasoline in that white pail."

I didn't point out that it was the same stuff they planned to use to burn her to a clue-less crisp, but I sensed her shudder.

I said, "I think it'll burn hot enough to eliminate any evidence that could lead to you."

"What about all the blood we just buried in the clearing back there?" she asked.

"I don't think anyone will look any further than the van," I said. "I haven't left any fingerprints on their driver's licenses. I'll use my gloves when I take those out of the wallets and leave them on the road. Even out here the fire and smoke will attract attention pretty quick. These are Forest Service roads – somebody will check it out. And if some smart cop doesn't come up with the Roaster Rapists connection right away, I know someone who can discreetly tip off the FBI. The whole thing will focus on Huntsville and the other victims after that."

She was quiet for a moment, then she said, "You need me to ride your Harley."

I nodded.

"It's heavy," I said. "Nearly twice as heavy as your sportbike."

"I can do it," she said.

I didn't doubt her for a minute. Anyone who can handle a wickedly fast Kawasaki wouldn't have trouble with the Harley. Unless it fell over on top of her. I slipped into my jacket and gloves, then backed the bike out onto the road and climbed off. She lifted a knee to straddle the seat, but a shot of pain made her drop her leg. She caught herself with the handlebar and stood for a minute with her head down, her breath hissing through her clenched teeth.

"Guess I need some help here," she said, raising her head.

I walked around to the other side of the bike and reached across to steady her shoulders. When she lifted her knee this time, I put a hand under her calf and helped her stretch her leg over the seat. She settled down carefully, denying the pain by breathing through her clamped jaw. She lifted her right foot onto the floorboard, then looked up at me. I reached into the van and retrieved her helmet.

She eased it onto her head. A quick groan escaped her lips when she squeezed it down over her swollen jaw. She let the straps hang. She lifted the bike off the side stand and balanced it with her toes on the gravel.

Before I could give her any instructions, she turned the ignition on, flipped the run switch from *off* to *on* and started it up. I grinned.

"Stop short of the main road, where any passing cars can't

see you," I said. "Shut it off and wait until you see the smoke. Ten minutes, tops. OK? Then ride out and turn left. Two miles. You'll see me standing by the road."

She gave me a brief, emphatic nod.

I grabbed my helmet, jumped back in the van and drove to the end of the gravel. She followed a hundred yards back and stopped when I stopped. The Road King's headlight winked out. Good girl.

I drove to the red clay road I'd seen earlier. Nothing like driving a van full of bodies to raise your heart rate and get you checking the rear view mirror every two seconds. Fortunately, I made it without seeing another vehicle and turned into the woods.

Well in from the paved road, I stopped. Belated second thoughts about how well the nice smooth clay outside would show footprints set me scrounging for something to wrap around my boots. Those damned CSI shows even had me worrying about evidence now. Gloves still on, I ripped four strips of duct tape from a roll I found next to the mattress and stuck two on the bottom of each boot. Not the best solution, but it should make my footprints untraceable.

My initial plan was to let the fire do all the work, but when I spotted a rag stuffed in a pouch on the back of the passenger seat, I used it to wipe down the steering wheel and anything else I might have touched before I donned the gloves. Next task was to find an ignition source. One of them had to have matches or a lighter. What are the chances that all three of these morons were non-smokers? The second pocket I searched yielded a disposable butane lighter. I flicked it and was rewarded with a satisfying flame. I stuffed it in my pocket.

Working quickly, I extracted the three driver's licenses and threw the wallets on the bodies. I pried the lid off the gasoline mix again. Stepping inconsiderately on the bodies, I sloshed it front to rear. The fumes were so toxic they burned my eyes and nearly triggered a coughing fit. I slipped twice on the uneven footing, but I coated everything liberally without spilling any on myself. I tied the rag around the handle of the shovel, dipped it in the last of the goop and left it on the ground.

Standing clear, I picked up the shovel and took out the lighter. I thought for a second, then cursed my stupidity when I realized I'd left the driver's licenses and my helmet on the front seat. I retrieved them, tossed the licenses on the ground where they wouldn't burn but couldn't be missed. I looked at the three plastic cards in the red dirt and decided to add a couple of the wooden stakes. For good measure I popped the fake magnetic sign off the back of the van and threw that on the evidence pile too.

I put on my helmet, then stood there for a moment while I ran another mental checklist. Couldn't think of anything. Time to roll.

I lit the rag on the shovel handle and almost burned myself when it ignited with a whoosh. Whatever they used, that stuff was the arsonist's dream accelerant. I stepped back until I was almost in the woods and launched the shovel like a flaming spear into the van.

I spun and lifted my boot to run, but the whole thing went up with a huge thumping *whooomp*. The shock wave slammed me down like a backhand from a giant. The thick bed of pine needles covering the ground under the trees cushioned my landing, but a glob of burning gel splashed onto my boot. I slapped at it with my gloved hand and only managed to spread the fire around. I finally smothered it with a handful of dirt. I pushed myself up and shook my head in amazement. Whatever those idiots mixed in the bucket, it was hot. A couple of white phosphorus grenades wouldn't have created a fire that intense. I stripped the duct tape from the soles of my boots, wadded it into a tight ball and pitched it into the blaze.

Then I scrambled to my feet and ran for the main road, a task made easier by the way the forest service had planted the pine trees in nice straight rows. Winter Rose was waiting astride the Harley. She'd had the presence of mind to keep the bike on the pavement to avoid leaving tire tracks in the clay shoulder. I threw a leg over the tank and she pushed herself slowly and carefully onto the backseat. I kicked the bike into gear and we pulled away.

I felt her shift on the pillion now and then, and once when there was no traffic, she stood on the passenger foot boards and let the wind wash over her for a couple of minutes. Otherwise she rode in stoic silence. Tough woman. I bought some aspirin and bottled water for her at a little country store twenty miles down the road. As we passed by Augusta, I tapped her knee lightly to get her attention.

"Hungry?" I said.

We rolled on so far that I thought she hadn't heard me. I was just about to ask again, when I heard her reply, nearly as faint as a whisper.

"Milkshake?"

What the hell was I thinking? She'd like a double cheese-burger? A milkshake, of course. She couldn't chew with her jaw swollen like that. I pulled into a convenient Dairy Queen and picked up a small vanilla for her. We sat at a rickety picnic table by ourselves, behind the property where they had left a shady row of sweet gum trees. While she sipped her shake, I told her about my old friend Perry Lukens.

"He's a retired Special Forces surgeon," I said. "He's the best."

She turned her head looked up at the trees while she thought about it. When she brought her gaze back to me, I could see the "no" on her face. Before she could speak, I raised a hand and added, "He works for himself and he knows how to keep his mouth shut."

She sat silently for another couple of minutes, slowly turning the milkshake cup on the table. Finally, she took a deep breath and nodded once. I pulled out my phone and called Perry. He agreed to meet us at my house.

CHAPTER 2

I RODE STATE ROAD 25 south from Augusta, jumped on 80 after Statesboro and stayed five over the speed limit all the way down past I-95 to Route 17. The Interstate takes all the trucks and snowbirds, leaving Route 17 the crumbs of local traffic. Cruise down that old road at the posted 45 mph and what you'll see is mostly pine forest and marshland with a scattering of transmission shops, used car lots, family restaurants and little churches. Lots of little churches. Wooden churches with peeling white paint about the size of the average two car garage, red brick churches with slate covered steeples and arch-fronted concrete churches made of stucco covered cinder block. Show me a photo of any picturesque little church anywhere in the world, and I'll find you one like it on a back road somewhere in Georgia.

I turned off Route 17 at an intersection where the corners are occupied by a boarded-up BBQ joint, a mom and pop convenience store owned by a South Korean family whose unfailing politeness makes a Canadian tour guide seem rude by comparison, and of course two churches. The cross road is called Sky Hill Lane, although I've never been able to figure out where the

"Hill" part comes from, because you'd need a surveyor's instruments to detect any rise in elevation.

I rode past the first church, which grandly calls itself the "New Reform Pentecostal Church of the Holy Gospel," but is lodged in a pre-fab metal building that looks like a roller rink with one big stained glass window. I turned into the driveway behind the other church, on the east side of Route 17.

"I don't need a church," she said, staying seated when I cut the engine.

"It's not a church," I said. "At least not anymore. It's my house."

"*This* is your house?" she asked.

"You bet," I said. "Go ahead and dismount."

As I held the bike steady, Winter Rose climbed off and stood in the drive, helmet in her hands. A look of amazement spread over her face, in spite of her battered lips and jaw.

"You live in a church!"

"Yeah," I said, "but not just any church. This is the church my mother dragged me and my twin brother Virgil to every Sunday as kids. Man, I hated it."

"So you bought it?" she said, walking back out the drive a bit to get a better look at the place.

"Better me than the State of Georgia. The highway department was the next highest bidder when the property was auctioned off. They wanted to tear it down and build a maintenance facility here. After I outbid them, they bought another place about three miles down the road, in a better location for them, closer to 95."

Winter Rose looked over at the old church marquee, which I had left out by the road. It was still decorated with three purple crosses and a bouquet of white lilies.

"Life's an adventure – make yours a damn good one," she read aloud.

"I found a cardboard box full of plastic letters when I was clearing stuff out. So I put my own messages up there now," I said. "Probably not one you needed to see today, but it's better than the trite crap Pastor Jameson used to come up with, like 'Exposure to the son may prevent burning.' "

I unlocked the door and pushed it open.

"Come on in," I said, moving to one side to let her by.

She stepped around me – and stopped. She stood there silently for a moment, taking it in. Then she looked over to me and said, "You're right. It's not a church anymore. You've made it into a house."

"Actually, I hired an architect for the makeover. Turned out great, didn't it?"

I have to admit, I'm still pleased by the results. The front aspect of the church – two tall arched windows of cut glass flanking a larger arched door – had been retained, so it still looked like a little white-painted, wooden country church. The inside had been gutted, with most of the pews going to the chapel in a halfway house run by my brother Virgil, along with the altar and a stained glass window in the shape of a cross that had been mounted high on the back wall. A modern kitchen had been installed where the altar had been, and the main part was now an open area for both living and dining. The high vaulted ceiling made the space airy and inviting. I'd had new floors laid over the old, made of real hickory with dark knots and bold grains swirling around the edges of throw rugs I'd sent back from Turkey, Fiji, Thailand, Egypt and other places I'd traveled over my years in the Army.

Peter Lik's *Tree of Life* photograph hangs on the side wall of the living room, between two tall, narrow windows with more cut glass. It is a huge, stunning print that invites you to climb right onto the lush green grass in the foreground and bask in the golden glow beneath the branches. On the facing wall I've hung a poster size print of a photo I took myself during a ride out to the west coast. It's another tree, a lone cottonwood by the side of Highway 50 in Nevada, festooned with shoes. All kinds of foot-wear – sneakers, flip-flops, dress shoes – hang from its branches like overripe fruit. The absurd contrast of the two trees always reminds me that if you get through the day without at least one good laugh, you're taking life too seriously.

My only other wall hangings are antique maps. One is a mosaic of original Arbuckle coffee card maps. As a kid I'd collected all fifty in the series of state and territory maps, which were included with packets of Arbuckle Ariosa coffee in the 1880s. I'm always reminded of the power of history to dress up the truth when I see the map of Oklahoma which, at the time it was printed, was simply called *Indian Territory*. My other treasure is an original Johann Baptiste Homann map of eastern North America, drawn in 1720. It is an exquisite creation, with incredible detail and colors still bright after centuries. I bought it at an auction for $2,500. The item which sold immediately after my Homann map was a baseball signed by Micky Mantle. The damn baseball went for $6,700. I wasn't really surprised. I often find that what is important to most people is different from what is important to me.

Off to our left, a slab of Italian granite matching the stone in the kitchen is flanked by a pair of the old pews, forming an extra large breakfast nook capable of seating ten, though I'd never served bacon and eggs to more than two.

"Down that hall," I said, "is the new section of the house,

which was added during the renovation. It's got the master suite, a guest bedroom and a second bath. Out back is a separate building, also new. It covers a big patch of the old church parking lot and has a three bay garage with a large workshop. I use the space over the top of the garage as a gym.

As I started to close the front door, Doc Lukens turned into the drive.

CHAPTER 3

I CAN WALK NORMALLY today because five years ago Dr. Perry Lukens kept them from cutting off my right leg just above the knee. On the way back to base after a mission to ambush and destroy a suspected insurgent weapons shipment, I was riding shotgun in a Defender – the lightweight special ops vehicle built for the Rangers by Rover – when a roadside bomb blew off the right front wheel. The mass of the vehicle absorbed a good deal of the blast, but a piece of shrapnel, about the size of a silver dollar, tore away most of my knee. Three other surgeons in the combat support hospital wanted to amputate. Doc Lukens said no, for which I'll be eternally grateful.

The result is an ugly mess of scars and dimpled transplanted skin, but it works. I've learned how to walk on the metal joint without even a hint of a limp. I haven't mastered running quite as well. Tendon and muscle damage makes it hard to swing my foot forward smoothly when I'm in a hurry. Heat doesn't bother me much, but a sudden cold snap will make my entire right leg ache like a son of a bitch.

After docking his big white Lincoln Town Car behind my bike, the doctor reached into the back seat and pulled out two large, over-stuffed leather physician's bags. He walked through the door, ignored me except to shove both bags into my hands, and focused on Winter Rose.

"Doc Lukens," I said, using the bag in my right hand as a pointer, "this is Winter Rose."

He held her by the elbow with one hand, gently cupped the other on the side of her head, and ran his eyes over the damage done to her face. The swelling looked about the same, but the dark bruises on her skin were now tinged with a ghastly looking saffron. He shook his head slowly and said, "Ah, my dear, my dear. Come, come. Let's get you fixed up."

The tension slipped visibly from her shoulders and I could tell that Winter Rose was already transferring her trust to Dr. Lukens. I wasn't surprised. He wasn't simply a superb physician, he *looked* every bit the part. Fifty-something and trim. Maybe half an inch shorter than me, which put him a hair under six feet. He'd been a varsity squash player during his pre-med days at Yale, and although my knee kept me from court games, I heard that he still swung a mean racquet. He was impeccably dressed as always. Gleaming burgundy leather loafers, pleated gray trousers that hung just so, perfectly cut navy cashmere blazer and a flawlessly smooth white shirt, open at the neck. A perpetual smile had etched crow's feet around his eyes and creases into his cheeks. He had a full head of hair as white as a virgin snowfall and soft blue eyes topped by eyebrows like fuzzy white caterpillars. He looked as clean and warm and inviting as a freshly made bed with the covers turned back and a chocolate wrapped in gold foil on the pillow. He and his wife Marietta were childless, but Doc Lukens was everybody's father.

He slipped the helmet from her hands, held it out to me, saw that both my hands were full with his bags so he lifted my elbow and wedged it under my left arm. Rather belatedly he glanced at my face, then looked more closely at my forehead.

"Wash the gun powder out of that burn," he said, "and dab some Neosporin on it." He turned back to Winter Rose and said, "Now then, my dear, a lovely, long hot shower and a soft clean robe."

Doc Lukens guided her straight down the hall to the guest room, familiar with the layout from his frequent visits. I set his bags inside the room and gently shut the door for privacy. A couple of minutes later a rush of water through the pipes told me she was in the shower. If it was me in her place, I'd be in that hot shower for an hour.

I sniffed my own shirt and got a snoot full of cordite, burned oil and the brassy odor of dried blood. The smell flashed me back to Iraq for a split second, disoriented and blinded by smoke, pinned again in the burning Humvee. I shook it off and went into the master bath to wash up. After a quick shower, I found a tube of Neosporin and spread some on the patches where the two muzzle blasts from the Python had burned my forehead and chin. In the mirror they didn't look too bad, but hats and helmets were going to be a shade uncomfortable for a couple of days. My clothes – which turned out to be clotted with more blood than I thought – went into a heavy plastic bag for disposal.

I pulled a fresh uniform from the closet and for the last time in my life dressed in an Army uniform. In the kitchen I made myself a ham sandwich on some nice soft whole grain bread with a generous slab of extra sharp cheddar. I sat in the breakfast nook and munched.

The pew I was sitting in was the same one our family had occupied every Sunday for most of my childhood. Fashioned from dense, dark oak, the aisle side featured a cross elaborately filigreed with leafy vine, hand carved in the days before lasers. A little brass plaque, inscribed with the number "6," worn and polished by countless fingertips, was still screwed to the thick wood.

Maybe it had been a mistake, using this particular pew in the house. Every time I sat in it, some painful memories came flooding back. My brother Virgil and I fidgeted through Sunday services in it. We played around, like brothers everywhere, eventually drawing a fiercely whispered "shush!" or "stop!" from our mother. Or worse, the wrath of our father.

Sunday by Sunday, I gradually understood that all four of us had different reasons for being there. My mother was the believer. Jesus guided everything in her life. He rewarded her good deeds with happiness, punished her transgressions with misery, including the sexual humiliations my father forced on her, the beatings he periodically inflicted on all of us and most especially her cancer. She believed these were punishments from on high; punishments she deserved.

For my father, that little church was the world's best disguise. People watched him bow his head in prayer and thought him the epitome of Christian strength and piety. "That man is a rock, an absolute rock," they whispered as he gently helped my mother to her seat each week during those last hellish months.

Virgil believed my father was the devil himself. It all made sense to him. Heaven and hell, good and evil, God and the Devil. Life is a constant battle, a test by God. And Virgil was determined to be on the right side. Toward the end even Virgil gave up on that pew, though. He switched his allegiance and found his solace over in the massive stone Catholic cathedral on East Harris Street.

Me? In all of those hours on that hard oak bench, I listened to a lot of people who claimed to know what God wants, often in amazing detail. But I was never convinced that they knew any more than I do on the subject. All I know about God is that I don't know anything for sure. The only thing that has always made sense to me is the golden rule: do unto others as you would have them do unto you. Or if you prefer modern English instead of that antiquated "unto" crap: treat everyone the way you want to be treated. It's the old military KISS principle applied to religion – Keep It Simple, Stupid. I may not always follow it, but I've yet to find a situation where the golden rule doesn't work.

I didn't know it at the time, but the transformation of that little church into my home started one day when I was fourteen. It happened in the cottage that used to stand in the empty lot behind the church. That day three escapees from Ware State Prison up near Waycross crossed paths with Pastor Gerald Jameson and his family, who lived in the cottage. Two of them, Cletus Trowall and Willie Johnston, were six years into twenty-five-to-life sentences for first degree murder.

Cletus was from Wallahatchee, a pleasant little wide spot on a back road about halfway between Waycross and Tifton with the ubiquitous church, a grease blackened three-bay garage without gas pumps and a small supermarket with a sun-faded RC Cola billboard mounted on the roof. Cletus was a slightly built white man, burdened with the twin resentments of being short and poor, both conditions in his mind being totally unreasonable and not at all his fault. He killed a man in a bar over a $20 bet on a high school basketball game. When the man refused to pay, Cletus slipped out to his truck, retrieved the old worn .38 revolver he kept in the glove box, marched right back in, spun the man around on his stool, jammed the barrel into his chest and fired all six bullets as fast as he could pull the trigger.

Willie Johnston was a beefy black man in his mid twenties, whose zenith in life was the year he starred as a linebacker in high school. A shattered ankle in his senior year had dashed his hopes of a football scholarship to UGA and, once outside the cocoon of the football program, even a high school diploma proved beyond Willie's grasp. Willie Johnston beat his girlfriend to death with his fists, the culmination of a tragically common escalation of domestic abuse. When the cops knocked on the door, Willie was watching TV, drinking the beer she had told him to get up and get for himself.

Both men were technically eligible for parole after seventeen years, but they had already spent weeks in solitary for fighting. Neither had any illusions about getting out early.

A third man named Purcell Jenkins led the breakout. PJ, as he called himself, was clever in a street sly way and smart enough to hide his viciousness under a veneer of affability. He had a large head with round cheeks and a wide smile that was engaging at first glance, but if you looked closer, the smile only added to the menace lurking in his eyes. Purcell was serving life without parole for the brutal rape and murder of two University of Georgia coeds, who'd had the lethal misfortune of a chance encounter with him after their car broke down while they were driving home from Athens for Christmas.

Late one afternoon, the trio bluffed their way out the prison gate with the unwilling help of the assistant warden. They piled into his car and took off, ejecting him from the back seat at about sixty miles an hour. Against the odds, the assistant warden survived and flagged down a trucker who helped him sound the alert. With an ever growing line of police cars trailing about an hour behind them, Cletus, Willie and Purcell pulled up at the convenience store across from the church in search of beer and cash. After pummeling the lone clerk unconscious, they helped themselves to both commodities and were about to depart when the Reverend Jameson had the extreme misfortune of arriving home with his wife, Grace, who taught music and played the organ on Sundays, and his fourteen-year-old daughter, Ellie, a shy, slender girl whose unusually husky voice might just possibly have matched her dreams of singing professionally.

At the sight of the two women, the convicts hastily dumped their cartons of beer in the trunk and trotted across the street to intercept the family. Arming themselves with knives from the kitchen, they made the next forty-five minutes seem like an eternity in that house. Finally, Purcell forced Pastor Jameson to lie down next to the violated bodies of his wife and daughter.

He laughed and said, "Well now, preacher, your turn."

Purcell carefully placed the tip of his knife over the pastor's heart with his left hand and lifted the heel of his right hand to pound the blade in. Suddenly, the police who had been tracking the escapees breached the door and rushed in with guns drawn. When Purcell leaped for the closest deputy with the knife held high, three of the cops – Ware County deputies who didn't like escapees making them look bad – opened fire. For ten seconds the room was a war zone. Later investigation determined that a total of twenty-seven rounds were fired, seven of them striking and killing all three felons. The pastor's only good luck that day was that he was on the floor, below the deputies' broad spray of fire.

On the Sunday following the double funeral of Pastor Jameson's wife and daughter, the little church was packed. Virgil and I were there, with ties knotted around our skinny necks and faces scrubbed squeaky clean. Pastor Jameson entered the church from the vestibule and slowly climbed the steps to the pulpit. He was visibly hunched over, as though he were carrying the bodies of his wife and daughter on his narrow shoulders. He stood there silently for a few moments, looking around the church helplessly, like a man lost in a foreign country where he doesn't understand a single word. Unable to speak, he started crying. At first, we quietly let him sob.

Then my mother said, "God bless you, Pastor!"

Others picked it up.

"Jesus loves you!"

"Take strength from the Lord, for He is our savior!"

But Pastor Jameson raised a hand to stop them. When silence reigned again, he spoke in a low voice, almost a whisper.

"No god," he said, "would have let that happen."

I thought it was the first raw truth I'd heard in that church, but everyone else present that day was stunned. Those in the front rows had heard him clearly, but the rest thought surely they were mistaken.

The pastor raised his head, straightened his back and grabbed the brass rail of the pulpit with both hands. Looking up toward the heavens, he shouted this time, his voice thundering through the church.

"No god can be so cruel!"

He lowered his chin and leveled his gaze at us. When he spoke, contempt twisted his voice nearly into a snarl.

"No *loving* god would have let those… those *animals* do that to my little girl. To my wife. Not to Ellie. Not to Grace."

More tears streamed unheeded down his cheeks. He looked around the church like he had suddenly awakened in a strange room surrounded by people he didn't know. His eyes locked on the doors in the rear of the church.

He said, "There is no God."

Then he left the pulpit and walked out without another word.

He had been a popular and well-loved pastor and his loss of faith turned out to be highly contagious. One after another, it hit the parishioners like a virus. More and more stopped coming each Sunday, until finally the doors were locked. Ten years ago the empty church was put up for sale.

Now I eat my sandwiches on the same hard bench where I listened without conviction to Pastor Jameson and I am no closer to understanding what the hell is on God's mind. Generally, that doesn't bother me at all.

CHAPTER 4

A T EXACTLY 1630 hours on Friday, the 24th of May, I entered Colonel Forwin's office in the orange-roofed brick headquarters building of the 1st Battalion, 75th Ranger Regiment on Hunter Army Airfield. The normally spacious room was packed. The colonel's desk had even been shoved back against the wall to make more space. Jammed shoulder to shoulder, two and three deep around the periphery wherever they could find room to stand, were men and women in an assortment of uniforms and civvies: mostly Army, but also a couple of the tan tunics of the Marine Corps and a bit of Air Force blue.

I saw Norm Windhorn and Jeremy Tanner, a pair of Rangers who had been with me on my first Iraq tour. Next to them was Captain Jim Drake, a young officer from Texas who was going to make an excellent battalion commander someday. Adrienne Lewis – a stick thin matron with short curly hair dyed as dark as black shoe polish, who some claimed had been head of personnel for the regiment since Eisenhower was president – was there too.

Off to the side, where he could observe everyone and still be close to the door, my friend Magnus Magnusson towered over everyone else. Hear him talk, and you'd swear he could have been a dialogue coach for the Coen brothers' quirky movie *Fargo*. See him in street clothes, with his wide smile and the disarmingly innocent look of a blue-eyed, blond-haired Minnesota farm boy, and you'd never guess he's a decorated former Navy SEAL. Imagine him vaulting from a Viking ship swinging a massive sword and you'd understand why his nickname in the service was Magnus the Magnificent. I've served with many outstanding men and women over the years, but there is no one I'd rather have at my side than Magnus.

Genetics blessed him with a six-four frame, broad shoulders, a deep chest and the long reach of a professional boxer. Three months shy of twenty eight, Magnus hones those gifts with daily workouts of swimming, weightlifting and wall climbing. His nutrition plan consists of three simple rules: graze lightly throughout the day, avoid sugar like poison and drink lots of water. It might not work for everyone, but it keeps Magnus at two twenty-five with about eight percent body fat. On the Tybee Island beach near his house, women stare long enough to irritate their husbands and men wonder if that isn't what's-his-name, the new linebacker for the Falcons who nearly cut Tampa Bay's fullback in two, he hit him so hard.

I've seen Magnus toss three axes – one after the other, with the nonchalance of a pub champion throwing darts after his third Guinness – into the center of a target from twenty feet, but normally he relies on a Wilson Spec Ops 9 semi-auto. A full load in the butt of the custom pistol, one in the chamber and two extra magazines gives him forty-nine rounds. For backup he wears a pair of compact Colt 1908 pocket pistols in .32 caliber, locked and loaded with one round in the chamber and seven in each magazine. His father, who had been a C-48 transport pilot in the Army Air Corps during WWII, gave the pistols to Magnus the day he became a SEAL. Magnus had never told me exactly how his Dad had gotten his hands on two of them, much less a sequential pair stamped *Property of United Air Lines*, but Magnus loves the slim little guns. He wears both of them at the same time because he doesn't like the unbalanced feeling of wearing a back-up piece on only one ankle. He says two feel just right, and after running out of ammo during a firefight in Afghanistan, his motto is, "Can't have too many bullets, dont-cha know."

When he's not riding his Harley Ultra Classic, Magnus runs a one-man security service. A starlet he met in Iraq of all places had urged him to start the business and now he has a select clientele of celebrities and CEOs around the country. Word of mouth gets him all the work he wants.

I moved slowly into the room, shaking hands and exchanging a few quick words. Near the back of the crowd I found Uncle Gil. In the Savannah papers he's regularly called a "prominent citizen" and "a mover-and-a-shaker." He's Chairman of the Police Advisory Commission and generally a big brick in the Savannah establishment. Gilbert Rumsdale is from old, old money and a line of southern military heroes, including a couple of lesser known Civil War generals. In the watch pocket of his ubiquitous three piece suits, he carries an exquisite gold Patek Philippe, purchased by his great grandfather on the day of his grandfather's birth, July 17, 1919. Uncle Gil inherited the watch on his twenty-first birthday and still uses it every day, if that tells you something about the staunchness of his family connections.

Uncle Gil is anything but a pampered rich kid, though. The Rumsdale family fortunes waned over the generations, and by the time Gilbert was a young man all that remained was a hollow financial shell and a sterling silver reputation. Before I was born, Gilbert had tried to revive the military service tradition as a start on rebuilding the family standing. Unfortunately, at West Point he was caught up in an exam cheating scandal with another cadet. In spite of his protests of innocence, he was booted out, less than six months from graduation. It didn't help that the other cadet was exonerated, leaving him to take the humiliation alone. For years he followed the career of that cadet, marking the man's promotions against his own success, until Gilbert eventually left him behind.

The whole affair only strengthened his determination to restore his family's place in Savannah society. He came home, borrowed every dollar he could using the few remaining family assets and sunk the money into real estate, mostly commercial. This time the gods of fortune smiled on him. A favorable market, an eye for the right property and a willingness to work fourteen and fifteen hours a day made him a rich man inside ten years.

In Savannah, there's nothing like being old money *and* new money. Even the real estate slump that nearly drove the whole nation into depression in 2007 didn't slow him down. Now he owns land and property all over the state, including two pulp mills, a hospital and six associated clinics, and one of the largest assisted living facilities in the country. His dream was to follow the likes of Jimmy Carter and Roy Barnes to the splendid thirty-room Greek Revival style Georgia governor's mansion in Atlanta, but his forte turned out to be wielding power behind the scenes. He worked his way up through the hierarchy of the Republican Party far enough that he bought a townhouse in D.C. to make his frequent trips there more comfortable.

"Give your Uncle Gil a hug," he said now, wrapping both arms around me like a wrestler. He broke the clinch, then straightened his arms with both hands on my shoulders.

"A real hero retires! Who would have believed it when you were a little squirt in diapers?"

Virgil and I have always called him Uncle Gil. We didn't learn that he wasn't really our uncle until we were six years old. Our father told us, during one of his all-too-frequent tirades at the dinner table. After he stormed off and our mother dried her tears, she told us that Uncle Gil had always been like a brother to her so he was as good as an uncle and we could still call him that. We did, because he always had that essential uncle-ness to us: someone you could tell stuff you wouldn't tell your parents; someone who would cut through the bullshit and give you the straight scoop. Someone you could trust. With our parents, Virgil and I really needed an uncle.

Gilbert Rumsdale looked the part of the wise and kindly uncle too. He wasn't what you'd call athletic, but he was about my height and reasonably trim. He was ageing gracefully, although his neatly cropped beard was more salt than pepper these days.

He turned me to face the light from the window and frowned. With one finger he carefully drew air circles around the scorch marks on my face.

"You fall off that damn bike?" he asked. His tone had that unique quality only a parent or favorite uncle can manage: equal parts suspicion and concern.

I flashed a quick smile and probably only managed to look guilty. Just like any kid in a similar situation.

"Nah," I said. "Just stood too close to a fire. It's nothing."

He leaned closer to check for himself that it was only

superficial damage. Apparently satisfied, he nodded once and let me go. Then he craned his neck to look around the room.

"Virgil's not here?" he said.

I shrugged.

"Didn't expect him," I said. "He's never been comfortable on a military base." I paused to change subjects, then I said, "Can I talk to you about something after the ceremony?"

"Sure," he said, "Anytime. You know – "

Just then Colonel Forwin came through the door and someone shouted, "Ten-shun!"

Uncle Gilbert whispered, "Later." He stepped back and left me front and center in the room.

Colonel Forwin marched right up to me and grabbed my hand in both of his before I could salute.

"Last chance, Master Sergeant Keane."

I had to smile at that.

"No sir," I said. "If I stay in, the Army will keep me behind a desk until I'm a petrified lump."

He grinned back at me and dropped his left hand to pat his stomach.

"I know what you mean," he said. "I'm turning into a lump behind a desk myself."

He gave a little shake of his head to show the levity was over, then he leaned in a bit closer.

"I'm going to miss you, Roman," he said.

"Thank you sir," I said. "I'm gonna miss you too."

Funny, but I really meant it. In just over twenty years of Army life, I had discovered that you had to take officers with the proverbial grain of salt. They lived in a world of their own and it didn't always run parallel to the practical world the rest of us lived in. Colonel Forwin was a welcome exception.

Lean by the current national standards, Colonel Forwin was round-cheeked for a Ranger and perpetually fighting to maintain his weight. The extra pounds he carried around courtesy of his desk time lent him a cheerful countenance that led many to assume he was an easy-going guy they could take advantage of, a mistake they only made once. A fondness for food aside, he was one of the most dedicated and capable officers I had ever known.

"In two weeks," he said, "you'll be bored stiff."

I thought about this morning's ride on the Road King and smiled.

"No sir, I don't believe so."

I could tell he didn't believe me, but he clapped me on the shoulder and said, "OK, then, let's proceed."

He stepped to his desk and picked up a single sheet of paper that was ready on his blotter. My career in the Army – closed out on one page with a couple of simple sentences in black and white. He snapped to attention and raised his hand in salute. Everyone in the room followed suit, noisily stomping the floor as they slammed their boot heels together.

In his penetrating command voice, the Colonel said, "Master Sergeant Roman Keane, serving with you has been our great privilege."

I returned the salute with a sudden upwelling of emotion that surprised me. Colonel Forwin released the salute and ordered the room at rest.

After a pause to make sure he had everyone's attention, he said, "I have to laugh whenever I remember that 'Army of One' bullshit the recruiters came up with a few years back. I know it must be at least an Army of Two, because behind every good officer in this Army, there's an even better NCO keeping his ass out of trouble."

That got him the polite laughter you might expect. He waited until the room was quiet again before he resumed.

"When I was a green company commander in 1990 I met a young Staff Sergeant named Roman Keane. Even back then, you'd swear he'd been born a Ranger – like he'd grown up with an M-4 in his hands and a 'Follow me!' look in those compelling eyes of his. I remember he was quiet, but he radiated confidence the way the sun radiates heat. Three months later, he saved my life in Kuwait."

He moved to a position in front of his desk and stood with his hands on his hips, knuckles folded under.

"I was leading a platoon-sized Ranger force on an ambush that was supposed to catch the elite Iraqi Republican guard with their pants down and their nifty red berets off. But the intel was faulty. We inserted by helicopter just after dark. Then we moved twelve clicks through the desert, fast and quiet. We set up as planned at the ambush site and waited for dawn. But when the sun came up it all went to shit.

"The Iraqis ambushed us. What looked like a good L-shaped offensive position at a crossroads turned out to be a defensive death trap. They were behind us, with good cover. We lost six good men in as many minutes when the shooting started. In twenty minutes we were down to half strength. I took a round through the thigh and almost bled out in the sand. Sergeant Keane tightened a tourniquet down on my leg. The M-60s were down to one short belt each. Everyone was on their last magazine. Air support wouldn't reach us for another half hour. The closest artillery wouldn't be in range for another hour. We had minutes, not hours. Time was running out.

"That was when Sergeant Keane came up with a plan. Everyone in this room is probably aware of his nickname, the Road King, but not all of you may know why we call him that. It's not because of the hot-rodded Harley parked out front. It's because he's got a map in his head of everywhere he's ever been. A photographic memory for places. Perfect recall of every road, every town, every feature. And he has this extraordinary ability to read a map and see the terrain in his head. When he scans the ground in front of him, it's like he's got remote cameras that check every spot and send back information on cover, field of fire and target visibility. Well, Rangers – and guests – I can tell you the Road King put his unique ability to good use that day. He scanned the map and discovered a tiny, nearly non-existent route off the kill zone and around the enemy's flank. He selected two volunteers and collected all the ammunition we had left."

The Colonel stopped and looked over the gathered men.

"I see that both of you who went out with Sergeant Keane are here today," he said. All eyes went to Windhorn and Tanner, who nodded in acknowledgement. No one smiled. We were all back there in the desert for the moment.

"I remember the mission briefing he gave you. He described the nearly impossible route you would follow, crawling through small gullies that were barely more than sandy washes. Then he said, 'Here's the plan: we move fast, get close, kill them all and come back alive.'"

Colonel Forwin paused. I fidgeted. I knew he couldn't resist telling the story again, especially not at my retirement, but it got more dramatic every time.

"That's exactly what happened," he said. "All three Rangers made it around the enemy flank. When the shooting stopped the body count stood at nineteen – all of them Iraqi. All three

Rangers came out alive – without a single round left in their weapons. Sergeant Keane's bravery and leadership was in the finest tradition of the U.S. Army."

He frowned, then looked my way and said, "I put all that in my recommendation for the Medal of Honor, too, but they kicked it down to the Distinguished Service Cross."

The colonel called the room to attention again.

"Now it's time to say goodbye," he said. Then he said the required words, handed me my paper and with the DSC on my chest and a titanium knee in my right leg, I officially became Master Sergeant Roman Keane, U.S. Army Retired.

The colonel winked and in a more normal speaking voice, that still made it undiminished to the corners of the room, he said, "I'd come to the party at the G-String tonight, but I wouldn't want to inhibit all these other characters who can't wait to be there."

He shook my hand one last time, then pivoted on his heel and left the room. The well-wishing lasted another half hour, spilling into the hall and finally down to the lobby. As the last few people left, I managed to get a moment alone with Gilbert Rumsdale.

"You've still got friends at the FBI, Uncle Gil?" I asked.

"One of my brokers is married to the Assistant Special Agent in Charge of the field office in Atlanta," he said. "He and I play golf a couple of times a month. His tee shots are killer, but lucky for me he can't putt to save his life. Why, you looking for a job?"

"Me?" I said. "Working for the FBI? No way. I'm going riding."

He made a face like he'd just gotten a whiff of spoiled milk.

"I don't get it, Roman. You'll be out in the weather on that bike, either too hot or too cold. Take the time off you deserve and travel, but for God's sake drive a car. Go in comfort."

I grinned. This wasn't the first time Uncle Gil had tried to dissuade me from riding, although usually he argued from the safety angle.

"Too much comfort is like too much sugar," I said. "It'll sap your energy and turn you into a lump."

"But what about when it rains? You'll be soaking wet!"

I shook my head, still smiling. I've ridden my share of miserable miles, unprepared for rain or cold, but I'd quickly learned how to cope with the elements. With the right gear, a rider can stay comfortable in some surprisingly nasty weather.

"Waterproof boots and raingear, Uncle Gil. Besides, what's the point of touring the country cocooned in a car, sealed against all sounds, smells and storms? You might as well watch the whole trip on TV."

"OK, OK," he said. "I give up." He extended his hand and said, "But promise me you'll think of me now and then. And when you do, ride safe."

I took his hand without hesitation and said, "Deal."

He gripped my hand hard for a moment, then let it go.

"So," he said, "what's this about the FBI?"

"I'd appreciate it if you mentioned a... ah... situation for me."

"A situation."

"Exactly, a situation."

"This would be a 'situation' the FBI is interested in?"

"Yeah. Well, they would be... if they knew about it."

"And you want me to let them know about it?"

"Discretely," I said.

"By discretely," he said, "I take it you mean anonymously."

I nodded.

He blew the air out of his lungs, shrugged his shoulders and said, "OK, give. Who did you kill this time?"

I told him. It took ten minutes, during which time he listened quietly and didn't interrupt with a question until I described leaving the dead men's driver's licenses on the road near the van.

"Damn!" he said. "You never do anything by halves, do you Roman?"

I shook my head, kept my mouth shut.

Uncle Gil sighed.

"At least you cleaned up your own mess." He gave me a sharp glance and said, "You sure they're not going to find anything tying you and the girl to this?"

"It was one hell of a hot fire," I said. "That van went up like it had been hit by a missile."

He nodded.

"OK," he said. "I'll mention it to my friend. I'm sure he can keep the source anonymous. If everything is as you say, I imagine the FBI will just be glad to close the case and take the credit. The media, on the other hand, is going to go wild."

He pursed his lips and exhaled.

"Well," I said, "they'll make a big deal about it, but as soon as the bodies are identified the whole story will gravitate over to Alabama. That was home for all three of those boys."

He punched me lightly on the shoulder.

"Never a dull moment around you, Roman. Don't worry, I'll take care of this."

"It was great of you to be here today," I said. "Are you coming to the G-String later?"

"Wouldn't miss it," he said.

We shook hands again, then Uncle Gil left. I ducked into the men's room. I changed from my Army uniform into my new retiree uniform: scuffed leather riding boots, well-worn blue jeans and a plain black T-shirt. I folded the Army gear, stuffed it into the duffle I'd brought along, strapped it to the Road King's luggage rack and headed home to check on Winter Rose.

CHAPTER 5

DOC LUKENS HAD made himself at home on my sofa, neat stockinged feet up on the cushions, trousers carefully arranged to avoid any unseemly creases. The muted horns of Handel's *The Water Music* floated softly from the stereo.

I dropped my duffel in the hall and settled into one of the leather easy chairs that faced the couch.

He stopped directing the orchestra with his index finger and said, "Not that I mind lounging in this comfortable little church you call home, but really RK, you have a rather pitiful collection of classical compositions."

He picked up a plastic CD case from the coffee table and waved it at me.

"All I could find was this *Best of the Classics* CD. Doesn't that seem wrong to you? Can you distill Beethoven, Brahms, Tchaikovsky, Handel and Wagner onto one *Best of* disk? *Best of* the 70's or *Best* of Doo Wop, fine. But really, *Best of the Classics*?"

"Doc," I said, cutting him off, "that one disk pretty much covers classical music for me. What's that piece they used for *The Lone Ranger* theme song?"

"The *William Tell Overture*? By Gioachino Rossini."

"Yeah, that's it. I don't listen to much classical music, but I'd pay good money to hear what Mr. Rossini would have done with a couple of Stratocasters and a bank of Marshall amps."

I hooked a thumb down the hall.

"How's she doing?"

"Sound asleep," he said. "Down for the night, most likely."

"What about her jaw?" I said.

"Oh, I X-rayed that after you left. No break."

"What? You've got a portable X-ray machine in the trunk of that land yacht you call a car?"

He chuckled and shook his head.

"Quick drive over to the clinic, my boy. What's the sense in running your own place if you don't have a key to the back door? We were in and out in ten minutes and no one the wiser."

"Lucky for her you even remembered how to operate the machine," I said.

"All right, twenty minutes then, but that counts getting her started on antibiotics and giving her the morning after pill."

He pressed his lips into a thin line and shook his head in a quick little disbelieving motion.

"That is one strong woman, RK."

An image of her standing naked in the sand, eyes as hard as anthracite and my knife flashing in her hand, popped into my mind.

"You can say that again, Doc."

We had a quiet moment, both of us thinking about Winter Rose.

The silence was broken by Dr. Lukens clearing his throat.

"Is it the Chinese who believe that when you save someone's life you're responsible for them from that moment on?"

I sighed.

"I've heard that too. Or something like that, anyway."

"So?"

"You know I'll help her anyway I can. I don't know much about her yet. She rides, I know that much. She owns a seriously fast sportbike, although it's still somewhere in the woods outside Toccoa where they dumped it when they abducted her. I'm willing to bet she knows how to handle it. She had to ride my Road King out there while I moved the van. No problem, even on a gravel road."

"Ah, another biker. Why am I not surprised?"

"And an aviator," I said. "Did you know that she was a gunship pilot?"

"Really? But then again, I guess I'm not surprised at that either. She's an extraordinary person."

I nodded in agreement.

"Beautiful, but hard as an anvil."

I remembered that she had been a captain before she left the Army. "She was a commissioned officer," I said. "She got out about a month ago. Didn't say why exactly, just that she was finished with it. Been living on her savings while she figures out what's next."

He considered that briefly, then said, "Commissioned officer? So she must have a college degree of some sort. A Georgia school, I think. Her accent is slight, but definitely from this part of the country. Where's she from? She has a Eurasian look. Very exotic."

I shook my head.

"I made the same mistake. She's Cherokee, Eastern Band."

"Ah! Of course! Cherokee."

Another silence settled between us while we thought about the implications of Winter Rose's condition.

Finally Doc Lukens said, "She'll have people up in North Carolina. People who can help her. She'll need to go there."

I nodded.

"Yeah."

"Sooner would be better than later."

I nodded again, an eyebrow raised in inquiry this time.

He clasped his hands and rubbed them together, like he was kneading a clay ball between his palms. I knew it was a sign he was wrestling with some inner conflict, so I sat quietly.

Finally, he relaxed his hands and said, "Listen, Roman. I can't violate her confidence, but you apparently intervened relatively early in the assault. And her… ah… physical injuries are not as severe as they might have been. She's young. Resilient. Physically, I think she will recover with extraordinary speed. She may not admit that she needs help. In fact, I can practically guarantee that she won't. Don't be fooled, RK."

I turned my head and regarded Doc Lukens steadily.

"I just want to instill a proper sense of urgency," he said, raising a palm to erase any accusation of lack of concern on my part. "Her rapid physical improvement may lull you into thinking she's fine, but this, this… assault isn't something you simply put out of your head."

"Got it, Doc," I said. "I won't let her – or you – down."

He smiled benevolently.

"I never had the slightest doubt, Roman."

To change the subject, he said, "So I understand the G-String will finally host a real, honest-to-God stripper for your retirement party tonight."

I laughed. "I'm sure the young lady would be insulted to be called an honest-to-God stripper, but you're right – we do have a dancer. Magnus talked one of his friends into dancing tonight."

The G-String is my private club on the Little Ogeechee River about fifteen miles southwest of Savannah, a combination of hobby, hide-out and investment. Sounds like some sleazy strip joint, doesn't it? Everyone thinks that first time they hear the name – I picked it to keep the damned tourists and the Bible thumpers away. Actually, it's a reference to the fourth string on a guitar, not the infamous less-than-nothing stripper's outer wear.

Apparently the G-String is a regular topic of discussion for the Savannah Ladies Auxiliary of Bull Street, although none of the members have ever visited the club. A friend told me that Belinda Somerset, the Auxiliary President, stood up at a recent meeting and declared the G-String, "A disgraceful drug den where depraved men in dirty T-shirts and greasy dungarees gawp at naked women."

Man, I had to laugh at that. The insufferably self-righteous never let ignorance stand in the way of their cause. Mrs. Somerset could hardly be farther off the mark.

I bought the place twelve years ago, as an investment. It was a little fish camp in the woods, half a mile back from Route 17 on a dirt road, unused and overgrown. I got it for a song. I rebuilt it over the years, so I could have a quiet spot to hang out with friends and listen to some good music. A source of perpetual expenses and no income, it makes a nice tax shelter too.

The G-String's not big: seven booths with black vinyl seats and polished oak tables, a narrow bar made from more of that exquisite Italian granite – a slab of black-and-gold-speckled green in this case – and a couple of picnic-style wooden tables out on the deck facing the river. The booth closest to the door is my "office," and everyone knows to leave it vacant for me.

Most of the booths have a good view of the wall-to-wall stage at the end of the building, where a buddy from the Hunter

Army Airfield facilities maintenance section installed a slick set of computer controlled lights and a sound system that I suspect could shred Kevlar if I cranked it up to full volume. The stage is occasionally taken by a guitarist or singer working out some new stuff. *Up and coming* would be the best way to describe them, although one well known singer stayed at my place the winter before last and wrote enough songs at the keyboard on that stage to fill a new CD that stayed in the Billboard Hot 100 for thirteen weeks, largely on the strength of the title song, *Blue Jeans and Black Leather.* She still calls sometimes, just to talk now, but hearing her sing "*long rides together, in blue jeans and black leather…*" on the radio always brings a smile to my face.

"The show starts at 9:00, Doc. Gives us plenty of time to eat. I could grill a couple of filets?"

Perry swung his feet to the floor and slipped into his loafers.

"Let me check on the patient," he said standing easily, "then I'll make the salad. Do you still have some of that lovely Gouda that lass in Amsterdam sends you?"

Perry assembled the salads in the short time it took to grill the steaks and then we ate quietly, Australia's Tommy Emmanuel turned low on the stereo. I left for the G-String about quarter to nine. Dr. Lukens planned to stay until I returned, in case Winter Rose needed him. She was still sleeping peacefully, so we both thought he'd have a nice quiet evening. I should have known better. One of the things they hammer into you from your first day at the Ranger School in Fort Benning is to expect the unexpected. But after Winter Rose I'd never have guessed that more trouble was careening my way. Who expects to be struck by lightning twice in the same day?

CHAPTER 6

MAGNUS'S FRIEND RUBY danced her first set to Gary Moore's *Still Got the Blues*, dressed in a tight black leotard that covered everything but the imagination. Her choreography matched Moore's soaring guitar, a ballet of erotic athleticism. When the music stopped all of us sat for a moment in the steamy silence, then we leaped to our feet and clapped like mad. Ruby's face lit up with a relieved smile. Magnus told me she'd been very nervous about performing – she's a physical therapist at the VA hospital in Augusta, not a professional dancer.

She rose so easily it seemed an act of levitation, blew us all kisses and skipped off the stage. She mocked us all playfully in the second set, dancing with a Ranger T-shirt over the leotard. The heavy beat of George Thorogood's *Bad to the Bone* throbbed from the big Maranz speakers bolted high on the walls. Ruby looked anything but bad. Until that performance, I didn't realize you could laugh and pant at the same time.

She came out on fire for the final set, with Stevie Ray Vaughan and Double Trouble hammering out *The House is Rockin'*. Everyone started clapping and stamping their feet in time with Chris Layton's drums. Ruby wore five inch stilettos and a red bikini for this number, revealing a trim, muscular body worthy of a world class sprinter or an Olympic gymnast. Covered in a smooth sheen of sweat, she glowed in the stage lights and radiated an eroticism that reached out with velvet fingers and grabbed you by the crotch. I could feel the heat of the room in my throat as I breathed. Outside, the evening was cool enough to draw Savannah's residents out to their porch swings for a breath of soft spring air, but here in the G-String the air conditioning wasn't even close to keeping up.

About six bars into Stevie's guitar solo, some loony with a gun slid into my booth and aimed it at my chest.

CHAPTER 7

I WASN'T SURE IF it was good luck or bad, but I had the booth to myself. Uncle Gil had been sitting next to me, but he'd moved up to the bar for a drink between sets and was still there, perched on one of the stools with his back against the bar. The seat opposite me faced away from the stage, so naturally it was empty until this guy slid into it.

He held the gun in both hands and braced his elbows on the table. I could see it was a black Colt .45. An excellent pistol, but probably not the choice of most lunatics. His hands twitched and I caught a glimpse of white lettering on the left side of the slide. I couldn't read it in the shadows, but I knew the script marked this pistol as a Clark Custom Combat. Definitely a serious shooter's gun. Not that it mattered much whether he could shoot or not – from this distance a blind monkey missing three fingers could put one through my heart.

Over the guy's right shoulder I could see Ruby dropping straight down from a high kick into a full split. She still had 100% audience concentration. Hand clapping escalated to feet stamping. The floor vibrated under my boots, like the prelude to an earthquake. Even if the earth suddenly split apart and a chasm swallowed up the entire building, I suspected no one would have torn their eyes away from Ruby.

Except Magnus. Somehow he saw what was going on in spite of the low light away from the stage, and moved sideways to line up a clean shot. The Wilson had materialized in his right hand. It was comforting to have him back me up, but I waved him off with a small shake of my head. The hammer was down on the Colt pointed at my chest. Since it's a single action pistol, nothing was going to happen too quickly. Depending on whether or not there was a round in the chamber, the guy would have to either cycle the slide or cock the hammer before he could shoot. Either way, the Colt wasn't ready to fire yet. I was pretty sure I could disarm him before he corrected the situation. I rested both hands carefully on the table within quick reach of the .45, and took a closer look at the man opposite me in the booth.

He was hollow-cheeked and his chin was smudged with something dark. Hard to tell exactly what it was in the dim light; oil or something grimy. Veins of gray streaked the untidy brown hair that sprouted like wild brush from beneath the greasy Atlanta Braves ball cap jammed low on his head. What looked like dried blood crusted his hair into spikes on the left side. A scruffy beard added to an overall homeless look. His body odor reached across the table and poked a rude finger up my nose. Every time he exhaled, the stale stink of whisky wafted across the table. One good spark and he'd probably burst into flames.

A plain gold wedding band circled the ring finger on his left hand, but no wife in the world would have let him out of the house wearing a business suit and a baseball cap. The suit was bluish gray with fine white pinstripes. I'm not what you'd call a connoisseur of fine suits – I own one black leather blazer and there's a lone silk tie with a subdued silver and burgundy print somewhere in the back of my closet, in the remote possibility that I ever need to show up somewhere in a coat and tie – but his suit must have been worth at least three grand when he bought it. Now it looked like he'd slept in it for a week. Crust on the left lapel looked suspiciously like dried vomit. His white shirt hadn't been cleaned for at least as long as the suit.

The music stopped and I risked a quick glance up. Ruby finished the set with her legs spread and knees locked, looking back over her shoulder at the room. She was breathing hard, but smiling happily. Her new fans were out of the booths and on their feet cheering and whistling.

I wanted to join them, but the big black hole in the barrel of the Colt pulled my attention back to the booth. The guy's eyes were hidden in deep shadow beneath the bill of his hat, but I could feel him staring at me intently. I tried to look unthreatening, although my friends tell me I could be a star playing an assassin for Hollywood. I was born with a condition called heterochromia iridium. My right eye is light green and my left is dark brown. When I'm tired or pissed off, both eyes are imbued with the intense luminosity you see in border collies and some sled dogs. When that happens apparently neither eye looks the least bit warm or inviting. In the past it has proved to be a useful thing when I needed to freeze a soldier with a hard look. Right now I was just puzzled, so I gave him a smile, hoping that might help.

That's when he surprised me. He started crying.

Tears welled up on his lower lids, overflowed like a dam bursting and streamed down his cheeks. Without breaking eye contact he lowered the gun to the table and laid it down. He laced his fingers together and pushed it across with his knuckles, until it was directly in front of me. He licked his lips to get a little lubrication, but his tongue looked as dry and rough as a sheet of 80 grit sandpaper. He closed his mouth and worked his throat like a man trying to dry swallow an aspirin. He tried to speak again, just as the applause for Ruby finally died. In the sudden silence, his voice was hoarse and a bit scratchy, but otherwise clear as a bell.

"Kill me, RK. Please, kill me!" he said.

CHAPTER 8

"ACE!"

I couldn't believe it. This whacked out bum was Ace Emory? I hadn't recognized him until I heard his voice. Didn't have a clue. But then I hadn't seen him in what, five, six years? He was younger than me, but he looked like an old man. Hell, he looked ready for the grave.

"Ace!" I said again, shaking my head.

He pulled the hat from his head, locked his red, sunken eyes on mine for a brief second, then looked away.

"It's been a long time since anyone called me that," he said.

He pressed his hands to his chin, fingers still locked around the hat. The contact made his whole upper body shake as he fought to contain the tremors in his hands.

I quietly slipped the pistol off the table and held it out to Magnus. He reached over, took it out of my hand, and stepped back. I kept my eyes on Ace, but in my peripheral vision I saw Magnus pop the magazine and rack the slide back. He checked the load in the magazine, sniffed the empty breech and shook his head to say "not fired."

A few seconds ago the G-String had been rocking loud and

hard. Now the music was off and an edgy silence had descended. One by one, the guys elbowed each other and pointed, and the general hubbub died away. Ruby slipped quietly into the ladies room to change. Everyone seemed to be holding their breath. A few of these men knew Ace personally. Most of the rest knew *of* him.

I leaned forward and said, "Ace? What happened man?"

He dropped his hands and looked at me with a bleakness I had only seen before in men dying on the battlefield, eyes barren of all hope. I believe he really did want me to kill him. I have near perfect memory for every road I've ever ridden, but I couldn't imagine a road that could have led him to this.

I met Ace in the Army, back in 1995. He'd enlisted after graduating from LaGrange College, partly out of a patriotic sense of obligation, partly in rebellion against the 9-to-5-office-and-house-in-the-suburbs life he imagined would follow his degree in accounting. His real name is Alan Carson Emory. Of course we called him Ace, but not just because of his monogram. He was one of those rare people you would call a natural shooter. Give him a weapon of any kind – handgun, rifle, or even a shoulder-launched missile – and Ace would score a bull's-eye with the first shot. He said he'd always had this phenomenal hand-eye coordination, this blinding speed. Even as a kid they called him Ace because he could always win at tennis, or any game with a racket. He was in one of my squads for a year or so, then he left the Army and became a financial manager. I'm not sure where the hand-eye coordination thing fits with making money, but he was an ace at that, too. Maybe it was just his killer instinct.

"Ace," I said, "whatever you need, I'm here."

He smiled then, a tight, thin movement of the lips that

barely made it into the category of a smile. He leaned forward, and I thought he was going to relax. He was with friends now, right? But he kept falling. Before I could catch him, his forehead hit the table with a whack like a bowling ball dropped on an oak floor.

"Magnus!"

He was already reaching for Ace as I scrambled out of my side of the booth.

We lowered him gently to the floor. I searched the room for George Bentana, a paramedic with Charlie Company. I'd seen his silver '78 Honda CBX Super Sport out front earlier, so I knew he was here. I spotted his thick bushy eyebrows and dark hair as he snaked his way to the front of the gathering crowd.

I moved aside to give him room and said, "Over here, George. Take a look."

George crouched over Ace for a few minutes, doing all the usual first responder things like checking pulse, respiration and pupils. The rest of us bit our tongues and let him work without distraction.

George stood finally and said, "Steady pulse and good respiration. He's out cold, but he's not gonna check out tonight."

"Thanks," I said. "Anything else?"

"He's gonna have one hell of a knot on his forehead tomorrow and a headache to go with it," he said. "An IV to get him hydrated would help. Oh, and I wouldn't risk any open flames near him until he dries out."

"OK," I said, "let's get him onto the bottom bunk in the Snore Room. I'll get Doc Lukens to check on him there."

Magnus slipped his hands under Ace's armpits. Bentana took Ace's legs and we headed past the restrooms to a door marked "storeroom." A bunk bed had been wedged in the cramped space with the paper towels and mops – my solution for friends who had one too many. I forget who called it the Snore Room first, but the name had stuck.

I pushed open the door and flipped on the light. I stepped back to allow Magnus and Bentana to carry Ace into the little room. With Ace's feet still outside, the little procession came to an abrupt halt.

"Uh, RK," Magnus said, "small problem here."

I eased through the door and leaned in to see what Magnus meant. To my surprise, someone was already in the bottom bunk. I lifted the blanket.

"Damn!" I said.

It wasn't someone, it was something. While I was away the contractor I'd hired weeks ago had finally started work on replacing the old fixtures in the restrooms. Apparently the lower bunk had looked like the perfect spot to store the new, unboxed units. Two sinks and a urinal were lined up on a drop cloth carefully laid over the mattress. Glancing around, I could see that there really wasn't anyplace else. I dropped the blanket back into place over the fixtures.

"Top bunk," I said. "When Doc Lukens gets here, he'll just have to work with it."

I slipped my arms under Ace's waist and the three of us wrestled him onto the upper bunk. We got him stretched out as comfortably as possible, then I pulled my phone out and called Doc Lukens.

"Another casualty?" he said when I got him on the line. "Mayhem has followed you into retirement, my dear boy. Let me check on patient number one, then I'll pack up my medical kit and head your way."

Everyone was waiting quietly when we stepped out of the

Snore Room, the party already forgotten. I wasn't surprised — these are men and women who would drop everything to help one of their own.

Uncle Gil rose from his seat at the bar. He had his gold pocket watch in his hand, but slipped it casually into his vest as I approached.

"Roman," he said, "I thought for sure you'd miss the excitement when you retired." He gave me a quick smile. "Wow, was I ever wrong. Listen, I hope that young man is all right, but I've got to be going. Business meetings in the morning, then an afternoon flight to D.C."

"He'll be fine," I said, hoping I was right.

Uncle Gil slipped out and I turned to the rest of the guests.

"He's going to be OK," I said. "We'll find out what happened and let you know."

"You sure, RK? Cause we don't mind… you know… hanging around a bit if you need us."

I recognized a Special Forces sergeant named Cecil Slattery from Fort Stewart, sitting on the edge of a booth with his arms crossed. His biceps nearly popped the sleeves on his shirt and his hands looked hard enough to use as shovels.

"Thanks, Cecil," I said. "Doc Lukens is on the way. There's nothing else we can do right now."

Reluctantly, they started trooping out.

"One thing," I said.

When all the faces were turned toward me again, I said, "Most of you know Ace was a damn good man. One of us. I don't know what happened to him, but I want the option of surprising whoever did it. Keep this to yourselves."

There were no startled looks, no questions. Everyone nodded quietly and headed for the parking lot. From the porch I watched them saddle up. These weren't the hard drinking bikers of the movies. They were soldiers, and other professionals, who gathered at the G-String for the music and the company, not to get blasted. I was a little concerned that tonight's festivities might have encouraged more drinking than usual, but I saw no sign that anyone was having difficulty. A Suzuki Hayabusa and Honda sportbike of some kind purred out before the others even cranked up. Nobody had particularly loud pipes in this crowd, but the rumble of exhausts rose steadily as the bikes were started. A trio of Harleys left together, followed by somebody on a sixties vintage BMW boxer. A sleek Victory Vegas slipped out ahead of a Yamaha FZ-1 and one of those huge Kawasaki Vulcans.

When the noise died, there were two bikes and two cars left in the glare of the security lights. The Road King was mine, the big blue Harley Ultra Classic with fishtail pipes was Magnus's. He calls her Eloise. At one time or another all of us had asked who Eloise was, but all Magnus would say was that she was someone he didn't want to forget. And when someone of Magnus's size and armament gives you that *subject closed* look, you rub your sweaty palms on the sides of your pants and say, "So… ah, how 'bout them Braves?"

After the drone of the last bike subsided into the night, I realized I could hear the wind in the trees. I glanced up. Low bands of dirty gray clouds tumbled across the night sky and buried the moon. I was wondering how soon the rain would come when Ruby stopped beside me. Her face was freshly scrubbed and she had her hair tied up in a ponytail. She was dressed in black tights, Reeboks and a pale blue fleece jacket. The sports bag looped over her shoulder must have contained her costumes. I didn't know what Magnus had arranged with her in the way of payment, but I made a mental note to double it.

"Thanks, Roman," she said. "I had fun." Then she frowned and quickly added, "Up to the end, anyway."

I gave her a quick hug and a smile.

"You blew us away, Ruby!"

"I did? Really?"

"Absolutely. Any other night that bunch would have carried you out on their shoulders."

"Wow! Thanks!" she said.

When she smiled I suddenly understood that people really can beam.

"You're welcome here anytime, Ruby," I said, "and don't worry about Ace – we'll take care of him."

She stood on her toes and gave me a peck on the cheek, then walked over to one of the two cars in the lot, a little yellow and black Mini Cooper tucked away in the corner. She chucked her bag inside, backed out like a state trooper in a hurry and zoomed off with a little chirp of rubber when she hit the highway.

Magnus joined me on the porch.

"Makes you wonder, ya know?" he said. "Can things get any fucking worse for a guy?"

Magnus grew up in western Minnesota, on a dairy farm near the town of Elbow Lake. He's the middle slot in a family of five, all boys. One of his brothers was killed by a drunk on a snowmobile, but the rest are all still in Elbow Lake, either working the farm or raising their own families near by. The Navy was Magnus's ticket out, but it didn't change his happy, open Minnesota demeanor much. And the SEALS, who must have kidded him unmercifully, didn't eliminate his singsong rural accent but they did manage to add a number of profanities to his vocabularies that were probably never heard on the Magnusson farm. Sometimes he blends them with the colorful colloquialisms of the region.

Actually, it was hard to imagine things getting any fucking worse for Ace.

"Yeah, Magnus," I said, "you're right. Let's check his car. Maybe it'll tell us something."

We stepped off the porch to the only car left in the lot, Ace's ink blue BMW 740i. It was off to the left of the steps, carelessly parked with the hood nearly under the porch. The G-String lights were bright enough for me to check the peeling City of Savannah parking permit in the lower left windshield. It had expired two years ago. The driver's door was wide open, but the interior lights had already timed out. When Magnus opened the passenger door they came back on.

A miniature dream catcher hung from the rearview mirror. Magnus unhooked it and held it closer to the light.

"Spendy looking," he said. "Not the usual cheap trinket."

I took it from him, held it closer to the light. He was right, it was beautifully made. White fur had been carefully stitched to the rim and the webbing inside was woven into a five-petal design with a small cluster of yellow stones in the center.

"It's Cherokee," I said. "It was hanging there last time I saw Ace. In fact, he told me he's had it in every car he ever owned – for luck. Guess it didn't do much for this poor Bimmer."

I hung it back on the rearview mirror and continued our examination of the car.

The black leather had seen better days. Dirty foam padding erupted from splits on both sides of the driver's seat. The steering wheel was shedding leather like a molting snake. Too many summers in the relentless Georgia sun had spidered the dash with cracks and cooked the color out of the carpeting. The floor was littered with red cardboard French fry boxes and greasy burger wrappers. The car had a rancid, unwashed smell, like a dank cave where some animal had crawled to die.

"Whew!" Magnus said, lifting his head to suck in some fresh air from outside the car. "Your friend's life was in the sewer, dontcha know."

I straightened up and banged my fist on the car's roof.

"I know, God damn it!" I said. "I know!"

Magnus clamped his jaw tightly and looked at me like I'd slapped his face.

"Sorry, Magnus," I said, "I'm not mad at you. I'm mad at myself. How could I let a friend – a friend who lives right here in my home town – get into this condition?"

Magnus shrugged his big shoulders.

"When was the last time you saw him then?" he asked.

Good question. When *was* the last time I saw Ace?

"It was right after he bought this car," I said, after casting back in my memory.

He popped the glove box, checked the leather bound owner's manual.

"This is a 2000 model," he said.

Before 9/11, even longer ago than I thought. I remembered seeing the car then, gleaming in the sunlight. I was having a sandwich at one of the sidewalk tables at Café Ambrosia on East Broughton. Ace pulled to the curb, lowered his window and called over to me. We chatted for maybe half a minute, just hey-nice-car-let's-get-together stuff, until traffic started to move, forcing him to pull away. I remember he looked good – the prosperous kind of good that a steady stream of money brings. Expensive haircut, clear eyes, easy smile. Nothing like the desperate wreck lying on the bunk inside.

"You've served two tours in Afghanistan and another in Iraq since then. You had all those months of rehab up in Augusta, eh. And what about the time you spent with the Aussies? You were on the other side of the world when this guy was self-destructing."

He was right, but Ace was my friend. Why didn't he get in touch? Even the other side of the world is only two seconds away by phone.

"Doesn't matter," I said. "If he'd called, I would have come."

More to the point: if *I* had called my friend once or twice over the years, maybe his life wouldn't be in the crapper today. I didn't like what that said about my value as a friend.

I swept my arm out, taking in the G-String and the land around it.

"Do you know Ace told me to buy this place?" I said.

"For crying out loud! That guy's your money man?"

"My money man?" I said with a laugh. "Yeah, I guess you could say he's my money man. Was in the beginning, anyway. After the Army, Ace worked for Charles Schwab for a couple of years, then started his own financial management business. Had a nice office in the historic district, on East Bryan Street. Made a ton of money. A ton."

I leaned into the car and pressed the trunk release button. The trunk lid rose an obedient inch and we both headed for the back of the car.

"I don't tell most people this, but when my mother died I inherited a good piece of money. For a long time, it was just sitting in the bank. Then Ace gave me some advice. I'll always remember what he told me – "

Magnus lifted the trunk lid and I stopped talking.

I don't know what I expected to find, but it wasn't a trunk full of clothes. Shirts, jeans, underwear, socks – all the stuff you normally keep in a dresser at home. Far in the back was a plain white Bell motorcycle helmet, along with a well-worn brown leather jacket and a pair of boots. The motorcycle gear brought back an image of Ace on an old Triumph Bonneville.

"What were you going to say, RK?" Magnus asked, as I gently pushed the trunk lid down. "About what he told you?"

"He told me it's only green paper until you buy something with it. He said, 'Buy land, preferably waterfront.'"

"Oh yeah? A good advisor, then?" he said. He inclined his head toward where Ace still lay inside the G-String. "So, how come he wants to die?"

I shook my head.

"I don't know, Magnus, but I'm going to find out. First thing I've got to do – "

I never finished that thought, because a big black crew cab pickup charged into the G-String parking lot. It jerked to a stop facing Magnus and me, kicking up gravel and sending clouds of dust billowing. Doors on both sides of the trucks opened simultaneously. Four dark figures stepped out. Squinting against the glare of the truck's headlights I saw they had the bulky look of men in body armor. When they moved closer I could see they all held assault weapons across their chests.

CHAPTER 9

THE ALARMS IN my head clamored a noisy get-the-hell-out-of-here warning. Magnus and I ducked behind Ace's car and sprinted for the door. We dived into the building. I slammed the heavy oak door behind us and we low crawled toward the bar.

The men outside, whoever they were, opened up. To my surprise, the chatter of their guns sounded no louder than someone drumming on the hood of a car with wooden sticks. Silencers on 9mm Heckler and Koch MP-5's, I thought, judging by my brief glimpse of fat barrels on stubby machine guns as I shut the door. Nothing heavy enough to punch through the cinderblock walls of the G-String, but the front windows shattered under the fusillade, scattering shards of glass down on us. We scrambled behind the bar.

After half a minute of curiously muted bedlam, there was sudden silence. One magazine gone for each of them, most likely.

Magnus whispered urgently, "Who *are* those guys?"

I don't know if he was intentionally mimicking the line from *Butch Cassidy and the Sundance Kid*, but I nearly laughed in spite of the situation. Magnus reached up cautiously over his head and felt around. His hand came back down with the .45 that Ace had brought in earlier. He handed it to me, then pulled out his Wilson.

I checked the magazine on the .45. Full load of semi-wad cutters. Target ammo. Not going to be much use against body armor. I reinserted the magazine and jacked a round into the chamber with the slide. I would have traded the wad cutters for full metal jackets, but the heavy pistol had a familiar, reassuring feel in my hand.

Magnus watched me check the .45.

"Yah. Okay. Two guys with handguns against four guys with automatic weapons. Not too good a deal. And who has access to HKs with silencers like that?" he said. "If I had my damn druthers, you know I'd have more firepower."

"Relax, Magnus. We've got a good defensive position."

It was still quiet outside, but I knew that wouldn't last long.

"Good…" I said, "but we'll have better cover on the far side of the stage."

Magnus nodded once and slipped away without a word. He knew the real reason I was spotting us where I did. Those guys were after Ace. Moving to the stage let us cover the door to the storeroom and still have a bolt hole out the backdoor if we needed it.

Just as we made it to the stage, the door finally gave way, splintering under a relentless stream of bullets.

They stormed in quickly, but with good tactical movement. Red dots from laser sights danced from spot to spot as they cleared their way along the booths.

I lined up Ace's .45 over the top of the stage and fired three rounds at the lead intruder.

Bam, bam, bam!

The .45 sounded like a howitzer compared to the silenced MP-5's. Magnus blasted the second man in line. Both targets staggered backward as our rounds smacked into their armored torsos, but neither man went down. One man's sleeve blossomed red from Magnus's shot, but otherwise we hadn't done any damage.

Magnus and I flattened ourselves behind the stage and scooted further back behind the big speakers a split second before all four of the gunmen sprayed a withering fusillade in our direction. The firing continued non-stop for another minute, in rapid bursts that kept our heads down. When the barrage abated, I risked a quick peek. Another spurt from an MP-5 nearly took my head off. I poked the .45 over the edge of the stage and loosed off another three rounds. Magnus rolled on his back, held the Wilson over his head and sprayed the rest of the magazine using his thumb on the trigger.

I wiggled over to the edge of the stage. I glanced at Magnus. He nodded, held the reloaded Wilson up again and loosed off another barrage. As he fired, I stole a quick glance around the end.

"Magnus!" I said when he paused for a second. "They're gone!"

I scrambled to my feet, the .45 in a two-handed grip. The pungent stink of cordite hung heavily in the air. Hundreds of bright brass shell casings sparkled on the floor. The entire stage looked like mad men with hatchets had hacked it into splinters. The big Maranz speaker high on the wall, near where Magnus and I had taken cover, was completely shredded. Lines of bullet holes pocked the walls over the booths. Three random holes starred the mirror behind the bar.

The men were indeed gone. I lowered the .45 and clicked the safety up with my thumb.

Magnus holstered his own pistol and said, "Can you believe it? Those guys were wearing military body armor, eh?"

I nodded.

"They moved well too," I said. "Silent commands."

Magnus shook his head gently, trying to clear his hearing. Firing any handgun an enclosed space will make your ears ring. Even loaded with wadcutters, Ace's .45 was an acoustic sledgehammer. Magnus's 9mm wasn't much quieter and he'd ripped through two magazines.

"In and out fast," he said, working his jaws and poking a finger in one ear.

I nodded again.

"And they had a fortunate tendency to shoot high. Otherwise, they were damn good."

Then he touched my shoulder. I turned his way, followed line of sight.

The door to the storeroom hung open about six inches, the jam splintered.

"Oh, shit," I muttered, fearing the worst.

I pushed a shoulder against it, edged carefully in and felt for the light switch with my fingers. The bare overhead light hit the room with a bright glare that made me blink. More shell casings littered the floor, and the stink of cordite was even stronger in here, maybe because it was such a tight little space. Magnus crowded in behind me. We looked up at the top bunk. Ace's lumpy form lay motionless. Magnus reached a hand out to lift the blanket, then suddenly jumped back.

Ace sat up. He looked like a corpse coming unexpectedly to life in a morgue.

"What... hell?" he said, barely coherent.

I ripped the blanket off the bottom bunk. Not a single piece over six inches in diameter remained in the piles of shattered porcelain. One of the intruders had burst into the storeroom and emptied a magazine into the bottom bunk. The light, I thought. The light was off when I came in just now. If the shooter had turned the light on, he would have realized his mistake.

"Ace," I said, "if you have the nine lives of a cat, you're down to eight." I reached up to help him down. "Come on, let's get out of here."

Magnus and I hauled Ace down from the bunk. He was weak and shaky, but at least he was conscious this time, so the process was a little smoother than getting him up there. We supported him between us and shuffled through the carnage of the G-String like an entry in a three-legged race.

I half expected to see a squad of police cars in the gravel parking lot, but it was deserted except for our bikes and Ace's car. My ears were ringing from the gunshots, but I guess the silencers on the HKs and the heavy cinderblock construction of the G-String had contained the noise. I glanced toward the road and thought the half-mile of woods between here and the main road had worked in our favor too. Quiet reigned in the night, except for the wind, which gusted even stronger than earlier in the treetops. The low clouds had multiplied into a solid overcast.

Ace's car looked like it had been caught in a war zone. All four doors stood open and the trunk lid was up. The clothes and gear Ace had in the trunk were strewn all over the parking lot. The windshield was stitched with bullet holes and the headlights had been shot out.

"Somebody's pissed at you, Ace," Magnus said. "You bet. Really fucking pissed."

Ace gave a grunt of dismay and pulled away from us. He staggered forward a couple of steps, then fell to his knees with a crack that sounded painful. He pawed at the pile of clothes.

He gathered pieces seemingly at random, tucking them under his arms, then dropping them without noticing as he picked up something else. I knelt to help him. Close up I could see the tears in his eyes, and I realized that this was all he had. A lifetime stored in the trunk of a car, and now it was spread all over the gravel like garbage from an upended dumpster.

To add insult, a few fat drops of rain fell from the dark sky. Time to go, I thought. We wouldn't be so lucky if they came back again. We slammed the doors and started throwing the clothes back in the trunk. I grabbed Ace's old leather jacket from the pile and pushed it against his chest.

"Put that on," I said.

I rooted around and finally found his helmet, which had rolled beneath the bumper. I helped Ace strap it on.

"Grab our gear from inside," I said to Magnus. "I'll call Doc Lukens and tell him where we're going."

"Not to your place, then?" Magnus asked.

I paused. Normally I wouldn't have hesitated to fill Magnus in on the events from earlier in the day. I trusted him completely. But this was different. Winter Rose desperately wanted her private life to stay private.

"Let's just say Ace here is my second save of the day. The Doc's at my house now tending to the first."

"*Second* save, he says," Magnus said, raising both eyebrows in surprise. When I didn't elaborate, he shrugged his shoulders. "So, what's the problem? Move the first guy to the couch."

I smiled in spite of the situation.

"Yeah, well, the first guy is a young lady who needs her privacy."

Now it was Magnus's turn to smile.

"Well, then. Two rescues and one's a woman, he says."

"Down boy," I said.

He waved a hand.

"Just kidding. So, where we gonna stash Ace, then?"

"Virgil's," I said.

"Virgil's!" Magnus said, the grin springing back even wider. "Won't he be pleased?" He spun around and went in for our helmets and jackets.

While Ace fumbled into his gear, I called Doc Lukens. He was still at my house when he answered my call. Everything was fine, but Winter Rose had been awake when he'd gone to check on her. He'd given her another small sedative and she'd just fallen asleep again. He took the change of location in his stride.

Magnus hurried out with our riding gear. He donned his own while I kept a wobbly Ace on his feet, then Magnus propped him up while I shrugged into my jacket and strapped on my helmet. After Magnus had his Ultra cranked up, I guided Ace over and got him settled on the passenger seat. On a whim, I ducked into the front of Ace's car and retrieved the dream catcher from the mirror. I stowed it carefully in my left saddlebag, wedged between my chaps and side of the bag. Maybe it would bring his next car better luck.

I lifted the Road King off its side stand, started up and kicked it into gear. Just before the main road, we stopped for a moment while I wrestled the old wooden gate across the road. I had opened it years ago when I bought the property and never closed it since, but still had the "Private Property" sign screwed to the top board and I figured it would keep people out until I could do something about all the bullet holes. Magnus waited patiently with Ace until I was back aboard my bike. As I let the clutch out, the black sky opened up like a busted dam, unleashing a cold spring monsoon.

CHAPTER 10

A BRONZE PLAQUE SCREWED to the faded blue paint of the front door at Virgil's halfway house quoted Abraham Lincoln:

IT HAS BEEN MY EXPERIENCE THAT
FOLKS WHO HAVE NO VICES
HAVE VERY FEW VIRTUES.

Below the plaque a hand-lettered sign was taped to the door, apparently written by one of Virgil's volunteers on the back of a wrinkled piece of recycled typing paper. It said simply, "Ring bell for help."

I stabbed the button once.

We huddled from the downpour under the shelter of the little porch. Magnus and I probably looked like motorcycle zombies with our soggy leather jackets, soaked jeans and helmets still dripping from the rain, each with an arm around Ace, who had managed to stay awake on the short ride over from the G-String but now hung between us limp as a fresh corpse. A lone eighteen-wheeler rumbled over our heads on the Truman

Parkway, laying down a nose-clogging fog of diesel smoke. Pale moths flickered through the raindrops around a light fastened to the left of the door. Under the light a smaller bronze plaque proclaimed the old frame house to be St. George's Rescue Mission. Few people, even the volunteers and "guests," know that St. George is the Catholic patron saint of highways. I've always wondered how you get to be patron saint of the highways. And is there also a patron saint of cars? Or motorcycles? Or even strip clubs?

My brother Virgil chose the name St. George's the same day that I put the sign up on the G-String. I'm sure his choice was as tongue-in-cheek as mine. We're different in more ways than most identical twins, but we share a certain sense of the ironic.

Virgil's Jesuit career has not exactly followed the usual pattern. At times he's been their shining star, but his propensity for free thinking periodically gets him in trouble. If the Jesuits had stripes of rank on their cassocks like the Army, Virgil's would have to be attached with Velcro for easy removal.

The sermon incident from three years ago is typical Virgil. It started when he was invited to deliver a series of sermons at the Cathedral of St. John the Baptist in Savannah, the same church he had sought refuge in as a kid. The pulpit is not the usual haunt of a Jesuit, but Virgil's inspiring talks at Jesuit retreats were well known. One Sunday, while looking out on a sea of bored, empty faces, Virgil departed from his planned remarks. He later claimed that half of the congregation was actually asleep at the time, but the Jesuit hierarchy felt that was scant justification for pounding both fists on the pulpit and shouting, "Eternity is a long fucking time, people!"

I thought the line was great. In fact, I used it to good effect during a mission briefing and for a short time the phrase could frequently be heard around our company area. One Ranger liked the phrase so much he added it to the death's head tattoo on his shoulder, in an elaborate script that looked like it had been lifted from an old Bible.

The eternity sermon by itself would have simply gotten Virgil busted down a figurative rank or two. The hangman's noose debacle pushed things over the edge.

At the start of mass the following month, instead of crossing himself as usual when he genuflected in front of the altar, Virgil jerked his right arm straight up into the air, cocked his head to the left, closed his eyes and stuck out his tongue. He made the same gesture in place of the sign of the cross numerous times as the mass progressed.

The congregation was thoroughly bewildered by the time Virgil started his sermon. Their frantic whispers had risen in volume each time he repeated the strange little ritual and an urgent buzz rumbled through the church. Virgil climbed to the pulpit and raised his hands for silence.

"Let's play *What If?*" he said.

He lowered his hands.

"Just imagine this *What If?*"

He paused until he saw all faces riveted on his.

"What if Jesus had been hung instead of crucified. Would we make this sign after each prayer?"

He repeated the gesture he had been making. This time he gave it his best dramatic effort: lips stretched in a gruesome grimace, tongue thrust out, eyes bulging and neck tendons straining.

"Would the rosary have a hangman's noose on the end?"

He pointed toward the back of the cathedral.

"Would we dangle a rope from a gallows high above the altar, instead of the crucifix?"

Naturally, people were horrified, the cross being the sacred symbol of Christianity. Virgil's point was that it was an instrument of torture and execution, and merely the most common device in use at the time.

"What if the timing was different?" Virgil asked. "Closer to present day? Would we wear little golden rifles on delicate necklaces if Jesus had been executed by a firing squad? Or dangle miniature electric chairs from our rearview mirrors?"

At a Jesuit hearing later, Virgil claimed in his defense that he had noticed many women, and even a large number of men, wearing crosses as jewelry. Some encrusted with diamonds. He had even seen belly button jewelry in the form of a cross. The notion of a sacred cross or holy crucifix had been perverted beyond reason, he said. He just wanted people to reconsider what the symbol of the cross really meant.

Of course, it didn't help that many of the kids took to the notion with enthusiasm and choked themselves with imaginary ropes whenever they genuflected for months afterwards. The Jesuits decided it was time to stash Virgil out of the public eye for a while.

One of their bean counters suggested turning this house into a rescue mission and putting Virgil in charge. It had been left to the Church by an ornery old recluse who wouldn't budge, even after the city built a flyover for the Truman Parkway right across his roof. For Virgil, it was like being thrown in the proverbial briar patch. He promptly turned it into a very successful halfway house for addicts and alcoholics. He's been tending the vice-ridden ever since.

We heard a metallic double click as a deadbolt worthy of a

New York apartment was released, then the front door opened and my brother filled the entrance. He was dressed in his version of Jesuit priest attire: blue jeans, purple Crocs and a short-sleeved black shirt with a crisp white clerical collar. His hair was the silver of brushed aluminum like mine, but he wore his Jesus long while mine was still Ranger short. We shared clothes all the time as kids, but these days he couldn't squeeze into my jeans without divine intervention even though he was dieting again.

Virgil's right eye is brown and his left is green, the mirror image of mine. My mother told me that to tell us apart as babies she recited a little rhyme she made up, "Roman Keane, right eye green." When we were kids Virgil and I had a secret ceremony; a rite we performed whenever life around our tumultuous house was too much for one young boy alone. Hiding behind the garage, or down in the basement or up in our room, we pressed our foreheads together to line our eyes up – green to green and brown to brown – and chanted, "Eye-to-eye, heart-to-heart, brothers forever." We haven't done that since our father's death, more than twenty years ago.

Virgil examined Magnus and me with our burden.

"Roman," he said. He made a show of checking his watch. "Seven hours a civilian, yet you look like you've just dragged your ass off the battlefield."

"Good to see you, too, Virg."

He smiled at me to take the sting out of his greeting and shifted his gaze to Magnus.

"How are you, Mr. Magnusson?" he said.

"Can't complain, Father Keane, can't complain," Magnus said with his broad grin.

"Let's see what you have here," he said, turning his attention to Ace.

Virgil slipped a pair of slender reading glasses from the open ended case clipped into his breast pocket, perched them on his nose and tilted his head back to look through the lenses. He gently lifted Ace's eyelids one at a time to check his pupils.

When he finished, he looked quietly at me and said, "Well?"

"Drunk, dehydrated, depressed. Doc Lukens is on his way over to have a look."

"Stability?" Virgil asked.

"He won't die on you, unless someone kills him first."

Virgil lifted an eyebrow.

"He used to be as solid as they come," I said. "Somehow he got mixed up in something so terrible he wants to die. And somebody else wants to make sure he does. They just tried to kill him over at the G-String."

Virgil looked quickly around the dark neighborhood, like a team of assassins might be lurking out there.

He stepped aside and said, "Better come in, then."

As I squeezed by, Virgil planted a hand on my shoulder and said, "Still a lightning rod for trouble, aren't you Roman?"

CHAPTER 11

S T. GEORGE'S WAS surprisingly spacious once you got past the cramped entranceway. It was another sore point with his Jesuit superiors, but Virgil refused to turn his share of our mother's estate over to the church. Instead of divesting himself of the modest wealth by donating it, he simply stuffed it into a money market savings account and used the interest as he saw fit. To upgrade St. George's, for instance. He had completely renovated the interior, opening the available space into an office, a lounge and a big kitchen. In the back, ten individual rooms had been created, barely large enough for a single bed, a chair and a small table, but providing each patient with a private living space. Each room had a window and a footlocker. Pastel yellow walls and earth-toned bed covers with matching throw rugs kept them from looking like barracks or cells. Two doors opened as we passed, and sleep-tousled patients looked out curiously.

"Back to bed," Virgil said gently. "Remember, we get the same respect we give."

There were one or two last looks, but everyone obeyed.

Virgil lived in a room at the back, hardly larger than the

others. Beyond his room, the back porch had been enclosed and now served as a chapel. A bronze plaque on the chapel door was inscribed with this quotation:

How far you go in life
Depends on your being
Tender with the young,
Compassionate with the aged,
Sympathetic with the striving and
Tolerant of the weak and the strong,
Because someday in life
You will have been all of these.

It was another favorite of Virgil's, not from the lips of a preacher or a pope, but from the pen of George Washington. I had donated the worn oak pews, as well as the polished granite altar and the stained glass cross that had been mounted in the wall behind it, when I had remodeled the little church that was now my home.

We moved Ace into the last room in the place, situated directly across the hall from the chapel. By the time we had Ace settled into the narrow bed, Doc Lukens rang the doorbell. Virgil asked Magnus to bring him back. When Doc Lukens came dripping into the little bedroom with his bags, Magnus and I moved back to the living room to give him and Virgil space to work. I scooped up Ace's sodden clothes on the way out.

Moving quietly to avoid disturbing the other St. George's residents, we went straight to the kitchen, where I dumped the wet clothes in the sink. Magnus flipped on the lights and I started going through the pockets. I lined each item up on the counter as I fished it out. In right front pocket of the slacks I found a plain metal key ring with the key to the BMW and three house-type keys. His wallet was in the right side back pocket. It was an old bi-fold style, good leather but well past its normal service life. The wallet held Ace's driver's license – still valid and with a motorcycle endorsement – an expired platinum Delta SkyMiles card from American Express and three one dollar bills.

In the left side back pocket, I discovered a slim softcover notebook. It was creased and damp, but readable. Only the first page contained any entries, a list of six names and addresses. I had just begun to read through them when Virgil and Doc Lukens joined us.

"What's the diagnosis, Doc?" I asked, setting the notebook down with the rest of Ace's things.

"Severe dehydration, moderate malnutrition and alcohol poisoning. Hate to think what his liver looks like. I've got some fluids started. I'll pump as much as he can take into him tonight."

Doc Lukens agreed to stay until morning. Virgil explained that Ace had taken the last available bed, but that the couch wasn't too uncomfortable.

"Wouldn't be my first night on a couch, Father Keane," Doc Lukens said.

Virgil and the Doc went off in search of sheets and a blanket.

Magnus and I turned back to the row of items from Ace's pockets. What the hell had Ace gotten himself into?

I held Ace's driver's license up to the light. A younger, cleaner version of Ace looked out at me from the photograph in the corner. I checked the address: 754 Whitaker Street. He'd lived at that address when I'd seen him last, a nice two-story house facing Forsyth Park. If he was using his car as a clothes closet, I'd be surprised if he still owned the house.

I stuck the license back into the wallet and picked up the

notebook. I glanced at the list Ace had written on the first page, then flipped through the rest of the pages to make sure he hadn't made any other entries. The rest of the pages were blank, so I turned back to the list.

Six names, six addresses. I read through them one by one as Doc Lukens arranged his gear by the couch. I recognized only one name, Linc Price. Like Ace, he was another a vet I had not come across in years. The rest of the names and addresses didn't mean anything to me.

Until I read the last one. My heart nearly stopped when I read it: Brad Beardsley, 27 East Perry Street, Savannah, Georgia.

Virgil, who had returned to the living room with sheets and a blanket, sensed something was wrong immediately. The brother connection was never turned all the way off.

"Roman?" he said, passing the linen to Doc Lukens.

"Virgil," I said, handing him the notebook, "look at this."

I pointed out the last entry in Ace's list. Virgil held the notebook with two fingers while he fished his reading glasses out of his pocket. When he got them open and settled on his nose, he glanced at the page.

"Brad Beardsley?" he said. "Should that ring a bell?"

I pointed again. "Not the name, Virgil, the address."

He read the address. A silent moment passed while his tired mind processed the information. His face turned white. He threw the notebook down like it had suddenly turned into a poisonous snake.

"What is this, Roman? What?"

I was as stunned as Virgil.

The house at 27 East Perry Street was where Virgil and I grew up. It was also the house where I killed our father.

CHAPTER 12

ONE OF US was bound to kill him. And if I wasn't ordained for that horrible act right from the moment of our conception, I think I was chosen for it at birth.

Virgil was born one minute and thirteen seconds after me; less time than it takes to warm a cup of coffee in a microwave, but that interval defined us. We were identical twins, but I was the older brother and he was the younger. He and I always armwrestled to a draw and raced to a dead heat on our bikes, but Virgil was the follower. Our mother, Elizabeth Caswell Keane, saw to it that I never pulled rank but it was always Virgil who deferred and I who decided. And I was the one who protected us from the one man who we should have been able to count on to protect us.

Our father, Randall Keane, was a workingman who married up. He sold pharmaceuticals for a living, servicing hospitals and physicians as far south as Miami. It earned him a middleclass tax bracket, but that was a long way from serious money. My mother was from serious money. She was from an old southern family with old southern money and, more importantly, old southern society. Her father was Tilman Caswell III, chairman of the board of the largest bank in Savannah, the largest holder of riverfront commercial real estate and owner of five downtown office buildings. A lot of rich and powerful people in Georgia, Florida and South Carolina called him sir; Virgil and I called him Grandpa Tillie. Both of us were named after him, Roman Tilman Keane and Virgil Tilman Keane.

I loved that old man. Now and then on a Saturday morning he would take Virgil and me up to his office where he'd bring the old oil portraits on the walls to life with stories about Caswells who took part in everything from naval battles to mergers. My favorite stories were about Lawson Caswell, who entered the Civil War as a lieutenant in the 3rd Georgia Infantry under Ambrose Wright. By the end of the war, he had fought in seven major battles, been wounded twice and had been promoted to colonel. He was twenty-four when he returned home to Savannah.

In a safe in his office, Grandpa Tillie had the LeMat revolver that Colonel Caswell had carried throughout the war. It was a strange and wonderful pistol, so worn with use and time that it looked like it was made of polished pewter. The cylinder carried nine bullets instead of the usual six, and underneath the main barrel was a second barrel, shorter and fatter, that fired a single round of buckshot. Everything about that pistol fascinated me. Grandpa Tillie told me it was made in Paris, then sent to England, then to Bermuda. From there a blockade runner brought it to Savannah. The Saturday mornings I remember best I sat with that revolver cradled in my hands and listened to Grandpa Tillie tell Virgil and me tales of Lieutenant Caswell at Second Manassas, or Captain Caswell at Antietam, or Colonel Caswell at Gettysburg.

One summer Saturday when we were eight years old, he sat

Virgil and me down on a shady bench in Johnson Square, an arm around each of us, enveloping us in the sweet cherry aroma of his pipe tobacco.

"You boys listen carefully," he said. "Hear me now?"

He made us sit still until he had our attention.

"You come to me if your daddy gives you trouble," he said. "Come right to me. I'll take care of everything."

Virgil asked, "What kind of trouble, Grandpa Tillie?"

The old man just shook his head and said, "You'll know when it comes your way. For now let's just call it big trouble, boys. Anything you can't take to your momma."

He knew, I think, that my father could marry a Caswell but never *be* a Caswell. Maybe he suspected my father had deeper flaws, too. Unfortunately, Grandpa Tillie died that winter. The trouble began soon after. My father discovered the old man had wrapped all that lovely old family money in trusts guarded by old family lawyers and stern-faced old family accountants, all determined to keep him from getting his "grubby hands" on any of it.

From that point on, Virgil and I grew up with my father's abuse. To us the twisted arms, the head slaps and the periodic lashes with the heavy belt passed for nearly normal. At least once a month the door to my parents' bedroom slammed shut and we cringed while he shouted in rage and she screamed in fear. We huddled miserably together and listened with dread to the muffled thumps, the groans, the terrible silence afterward.

When we were thirteen, tall and strong for teenagers and young men in our own minds, I was the one who first stepped between my father and my mother.

My mother tried to push me away and said, "Roman, no!

You don't understand, I know, but this is my... my penance. This is what I deserve."

My father slammed a hard fist into my stomach that doubled me over in pain and drove every breath of air from my lungs. "Get out of here, you little punk!" he said. "It'll take a bigger man than you to stand up to me."

After that, I became his favorite target. When we heard our father's footsteps thumping up the stairs after he had agitated his dark demons with a flask of Johnny Walker, I always took the first and most vicious wave of hatred. By the time he turned to Virgil, our father's fists had slowed and his alcoholic rage was washing away like the outgoing tide.

When we were nearly fifteen, Mom came down with pancreatic cancer. Our father transferred his attentions, and his sexual aggression, to Virgil. Virgil rationalized that he was finally getting his due. Six months later Mom died. My father played it for all it was worth: rumpled dark suits, "forgetting" to shave for that how-can-I-go-on look, prayer meetings in the parlor, grateful acceptance of countless tuna casseroles and tinfoil-covered paper plates of home-baked sugar cookies that he dumped straight into the trash can as soon as the front door closed. Less than a week after my mother's funeral, our already tilted world turned completely upside down.

CHAPTER 13

I REMEMBER THE WEATHER that day, the thirteenth of August: windy, with low dark clouds that spit fitful sprays of rain before unleashing a torrent of rare summer hail. It caught me a mile from home on my bike and pelted my head like pebbles pitched from an airplane. I'd been working at Uncle Gil's, but had left early to check on Virgil. He had stayed home since the funeral, afflicted by something: flu or maybe just heartsickness. Either way, he wouldn't eat, looked like hell and slept like the dead.

With one hand shielding my eyes, I pedaled hard through the pinging hail. I wheeled my bike straight into the garage, surprised to find my father's black Seville parked there. He had left to service his pharmaceutical clients in Miami and Fort Lauderdale on Wednesday and wasn't due back until late on Saturday.

Inside the house I found another surprise – Virgil wasn't sleeping. His bed was unmade, sheets rumpled and blanket on the floor. I picked up the blanket and the alarm bells that were already ringing in my head turned to sirens. A splash of congealing blood wet the floor next to the bed. More of it stained the blanket I was holding.

I flew down the stairs, hardly touching the steps with my feet. I checked the kitchen, the living room and the dining room. All empty. Puzzled, I tiptoed toward the back of the house. Toward my father's den.

It was the last place I expected to find Virgil. My father reserved that room, downstairs at the back of the house, for himself. And knowing the kind of pain he could inflict with his big hands and powerful arms, we tried to avoid stirring his wrath.

The den was generously proportioned, with thick wall-to-wall carpet, floor-to-ceiling wood paneling, a heavy desk and a massive leather couch that would have looked more at home in an Ivy League library. Naturally we snuck in from time to time in spite of our fears.

Our objective was always Colonel Caswell's LeMat pistol, which my father had somehow managed to wrestle from the Caswell lawyers. The priceless revolver was still nestled in the beautiful walnut case Grandpa Tillie had had made for it, but my father kept it open on his desk instead of locked away in a safe. He'd convinced a local gunsmith to cast bullets and percussion caps for it. He didn't have the nerve to actually fire it, but Virgil and I had breathlessly cracked the door just a hair one night and discovered him sitting alone at his desk cocking and uncocking it.

On the wall to the right of the door was a small but elegant gun case. Through the cut glass doors three shotguns were visible. A 1926 Ithaca double barrel in the classic side-by-side configuration that had been Grandpa Tillie's favorite duck hunting gun, an over-under skeet gun and a modern Remington pump. I knew they were there for looks – my father had tried trap shooting once, but couldn't hit a damn thing. He'd bragged that they were always loaded, though. I checked once, and discovered he was telling the truth about that at least.

I put my ear to the door. Silence. No, wait. A voice, laughing. And something else. A small child sobbing? With a shock I realized it was Virgil. I threw the door open and everything froze. Since that day I've seen the horrors of war in Iraq and Afghanistan, up close in hot, loud and messy Technicolor, but nothing has yet displaced that tableau from my memory.

Virgil knelt on the floor, a rope around his neck pulling his upper body over one of the padded arms of the couch. His hands were tied behind his back. He was wearing only the tops of his pajamas. Blood leaked from his smashed nose and split lips. Tears streamed from his eyes. The look on his face was a heart breaking mixture of agony and humiliation.

My father stood behind Virgil, tucking himself back into his trousers.

He snapped his head up. The surprise in his eyes changed quickly to a smile. Not the kind of smile your normal dad gives his son. A Charles Manson smile, midway between sinister amusement and utter contempt.

"Perfect," he said. "Both my little snots right where I want them."

I stepped over to help Virgil up, but my father had other plans. He snatched a pistol off the desk and pointed it at me. I started to raise my hands, but he pulled the trigger. Instead of the loud bang I braced for, the gun made a p-phut sound, then I felt a sharp bee sting on my thigh.

I heard my father laugh. He held the gun up for me to see.

It was about the size of an ordinary target pistol, but it had a thick black cylinder under the barrel.

"Like it?" he said, his laughter subsiding to chuckles. "It's a dart gun. The Atlanta Zoo ordered it, for tranquilizing lions and tigers. They were supposed to get it today, but they'll have to wait until tomorrow."

I bent down and pulled the dart out of my leg. It was a small plastic hypodermic with a needle and a yellow plunger.

"I loaded that dart with a fascinating little drug called Tracrium," he said. "Hospitals use it in the operating room. Causes paralysis in about two minutes." He set the pistol on the desk. "Temporary, of course. Twenty minutes, half an hour at the most, but that's plenty of time. All the time in the world, in fact."

My legs buckled and I slumped to my knees. He knelt down next to me, grabbed my jacket and jerked my face right up to his.

"Guess who I talked to?" he bellowed.

He shook me back and forth so hard I bit my tongue when my jaw clanged shut. He pulled me face-to-face again, his eyes bulging.

"That shyster Caswell lawyer, that's who! He showed me your mother's will."

He lifted me another inch and shoved his forehead against mine.

"Know what that bitch did?" he shouted.

I was too frightened to answer, or even shake my head.

"Do you know what that bitch did?" he screamed.

I dared not speak. I turned my head to the side, a careful quarter inch one way, then the other.

"She left it all to you two punks. Know what she left me?

Me? Me, her loving husband? A trust fund! A damn trust fund, so I can make sure we all live here in comfort."

Flecks of white foam clung to his lips and his hot breath rasped in my face. I tried to push him away. My arms felt like they were made of stone.

"She didn't count on one thing: if you both die at the same time, I get everything. The money, the investments and the fucking house!"

Without turning my head too far, I looked cautiously around for something I could hit him with, anything to knock him down so I could untie Virgil and get out of there before the drug kicked in completely.

"Well, guess what? When I get home tomorrow, I'm gonna discover a tragedy. The world's biggest heartbreaking mother of a tragedy."

Nothing right at hand. The gun cabinet was slightly beyond reach, just over his left shoulder. But the glass doors were open.

"Imagine this, boys," he said, throwing a hard glance at Virgil then drilling his eyes back into me. "The hardworking father – Mr. Reliable, old Mr. Dedication – comes home from business and opens the door to his den only to discover… his poor twins dead!"

I rehearsed the move in my mind: lean forward, use my weight to get my father off balance, reach out and grab one of the shotguns by the stock. Remember to lift it slightly to get the butt clear of the cabinet.

"A double suicide!"

"That's stupid!" I yelled. My hot breath ricocheted off my father's face. "You'll never get away with it. They'll know what you did to Virgil."

He didn't even flinch.

"Oh, they'll find out what happened to Virgil, all right. I'm going to tell them myself."

That chilling smile crept back onto his face.

"That's the beauty of my plan," he said. "I'm going to tell them all about the sick things *you* did to your brother."

The smile expanded into a victory grin.

"And I'll make sure the evidence backs me up – a bit of Virgil's skin under your fingernails, a strand of your pubic hair on his collar. It won't take much. They'll believe what I tell them."

He tilted his head back and laughed.

"After all, I'm the goddamned Rock of Gibraltar, the church-going family man everybody admires."

He was right. He could get away with it. I flexed my fingers, tried to will some strength back into muscles turning to feeble Jell-O by the drug he'd injected into my leg.

"I'll be devastated! I'll weep! I'll be inconsolable! I'll say, 'They were just boys. They didn't know what they were doing.'"

I measured the distance to the gun cabinet again with my eyes. Too far, too far.

"Know which gun you're going to use?" he said.

The Manson grin returned to his face yet again. He reached into the box on his desk and lifted out the LeMat pistol.

"This one!" he said flourishing the pistol. "The famous Colonel Caswell's own revolver! Hah! The family heirloom! This story will live forever in Savannah history. For fucking ever!"

Last chance, I thought. I sagged into him and hung on until my weight dropped him back onto his heels. Then I lunged up for the gun cabinet.

My arms moved in slow motion. It felt like gravity had somehow tripled. My hands came up short.

My father grunted with surprise, then recovered and levered himself upright. He cocked the pistol. It was a hundred and fifty years old, but it worked perfectly. The hammer locked back with an ominous metallic clack. He turned the barrel toward my temple.

I stretched desperately. My fingers found a tenuous grip on the stock of the Ithaca. I leaned into it, got a solid grip, then pushed off. Somehow, the gun cleared the cabinet.

My father realized what I was trying to do. He dropped the pistol to the floor and shifted his hands to the shotgun. We wrestled it between us, barrels up. His eyes glared at me like hot white buttons. His lips pulled back from his teeth. I felt the cool metal of the Ithaca's barrels sliding along my cheek.

"Think you can beat me, boy?"

I strained against him until I heard sinew pop in my shoulders.

"You want the shotgun instead of the pistol? Fine by me!" He pushed harder.

I shifted one hand high up on the shotgun, but my strength was draining away. The twin muzzles of the shotgun scraped along my chin and slid against my neck.

"Say goodbye!" he said, reaching for the trigger.

With nothing to lose, I stopped pushing and dropped all my weight onto the gun. I gained an inch before my father caught himself, but it was enough. I rose up as high as I could reach on my knees and rammed my forehead into his nose.

In the split second his head was back, I shoved the shotgun under my father's chin and reached down blindly with my right hand. I fumbled frantically and found the trigger guard with my fingers. I jammed them through the metal ring and pressed down.

Both barrels exploded.

My father's face disappeared. Chin, mouth, nose, eyes – everything. A warm red mist blossomed into the air like a cloud of tinted steam. I felt it settle wetly on my face, but otherwise the world seemed to have stopped. After the deafening crash of the shotgun, there was total silence.

In my memory, I always see it like a witness rather than a participant, as though I'm looking at a photograph of the scene taken from near the doorway. Maybe that's how I cope with an image that refuses to fade with time – by adding some distance. I see all three of us on our knees. My father and I are locked in a morbid embrace, both of our hands on the shotgun; Virgil is still tied-up and bent over the couch.

I thought the phrase "death grip" was only an exaggeration, but the shotgun was seized like a vise in my father's dead hands. I let go.

My hands didn't obey. My fingers wouldn't open. The drug my father had injected into my thigh with the dart gun had taken full effect. I could breathe and, strangely, my eyes swiveled freely, although I couldn't seem to control them properly. Otherwise, I couldn't move. I tried so hard. I stared at my hands and willed them to move. But I couldn't let go of that shotgun.

We held each other in that unwilling embrace for long seconds, then he slowly toppled, pulling me inexorably along. He thumped down on the carpet and bounced once, spraying a gout of blood from the remains of his head before he settled for good.

The impact dislodged my hands from the shotgun but I landed on my right side, facing my father's mangled corpse. My eyes wandered over the shattered remains of his head, only inches from my own. I shut them, but they opened again, involuntarily. The drug locked my eyelids open. A quick blink was all I could manage. Of their own accord, my eyes turned back to my father's ruined face. They surveyed the jagged stump of jaw, one molar sheared cleanly by the buckshot, roots and silver metallic filling exposed. My eyes lingered perversely on the raw lump of meat that remained of his tongue. In far too much detail they examined a spongy glistening glob of brain, hanging loose from the shattered skull. They marveled at the right ear, curiously untouched by the carnage that wasted the rest of my father's head.

Finally, I forced my eyes to look down.

I could see my father's hands still locked on the shotgun. I could see my own hands, too. I tried to move them, but they may as well have been the bloody, lifeless hands of someone else's corpse. I could see my watch, an original Ball timepiece with a crocodile wristband Grandpa Tillie had left to me. The face was speckled with blood, but I could read the time. Ten minutes after four. If my father was telling the truth, I was trapped here next to his dead body until four thirty. At least.

Virgil called out, his voice pitched so high it was nearly falsetto.

"Roman!"

I could hear! Sounds had a weird echo, almost a vibrato, but I could hear.

"Roman!" my brother shouted again, hysteria sharpening his voice until it cut like a knife.

"Oh my God, oh my God, oh my God…"

Caked in my father's blood and shotgun-blasted bits of brain and bone, I must have looked dead to him.

His voice softened, the repeated litany running into one long word. Or maybe a prayer.

"OhmyGodohmyGodohmyGod…"

With my attention elsewhere, my eyes traveled back to the bloody ruin that remained of my father's head. I cast them down instead. Checked my watch. Four eleven. I would have moaned if I could have made a sound. My eyes gravitated upward again. I forced them down, let them wander in safer territory, away from the carnage that had been my father's head.

A wet sensation enveloped my right ear and the side of my head, where it lay in contact with the floor. I realized two things: first, I couldn't move but I could feel. Second, I was lying in a spreading pool of my father's blood.

Time slowed to a cruel crawl. To keep my eyes away from my father's corpse, I made myself follow the slow rotation of the sweep second hand on my watch. It creeped through three more minutes.

I heard a thump and a groan. Virgil, I realized, was trying to work himself free. He grunted hard and I could picture him pulling against the ropes. The back of the couch slowly crept into my field of view. Virgil was painfully dragging it an inch at a time across the thick carpet.

Finally I could see his face. And he could see my eyes. I stopped fighting and let them swivel freely.

"Roman!" he said, his voice cracking with relief. "You're alive!"

Pulling the couch had tightened the noose around his neck. His chest heaved and the breath rasped in and out of this throat. His face was nearly as dark as the burgundy leather of the couch. Tears flowed freely down his cheeks. With amazement I felt the wetness of my own tears.

"There is so much blood! Are you hurt?" he asked.

I tried to speak, got nothing. I rolled my eyes in frustration.

Virgil shook his head and said, "Sorry! Oh shit! Sorry, Roman. He shot me with the same kind of dart. I know, I know. You're paralyzed. It's like being halfway dead.'

He watched me carefully for what seemed like a long time but was probably less than a minute.

"You can blink, can't you? Are you hurt? Blink once for yes, twice for no."

I blinked slowly, deliberately. Twice.

"Thank you, Jesus," he said, dropping his head onto the cushion. After resting a moment, he said, "I can't get loose, Roman. I tried. Honest, I did."

It wasn't a question, but I blinked once. Yes. Yes, I know.

Virgil didn't look comforted in the least. His eyes were screwed nearly shut, his teeth bared in a grimace. With the rope tight around his neck he looked like he'd just survived a hanging. Barely.

"We have to wait, Roman. Whatever that junk was he pumped into you, it doesn't last long. Ten more minutes."

In spite of the circumstances, I would have laughed at that if I could. Grandpa Tillie used to hate it when someone told him a job would take ten minutes.

"Ten minutes is the kiss of death," he used to say. "If someone tells you something's going to take ten minutes, it's bound to take an hour."

Virgil and Grandpa Tillie were both right. The drug started to wear off in ten minutes. But it seemed like an hour.

I looked at my watch for at least the five hundredth time. The hands had barely moved, but while I was looking at my hand, my fingers curled. A few seconds later I felt my foot twitch. I closed my eyes. My lids stayed closed this time and I shut out the holocaust next to my face for a few soothing moments. When I opened my eyes again, I could turn my head an inch. Then I could bend my knees. I raised my hands slightly. I worked my right elbow under my body and levered myself off the floor.

I pushed my tongue against my teeth, pried my jaw open. I tried talking.

"Virgil…"

His name dribbled quietly out of my mouth, but I was alarmed when he didn't move. The rope was still so tight around his neck, and his forehead was wedged against the leather cushion.

"Virgil!" I said again, louder this time. "Virgil!"

I pushed myself to my knees, stood unsteadily. I had to loosen the rope around Virgil's neck. I lifted a leg to step over my father's body, but my toe caught on his arm. Off balance and still spastic from the drug, I fell hard. My knee jammed into his chest, forcing a horrid, wet burp out of his mangled throat. I scrambled up.

With un-cooperative fingers I picked at the knots on the rope choking Virgil. I fumbled uselessly until feeling suddenly flooded back. Like a switch had been thrown, strength flowed into my hands again and I finally got the rope off.

Virgil coughed. I touched his neck. A strong pulse throbbed.

I turned my attention to the rope tying his arms, but our father had tied what Grandpa Tillie derisively called a "hatchet knot." The kind you could only untie with a hatchet. The tangled rat's nest of rope he had wrapped and re-wrapped around Virgil's wrists was stubbornly effective. Finally finding the key strand, I worked the whole mess loose.

I pulled Virgil onto the cushions, propped him up against the back of the couch. His mouth hung open silently. He turned my way and his eyes scared me more than the faceless corpse of my father. His dark brown eye looked blank, as vacant as a black hole; his green eye radiated pure hysteria.

I grabbed his shoulders, brought my forehead to his.

"Listen to me, Virgil," I said.

A madman stared out from my brother's eyes.

I clamped down with my fingers. "Virgil!"

I saw a flicker of recognition, deep in his pupils. It disappeared, then came back. Stronger, now.

"Eye-to-eye," I said. "Heart-to-heart…"

He leaned into me. I felt his breathing relax.

"Brothers forever," I whispered.

He lifted his head, the mad light gone from his eyes. In its place I saw sadness and pain that I knew would haunt us both forever.

He threw his arms around me and held on like he was afraid he would die if he let go.

"Don't let them see me like this, Roman," he said. "Don't let anyone see me like this!"

CHAPTER 14

MAYBE I SHOULD have called the police, but I called Uncle Gil.

"He's dead," I said, when he answered.

He didn't ask who. He didn't ask why. Thinking back on it later, I figured he had been expecting this call would come someday. His only question was, "How?"

"The shotgun," I said, "he…"

"Stop!" he said. "Take a deep breath. Settle down. You're at home?"

I told him we were.

"Stay there. Don't do anything. I'm on my way."

We were sitting on the couch in the living room when Uncle Gil arrived. Virgil was drifting away again. He was motionless, nearly catatonic. I had my arm around his shoulders. Uncle Gil stopped short. Then he said what every southern Christian says when confronted with the unthinkable.

"Sweet Jesus!"

He went down on one knee in front of us. He searched Virgil's face, put a hand gently on his shoulder.

"Virgil?" he said softly. "Virgil?"

He shifted his gaze to me. He started to reach out, but stopped short. I looked down at myself for the first time. I looked like I'd been standing in front of a fire hose spewing blood and ground up body parts. My shirt was soaked. I could only guess what my face looked like.

"Are you all right, Roman?"

I nodded, my jaw clenched tight. I was on a tightrope. I was afraid if I opened my mouth, everything would come gushing out – vomit, screams, curses, everything I was holding back.

"Where is he?"

I motioned with my head toward the den.

"Stay here. Don't walk around. Try not to move at all."

He walked quickly to the den. I don't know what he did in there but he was gone a long time. A wave of nausea swept over me when I finally became aware of how I smelled. I coughed and nearly lost it, but I clamped down hard and managed not to puke. Uncle Gil finally came back.

He walked quickly past me, holding out a hand like a cop stopping traffic. He disappeared into the kitchen and came back with a black plastic garbage bag. He fumbled with it, pulled it through the air to open it wide.

"Take off your shoes, pants and shirt, Roman. Drop them right into the bag."

I did as he said. He looked at me for a long moment as though I had suddenly been replaced by a complete stranger, then he said, "Take a shower and put on fresh clothes. Make it fast. You too, Virgil."

We both rose obediently and headed for the stairs. I was functioning on automatic now, willing to go where he said, do what he instructed. In the bathroom, I caught a glimpse of my face in the mirror and realized why Uncle Gil had looked at me so oddly. My hair was pebbled with white bits of bone and gray blobs of brain matter. My eyes had that lost, hollow look you see on people they pull from collapsed buildings. In the shower I washed up quickly, revived a bit by the hot water. After a shower Virgil looked better too, but he kept his head and eyes down and refused to speak. I guided him down the stairs.

Uncle Gil was talking intently on the telephone as we entered the living room. When he saw us, he said, "Go ahead and set it up – and thanks, hear?" to whoever he had on the other end of the line. He replaced the phone in the cradle, then he sat us down again on the couch.

"Here's the plan," he said to me, after casting a worried glance at Virgil. "I get you and Virgil out of here, then call the police and tell them your father killed himself."

"But won't they know that we were…"

"No," he said, holding up a hand to cut me off. "Trust me. I'm going to call in every favor I'm owed, and I'm owed a lot. The right people will accept my version of things. You and Virgil were not here. Where was your father supposed to be?"

I looked toward the den, where he sprawled faceless in an ocean of blood. "On a sales trip," I said.

"He came home early?"

I nodded.

"Perfect!" he said. "So, here it is: you and Virgil were working at my place. Your father was gone, so you asked me to drive you home. I did, and when we got home we found your father had committed suicide. Got that?"

"Yes," I said, "but Virgil was home all day."

"No matter," Uncle Gil said, "you two look so much alike everyone will assume you were both at my offices today."

He pushed forward until he was sitting on the edge of the couch and turned to face me.

"Here's the kicker, though. I can cover all this up, contain the evidence, make sure the report reads what I want it to read. But – and this is crucial – only if I control everything that's said. If the police question you and Virgil, they'll get... all that." He pointed at the den. "Believe me," he said, "they'll get the truth. And once the police have the whole story, so will everyone else in Savannah."

I slumped back on the couch. The whole world seemed to be spinning madly down a powerful whirlpool. Virgil and I were going to be flushed into the vortex and drowned.

"What should we do?" I asked, embarrassed when my voice cracked and tears blurred my vision.

Uncle Gil said, "You're both almost sixteen, right?"

"Next month," I said.

He clapped his hands together and said, "All right! This might just work! From now on, you're both *seventeen*. I'll get someone to fix the records later, but you need to be at least seventeen."

I trusted Uncle Gil more than any adult in my life. I nodded and said, "OK." Besides, I couldn't let Virgil be dragged through the horrible gauntlet of reporters and police. He wouldn't survive.

Uncle Gil glanced at Virgil, then looked back at me.

"Here's the bad news," he said. "You and Virgil have to split up."

I opened my mouth to protest, but he raised a hand.

"I know," he said. "It's the last thing I want, too. But do this for me, all right? Just listen to what I have in mind. I think you'll agree it's best for both of you."

"Virg?" I said, leaning close to his ear. "What do you say?"

In a strangled voice that nearly broke my heart, Virgil said, "Don't let them find out, Roman. Get me away from this place."

I looked back to Uncle Gil.

"What's the plan?" I asked.

"Right!" he said. He stood up, rubbed his hands together and pointed at Virgil. "Today – tonight, that is – Virgil leaves for Louisiana."

"Louisiana?" I asked. Born and raised in Savannah, we had no ties to Louisiana. Or anywhere outside of Georgia, for that matter.

Uncle Gil smiled, apparently pleased by my surprise.

"See?" he said. "Totally unexpected, and therefore perfect." He put a hand on Virgil's shoulder and paused to get his attention.

"Tomorrow you'll enter the St. Charles College in Grand Coteau, Louisiana. To become a Jesuit Novitiate."

"A Jesuit?" Virgil asked, a bit of life creeping back into his voice.

"It's the first step," Uncle Gil said. "It's a long path, ten years or more."

"But I can't just show up. They won't take me! I'm just a kid."

Gilbert put his hand up again, like a policeman stopping cars on the street.

"You're seventeen," he reminded us. "That's the minimum age. And you *will* be accepted. I know someone in the archdiocese – someone high up – who owes me a favor. We'll get you on a plane tonight, and I'll get everything sorted out first thing tomorrow."

Virgil sat up straight. He threw his arms around Uncle Gil and said, "Oh, God! Thank you! Thank you!"

After a moment Uncle Gil disentangled himself from Virgil and turned to me.

"I just don't see you in the priesthood, Roman."

I shook my head. "No," I said. "Sorry, but that's not for me."

He clapped me on the shoulder.

"That's all right," he said. "I have friends in the military, too. Which would you like, Navy or Marines?"

I knew exactly what I wanted to be. I had seen men from an elite military unit around Savannah and at career day at school. Quiet, intense, competent looking.

"The Army," I said.

Uncle Gil frowned, probably because of his experience with the Army at West Point. But then he shrugged his shoulders.

"All right, Army it is then. I can get you into the next basic combat training camp at Fort Benning, if you're sure."

I nodded positively.

"I want to be a Ranger," I said.

CHAPTER 15

I REALIZED MAGNUS AND Doc Lukens were looking at Virgil and me oddly. I wondered how long we had been locked in our trance, re-living that terrible night. I shook my head to break the connection with my twin.

Well," I said, trying not to give away the turmoil those memories had stirred up. "The house on East Perry sat empty for nearly three years before it was sold. Uncle Gil handled the sale. I don't remember who bought the place, but I don't think it was anyone named Beardsley."

Virgil nodded. "No, it wasn't Beardsley. It wasn't a person – it was an organization. I remember Uncle Gil telling me that word spread quickly about a gory suicide, so the house was shown to lots of curiosity seekers but no real buyers. Besides that, it was on the National Historic Register and it needed a lot of work. Uncle Gil called it the triple whammy."

"So who bought it?" Doc Lukens asked.

Virgil shook his head. "Some non-profit organization. I just wanted to forget that house, so I didn't pay much attention. Something to do with Ireland or Irish immigrants, I think."

"It's been over twenty years," I said. "I wonder who owns it now. I'll ask Uncle Gil tomorrow."

Virgil picked Ace's wallet up again and continued his search. He found an expired library card, a photo of a woman and a young boy and coupons for special offers at Denny's and Burger King. Tucked away behind the empty slots where normally a man would store his credit cards, Virgil found a wrinkled business card with Ace's name and the title Financial Advisor. The address was on West Victory in Savannah.

"West Victory?" Magnus said. "That's what, three miles from here, eh? Why don't we…"

Doc Lukens cut him off with an exaggerated yawn and a pointed look at his wristwatch.

"One thirty in the morning, dear boy!"

He stood up and carefully adjusted his cuffs to drop properly over the top of his polished loafers.

"Would you help me with these sheets, Father Keane?" he asked Virgil. When the fold-out was made up, he told me he'd be around to check on Winter Rose later in the day.

"Much later," he said, settling onto the mattress with a tired sigh.

"Let's all get some sleep," I said, rising too.

"So, want me to stand guard here?" Magnus asked, smothering a yawn himself.

"Stand guard?" Virgil said, immediately on alert. His eyes swiveled from Magnus to me. "Somebody might still try to kill him?"

I shook my head.

"Relax, Virgil," I said. "The danger's gone. Whoever tried to kill Ace, they think he's dead. Besides, nobody followed us here from the G-String in that downpour. I checked."

Magnus stood and stretched, back arched and arms high over his head. He rolled his head from side to side and blinked once, like a big cat after a long hunt.

"OK, I'm headin' home, RK."

"Go ahead, Magnus. And thanks."

He flashed that big Magnus smile.

"Think I would have missed that, then? A beauty of a dancer, a maniac with a gun and one hell of a fire fight. A guy couldn't ask for a better time."

He picked up his jacket and helmet. I grabbed my own gear and followed him out the door. Magnus and I rode home in the rain to our own beds. It wasn't until much later that same day that I wished I'd listened to him about setting a guard.

CHAPTER 16

I WAS OUT OF bed by five thirty – force of habit, although I wondered how long that would stay with me now that I was a civilian. I had a weather station mounted on the steeple up where the cross used to be, with a little readout panel on my bedside table. It showed a brisk wind nudging 15 mph and an outside air temperature of 55°F. I padded to the window, limping as usual until my right leg warmed up. The architect I'd hired to transform the church into a home had taken advantage of the view out back. On the side opposite Route 17, the church property abutted a small forest of pine and swamp oak on the edge of a slough of the Ogeechee River. The cold front that had dumped all the rain on us last night had barreled out to sea, leaving behind a brilliant starry sky and freshly scrubbed air. I brushed my teeth, dressed quickly in shorts, running shoes and a tank top. With a towel around my shoulders I stopped off in the kitchen for a glass of cold water and washed down half a banana and a multivitamin. I put my ear to the door of the guest room where Winter Rose was sleeping – all quiet – then slipped out to the gym over the garage.

A pair of huge windows on one wall of the gym provided the

same wooded view as the master bedroom. The other walls had smaller windows and were taken up by racks of free weights, a spa-quality universal weight machine and a mechanized climbing wall that Magnus had talked me into buying. He used it as often as I did, which I'm sure he was figuring on all along. A cabinet held a Bose sound system for the iPod. Padded rubber flooring and a billboard-sized mirror completed the real gym look, although I was determined it would never have that genuine sour gym smell. This gym was my biggest luxury. I cued up one of my workout playlists on the stereo and warmed up with some push-ups while Jimmy Thackery picked his way through *It's All About My Girl.* By seven I had finished my workout.

I showered quickly as usual, enjoying the tight buzz that follows a hard session with the weights. After I toweled off, I dressed in jeans and a pair of black Merrell's. My plain T-shirt had a pocket for my reading glasses – a curse I shared with Virgil, and just about everyone over the age of thirty-five. My one concession to fashion was a black leather belt I had found in Australia, with an intricate hand carved weave and a small silver buckle.

The sun was high enough for its first orange rays to flicker through the cut glass of the high arched windows of the living room while I waited for the coffee to finish percolating. When the dark brew was ready I filled a mug, but before I could savor that first sip my phone chimed. I checked the screen and saw the photo of Uncle Gil smiling at me.

"Good morning, Uncle Gil."

"Good morning yourself, Roman. I hope I didn't wake you up. You're probably sleeping in now that you're retired."

"Not likely," I said. "Early rising is in my blood."

He chuckled.

"Mine, too," he said. "A blessing and a curse, as they say. Listen, I'm glad I caught you. That matter you asked me to have my friends at the FBI look into? They are on it like a swarm of bees."

"That's great. None of us are going to see our names flashed on TV, right?"

"Definitely not – the deal was total confidentiality. My guy in the FBI will keep both of us and your girl out of it. He says it won't be a problem – your information made him look very good."

"I really appreciate it, Uncle Gil."

I paused for a moment to signal a change of subject, then I said, "You probably don't know the answer to this question, but who owns my mother's old house now?"

"The house on East Perry? The one where…" He let the rest of the thought go unspoken.

"Yeah, that one. It's no big deal," I said. "It came up in conversation last night and Virgil said some Irish non-profit bought it. I just wondered who they are and if they still owned it."

The connection was quiet for a moment while he pondered the question. Finally he said, "I remember it took forever to sell that house. Virgil's right, it finally went to a non-profit. Funny name, full of D's and E's – Diddleeaidee. Something to do with Irish musicians. We've got so many Irish organizations in Savannah, I didn't pay much attention."

"Really?" I said. I'd never heard of it, but then I stayed well away from that house.

"I think they still own it," Uncle Gil said, "but as I recall they were represented by some fellow named Martin in Atlanta. I can check on it later if you'd like."

"If you get the chance, that would be great."

"No problem. Say, how's that fellow Ace Emory? What a shock to see him in such bad shape."

"Doc Lukens saw him last night. I'm sure he's doing much better today."

"I'm relieved to hear that. I really felt bad. I did a little business with him a few years back, you know."

"Really? I didn't know that."

"Oh yeah, his advice helped me stay on my feet when the real estate market first tanked during the mortgage meltdown a few years back."

Uncle Gil cleared his throat and added, "And then I didn't even recognize him last night."

"None of us did, Uncle Gil. He sat down right in front of me and I still didn't realize it was him."

"Fine thing we did, huh? To let our friend get to that point?"

"Yeah," I said, "but I'll stand by him now."

"Me, too. Let me know if you need anything. I'd be glad to help out. He staying with you?"

"No, he's over at St. George's.'

"Really? Virgil's halfway house?"

I told him about the shootout and attempt on Ace's life at the G-String.

"Incredible," he said. "You have no idea who it was?"

I shrugged. "No," I said. "Not who, not why."

"Well," he said, "I'm glad to hear he's recovering and in good hands."

"Come on over to St. George's for lunch. You can see him for yourself. I'm sure he'd appreciate it."

"I don't know. I wouldn't want to intrude."

"It's barbecue day."

"Really? The good stuff?"

"Straight from old Betty's fire pit."

"Count me in, then. Oh, and Roman? You're supposed to be retired. You've got to pace yourself now, son."

I laughed.

Winter Rose came out of the guest room as I ended the call and joined me at the breakfast nook. She looked amazingly improved this morning, a tribute to both her constitution and Doc's ministration. Much of the swelling was gone from her jaw, although the surrounding skin was now a spectacular purple and blue. She still had a lump in her upper lip, but it was much reduced. Her eyes were puffy from the sedative-induced sleep and lined with dark shadows. White dressings circled both of her wrists like sweat bands, covering the damage from the ropes. I assumed she had similar wrappings on her ankles, hidden by the sweatpants I'd set out for her, along with the fresh T-shirt she was wearing.

I poured some coffee into another mug for her.

"Cream and sugar?" she asked, looking around the countertop.

"In the fridge," I said, "middle shelf on the door."

She mixed both in until the coffee was about the same shade as her skin, then slipped into the breakfast nook opposite me.

"While I was sleeping I remembered you," she said.

"You dreamed about me?"

She held the mug in both hands with her elbows braced on the table and looked at me over the top of the rim. She shook her head.

"Not dreamed. Remembered. I saw you at Ops over at Hunter a few months back. Your face was camouflaged, but it's hard to miss those eyes."

I nodded. "I was evaluating a platoon sergeant who was

conducting a field exercise that day. We were waiting to board a Blackhawk lift out on the tarmac. I remember seeing you that day, too."

She met my eyes. "I'm surprised you recognize me now. I look like I'm the only survivor of a big crash."

I stifled a smile and didn't tell her that actually I'd recognized her when she was standing naked in the bright sun, bleeding and holding my knife.

"In a way, you are," I said. "The sole survivor."

Her eyes widened and the mug stopped halfway to her lips.

I said, "Here's a life lesson I learned the hard way – surviving is always good. Everything else is just details."

She took another sip, then she nodded. "I'm… I'm fine," she said, "really."

She put the mug down and used the heels of her hands on the edge of the table to push herself back in the seat. She looked at me quizzically.

"How about you?"

"Me?"

"Yeah," she said, holding the same intent gaze on me. "Doctor Lukens said he didn't know the details about how you rescued me, but not to… not to worry about you."

"He's right. Those boys got what they deserved. In fact, all three should have gotten the same treatment you gave the last one. None of it's going to keep me up nights."

She nodded slowly and put her mug down. "Doctor Lukens also told me you retired yesterday. I guess I sort of messed up your big day. Sorry."

I had to smile at that.

"No sweat," I said. "The retirement went off without a hitch. Now the retirement party… that was another story."

I told her about Ace and his unexpected appearance and the shoot-up that occurred afterward.

"Wow," she said. "Is this what you plan to do in retirement? Rescue old friends and almost acquaintances from dire difficulties?"

I laughed.

"Not exactly. I always wanted to tour the country on a motorcycle. Thanks to my mother's family and Ace's advice, I've got the money to do it."

I snapped my fingers.

"Hey, that reminds me. I want to show you something Ace had in his car. Be right back – it's still in my saddlebag."

I slid out of the pew, went out the front door and opened the left saddlebag on the Road King. The little dream catcher was still trapped safely between my rolled up chaps and the side of the saddlebag. I pulled it out carefully and walked back inside. Winter Rose was at the sink, rinsing out her mug, when I got back to the kitchen.

"Ace had this in his car," I said, letting the dream catcher dangle from my index finger. "It's nicer than your run-of-the-mill trinket. Ever seen one like it?"

Winter Rose turned her head to look, then she gasped. She dropped the mug into the sink with a clatter and clamped both hands over her mouth. The blood drained from her face and I thought she was going to faint.

I took a quick step to help her, but she held up a palm, leaned back against the counter and took a few deep breaths to compose herself. Her eyes never left the dream catcher on my finger, as she pushed herself away from the counter and tottered toward me like someone who had suddenly forgotten how to walk. She reached out with trembling hands and unhooked the dream catcher from my finger. She held it up to the light streaming through the front window arches. I watched her eyes run over the white fur circle enclosing the five-petal flower, the little cluster of yellow beads in the center and the two feathers hanging underneath.

Then she closed her eyes and made a little noise in the back of her throat that was part hum, part moan. She pressed the dream catcher against her breast and covered it with her hands. She swayed and nearly lost her balance before I steadied her. I guided her back to the breakfast nook and helped her slide into the pew.

She laid the dream catcher on the table and smoothed it out carefully. She knuckled her eyes, then placed her hands flat on the table on either side of the dream catcher, fingers and thumbs out to form a frame around it.

"My mother made this for me," she said.

I passed her a napkin and she wiped her eyes and face. She sniffed discreetly so I handed her another one, which she used to blow her nose. I took them both back and dropped them in the trash.

"She made hundreds of them, to sell to the tourists, you know. Hers were all small like this, but they were the best. Most dream catchers just look like spider webs, but my mother made the web look like a flower. See?" she said, tilting it toward me. "Not just any flower, the Cherokee Rose. You can tell by the number of petals – five – and by the yellow center."

"But I found that one hanging from the rear view mirror in Ace's car," I said. "Why do you think that's the one she made for you?"

She ran her index finger around the outer rim of the dream catcher, lightly stroking the fur.

"My mother made this dream catcher for me before I was born. She used fur from a white fox, to symbolize the winter snow because I was due in December," she said. "I was born in the middle of a snow storm, actually. That's why I'm called Winter Rose. This is the only one my mother ever made with white fox fur. All the rest were finished with brown rabbit fur."

It did seem like it might be one-of-a-kind, but I wondered if it was actually the same dream catcher. After all my time in the Army, I would have been more convinced if it had a serial number. I stroked the fox fur. It *was* unusually thick and soft, even after all these years.

"But I can see that you'd never sell it," I said, "so how did it end up in Ace's car?"

"My brother!" she said, narrowing her eyes. "Well, my cousin, really." She saw the question in my eyes and sighed. "My parents both died when I was very young, so I was raised by my mother's sister and her husband. Long ago, that was common practice among the Cherokee. Aunts and uncles raising kids instead of their biological parents, I mean. Anyway, my aunt and uncle already had a son, who was two years older than me. They insisted that I call him my brother. Kept after me to pretend we were just one happy family."

She cut a hard glance my way and I saw the lava bubbling in her eyes again.

"We weren't happy, though. My so-called brother has what they politely call abuse issues. He was an alcoholic by the time he was twelve. Then it was cocaine. Then crack."

She took a deep breath and blew it out noisily.

"He stole the dream catcher from my room when I was seven. He sold it to some tourist kid in town."

"Ace," I said. "I think he's a few years older than you. That would make him about nine or ten at the time."

She nodded. I could see her thinking about it for a minute. Then she asked, "He's had it all this time?"

"I can't say for sure, but I think so. He said he's had it in every car he ever owned."

She picked the dream catcher up and looked at me through it.

"There's one more thing," she said. "Something I never believed."

She lowered the dream catcher, hesitating.

"One more thing?" I asked.

"I was so upset at my brother selling it, that I refused to speak at home. My adoptive parents finally took me to a medicine woman. Margaret Keystone."

She sighed. "I hate to think about how rude I was to her," she said. "She tried to help, but I was so angry back then, and not just about the dream catcher. About losing my parents, school, other kids. I was angry about… about just being Cherokee. I wanted to be Barbie, not Cherokee." She gently shook her head. "I was an idiot."

She closed her eyes. Maybe she was wishing she could go back and do things differently. I kept quiet. I knew going back never works.

"Anyway," she said, opening her eyes again, "Miss Keystone burned a little pile of twigs and poked through the ashes. She told me not to be sad. She said the dream catcher was not lost, that others needed it more than I did. She said it would return to me one day."

She buried her face in her hands, then rubbed her palms

slowly all the way back to her ears, as though she wanted to wipe her face blank and start with a clean slate.

"I laughed at her. Told her it was mystical Indian bullshit." She smiled sadly at me then said, "I thought she'd scold me, but she didn't. She just nodded and stirred the ashes into the dirt without a word."

Winter Rose held the dream catcher up again, let it swing gently from her finger. Her face reflected equal parts astonishment and acceptance now.

"And here it is," she said.

I watched it swing like a pendulum.

"I guess you want to meet Ace, then," I said.

She stood up quickly.

"Can we stop by my apartment on the way? I need to change clothes."

CHAPTER 17

WHEN VIRGIL ANSWERED the door at St. Georges and saw Winter Rose standing next to me, he smiled broadly.

"My brother never ceases to surprise me," he said, extending both hands toward Winter Rose.

"Winter Rose Ridge, this is Virgil Keane," I said, making the introductions. "*Father* Virgil Keane, to his flock."

Winter Rose looked from Virgil to me and back again. I could see her adjusting for the differences in weight and length of hair, then her eyes widened as she realized Virgil and I were twins.

"Nice to meet any brother of Roman's," she said, letting Virgil take her hand. "A priest, huh? I hope you're not full of religious crap."

Virgil threw his head back and laughed. He held her hand in both of his and said, "Never fear, Miss Ridge. We Jesuits have a well-earned reputation for cutting through crap, religious or otherwise. Come in, come in. Everyone is welcome at St. George's."

He drew Winter Rose inside. I saw him glance at her swollen

lip and the vivid discoloration on her jaw. I knew he had seen too many women in similar condition over the years. He raised an eyebrow at me as I followed her in, and I knew I'd have some explaining to do as soon as he got me alone. To forestall the inevitable, I said, "She's here to see Ace, not you. How's he doing this morning?"

"Resting comfortably," Virgil said, guiding us into the sitting room. He got us settled in chairs, then said, "Doctor Lukens removed the IV during the night and stayed with him until eight o'clock. We got him into the shower, then put him back in bed. I think he's still asleep."

"We'd both like to see him, if he's up to it," I said.

Virgil glanced quickly at Winter Rose's face, then said, "Is he… are you…"

"Is he what?" Winter Rose asked, tilting her head in question.

"Damn it, Virgil," I cut in, "Ace isn't her husband and he didn't beat her." I stepped in front of Winter Rose and said, "You'll have to excuse my brother. He assumes the worst when it comes to domestic abuse."

I punched him lightly on the arm to take away any offence.

"Usually he's right. Why don't you wait in Virgil's sitting room? I need a few minutes alone with Ace."

Virgil graciously took Winter Rose's elbow. "I promise to neither pry nor preach, Miss Ridge. Come and sit with me. I'm sure you'll enjoy some pleasant conversation with the *civilized* Keane brother."

I rolled my eyes and headed down the long hall to Ace's room, all the way down by the chapel. Two other guests passed me along the way. They both said hello and did a double take when they realized I must be Virgil's brother, but in keeping with the privacy policy Virgil enforced at St. George's neither one interrupted my progress. I knocked on the door. To my surprise, Ace immediately called out, "Come in."

Ace was sitting up on the bed, both feet on the ground. He was gray around the gills and his eyes were sunk so deep in his head he looked like a recently liberated prisoner of war, but at least he was functioning again. He had managed, probably with Virgil's help, to shave. His hair was clean and combed back over his ears.

There were a couple of small wooden chairs in the room, refugees from someone's old dining room set. I pulled one over next to the bed and sat. I tried for the relaxed and casual look to put Ace at ease, my left ankle crossed over my right knee.

"Quite a night, Ace," I said. I smiled gently. "So... what the hell's going on?"

He blew the air from his lungs, filled them back up. He looked out the window, down at the rug, flexed his hands and examined his fingers like he'd just discovered how they worked. Finally he sighed and looked up at me.

"At first it was a straight forward financial management deal, RK," he said. "It's what I'm good at." He cast his eyes to the floor again. "Was good at."

I said, "I know you're good at it, Ace. I took your advice, and look at me – a common foot soldier and I'm rich."

He snorted.

"You're not rich, RK. You're well-off. There's a big difference. Besides, your nest egg was inherited."

"Yeah, but that nest egg is worth nearly five times what it was when I got it."

"Really?" he said, unconsciously straightening his spine. "Five times?"

"You told me to buy waterfront and gold, that's what I did."

"Wow."

"Yeah, wow," I said. "Now what about this deal you mentioned. Why don't you just start at the beginning?"

He slumped again. "Right. It started with an investment company out of Atlanta, RK. Called Vet Invest."

Ace shook his head.

"I was like some rube who falls for the three card Monte scam. But you've got to realize I was desperate. My family was gone. I owed everybody. Everything I touched turned to shit."

"What do you mean your family was gone? Your boy, Brett? And Marilyn? Marilyn left you?"

Ace hung his head. His shoulders shook. A sob burst out of him and he rocked like he'd been shot. He looked up at me and his face was pure anguish.

"I killed her, RK. I killed her!"

"No!"

"Yes, yes. I killed her."

I moved over onto the bed next to him, put an arm around his shoulders.

"All right, Ace," I said, when the racking and snuffling finally ran down. "Tell me all about it."

He rambled through the telling, but I finally pieced it all together. The Midas touch had suddenly deserted him about three years ago. He had appeared to be doing fine, then he had made a couple of inexplicable mistakes. Those spawned more mistakes – bigger mistakes. Clients started leaving. His confidence, his biggest asset in the world of high finance, had faded after his two biggest clients pulled out. It was just a bad patch, he told himself. He figured he'd work his way through to the other side. He came to work earlier and left later.

The real problem had started with the booze. It began with

a quiet drink at his desk while he was working late after dinner. Then the scotch had become dinner and the drinking began consuming the evenings like runaway brush fires. He rarely saw his son Brett, who seemed to have morphed overnight from an enthusiastic kid into an angry, sullen teenager.

It had all come crashing down the night Marilyn showed up at the office. They were supposed to go to a dinner party at her boss's house, a semi-formal affair where she fully expected to be named a partner in the law firm where she was an associate. They were late, but they could still make it. Ace insisted on driving. She said no, but he claimed he wasn't drinking, that he was OK to drive.

On the way to the party, he had lost control of her Lexus. The car left the road, flipped on its back, landed upside down on a wall of rip-rap by the water. The airbags inflated as designed, but the passenger side of the roof collapsed, speared by a pyramid-shaped block of granite. Marilyn had died on the scene of massive head injuries. Ace wasn't even scratched.

"It happened less than a mile from her boss's house, RK. One of the other guests saw the wrecked car and called the police. I woke up by the side of the road with attorneys all around me. Your uncle was even there. Mr. Rumsdale. He took a silver flask from his jacket pocket and gave me a drink. It gave the attorneys enough to invalidate the blood test later."

I didn't say anything, amazed that Uncle Gilbert's quick thinking had rescued not only Virgil and me, but also Ace here, too. He hadn't mentioned that part when I talked with him earlier this morning. He kept our secret all these years and I guess he meant to do the same for Ace.

"That clever little maneuver kept me out of jail, but it didn't bring Marilyn back," Ace said, slumping in his chair. "And in the end it didn't matter anyway. Word got out."

He lifted his head to look at me. If you had to choose a picture to illustrate the word *abject*, you couldn't do better than a close-up of Ace's face at that moment.

"They didn't charge me, but now I was the drunk who crashed his car and killed his wife. You know this town, RK. Bad news travels fast. My remaining clients left in droves. I lost my wife, my son, my house, my office in the Johnson Building. Everything."

"Man, I'm sorry. I wish I'd been there to help."

He held both palms up and shook his head.

"You weren't even in the country. Besides, I was so intent on digging my own grave I'm not sure anyone could have helped."

I tried to believe that, but couldn't. Ace had been a good friend and a good advisor. I should have kept in touch over the years.

"OK," I said, "let's get back to this Vet Invest deal."

He lowered his eyes and was quiet for a long time. I thought he might be drifting away, but then he spoke in a low voice and I realized he had just been assembling his thoughts.

"It started when Emil showed up. Emil Novak. At first he was the answer to my prayers. I was sitting there in my crummy little rental office one day. You know what I was doing? Reading my eviction notice! He came in wearing a suit and tie, like a banker with his old leather briefcase. He said he represented a group called Vet Invest."

"Vet Invest?" I said. "Some kind of financial group for veterans?"

"Exactly!" Ace said. "The organization was started with a core donation by an anonymous benefactor to help veterans improve their finances. It let veterans pool their resources so their investments had more earning power. Like an investment club for whatever they could save from their compensation benefits."

"But that would be a good…"

He gave me a resigned nod.

"It was good. At least I thought it was too. Then one day, about six months after that first meeting, Emil came in with his goons. No suit, this time. Leather jacket, black turtleneck. Jesus, he looked so mean, so dangerous. But quiet, you know? Novak laid it all out. A lot of the Vet Invest club members were either totally fake or they were real vets who weren't actually entitled to compensation benefits. These guys had scammed the whole thing. And my name, my signature, was all over it. On contracts, deposit slips, transfer orders."

"How many?"

"How many what?"

"Vets, Ace. How many vets are they using like this?"

"I'm not sure exactly, but I remember Emil insisting on a toast when we went over 2500 members. Before you ask, I don't know how many were just plain made up and how many are real people. From all over the country, though. Thirty-nine states out of fifty."

"Thirty-nine states?" I said. Shit, I thought. I figured this would be a Georgia thing, a Savannah-Atlanta connection that I could shut down quietly. Maybe, with a little more help from Uncle Gil. But this is huge. In my mind I saw the whole thing spiraling out of my grip as the FBI, the Secret Service and any other outfit in the federal alphabet soup, with an interest in interstate white-collar crime, jumped in with both feet.

"How much?" I asked.

"Well, you gotta understand, the monthly benefits vary for

each Vet, fake or not. Some only got eighty or ninety bucks, some got thousands."

"How much, Ace?"

"Nearly eight hundred grand a month."

"Eight hundred grand?"

I nearly shouted the number, then lowered my voice with an effort.

"Almost a million dollars a month, Ace?"

He pressed his fingers to his temples and rubbed, like he was trying the erase all the bad news stored in his brain.

"Not quite, but eight million total last year," he said.

"Eight million!"

"I know, I know. When you say it out loud, it sounds just like what it is – a crime. But I swear, RK, it didn't start that way. And Emil said it was a victimless scam. Nobody got hurt, he said. The government would just waste the money anyway, he said. I… I was an idiot. I convinced myself I didn't have a choice. I just buried my head in the sand."

"OK," I said, "so where did all the money go?"

"Offshore. The Cayman Islands."

"Offshore?" I said. "As in untraceable offshore?"

Ace gave a little negative shake of the head.

"Not exactly untraceable. I traced it through two shell companies: one called Top Rank Investments in Delaware and another called General Finance in Wyoming. Both are Limited Liability Companies with anonymous owners."

"Anonymous owners?" I said. "How in hell can the owner of a company be anonymous?"

Ace shrugged his shoulders.

"That's the law in those states," he said. "Nevada and

Oregon, too. They only require the name and address of the company's registered agent, and of course those were false."

I rubbed my face and shook my head in a futile attempt to clear my brain.

"You said not exactly untraceable," I said. "What did you mean by that?"

"I traced it in and out of those shell companies. I got as far as one particular bank in Grand Cayman. I couldn't find out who owned the account or even the number of the account. All I know is that it's twelve digits or a combination of twelve digits and letters. And even that number may lead to another blind account in another bank. Whoever is running this operation is very, very secretive."

I took a deep breath and let it out.

"But something else happened, right? Something worse than stolen money. Something that ended with you begging me to kill you."

Ace hesitated, then he said, "Every month, they printed a new list."

"A new list of what?" I asked when he stopped.

Ace looked pained for a moment, then explained.

"A list of new members. The way it worked, RK, they must have somebody with access to the Veteran's Administration records. First level access, by an insider deep in the VA."

He sighed and I got the feeling he'd thought about this long and hard without success.

"Whoever it is, they went into the VA computer system and set up the fake accounts. But see, there are big risks either way."

"Either way?"

"Fake names altogether, or real names with fake injuries. If they set up totally fraudulent accounts – fake names, fake service records, fake addresses, fake injuries – then they have to keep up with the routine inquiries from the VA, like follow-ups to verify contact information and surveys to check quality of health care. Some of these inquiries are just bureaucracy in action, some are to catch exactly these kinds of scams. Anyway, the more totally fake accounts you have, the more work you have to do to keep them straight."

"And that was your job?"

He shook his head. "No, no, RK. I was just the money manager. I made the actual investments. They moved a guy named Dalbert into my office to keep track of the personal information – fake and real."

"On the same computer you used?" I asked.

"Oh, shit! My laptop! I left it on my desk when I ran out. My cell, too."

"Relax," I said. "I'll get them for you. Let's get back on track. You were telling me about this guy Dalbert's job."

Ace swallowed a couple of times and looked around the room, like there might be a bottle sitting handy someplace. I poured him a glass of water. He took it with trembling hands and drank gratefully. After he set it down he continued.

"Like I said, Dalbert kept track of the Vet Invest membership. His job was to make sure the VA didn't get wise. See, the advantage of taking over the service of a real soldier is that there's less false information to keep track of. You take a real vet, give him or her fake injuries and start collecting their benefits. The VA corresponds with Dalbert from the beginning and the real soldiers never even know that benefits are being collected in their names."

"But the VA might actually get in touch with them someday?"

"Right! And then the shit hits the fan because the real guys are going to say what the hell are you talking about? I'm not injured. I don't collect any benefits."

"So most of the members of Vet Invest are totally made up?"

Ace nodded.

"It's more work, but if there are questions from the VA, then Dalbert has the chance to make up answers."

"OK, I understand the fraudulent names and claims. What else was going on?"

Ace propped his hands on his knees and dropped his head. He looked like he was inviting the executioner to take the big swing with his axe.

"I know it was bad, Ace, otherwise you wouldn't have shown up at my retirement party with a loaded .45, begging me to kill you. Look, whatever it is, we can handle it."

"Emil's boy Dalbert is bright, but sometimes he gets so wrapped up in what he's doing, he makes mistakes. Yesterday morning, he gave me a new list — a copy he wasn't supposed to give me."

He paused.

"Something was different about that list?" I said. I had the notebook we had found in Ace's clothes last night in the back pocket of my jeans. I took it out now and showed it to him.

"Something different enough that you wrote down these names?"

He stared at the notebook like it was an artifact from another planet. I held it out to him. He took it warily and thumbed it open. He read the names and relief flooded across his face.

He said, "I forgot I had even written the names down. Here's the thing, RK. I usually didn't pay much attention to the names — the account numbers and amounts were more important to me. But this list had two names handwritten at the bottom. I recognized them both."

"And?" I said.

He pressed his palms against his temples. He started to speak, then stopped. He looked at me, raw-faced and hollow-eyed.

"I know them, RK!" he said. "Brad Beardsley and Linc Price. Both of them are real vets with disabilities. Both wounded in combat. Price was a helicopter crew chief and Beardsley was an infantry squad leader. I met them about five years ago when all three of us were asked to ride on a veteran's float in the St. Patrick's Day parade. They are supposed to be in Afghanistan, working for Falcon Security Services. But when I saw their names on the list, I called Falcon. I just wanted to warn them to get out of Vet Invest."

He braced his hands on the bed, as though the whole room might suddenly shift, throwing him to the floor.

"No one at Falcon's even heard of them. They've disappeared! Novak killed them, RK. I'm sure of it. He killed them and he's collecting their disability money!"

I didn't know Linc Price, but I had met Brad Beardsley. It wasn't the sort of name you'd forget, but the man was memorable in any case. A stocky redhead, he affected a self-deprecating humor that failed to mask a quick temper and a love of fighting. I'd heard his temper was bad enough that it finally got him invited out of the Army. I wouldn't have been surprised to hear that he'd gone back to Afghanistan as a civilian, in spite of losing his foot and lower left leg to one of the ubiquitous improvised explosive devices over there.

"You're positive?" I asked. "Never hired by Falcon?"

Ace shook his head.

"Any other company operating over there?"

No, again. "But," he said, "I found a friend of Beardsley's who said he got a postcard from Brad. That's how the story got started about them working for Falcon, RK. It just got spread around from there."

"So nobody would set off a stink about them being missing."

He nodded miserably.

"Both Brad and Linc were loners. No family – no really close friends."

"Nobody to dispute the story about working for Falcon in Afghanistan."

"Right."

I stood up and paced for a minute, then I stopped with my back to the door.

"So, let me get this straight," I said. "Apparently Novak is no longer content to make up fake vets or to make false claims on behalf of real vets. Now he's murdering real soldiers who are already collecting disability benefits from the VA. Specifically, he kills vets with no family or close friends. Then he continues to collect their money from the VA as though they were still alive."

I paused to see if Ace agreed. He nodded once, bleak mask still in place on his face.

"Why?" I asked. "The risk is huge. Why not stay with the fake name scheme and the fake benefits scheme. Why escalate to murder?"

"I don't know, RK, but there must be a reason. Like I said before, these people must have someone with complete access to the VA database. Maybe that person can reduce the risk by careful selection. If you assume that Beardsley and Price are typical victims, then they sought out single vets with no relatives. Vets with a high enough benefit payment to make it worthwhile. A lot of ex-soldiers fit that profile."

"Vets that nobody will miss," I said.

Ace nodded.

Damn. No wonder he asked me to kill him. Ace was in deep trouble. I thought for a minute, then decided I needed more information.

"All right, Ace, tell me more about this Emil Novak. For starters, what's he look like?"

"He's about five nine, maybe five ten. Slender. Sandy colored hair with a big bald spot in back. Wears glasses. Oval shaped glasses with gold frames. And he likes cowboy boots, wears them all the time."

"Sounds more like a guest at a dude ranch than a master criminal."

"You have to meet him in person, RK. He's intense."

I thought maybe I ran into him last night. I didn't get much of a look at any of the men who hit the G-String, but I remembered a flash of gold from somebody's glasses.

"Intense?"

"Hard, you know. He told me he grew up in the Czech Republic, in a state orphanage. He said the older boys taught him that you didn't have to be the biggest to survive, just the hardest. They must have really burned that into him. He never smiles."

I straightened my leg out to relive the ache in my knee. Sometimes it helped to rub my thigh just above the kneecap so I worked at the muscles with one hand while I thought.

"You said these guys must have access to the VA computer system. How hard is that?"

"That's just it, RK. The VA's database is extremely secure.

One hell of a lot of tax money goes into protecting that data. Hacking into it undetected would be nearly impossible."

"Nearly impossible," I said. "Not completely impossible. Could Novak do it?"

Ace frowned and shook his head emphatically.

"No way. When he needed information from the computer, he depended on Dalbert. I don't think he could even turn it on by himself."

"What about Dalbert? He good enough to hack into the VA system?"

"Maybe, but I don't think so."

"Why not?"

"Well, he's clever, but not smart, if you know what I mean. Novak has to stay after him, or he screws things up. He's quick with a keyboard, but I think he'd get caught if he tried something like that."

I gave up on the massage and flexed my knee a couple of times.

"OK, so there's someone else in this gang. Someone in the background who can access a secure government computer system."

Ace nodded.

"So who's the boss," I said. "Novak or this guy in the background?"

"Novak acts like he's in charge. He makes the decisions and gives the orders. Except once I heard him…"

"Except what?" I asked when Ace trailed off.

"Well, I didn't think anything of it at the time, but once I heard him tell Dalbert that the General was going to be unhappy."

"The General?"

"Yeah, like in the army."

"A real general?"

"I don't know."

"Could this 'General' be running things?"

"I don't know. I didn't really think about it until you asked. Novak kept pushing and pushing until all I could do is go along."

"Never met this General?"

Ace shook his head.

"No. Never. I only heard Novak say something like the General was going to be unhappy."

"Something like?"

"He said 'the General,' I'm positive of that."

"OK," I said, "Novak had three guys with him when he hit the G-String last night. Do you know them?"

"Yeah, I know them," Ace said. I could hear a tremor of fear in his voice. "One's a big guy named Ray Manion. Looks like a retired pro wrestler. Six three at least. Overweight, but a lot of muscle underneath. Barrel-chested. Shaves his head."

I nodded. I remembered he was the first guy out of the truck. Ace was right, he was large, especially wrapped in body armor.

"Then there's Bailey. I don't know his first name. They just call him Bailey. He never says much. Usually has a toothpick in his mouth and flicks it from side to side with his tongue."

"What's he look like?"

"Crew cut, medium build. Might be ex-military or police."

"What makes you say that?"

Ace shrugged.

"I don't know. Maybe it's just because he's not running his mouth all the time, but he also has a way of moving. Not fast, but… economically. Like he's had some training."

I nodded. That kind of thing stays with you.

"And the third guy?" I said.

"Cutcher. Daryl Cutcher. Moody bastard with bad teeth and a ponytail. He likes to carry a Smith and Wesson .44 Magnum. It looks like a damn howitzer hanging from his shoulder holster."

I tried to visualize the whole gang. They sounded like plain thugs, but I had to remember they were ruthless enough and clever enough to drive a good man like Ace right to the brink of self-destruction.

"OK," I said, counting them off on my fingers, "we've got Novak, Dalbert, Manion, Bailey, Cutcher and possibly someone Novak calls The General."

Ace bobbed his head.

"Yeah, that's all of them."

"And this gang has killed at least two vets, probably more."

He reached up, grabbed my shirt.

"I didn't kill anyone, RK! I didn't! Until I saw the list with real people on it that I knew, I told myself it was just a benefits scam."

I pried his hands loose and tried to ease him back down onto the pillow.

"I didn't mean *you* when I said this gang killed two veterans, Ace. I know you didn't kill anybody."

He stared wide-eyed at me, didn't relax at all. I pushed gently and he finally allowed himself to sink back. He closed his eyes and covered his face with his hands, like the see-no-evil monkey.

"They'll give me the death penalty," he said through his fingers. "They'll use the RICO Act and they'll fry me."

"Reek-o?" I said, "What's reek-o?"

"RICO, RICO," he said, as though I ought to know. When

I said nothing he dropped his hands and scooted himself up in bed.

"Racketeer Influenced and Corrupt Organizations," he said. "It's the law they use against the mafia and other organized crime. It means everyone in a gang is equally guilty of any crimes committed. I'm the gang's financial planner, for God's sake. They'll put the juice to me."

Now I recalled the law vaguely. If it was true, I thought, Ace could be found guilty and potentially get the death penalty. I also remembered that any organized crime prosecution I'd ever heard of depended on one crucial thing: a star witness. And the star witness is always given immunity. Maybe something could be arranged for Ace if I could hook Ace and his list up with the right person.

"Ace," I said, "where is the list Dalbert gave you?"

Ace shook his head.

"I don't know, RK!"

"You don't know?" I said, louder than I intended.

I hadn't thought it possible, but Ace looked even more miserable. For about the millionth time in my life I reminded myself that anger never helps. I took a deep breath to calm myself. I started again, more reasonably.

"What do you mean, Ace? The list wasn't in your pockets. Did you hide it somewhere?"

He was practically in tears now. He held his shaking hands out to me like a beggar.

"I put it in an envelope. Then I… I thought I was being so clever, RK. But I was drunk. And stupid. So stupid!"

"We've all done stupid things, Ace. It's not the end of the world. You must remember something about where you stashed that envelope."

"You don't understand, RK! I know where I put it *then*. I just don't know where it is *now*."

Oh shit, I thought. I know where this is going.

"You hid the envelope in a vehicle, didn't you? A car? A truck?"

Ace's head snapped up.

"Not a truck. An RV. It was the motorcycles, RK. I saw them and…"

"Not an RV? Motorcycles?"

"It was like an omen, RK." He shook his head. "I wasn't thinking clearly."

"Ace, there's nothing like being desperate and drunk to confuse the mind. But now you've got to focus. Where were these motorcycles?"

He closed his eyes. Pressed his fingers hard against his temples. I could almost hear the gears grind as he struggled to remember. Then his eyes popped open.

"Barbecue!" he said. "Betty Jo Bob's BBQ! They were parked outside the restaurant."

"Betty Jo Bob's!" I said.

"Yeah, that's it! I haven't eaten there in years, but I was driving by in a fog and it smelled so good. I remembered eating there with the guys so many times."

He started to drift away with the fragments of memory swirling through his mind, so I said, "Good news, Ace. You get to eat her barbecue today."

"Really?" he said. "Today?"

I nodded.

"Every Friday is BJB for lunch day at St. George's."

"Betty Jo Bob caters here?"

"I pay for it, Virgil sets the table. You remember old Betty, the owner? She brings it over herself." I checked my watch. "She'll be here in about three hours."

I almost laughed out loud because Ace actually licked his lips. Good barbecue will do that to you.

"OK Ace," I said, getting back on track. "You smelled the food, saw the bikes on the trailer and stopped. Tell me anything you remember about the RV. Make, color, anything."

Ace shut his eyes again. Did the finger-tapping thing on the brow.

"White? Some kind of brown trim? I don't know. Maybe that was it, but maybe that's some other RV I saw somewhere. It's no good, RK. I was wasted. My mind's a blank on the RV. All I remember is seeing a little door on it, down low near the back. I opened the door and shoved the envelope inside."

"How about the bikes," I said.

He thought for a moment, then said, "Harleys, I'm pretty sure. Big, lots of chrome. I remember they looked like shiny silver sculptures."

I stood up. I had more questions, but at least now I had an idea what this was all about. And I had a starting place – the list in the envelope. Betty Jo Bob might recall the RV towing the bikes that Ace described.

First, though, I wanted to take a look at Ace's office. I fished Ace's keys out of my pocket and held them up.

"One of these keys unlocks your new office? I'd like to take a look around," I said. "I'll pick up your computer and phone while I'm there."

Ace lowered his eyes.

"It's a dive, RK," he said in a barely audible voice.

"Don't worry about it, Ace. The road gets rough for us all now and then."

That got a grunt out of him, but he looked at me with gratitude and reached for the keys. He flipped through them quickly, then selected a worn silver Schlage.

"That's it," he said. "West Victory. Number, ah… 562."

I took the key off the ring and handed the rest back.

"Where's your son, Brett? Want me to get a hold of him? Tell him anything for you?"

I was trying to be helpful, but my offer pitched Ace back into the depths of misery.

"God, no," he said, shaking his head in short, quick strokes like an electric vibrator. "I'm the last person on earth he wants to hear from."

"Where is he?" I asked.

Ace covered his mouth with his hand, the speak-no-evil monkey this time.

"I won't contact him without your permission, Ace. I promise."

He dropped his hand.

"It's not that, RK. I… I don't know where he's living."

I sat back down and let the silence persuade him to tell me the story.

He rocked gently for a minute, then he said, "He was such a great kid when he was eight." Tears spilled from his eyes. "After he turned fourteen we did nothing but argue. After the car accident, we actually fought. Punched each other in the face! Ended up wrestling around on the floor. It was finally too much for me. I quit fighting. I just stopped and let him up. He stood up slowly. Then he called me a murderer and stormed out."

"You haven't seen him since?"

Ace shook his head, but a tiny kernel of hope blossomed on his face.

"The last thing I did for him – before everything went to hell – was to set up a trust to pay his way through technical school."

"Tech school? Which one?"

"Universal Technical Institute," he said. "They run the Motorcycle Mechanic Institute down in Orlando. Brett always wanted to work on motorcycles."

"So he went? Graduated?"

"With honors."

A brief flash of pride joined the hope in his eyes, then faded.

"I called MMI last year, told them I was his dad and that we had a family emergency."

"And?"

"They said he got offers from the Harley dealerships in Macon and Columbus, but I checked – he didn't go to work for either one. I don't know where he is."

I remembered little Brett, back when he was maybe three or four. A live wire. His middle name was Owen so, naturally, they called him Brett-O. He looked so much like Ace that Marilyn joked that it was a good thing she knew for sure she was the mother. Maybe I could help Ace find him, but that would have to wait. I stood up.

"I brought someone along who wants to meet you," I said.

"Me?" Ace said.

CHAPTER 18

VIRGIL AND WINTER Rose were chattering away like old friends when I came back into the main sitting area. Virgil's like that – another difference between us. He can talk to anyone and his natural state is animation. Mine is reserve. If I live longer than my small circle of friends, I'll probably turn into a taciturn old goat. Maybe that's the real reason I built the G-String – at least there I'd always have companions, if not friends.

When Virgil and Winter Rose saw me, they stopped talking and looked up expectantly.

"Well, he's awake and functioning," I said. "Ashamed, though, and scared."

"Scared?" Virgil said. "Scared of what?"

I shook my head.

"Scared of who is a better question. He got himself dragged into some kind of scam with a hood from Atlanta named Emil Novak."

I sat down on the couch next to Winter Rose.

"It must have been Novak and his boys who shot up the

G-String last night. They weren't messing around. Disciplined, well-armed and willing to shoot."

"But they didn't get Ace," Virgil pointed out.

"No," I said, shaking my head. "They did make that one crucial mistake. They assumed it was Ace under the blankets in the bottom bunk. He was saved by two porcelain sinks and a urinal."

I thought about that for a moment. It happens, sometimes, especially on a quick raid. It's even happened to me. You plan, prepare, rehearse. Then you go and the heat of the action stampedes the whole operation like a herd of wild horses and you're lucky to keep just enough control to get the job done and get out. Apparently, they didn't expect to find Magnus and me defending the place, at least not with the kind of firepower Magnus carries around as routinely as most people carry car keys and a wallet.

I shook my head and stood up.

"Ready to meet Ace?" I asked Winter Rose.

She said her thanks to Virgil, then followed me down the hall to Ace's room. When I knocked, Ace opened the door. I stepped aside, so he could see Winter Rose while I made the introductions.

"You!" Winter Rose said softly, a note of wonder in her voice.

"You!" Ace said more loudly, pure surprise in his voice.

They stared at each other in stunned silence, until I finally said, "You know each other?"

He said, "No."

She said, "Yes."

Then they both tried to explain at once. I cut them off and suggested we sit down and sort this out. When Ace was sitting on the edge of the bed and Winter Rose and I were perched in the chairs, I asked Winter Rose to start.

She was still looking at Ace like she'd seen a ghost, but she said, "We've run into each other twice before – literally."

If Ace nodded his head any faster, I thought it would come loose, fall off his shoulders and roll across the floor.

He said, "The first time was at my wife's funeral. Out at the street beforehand, actually. I was sitting in my car, trying to work up the courage to face her friends."

Winter Rose clapped both hands to her cheeks and looked horrified.

"Oh my God! That was your wife's funeral? I am *so* sorry!"

"Don't… don't worry about it," Ace said. "The whole thing was my fault. When I say courage, I mean liquid courage. Jim Beam. I thought I was at rock bottom, but what did I know?"

"So?" I said. "What happened?"

Winter Rose picked up the narrative.

"This was back in October, two years ago. I was training for the Chickamauga Marathon in November… out on a long run around the perimeter of the airfield at Hunter. I was about four-teen miles into it, out past the golf course and heading around the cemetery. I wasn't feeling very good, just trying to keep the pace up. The sidewalk was packed with people, so I swerved over to the street side of the parked cars."

"And I opened the door without looking," Ace said.

"I ran right into it," Winter Rose said. She smacked her palms together in the air. "Bam!"

"I was totally confused," Ace said. "At first I thought I'd had an accident – like I'd been driving. My shin felt like it was broken where the door caught it."

"Your shin!" Winter Rose said. "I thought you dislocated my kneecap!"

"I'm sorry!" Ace said.

"I know," Winter Rose said. "You looked so distraught!"

Looking over at me, she said, "Both of us felt like idiots. We apologized to each other about ten times, then we hobbled off in opposite directions."

"The second time we saw each other was less painful," Ace said.

"Well, physically anyway," Winter Rose said. "A couple of months later, I was just leaving the Toucan Café. The next day I was shipping out for my second tour in the Stan and I wanted the wasabi pea encrusted tuna they serve there." She smiled. "Last meal for the condemned kind of thing."

"I didn't know!" Ace said.

"No way you could," Winter Rose said.

"I saw her standing on the sidewalk out front," Ace said to me. "I honked! Honked, for God's sake. I never honk at anyone."

"I'm surprised you recognized me," Winter Rose said.

"I was having a good day, relatively speaking. Less alcohol, more food, so I was tracking better than usual. I was on my way back from the McDonald's on Water Ave, just around the corner."

"That's it?" I asked. "You've never actually met, just a couple of near misses?"

"Three, if you count this," Winter Rose said, holding up the dream catcher.

"My dream catcher!" Ace said.

"Actually, it's mine," Winter Rose said. "You've just had it on loan all these years."

"Yours? How do you figure?"

Winter Rose placed the dream catcher on the bed, midway between herself and Ace. "My mother made it for me," she said, "before I was even born."

"I bought it for my sister," Ace countered. "She was... she died of leukemia. We were on our way to Memphis, to St. Jude's. We were in a parking lot, waiting in the car while my parents were in at an information booth, asking about things to see and a place to stay. I saw this kid watching us, then he walked right up to the car. My sister, Sally, was in pretty bad shape by then. Gaunt, you know, kind of haunted looking. Anyway, this kid dangled the dream catcher on his finger and said it would cure her nightmares. I figured anything would help, so I bought it from him." He looked up at me, then over at Winter Rose. "Sally gave it back to me the night before she died."

Before they could get too wrapped up in the story, I stood up and said, "This is my cue to leave you two alone. Talk as long as you want. I'll be back later."

CHAPTER 19

AT THE CURB in front of St. George's, I straddled the Road King and pulled my cell phone out of my pocket. I was about to call Magnus when it started playing the opening bars to Lynyrd Skynyrd's *Call Me the Breeze*, the ring tone I use for the guys in Dahlonega.

I tapped the answer button and said, "Keane."

"Whoa! Gotta be weird not saying 'Master Sergeant Keane' when you pick up the phone, ain't it?"

I smiled. It was weird. I'd been a sergeant of one rank or another most of my adult life. It was going to take a while to become just plain Roman Keane again.

"I'm working on it, Ralph," I said. "How'd you make out?"

"Got it!" he said.

"No shit?" I said. "That's great! What kind of shape is it in?"

"Not bad, not bad. But listen, Sarge – I mean Roman – it ain't green like you said."

"What? You didn't pick up the wrong bike by mistake? You sure you've got the right one?"

"Has to be the right one. It was exactly where you said, but way off the road and into the trees. The key was still in it.

Ben – he's the only one of us knows how to ride them things – started it up. It chugged and sputtered a bit at first and smoked some for a couple of minutes, but then it cleared up. Runs fine now. Ben says it's a rocket."

In the background, I heard Ben pipe up, "It scared the shit outta me! I gave it the gas, you know, after it started running smooth. Damn front wheel came up so fast I almost looped it!"

"Don't worry, he didn't crash," Ralph said. "The bike's fine."

"But it's not green?"

"No, it's kinda… well, you'll see. You home now? We'll be at your place in about twenty minutes."

"Listen Ralph, I've got to be somewhere else for the next hour or two, but I really appreciate what you guys have done."

"No sweat, RK. We were looking for something to do anyway."

"Can you leave it in my garage?"

I told him where to find the key I hid in the woods out back and how to disarm the security system. I heard another voice in the background. It sounded like the phone was being covered, then Ralph came on again.

"Jack says we'll leave it in the garage, but we want an equal weight in beer as payment."

"Hah! Can't promise pound for pound, but you guys help yourselves to anything in the house."

"Really?"

"Beer or food," I amended hastily. "Anything you can't swallow is off limits. And listen guys, thanks again."

I went over the security system one more time with Ben. When I was sure they weren't going to be setting off any alarms, I hung up and called Magnus.

"You busy?" I asked.

"Just got back from my long swim," he said. "Not too choppy this morning. A guy couldn't complain."

Magnus's little house on Tybee Island is a "one-back," but it sits up on a rise and looks out over a vacant lot, so for now he has an ocean view from his living room. I knew he didn't buy the place for the view though. When the real estate agent showed him the public access right-of-way path to the beach right across the street from his house, he was already reaching for a pen. Magnus's neighbors think he's nuts, but unless a full-fledged tropical storm is bearing down on the island, he swims everyday when he's home. His "long" swim is a four miler, up and back the full length of the island. He does it once a week. He keeps trying to rope me into coming along, but so far I've managed to avoid everything but the "short" swims. One mile. Even that distance leaves me wrung out and wrinkled. It barely gets Magnus warmed up.

"Got time to meet me at Ace's office for a quick look around?"

"No problem. I've got to be up in D.C. for a job on Monday, but I'm yours to command until then."

"What's going on Monday?"

"Just a security job." He named an actress who I vaguely recognized. "She's filming in Georgetown for a couple of weeks. Got a stalking problem with a slightly rabid fan."

"Sounds like fun," I said. "Meantime, here's the address of Ace's office."

I gave it to him and he said he'd meet me there in fifteen minutes.

CHAPTER 20

"**A**CE WORKED OUT of this dump, eh?" Magnus said, after we parked our bikes across the street from the two-story brick building where Ace had rented an office.

"Back in '99, he had an office on the ninth floor of the Johnson Building," I said. "Over on West Bryan Street. It was a palace compared to this."

I looked left and right along West Victory. What I saw was a neighborhood that had slipped three or four notches below mediocre. The narrow sidewalks were crumbling and litter clogged the gutters. Cars zoomed right by the buildings at freeway speed, as though everyone wanted to pass through as quickly as possible.

The roof of Ace's building sagged in the middle, like a giant fist had reached down and given it one solid whack. The upper floor was a duplex residence, with black iron steps giving access on each end. Four businesses operated out of the ground floor: a tiny take-out pizza place called Pete's Piece-A-Pie, a pawn shop, a small convenience store called Maude's Grocery and, on the end of the building, Ace's office. All of them had their windows and doors covered with wrought iron grillwork. The pawnshop owner had added more security, in the form of an aluminum roll down shutter behind the grill.

At a gap in the traffic, we crossed the street and stopped by the door to Ace's office. Iron bars still protected the single window to the left of the door, but the top hinge of the barred gate over the door had been wrenched from the wall. Somebody had folded the iron gate against the bricks and wrapped a wire coat hanger around a convenient drainpipe to hold it in place.

A blue plastic sign with white letters, about ten by twelve inches, had been fastened at eye level over the peeling paint on the wooden door. In three lines it read, "Alan Emory, Debt Management, Pay Checks Cashed."

"I don't know Ace like you do, Roman, but moving from a plush pad in the old town to this place... well, that ain't too good a deal," Magnus said.

He was right, I thought. The Johnson Building, where Ace had his first office, reached for the stars and spoke confidently of money and power. This poor building knelt by the road in abject surrender and whispered, "Help me."

I had Ace's key in my pocket, but I checked the door first. A quarter inch gap showed at the jam. When I nudged the door with my elbow, it swung open freely. I leaned in cautiously. The fresh smell of death hit me before I could even flip on the lights.

Magnus moved in with me, the Wilson ready in his hand. He crossed the room to the only other door, yanked it open and checked the alley outside. He stepped back inside, holstering the pistol. He shook his head.

I found the light switch. Bright fluorescent lights flickered to life in the ceiling. Magnus and I stood together at the front of the room and looked around. The inside of the building was about what you would expect after seeing the outside. Dingy white walls, pale gray linoleum flooring missing half a dozen squares, a couple of putty colored filing cabinets against the back wall and a dented metal desk that could only have come from a government auction. A stack of three red bricks propped up a corner of the desk where one leg had gone missing. A cheap folding cot had been set up in the corner behind the desk, topped with a bare pillow and a tangle of flower print sheets. Last year's calendar was thumbtacked to the wall behind the desk, a give-away from the Savannah Chamber of Commerce. It was folded to show September, with an early morning aerial photo of the city in muted autumn colors and a soft mist on the river.

A dead body lay in front of the desk, in a coagulating mess of fluids and blood.

"Looks like a movie set," Magnus said. "*China Town* or *LA Confidential*. Maybe even something older, like one of the black and white Bogart movies."

"Except for all that red blood," I said.

I took two long steps toward the body, careful to avoid the splatter pattern spilling out from the head. I squatted to get a better look. Mid-thirties white man, carrying forty or fifty extra pounds. He was dressed in khaki pants with cargo pockets and a cheap gray sweatshirt over a blue T-shirt. His legs were twisted up beneath him, and he wore black Reeboks with black socks. His eyes were closed behind heavy black plastic framed glasses, like the kind Buddy Holly wore. A crusted glob of blood dangled from the bullet hole in his forehead like wax dripping from a candle. This had to be Dalbert.

"What's he doing here?" I said.

"What's he… ? Well, he's dead, dontcha know?"

"No, I mean *why* is he here? Somebody shot this man some time ago. Last night, probably."

"Oh, I see what you mean. Plenty of time to remove the evidence," Magnus said.

"Right," I said. "And presuming it's the same crew from last night, plenty of help."

Magnus lowered himself next to me.

"Ever seen him before?" I said.

"Nope," he said. "You?"

I shook my head.

"No, but according to what Ace told me this morning, his name is Dalbert."

I stood up, using both hands on my thighs and managing not to grunt at the pain in my right knee. Magnus stood easily and pointed at the body's legs.

"To land like that, a guy would hafta be on his knees when he got it."

He pantomimed aiming a pistol with his fingers and said, "Pow! One to the head. Yep. Execution style."

I tried to picture it. Gun to the head, the sudden shot, the fall of the body. Something didn't seem right. I leaned over again and took a closer look at the head.

"No powder burns," I said. "Ease around here, Magnus, and check this out."

When he was in place again I pointed at Dalbert's forehead.

"What's that?"

"That circle? I don't know. Weird, though, eh. Never seen anything like it before."

"Like a bruise," I said. "An abrasion maybe."

"Like a bruise, he says," Magnus said, nodding in agreement. "A bloody bruise."

"Entry wound just outside the circle. Looks like a 9mm."

"Probably. Too small for a .45."

Magnus held his right hand up, index and little fingers extended, the way the kids do at Texas football games. "If I had latex gloves, I'd give it the fingertip test. Index finger in the hole, it's a .45. Pinky size hole, then 9 mil. Looks pretty pinky to me. So, there you go. Course, it could have been a .38."

I had to smile at that.

"Where do you come up with this stuff, Magnus?"

He launched into an earnest explanation, but I held up a hand.

"Never mind," I said. I pointed to the relatively intact back of the head. "You're probably right. A hollow point 9mm would make an exit hole about that size. Same with a .38, but how many people carry a .38 anymore? A .357 would have punched a bigger hole on the way out."

We both stood up, looking around for the brass. Magnus spotted it, against the molding at the wall behind us. He knelt without touching his hands to the vinyl and read the lettering stamped on the back of the casing.

"Federal 9mm," he said.

At least that ruled out Ace's .45 for certain. Plus, the way he talked earlier, he didn't know Dalbert was dead. I tried to think of a reason why someone would kill Dalbert and leave him here in Ace's office. My best guess was Novak, shutting down the operation and setting Ace up to take the heat.

Magnus stood again, brushing dust spots off both knees.

"I've been in real dumps cleaner than this dump. Wanna bet we're leaving tracks everywhere?"

"You're right, but don't worry about it," I said. "But we do need to get out of here. Let me photograph that peculiar mark on the guy's forehead and check a couple more things, then we'll leave."

Using the camera in my cell, I got a reasonably clear close-up of the head wound. I stuck the phone back in my pocket and walked around the left side of the desk, away from the bloody carnage at the head end of the corpse, so I could search the drawers. To avoid leaving prints, I used my folding knife to open drawers and rummage around inside. The desk was recycled government issue with three drawers down the right side and one centered where you sit. None of them were locked, and all I found was the usual junk everyone accumulates in an office: stapler, a handful of ballpoints, rubber bands and a pair of scissors with blue plastic handles. No papers or pads, but an empty flask of Jim Beam lingered in the bottom drawer.

I turned to the filing cabinet behind the desk. If anything it was cheaper than the desk: vinyl veneer over pasteboard. Cigarette burns stained the top edge and two of the three drawers were too warped to fully close. Only the top drawer had anything in it: a row of manila folders, all neatly hand labeled. Using the blade of my knife, I leafed through them. As far as I could tell, these were Ace's day-to-day customers. The documents inside were copies of letters from banks, credit card companies and bill collectors. Paperwork brought in by his clients.

No phone and no laptop. Novak must have taken them. If he was planning to set Ace up as the fall guy for this operation, I wondered where they would turn up.

"Let's go, Magnus," I said, retracing my steps around the desk.

"We're not gonna wait for the police?"

"No," I said, "and we were never here, right?"

He nodded, trusting me.

"I'll make sure the police know about it later. Not right now, though. First thing they would do is slap a set of handcuffs on Ace and haul his ass off to jail. Before the police get involved, I want to talk to Special Agent Cushner."

"Cushner? Cute, kinda reddish hair?" Magnus said. "Great, let's go."

I shook my head.

"Not so fast. Remember Ace's car? The one sitting in front of the G-String full of bullet holes? So far we've been lucky, but the cops could show up there even with the gate closed and start wondering what the hell happened. If we're going to get Ace out of this mess, we can't have him tied to that shootout anymore than we can have him tied to that body. Can you get your friend Hernando out there? He deals in cars, right? Think he could stash it in his shop?"

"Hernando? He'll have it on a freighter to South America by three o'clock."

"That might be the best solution. Anyway, make sure he gets it out of the G-String lot. And grab anything you can salvage of Ace's, OK?"

"And the bullet holes in the building?" he said. "Won't the cops wonder about that?"

I grinned. "I know somebody who'll fix the windows and replace the door today. Anybody asks about the damage in the meantime, tell 'em it's just part of the décor."

"Sure," Magnus said grinning back. He pitched his voice ridiculously high and mimicked one of the biddies from the ladies auxiliary: "That G-String! It's just a sleazy strip club! Why, I wouldn't be caught dead in there!"

CHAPTER 21

"I'VE GOT AN opportunity for you, Big Al," I said, pushing the door open just enough to stick my head inside the tiny office.

"I told you never to call me that."

I smiled and slipped inside, careful not to bang the front of the desk with the edge of the door. The closet-sized office in Savannah was punishment for some supposed infraction of Secret Service protocol while she was assigned to the Vice Presidential Protection Detail in Washington, D.C. The story was that a certain protectee clamped a hand on her breast and she nearly pulled his arm off at the shoulder. The Secret Service may have demoted her, but standing up to him only raised my opinion of her.

Special Agent Alice Cushner leaned back in her chair, locked her fingers together, raised her hands over her head and arched her back. She did it to relieve the strain of working at her computer while jammed in that cubbyhole, but I enjoyed the way it stretched the top of her shirt across her chest. She caught me looking, stuck her tongue out at me and lowered her hands.

When Alice stood under the sign that read "You must be

this tall to enter the Secret Service," she had to have been wearing lifts. In her bare feet she would have to stand on her toes to break five two. She wouldn't tip the scales at much more than 110 either, but no one takes her lightly. I first met her at a martial arts competition in Atlanta, where she demolished five foes in a row and earned a standing ovation from the crowd. I've sparred with her many times since then, and each time I have been the humble student.

Her wavy, red hair is cut in a simple shoulder-length fashion and I've never seen her wear more than a hint of make-up, but she's one of the most beautiful women I've ever met. It's the smile, I think. It starts on her lips and lights up her face like a warm sunrise after a long cold night. Gives me a pleasant jolt every time I see her.

Unfortunately, I'm sure it does the same for her husband, Dylan. I met him once and couldn't understand the attraction between them, but then I could hardly be called an expert on matters of the heart. He's an attorney in Washington, D.C., a partner in a legal firm that works exclusively for the oil lobby. He's a workaholic with a skinny blonde secretary. When we were cooling down after a sparring session one day a couple of months ago, Alice admitted she frets a bit about exactly what services the secretary provides. The last thing I'd do is intrude on someone's marriage, so I didn't point out that the secretary sees Dylan ten or twelve hours a day while Alice has probably seen him ten or twelve times in the past year. None of that keeps me from thinking the bastard who said timing is everything was right on the mark.

She batted her eyelashes in an exaggerated spoof and said, "Are you just here to ogle, Master Sergeant Keane, or is there something the Secret Service can do for you?"

I slipped all the way into the office and closed the door behind me.

"Just plain Roman Keane, now Alice," I said.

"Right! Congratulations! Sorry I couldn't make your retirement party. I was in DC until late yesterday evening."

I waved the thought aside.

"Dull, dull, dull," I said. "You probably would have fallen asleep."

She giggled at that, a little stream of laughter that seemed to have a melody of its own.

"Oh, sure. A retirement party hosted by an Army Ranger with his own strip club? Dull?"

"I keep telling you, the G-String's not a strip club."

"Right. It's just a private club with a bar… *and* a stage… *and* a killer music system." She arched an eyebrow at me. "And a brass pole."

"There's no brass pole! As for the rest, it's an investment. Think of it as my work place, now that I'm retired from the Army."

"Hah! That'll look good on your new business cards. *Roman Keane – Have Gun, Will Travel – Inquire at the G-String.*"

I grinned.

"Not bad, but all I plan to do is ride."

She turned in her chair and pointed at the glossy black helmet on the bookcase behind her.

"My Softail's down in the parking garage, ready to go."

"You get that new seat?"

"More than half an inch lower and much narrower at the front. No more balancing on my toes. Remains to be seen whether or not it's crotch friendly on a long haul."

She put her forearms on the desk and got serious.

"Much as I enjoy the attention, I'm sure you didn't come to my office the day after you retired just to talk bikes or stare at my tits. You said something about an opportunity?"

"You still interested in identity theft?" I asked.

She nodded.

"Among other so-called white collar crimes, yes, of course. My boss keeps reminding me that the Secret Service is not just about protecting the president." She sniffed delicately and rolled her eyes around the tiny office. "As if I need a reminder from where I sit."

"How about identity theft leading to murder?"

The smile froze on her face and she stared hard at me until she was certain I was serious. She straightened up and pointed to the chair jammed against the front of her desk.

"Wedge yourself into that, Roman, and give."

I turned the chair sideways and sat.

"This is a big scheme involving identity theft to make fraudulent claims against the Veterans Administration – "

She held up a hand to stop me.

"I had a call yesterday, just before I left the office. Guy named Brian Blount, a special agent from the Department of Veterans Affairs. I met him last winter at a workshop on fraud and counterfeiting the Secret Service hosted. He works out of their Washington, DC, office. Highly strung individual, if you know what I mean. His friends call him 'Bulldog.' " She leaned back and regarded me thoughtfully for a moment. "He said he was looking into some allegations of identity fraud for the VA, possibly a scheme that covered the whole country. He said he was picking up some leads from down this way and wanted to know if I could assist him if he came to Savannah." She picked up a pen and tapped it gently on her desk. "He was pretty excited, but he didn't mention murder."

"At least two," I said. "No, make that three. Probably more."

She let that hang in the air before she said, "Uh-huh. And the source of the identity theft? Not state stuff, I hope."

I shook my head.

"Personal information stolen from federal government records."

She closed the lid on her laptop, pushed it aside and placed both palms on the top of her desk.

"I'm all yours, so talk," she said.

"Not so fast," I said. "A friend of mine is caught in the middle. I have to be sure he doesn't go down when the shooting starts."

She gave me a hard look. "Caught in the middle how?"

Good question. I took a deep breath and blew it out. I rubbed my chin and knuckled my eyes, all to give myself a few moments while I thought how to answer.

"Look," I said, "I don't want to sound like one of those idiots who gets on the news after Charlie is arrested with a gun in one hand and a bag of money in the other and says, 'My friend Charlie couldn't possibly do something like that – I know him too well.'"

"But?"

"But I believe my friend was duped into something he normally wouldn't have done. Then it was like the old fable of the tar baby – he just kept getting pulled tighter into the scheme. Finally, they had him wrapped so tight they could coerce him into anything they wanted."

"He was coerced?"

"Coerced. Forced," I said nodding vigorously. "However you want to say it, his life was at stake."

She drummed her fingers on the desktop. First the right hand, then the left, then the right again. She sighed.

"All right, RK. I know you won't hang me out to dry. Tell me what you have, and I'll keep it off the record for the time being."

"For the time being?" I asked.

"You and I both know there's a line out there I can't cross. I'll warn you if we reach it, but from that point on, all bets are off."

"Fair enough," I said, then I gave her the condensed version.

She fidgeted several times and said, "Oh, crap," twice, but otherwise listened stoically while I described the string of felonies that had occurred – and my failure to report them – since Ace showed up at the G-String. I finished up with Magnus and I finding Dalbert's corpse in Ace's office. By that time, she had her head in her hands and was probably contemplating her imminent dismissal from the Secret Service if she didn't read *me* my rights and then immediately go and arrest Ace.

I pulled up the photo I had taken in Ace's office on my cell and held the phone under her eyes. She studied the image for a few seconds, then gradually sat up, a new look of interest replacing the gloom on her face.

"This is the work of this Emil Novak character?" she asked.

"He's the logical candidate," I said. "I think he's closing down his operation by eliminating loose ends, starting with Dalbert."

"May I load this onto my computer?" she said, already hooking a cable into my phone.

"Of course," I said.

In less than a minute she had the photo displayed on her monitor. With a series of mouse clicks she enlarged the image until it filled the screen, corrected the exposure and sharpened the detail. The improvement was amazing. Within a small circle offset from the bullet entry hole, I could make out a crosshatch pattern of tiny diamond-shaped lines.

"Those look like abrasions, don't they?" I said, pointing at the markings without actually touching the flat screen.

"Or bruises, maybe."

She enlarged the area around the bullet hole until it lost detail, then backed it down a notch.

"Nice clean entry. Just comparing the size of the hole to the size of the eyeball, I'd say a nine millimeter."

"Magnus would agree with you, but he compared it to the size of his pinky."

"Ecch! He didn't actually stick his finger… ?"

"No, but only because I was there to supervise."

"Well, I think he's right, but what else do you see?"

I ran my eyes around the image. I saw a dark, almost perfectly round entry wound, slightly dimpled around the edges where the bullet pulled the skin inward; the curious circular hash marks slightly off-center from the bullet hole; a fuzzy eyebrow and one open, vacant eyeball. I shook my head.

"Come on, Alice, give. What am I missing?"

"Look at the markings, RK, and think about the order of events."

I looked again. Nice neat bullet hole, bloody hash mark shaped like a flat washer, no powder burns. Finally, I put it all together.

"All right," I said. "No powder burns, so the shot was fired from a distance. Three or four feet, anyway. The bullet hole is clean, so it came after the hash marks. That means the hash marks must have been made first, then the shooter stepped back."

"Yes! Very good! And look here; see how the bullet hole is partly in, partly out of the red-hashed circle? If this was a target, it would still count as a bull's-eye."

I looked at Alice in surprise, probably with my mouth hanging open.

"A target? You mean Novak put that red mark on the guy's forehead, then stepped back and used him for target practice?"

"Exactly! I'll bet you a hundred bucks that he made the mark with the barrel of the pistol."

She used the end of her pen as a pointer and traced a circle around the inner part of the red area.

"See where the skin is almost undamaged here? That could be from the hole in the barrel."

She pointed to the outer edge of the red area and said, "This circular area is larger than you would expect for the rim of a pistol barrel, though. Probably a fat silencer or some kind of flash suppressor."

"What is it?" I said. "Some hit man ritual?"

"Strange, isn't it," she said, shaking her head. "Let's see if Interpol has anything similar."

She clicked and pointed intently for five or six minutes, then crooked a finger at me. I leaned over so I could see her screen again. She had a rough looking character on the monitor, a gray haired guy with a hooked nose, deep-set eyes and a menacing scowl.

"Meet Caesar Kavinski, deceased. Emil Novak's former boss."

"Caesar?"

She snickered.

"Seems unlikely, doesn't it?" she said. "Maybe it's not actually his name. Maybe it's a self-bestowed title, like Duke or King."

"He looks – looked – like a tough customer."

Alice clicked a corner of the screen, which brought up a new page of text.

"He was convicted of three murders and executed – by firing squad. Guess they like the old fashioned way over there in the Czech Republic. But get this. Before his death, he was previously arrested for six other murders, but released for lack of evidence."

"Bad man, all right," I said. "I assume there's some tie-in with Ace's situation?"

She clicked again. The close-up photo of the gun shot wound she'd downloaded from my phone came up.

"OK," I said slowly, "that's the guy we think Emil Novak killed. Dalbert."

"Look again," she said.

I ran my eyes around the screen again, then it hit me.

"That's a different photo!"

"Right," she said. "See, the bullet hole is slightly further off center. This is one of Kavinski's victims."

"Now I get it," I said. "Emil Novak learned this weird game from this Kavinski guy."

She looked back at the screen and continued reading.

"It says Emil and Kavinski made a game of it. Maybe they made it up together. They actually had a name for it. Both of them were voracious chess players – guess what they called it."

I thought for a minute, then it hit me. The final move of a chess game.

"Czech Mate!"

She gave a lady-like little snort.

"Idiots. Anyway, Novak's wanted by Interpol. See?" She brought up a screen with what looked like a surveillance photo of a middle-aged man with a receding hairline and wire-rimmed glasses. "Looks kind of innocuous, doesn't he? But he's wanted by Interpol for *crimes against health and life.* That's the polite European way to say extortion and murder. I think he's using Kavinski's morbid signature on his hits. Your guy Ace has been playing with a very dangerous person."

We both looked at the picture of Emil Novak on her computer screen. She was right. Physically, he looked improbable as a serious criminal. But something about the whole package — stance, eyes, set of the mouth — said "don't fuck with me".

"If he's wanted there, how did he get here?"

She scrolled down a bit and pointed at the screen.

"Interpol traced him out of the Czech Republic by car using a German passport in the name of Dieter Gottschalk, then a train to Belgrade and another train to the Greek port of Thessaloniki. They think he bought his way onto a freighter bound for Halifax by way of Algiers. When the police finally got around to searching the ship in Nova Scotia, Novak was already gone."

"So he worked his way down to Savannah and set himself up in business here?"

"Why not?" she said. "Look at all the Ukrainians and Russians we've got running crime syndicates in the US now. We're paradise for them. Our open, democratic government is easy pickings for all kinds of scams: Social Security, Medicare, property insurance. You name it, they've tried it."

"I don't know," I said. "I think he's an action guy, not a planner."

"Somebody else is running the show, you mean?"

I nodded and told her about what Ace had said about

Novak deferring to someone he called the General, and the level of sophistication of this whole operation.

Al pursed her lips and scratched the back of her head.

"The General…" she said. "Another eastern European? Maybe. They've got plenty of ex-military types moving over into crime. But here's something else to think about: why the rough stuff? Killing isn't normally part of these types of scams. They're usually about money, not murder. Sounds like these guys were raking in the dough before they started killing. Why take such a huge risk?"

I nodded.

"That was my question, too," I said. "Although killing older vets who have no relatives may be less risky than you think. Lot of these guys are really alone out there. Besides, Ace says Novak has a couple of thugs working for him. He'll make sure they get caught first."

Alice reached her fingers for the keyboard.

"Oh, yeah. Novak's men. You said there are three more? What are their names?"

"Ray Manion, Daryl Cutcher and somebody known only as Bailey."

She rattled the keys and brought up a photo. Broad face, shiny head.

"Ray Manion," I said.

"Nasty man," she said. "Served eighteen months in the Carson City Correctional Facility in Michigan, after being sentenced to four years for assault with intent to commit great bodily harm. Clean since he completed his parole, though."

She typed some more.

"Daryl Cutcher. Now that's the kind of man mothers warn their daughters about. Twenty-eight years old, nine of them in prison. His record shows a steady escalation of charges, starting with grand theft auto and ending with his last conviction for robbery and assault with a deadly weapon. Must have been a bad boy in prison because he was never granted parole."

She clicked the mouse and Cutcher's photo appeared on the screen, an old booking composite photo, left side, right side and straight on. His narrow face had a flat, no-big-deal expression. High forehead, slightly crooked nose, sandy hair pulled into a ponytail with a red rubber band. He was wearing a dark tank top over his skinny frame. The top of some kind of tattoo was visible at his throat.

"Ace said Bailey might have been police or military at one time. Likes to chew on toothpicks, sports a crew cut."

She looked dubious, but flexed her fingers over the keyboard.

"Not much to go on. Let's start close to home."

She worked her way through Georgia, then South Carolina. She had a couple of hits we looked at more closely, but both of them were accounted for in the penal system. North Carolina was a bust too, then we struck pay dirt in the Florida records.

"Dennis Bailey. A warrant's out on him for – what else? – assault with a deadly weapon. Also possession of illegal fire-arms and explosives while a member of a militia group called the Federation of New Florida."

She glanced over at me.

"Ever heard of them?"

I shook my head.

"Me neither," she said. "Must be small time. There's a note here that he washed out of Marine Corps training five years ago."

"Doesn't take the Corps long to put their stamp on you," I said. "That would account for the feeling Ace had that the guy's ex-military."

Bailey's photo wasn't a booking photo. It looked like it might have been cropped out of a larger photo. Maybe a group photo for the New Florida boys. It was him though, right down to the toothpick. He had a disaffected, pissed off look that I guessed was his perennial expression. I could imagine how the Marine drill instructors had taken to it.

Alice cleared the screen and turned her chair to face me.

"Those are dangerous people, RK. If they are trying to kill your friend, his best bet is to turn himself in and get some official protection."

I blew some air out of my lungs and wiped a quick hand over my face.

"You're probably right, Alice. But here's the problem: I think this General – whoever he is – has set this whole scheme up so Ace will take the blame if they get caught. Maybe he's going to sacrifice Novak and the others too, but Ace for sure. I need some time to get Ace clear. If we can find the list that Dalbert gave Ace by mistake, maybe we can use it to flush the General out."

Alice shook her head slowly.

"A list that Ace *thinks* he stuffed in the side compartment of an RV towing a couple of motorcycles that was parked outside Betty Jo Bob's place a couple of days ago."

"Somebody wrote the names of the two missing vets by hand on the bottom. Maybe it was this General."

Her face brightened.

"You're reaching there, RK, but that list is important in another way: an analysis of the ink and the handwriting on the bottom could provide physical evidence implicating somebody. Maybe the General as you say, but I'd put my money on Novak."

"It's a start, right? Listen, I'm headed over to Betty Jo Bob's. I want to catch her at her place, see if that helps her remember the RV and the bikes. Want to come along? Then you could join us for lunch and talk to Ace? You might get something new out of him."

She spun her chair around and reached for her helmet.

"Betty Jo Bob's? I wouldn't miss it."

I smiled. Alice knew I paid to have a BBQ lunch catered at St. George's once a week. I did it for the Charlie Norwood VA Medical Center on occasion too, because I knew from personal experience how even a small treat could make a big difference during months of recovery. For Alice, the barbecue was just a convenient excuse to go and talk to Ace. I knew she'd help.

CHAPTER 22

BETTY GREETED US at the door of her place, Betty Jo Bob's Barbecue. The name always gets a grin from first-timers, who wonder what nutcase named his daughter Betty Jo Bob. Actually, it was Bob's Barbecue when she bought him out more than thirty years ago; she simply added her name to the front and kept the briquettes burning. Her real name is Betty Jo Bakersfield, but almost no one remembers that now. We all call her Betty Jo Bob. Slender, with paper-thin skin like worn parchment leather and warm blue eyes over a friendly smile, she was dressed casually in jeans, a plaid shirt and a wide brimmed straw hat. She knows all her regulars by name and treats everyone like family.

"Roman, good to see you. My word, Al, don't you look fine today? But girl, ain't you too skinny?" She gestured inside and said, "Goodness, ya'll come on in. You doing lunch with us here?"

"No, we'll join the crowd over at St. George's. I came to warn you there would be some extra mouths there today. Can you add enough to feed another five or six?"

She flashed her happy crooked grin and said, "I may not have much in this world, but I got plenty of ribs."

"Great, I'll give you some cash to make up the difference."

"Let me just let the girls know. Why don't ya'll on back to your usual table and I'll bring you something to drink. Sweet tea, right?"

"Thanks, Betty Jo Bob," I said. "That would be great."

I can sum up Betty Jo Bob's BBQ in one word: joint. Of course, I mean that in the best possible way. It looks and smells like a BBQ joint ought to, and the food is unbelievably delicious.

If we ever get three inches of snow in Savannah, the whole place will surely collapse in a heap under the extra weight. A good stiff wind might blow it over anyway. The outside is clapboard, weathered to a fine pale gray. You have to give the front door a hefty pull to get it open, because the usual spring mechanism has been replaced by a rope and pulley arrangement weighted with a 25 pound York dumbbell. Look up and you'll see exposed rafters blackened by years of warm rising soot. Each of the four corners of the big, open dining area hosts a pair of grandfather clocks, wound with rigid precision only by Betty Jo Bob herself. Diners plan their arrival for the top of the hour, just to hear the symphony of chimes. Strangely enough, it always reminds me of the Stone's *Honky Tonk Women* – powerful music that nearly stumbles over the line into noise.

The tables are all identical four-by-four squares of three quarter inch plywood covered with red and white checkered cloth. No two chairs are the same. A waitress brought the tea in big plastic cups while we were still pulling our mismatched seats up to the table.

A few minutes later Betty Jo Bob came over with a paper ticket in her hands and said, "I bumped up the ribs, the slaw and the stew. The extra cornbread's on the house. Want me to run it over in my van like usual?"

"I was counting on that, Betty Jo Bob," I said.

"Figured as much. When I saw you two come in on them bikes."

We chatted for a few more minutes, then I asked her if she remembered an RV that had been parked out front on Thursday.

"Well now, Roman. Well now. Let me think on it for one little bit. Thursday, you say?"

She cupped her chin in a rough red hand, let her eyes roam the room as though she was planning a round-the-world trip using the posters hanging on the walls.

"Pulling a trailer with a couple of motorcycles," I said to encourage her.

"Course it was," she said.

She gave a little snort and a shake of her head.

"Seems like nobody rides them fancy bikes anymore. They load 'em up on trailers, climb into their even fancier trucks and turn the air conditioning way up. I ain't exactly expert on the subject, but don't that seem contrary to the whole notion of riding them things?"

I had to smile at that. I prefer to ride, but lots of people trailer these days.

"Whatever gets them off the couch," I said. "At least they're out there."

"I reckon," Betty Jo Bob grumbled. Then her eyes lit up. She snapped her fingers and said, "Now I remember those folks. Older couple. Come up from Ft. Meyers. Nice people, laughed a lot." She took her hat off, ran her palm across her forehead and put the hat back on. "Don't know if this is any help at all,

Roman, but they talked about staying at some farm. They was gonna go up north. Gonna ride in Rolling Thunder."

"Rolling Thunder?" I said, sitting back in my chair. Alice and I glanced at each other, thinking of new possibilities.

"Yep," Betty Jo Bob said. "Half the Harleys in Georgia gonna be there, if you kin believe some folks."

The same waitress who served our tea poked her head into the room and told Betty Jo Bob everything was loaded up. Betty Jo Bob thanked her and rose.

"Reckon I best be on my way, then," she said.

After I paid the bill, Alice and I followed her to St. George's and helped her unload the food. By the time she left, the long dining room table was piled with enough food to feed an army. In addition to the extra ribs, Brunswick stew and coleslaw she promised, Betty Jo Bob had added a dozen ears of corn on the cob and a platter of cornbread muffins. The thick aroma wafting from the room had us all ready to stampede, so Virgil herded his regulars to their chairs and barely held them back long enough to say grace.

He crossed himself, and waited a beat for everyone around the table to follow suit. He bent his head and said, "Bless us, oh Lord, for these thy ribs." Then he snatched the topmost slab off the plate.

CHAPTER 23

VIRGIL WINKED AT me.

"Barbecue grace," he said, wiping a bit of sauce off his lips. "What? It's in the Jesuit manual."

After a moment of shocked surprise, the rest of us grabbed paper plates and reached across to serve ourselves. Every chair at the dining table was taken, so we left the regulars to the dining room and found space for ourselves in the living room. Winter Rose and Ace sat together on the couch and Alice nearly disappeared into the overstuffed easy chair. Uncle Gil and I dragged folding chairs out of the closet and set them up near the coffee table.

"I checked on your mom's old house," Uncle Gil said as we arranged our food on the table. "Nobody lives there, but it still belongs to that Irish non-profit group." He downed a couple of spoonfuls of coleslaw before he continued. "Apparently, they are not very active, except when they ramp up for the Irish Festival in February and St. Patrick's Day in March."

"So they're legit?"

"According to my sources. Small time, but then it's all volunteer so what do you expect?"

I wondered if there was a connection there. Irish musicians? It seemed impossible. More likely, Novak somehow knew the place was empty most of the time and used it for a mail drop without their knowledge. Easy enough, if you don't mind ignoring the postal regulations.

"Why did you want to know about that house?" Uncle Gil asked. "I would have thought that was a memory best buried."

I told him how the address had been used in the scam that had enveloped Ace.

"Hmm," he murmured. "Seems like a strange coincidence, don't you think?"

I nodded.

"Strange enough to bear further investigation," I said. "Monday maybe, I'll take a ride over there. Meanwhile, I'm going to enjoy Betty Jo Bob's feast."

I gnawed much too quickly through three ribs before I stopped to wipe up the sauce I'd slathered on my face. Just as I brought another bone to my lips, I saw a pickup truck through the front window. The same black truck from last night at the G-String. It jerked to a stop directly in front of St. George's.

I dropped the rib onto my plate.

"Take Ace out back!" I said, reaching over and yanking him unceremoniously to his feet. I thrust him toward Alice. One day of retirement hadn't blunted the authority of my command voice at all. Alice was on her feet before his plate hit the floor. She grabbed him by the wrist and ran toward the back. Ace stumbled after her like a string of laundry flapping in the breeze.

Winter Rose shot me a look that was all question.

"Go with them," I said. I pointed out the window where doors were flying open on the pickup. "Those are the same bastards who tried to kill Ace last night."

She disappeared after Alice and Ace.

I stepped quickly to the front door and threw the deadbolt. Then I turned to Virgil.

"Can you get them to their rooms? Quickly?"

Virgil, to my relief, didn't question or argue. He stepped to the dining room door and called for attention.

"Everyone to your rooms," Virgil said. Three or four forks stopped in midair, but no one moved.

In a reasonable facsimile of my army sergeant voice, he added, "Move your damn butts now!"

Apparently none of them had ever heard Virgil curse before. Eyes bugged all around the table for one cartoonish instant, then there was a clatter as forks dropped to plates and chairs scraped the floor. The total resident population of St. George's cleared the room in about five seconds. Virgil hurried behind them, making sure they were all tucked safely away.

The doorknob rattled, but the bolt held.

Uncle Gil was on his feet. Since he had been ousted from West Point he'd had little to do with the military, but he was president of the Savannah Rod and Gun Club and a nationally ranked skeet shooter. The look on his face said "my kingdom for a shotgun." Just as well he wasn't armed, I thought, remembering the automatic weapons and well-disciplined attack last night at the G-String. Too many innocent people here to risk any chance of another firefight.

A sudden pounding shook the door.

"Better open it," I said, "before they knock it down."

He crossed quickly to the door and flipped the deadbolt off. He opened the door and calmly said, "Yes?"

Emil Novak stood in the doorway. He inspected Uncle Gil briefly from head to toe, then pushed him out of the way and strutted into the room. Physically, I'd have put him down as blandly average. Medium height, medium weight. His receding hairline and wire-rimmed glasses would give most people a mild appearance, but he radiated an extraordinary intensity, as though he could burst into flame at will and burn you into a small pile of cinders.

"Where is Emory?" he demanded.

His three goons — minus the body armor from last night I noticed — filed in behind him and spread themselves out to the sides. I ticked them off in my mind, recalling the images from Alice's computer. Manion was on Novak's right, bigger than I imagined. He was nearly as tall as Magnus, but fifty pounds heavier. I guessed that Magnus was responsible for the heavy gauze bandage wrapped around his beefy forearm. Next to him was Bailey. Cutcher stood on Novak's left, rocking back and forth on the balls of his feet. All of them, including Novak, were armed with the same Heckler and Koch submachine guns they had demonstrated more than a passing skill with last night when they shot up the G-String. In the living room of St. George's peaceful halfway house, the weapons looked even more menacing.

Virgil returned to the living room. He tried to look casual, but he was breathing hard and his face was flushed. He had slipped on a black blazer over his black shirt and white collar, so he looked as priestly as he could on short notice. His long hair, blue jeans and bare feet in purple Crocs didn't project the standard clerical image, but Novak gave him a brief deferential bow anyway.

"Father," he said, "you have man here. He is called Emory. You must give him to me."

Virgil crossed his arms and kept silent.

Novak looked at each of us, one by one. None of us

answered. He turned back to Virgil. He shook his head like he regretted what he had to do. He took a deep breath and let it out slowly. Then he simply pointed a finger at Virgil. The one called Cutcher happened to be closest. He immediately stepped over and pushed the barrel of his H&K against Virgil's temple. His lips curled and he giggled, enjoying Virgil's alarm.

In a harsher, louder voice, Novak repeated, "Where is Emory?"

I moved forward, hoping to direct his focus on me instead of Virgil. Up close, Novak smelled of cigarette smoke. I noticed that the fingers of his left hand were stained yellow with nicotine.

"He's gone," I said. "He ran out the back as soon as you pulled up."

Novak looked over at Uncle Gil, who promptly said, "He's telling the truth. The guy you're looking for is already gone." He hooked a thumb down the hall over his shoulder and added, "That way."

Novak contemplated this information for a moment, then motioned all three of us toward the back.

"We search," he said.

Novak marched down the hall while his men prodded us along behind him. He threw open each door that he passed, a process made simple by Virgil's no-lock policy on the bedrooms of St. George's. At each intrusion he was met with indignant shouts of "Hey!" and "Get Out!" and a couple of "What the fucks?" In his wake Virgil calmed each resident with a finger to his lips and closed their doors quietly.

The hall ended with three doors, one on the end and two facing each other. The door on the right opened onto the chapel, the one on the left was the door to Ace's room. The middle door led outside. It was equipped with a commercial style latch, the kind you could push open from the inside, but required a key to be opened from outside.

Novak kicked the middle door open and stepped outside to look around, holding the door open with his hip. I couldn't see much from my position behind him, but I knew the back opened onto a tiny yard with an old wooden picnic table and a ratty umbrella. Virgil allowed his residents to smoke out there, but he kept it Spartan to discourage the habit. To get back in, they had to sign for the smoker's key from a volunteer at the front desk. It was wired to a ten-inch length of spruce 2 X 4, with "Smoking Causes Cancer" written on it in red magic marker. Virgil told me it didn't stop anyone from smoking, but at least nobody ever lost the key.

Novak shook his head and made an impatient sound deep in his throat. He stepped back inside and reached to push open the chapel door. Virgil quickly stepped forward to block him.

"That's our chapel," Virgil said. "Please do not defile it with weapons."

Novak glared at Virgil. I readied myself for a desperate lunge to come between them, but as I shifted my weight forward, Novak surprised me. He slipped the strap on the HK off his shoulder and handed it to one of his men. When the man had the extra weapon slung around his neck, Novak extended a hand toward the chapel door. I remembered that Novak had grown up in an orphanage and wondered if it had included a chapel too.

"After you," he said to Virgil.

Virgil led him into the chapel. I watched from the door, the fat muzzle of one of the silenced HK's jammed against my spine. Virgil walked ceremoniously down the center aisle, as though he was leading a procession into a grand cathedral on Easter morning. He genuflected in front of the altar, then spread his arms to invite Novak to conduct his search. It didn't take long. He looked down each row of pews – there were only three on either side of the aisle – and glanced into the narrow space behind the altar. He turned on his heel and marched back up the aisle. He shoved past me and retrieved his weapon.

There was only one door left – Ace's. As if to make up for his respectfulness in the chapel, Novak lifted his knee high in the air and slammed his boot into the door. The jamb shattered and the door banged open.

Alice sat up suddenly in the narrow bed against the wall. She had the covers drawn to her neck with her left hand, her fingers bunched tightly around the fabric. Her hair was tousled like she'd been in bed all morning. Dark smudges under her eyes gave her that exhausted, sickly look of an addict in withdrawal. She looked small and frightened.

"Who are you?" she asked in a high, anxious voice. "What do you want?"

Novak looked around hastily, then backed out. He fixed each of us with a penetrating glare.

"I'll be back," he said, sounding absurdly like Schwarzenegger in *The Terminator*. He stormed toward the front door, trailed by his men. Virgil and Uncle Gil followed them, cautioning the residents who poked their heads into the hall to stay in their rooms.

I stepped back into Ace's room and closed the door. When I turned to face Alice, she dropped the covers. She was fully dressed and held her Sig Sauer in her right hand.

"Close," she grinned. "Can you imagine the paperwork if I shot that asshole in here?"

"Quick thinking," I said, plucking a Kleenex out of the box

on the tiny end table. "But now wipe that mascara off your face and get out of that bed. Ace and Winter Rose have got to be pretty uncomfortable."

She laughed.

"You know where they are?" she said.

She swung her feet to the floor and holstered her pistol, then she quickly wiped away the black rings under her eyes.

"Virgil's idea, of course," I said. "Where do you think he got that altar? It used to be in the church I converted to my house. When we were kids, Virgil and I hid under it whenever Mom dragged us to her prayer group." I smiled. "There's a deceptively large space behind that granite front panel."

We charged out of the room and nearly collided with Virgil and Uncle Gil. We all skidded to a stop. Virgil shot me a mixed look that was equal parts, "see what you got me into" and "oh God, we are so lucky no one was killed." I knew the look well – I've lost count of how many times I'd seen it on his face since we were about three years old.

We opened the chapel door and ran down the aisle. I didn't stop to genuflect so I made it behind the altar before Virgil. I lifted away the panel concealing the space underneath.

Ace and Winter Rose blinked up at us. They were sitting with their knees up, jammed together like a couple of spoons in a narrow drawer.

"Up, you two," I said. "Time to go."

"Where are we going, RK?" Ace asked as he clambered out. I smiled.

"Letting those guys take another crack at you doesn't seem like such a good idea. How would you feel about a Blue Ridge run?" I said.

CHAPTER 24

AS WINTER ROSE extricated herself from beneath the altar, I asked Uncle Gil to go out front and keep an eye on the road. The last thing we needed was Novak and his gang returning with their guns and finding we had Ace here all along. He nodded and hurried off. Virgil gave me a dark look and said he'd better go smooth the ruffled feathers.

"Most of them don't do so well with unexpected changes in the menu. I can only guess how they'll handle sudden invasions of armed gangs."

A simple, "Sorry!" didn't seem adequate, but I said it anyway. Virgil just rolled his eyes and followed Uncle Gil. When the chapel door closed behind him, I sat everyone down in the pews.

"Well," I said when they were all settled in, "here's the situation."

I pointed at Ace.

"Against his will, Ace has become involved in a highly organized scheme that has defrauded the government of millions. Recently he discovered that the scheme went far beyond fraud. In fact, this gang has apparently murdered at least two Army vets, probably more. The initial proof of this is a list which includes the names of two murdered men that Ace recognized. The man you just met is Emil Novak, the gang's chief enforcer. He is closing the operation down. He's already killed one of his own men and now he wants that list and Ace."

"So, where's this list?" Winter Rose said.

I glanced at Ace, who hung his head.

"Ace… well, Ace has been having some problems with alcohol recently. He hid the list while he was running from Novak's men in a bit of a fog."

"Hid the list?" Winter Rose repeated. "Where?"

"On an RV headed for the Washington, D.C. area. The RV is towing a trailer with a couple of motorcycles. I think they went up to ride in Rolling Thunder."

"Oh no, Roman!" Alice said, her head suddenly snapping up. "I've come this far because you twisted my arm, but really… thousands of bikers riding in Washington, DC? Ace needs to turn himself in. Here and now."

I went down on one knee to put my face level with Alice's.

"You know the government will fry Ace. His name is all over this. If they have him in custody, they'll take the path of least resistance. There's only one way to rescue Ace: we need to flush out Novak's boss. To do *that*, we need to keep Ace alive and recover that list. Wherever it might be."

Alice put her face in her hands.

"Oh, God," she said.

"Remember what I said about this case being an opportunity for you?" I said. "I know you want to get back to DC. To the presidential protection detail. That's the Secret Service A-team, right? The Varsity?"

I knew that more than anything she wanted her career back on track. She had invested much of her adult life into the Secret

Service and, like too many talented females in male dominated careers, she'd run afoul of an unfair gender trap.

"If you break a major identity theft case, especially one involving the VA and murders of veterans, won't that get you off the Secret Service's blacklist?"

She met my eye for a split second and I knew she was hooked. I stood up again and looked over at Winter Rose.

"And you, Winter Rose... well, let's just say you need to put your life back on track too. The person who can help you with that is your medicine woman. Margaret Keystone, right? And she is on the Cherokee reservation, conveniently on the way to DC."

I took a big breath, put my hands out to include all three of them.

"We need to lose Novak and his boys while we get these things done. Well, is there a better way to drop off the grid than hitting the back roads on a motorcycle? Besides, when your enemy gets the better of you – as Novak has done twice now – it's time to do the unexpected. I say we hit the road. We run the Blue Ridge, then take the back way right into DC."

Alice sat back. Skepticism fought with enthusiasm on her face.

"Count me in," she said finally, "on one condition."

"And that is?" I said, folding my arms across my chest.

"I get to pull the plug whenever I see fit. If it looks like we can't recover the list – or we can't find the guy who's running the operation – then Ace surrenders himself into my custody."

We all looked at Ace.

"Your call," I said.

Ace looked hollow-eyed at each one of us. Then he said to

Alice in a shaky voice, "I agree. I… I appreciate the risk you're taking and I can't thank you enough."

I wondered if he had the mental and physical stamina for the trip at this point, but I hoped that it might actually be the best thing for him. A long ride had worked wonders for me in the past. Motorcycle therapy on the Road King health plan.

I turned to Alice. She still looked doubtful.

"Look," she said to Ace, "my risk is nothing compared to yours. This list? It's important because it's physical evidence – maybe a good lab can identify the person who wrote those names. But you? You're the shovel the government will use to bury the whole lot of them. Your testimony is worth way more than that list."

She paused to make sure she had everyone's attention, then focused back on Ace.

"At some point, Novak and his boss are going to re-arrange their priorities. They're going to take their chances on the list getting out and concentrate on eliminating you. Are *you* sure you want to be riding around looking for that list when you could be safe in protective custody?"

Ace took surprisingly little time responding. In a stronger voice he said, "Unless the authorities capture everyone in the gang – including Novak's boss – and recover that list, I'm the only person they've got to hang this on. What starts as protective custody would turn into a life sentence. This is exactly why I came to Roman in the first place, drunk or not."

It was the longest speech I'd heard from Ace since he appeared at the G-String. I took it as a sign he was improving. Alice took it as a sign that he knew what he was in for. After a brief hesitation, she nodded and gave me a discreet thumbs up motion.

I raised my eyebrows in question to Winter Rose. She turned her head to glance silently at Ace, then looked back to me.

"I'm in," she said, "but only if you don't leave me in Cherokee. All the way or nothing."

I smiled. I'd known her just over twenty-four hours, but I'd expected that's what she would say.

"How much time do you need once we get to Cherokee?" I asked.

"One night."

"Just one night" I said. "You sure?"

She nodded positively.

"I can always go back later."

"OK," I said. "We can break the trip into two days and spend the night in Cherokee."

"When do we leave?" Alice asked. "First light probably, since you've got that Ranger thing in your blood."

I shook my head.

"Right now," I said. "We need to get a jump on Novak before he finds out Ace was here all the time. Plus, there's your friend Brian the Bulldog from the VA. He's zeroing in on Savannah. He'll be on Ace's trail as soon as he finds Vet Invest."

Alice pursed her lips and nodded her head. "If he gets his teeth into this mess, he'll never let go."

"All the more reason to beat feet," I said.

I clapped my hands and stood up.

"Let's get our shit and roll," I said, heading for the door. I let Winter Rose and Ace go first, then stopped Alice with a hand on her shoulder.

"I want Magnus along too," I said. "You OK with that?"

She looked up at me with a tight smile and said, "He's

always a good man to have along. Do you think he'll be ready to go quickly?"

"He has a security job for some actress in D.C. starting Monday. I'll bet he's already packed. I'll call him in a minute."

When we got to the living room, we found Virgil trapped in the middle of a clamoring pack of his guests. He had both hands on the shoulders of one agitated resident, but he took a second to shoot me another dark look. I waved anyway. Uncle Gil was outside the front door, facing the street. He gave a little startled jump when I opened the door behind him. To cover his reaction, he pointed south.

"They went that way," he said, "tearing away in a big pickup truck. Sorry, I couldn't get a plate number."

"Thanks for trying, Uncle Gil," I said. "But it doesn't really matter. We're going to get out of here right now anyway."

"No police?"

"Think it would do any good?"

He thought it through for a moment. Then he shook his head.

"No, at least not as quick as you need."

"That's what I think, too. I want to get Ace out of here before those guys find us again. And I want another shot at them." So far, it was Novak two, me nothing. I wanted an opportunity to improve that record.

Uncle Gil reached an arm out and hugged me quickly.

"That's my boy!" he said, holding me at arm's length. "Self reliance is what made this country great. Go get 'em." He narrowed his eyes before he let me go. "You think Ace is up to it? He still looks like one hurting pup to me."

I looked sideways for a second while I thought about it. It's true, he did look like shit. And who wouldn't under the circumstances? I shook my head, though.

"Ace was a damn fine Ranger, Uncle Gil. And Rangers are expected to function when they're hurting. Part of the training. He'll reach deep and come through."

Uncle Gil searched my face for the truth. A tiny smile crinkled his lips and he nodded once.

"And once a Ranger, always a Ranger, right?"

I could only smile and nod, because he was right.

He slipped his pocket watch out of his vest, popped the cover and checked the time.

"Uh-oh, I've got to run. Plane to catch." He put the watch away and said, "I'll be in DC, but if I can help in anyway, call."

I hugged him back.

"Will do, Uncle Gil. Have a safe flight."

"Statistically," he said, giving me his best concerned surrogate parent look, "I believe my mode of travel is well ahead of yours in that department."

After Uncle Gil left, Winter Rose quickly stepped over and motioned me aside. When we were away from the others, she said, "Um, Roman, I don't want to sound ungrateful, but I don't do well on the back seat."

I smiled and shook my head.

"I assumed you'd want a bike of your own to ride. I'm sure there's something in my garage you'd like."

She chewed her lip in doubt, then decided she had to say more.

"Something, uh… non-Harley?"

I laughed quietly.

"Don't worry," I said. "I'm sure I've got exactly what you want."

She still looked worried, but accepted my assurances.

"But listen, you've got one more trip on the pillion. Ask Special Agent Cushner to take you by your apartment so you can get what you need for this trip. You two can go by her place, too. Then meet Magnus, Ace and me at my house. We'll leave from there as soon as everyone's ready."

She nodded and headed for Alice to relay the plan. I called Magnus and caught him up on events. While I was talking, Winter Rose and Alice rode off together. When I told Magnus what I had planned and invited him along, his response was simple.

"You bet!"

CHAPTER 25

FTER I ARRIVED home with Ace, all I had to do was pick up the tour bag I keep in the front closet and I was ready to go. What's the point of having a motorcycle if you can't just jump on it and leave? I've learned what I need on a trip by trial and error over the years. Now I keep things set up so I can take an extended ride at a moment's notice. In the left saddlebag I keep a rolled up pair of chaps, a rain suit in a pouch, a heated jacket liner in a stuff sack and a pair of cold weather gloves. The right saddlebag is reserved for my jackets, a thick Fox Creek leather jacket for cool weather, and a mesh jacket for hot weather. Everything else I need is in the tour bag, which I strap to the luggage rack.

Virgil had cleaned the clothes Ace was wearing when we brought him to St. George's and we had rescued his old leather jacket and helmet from the trunk of his car, so he had the basics. At my place we grabbed a couple of extra T-shirts, a sweatshirt that was tight on me but looked like it would probably hang loose on Ace and stuffed it all into a small duffle along with some toiletries I keep for guests. Magnus rode up about the same time we finished packing Ace's makeshift travel bag and, after a brief discussion, we decided to bungee Ace's bag to the top of Magnus's tour pack.

It was 1:15 by the time Alice and Winter Rose wheeled into my driveway. Winter Rose had a small set of throw-over saddlebags across her thighs and a small backpack on her shoulders. When Alice cut her engine, Winter Rose climbed off and looked around.

"You said you've got a bike I could ride, RK?"

I motioned her to follow me, and headed over to the side door of the garage.

Before I opened the door, I said, "You know you don't have to make this trip, right? You could relax in Savannah a few more days, then ride up to see your medicine woman. Stay here at my place if you feel safer. Let Doc Lukens look in on you."

"No," she said. "I want to go."

She stepped close so the others wouldn't hear.

"Look," she said, "I don't understand how all this ties together – my rape, your rescue, Ace's dilemma – but two things are clear to me. One, I need to see Margaret Keystone as soon as possible. Two, I want to help you help Ace."

She raised her hands, palms toward me, to stave off any rebuttal I might have made.

"I don't understand it. I can't explain it. Maybe it has something to do with the dream catcher... maybe if I help him get his life back, I'll get my own back too. I just know I want in on whatever you've got planned."

"Well, you've got the wrong brother if you expect me to explain the way life works. Virgil's the one with the answers to stuff like that. I go for a ride when I'm confused. You know, the motorcycle Zen thing. Give myself up to the bike and let the road work it out. I'm hoping it'll work for Ace. Maybe it'll work for you, too."

"RK, you'll never know how much I owe you – " she stopped and pointed at the garage door. "But I hope you have something that handles like my Ninja in there. I don't think I'll find much Zen lounging on half a ton of chrome with my heels in the wind."

I had to laugh.

"I get that, Winter Rose," I said. "Some friends of mine from the Ranger School up in Dahlonega drove down to Toccoa and found your bike."

Her eyes lit up – that golden fleck glow thing again, but happy this time.

"Really? That's wonderful!" The light in her eyes dimmed slightly. "Is it… was it wrecked?"

I shook my head and smiled.

"No. They said it's OK. They found it near the little roadside picnic area you mentioned. Your bike had been pushed over an embankment and was hidden among the bushes at the bottom. They wrestled it up to the road, knocked most of the dirt off and it started right up. Let's take a look – it's inside."

"Here?" she said, looking anxiously toward the door. "How…?"

I reached for the door, laughing.

"Typical Rangers. Three of them just picked it up, stuffed it in the back of their pickup and roped it down. They dropped it off a couple of hours ago and headed back to Dahlonega. All they asked for in return was an equal weight in beer. They took every bottle I had. Ate everything in my refrigerator before they left, too. There's nothing left in that kitchen but wrappers."

She cupped a hand to my cheek. For the first time since I'd

met her, she smiled like she meant it. Doc Lukens had worked wonders. The only external signs of her trauma were a bit of residual swelling on her lip and some yellowing along her jaw. She had a nice smile.

"Thanks for getting my bike back, RK," she said. "And for… for everything else."

What do you say to that? No problem? Any time? Those idiots in the van got exactly what they deserved. I only wished I'd gotten to them before they got to Winter Rose and their other victims. My role in their demise barely rippled the water on my inner pond. I wondered about the strange coincidence of wrestling another man in a life or death struggle for a gun, but like I'd told Winter Rose earlier, sometimes surviving is all that matters.

"I'm glad you didn't join your ancestors, Winter Rose," I said, pushing the door open.

The reference to Cherokee lore got me a brief startled look, then she caught sight of her bike and rushed over to it with a happy cry. While she checked it over and threw her saddlebags across the tiny rear seat, I raised the big overhead door. When the others heard it grind upward, they came over to join us.

The garage sits where the church parking lot used to be, so there was plenty of space for a building with three large bays and a workshop. I keep my car in the left bay, a Dodge Magnum in titanium silver with the big hemi engine and a set of Foose Nitrous wheels. Virgil says it looks like a hearse for rock stars, which makes me smile even more when I drive it.

My motorcycles are spread out across the other two bays. In addition to the Road King, the Harley-Davidson part of my small collection includes an original condition red and black 1957 Sportster XL that Special Agent Cushner covets. I've told her she can ride it any time she likes, but so far she hasn't taken me up on it. Afraid she might ding it up, but it wouldn't bother me. If you don't ride it, it might as well be gathering dust in a museum.

Three other bikes take up the rest of the space, one of the fuel injected Suzuki Bandits, a 1975 Triumph Trident and, my latest acquisition, a silver Kawasaki Concours 14.

Winter Rose's sportbike was on the end of the lineup. We wheeled it out into the sun to get a better look at it. Now I could see what Ralph and the guys from Dahlonega were talking about. Instead of the standard, hard-to-miss Kawasaki green, her bike had been painted flat gray. Devoid of graphics and chrome, it had the sleek, purposeful look of a military fighter jet.

"Six hundred cc?" I asked.

She shook her head and smiled.

"One thousand – it's a ZX-10R."

My turn to smile. The full liter Ninja is a rocket. About as subtle as a freshly sharpened chainsaw, it had the power to scare the pants of any unwary rider – male or female – who twisted the throttle with too much enthusiasm. No wonder Winter Rose had no problem riding my Road King.

"So, what's this, then?" Magnus said, running a finger along the cowling. "Rustoleum, eh?"

"That's exactly what it is, smart ass. It's already saved me from half a dozen speeding tickets. Look at my bike compared to yours. Which one do you think would catch a cop's eye going by at ninety? My gray shadow or your bright blue beacon?"

Magnus had the grace to give her a chagrined smile.

"Ghost gray it is then. But a spray can?" he said. "I know a painter who can help you go unnoticed with class."

"Maybe," she said, pulling on her helmet.

She flipped her visor down and disappeared behind its silver mirror tint. Suddenly I could see what she was going for with the whole package. The flat gray bike, gray riding clothes and flat black helmet with an opaque visor cloaked her in total anonymity. A blank slate. No need to be Cherokee or female or military. Just a rider. I understood it perfectly – that's a big part of why anyone likes to ride: you can leave the world behind on a motorcycle.

She threw a leg over the bike and hit the starter. The Kawasaki lit up with a deep growl. She blipped the throttle twice, then let it idle.

Even her voice was disguised by the helmet when she asked, "Are we gonna talk or ride?"

Magnus threw his head back and laughed. He whipped a big paw out and gave her a quick hug that nearly lifted her off the Ninja. He let her go and said, "You got that right, Winter Rose. Time to hit the road!"

CHAPTER 26

WE HEADED NORTH. Without discussing riding order, we slipped into the most logical formation. Winter Rose took point, darting out to scout the road ahead then falling back until she made contact with us again. Her sense of direction was almost as good as mine – probably part of what made her a good helicopter pilot. She rode like she had a GPS in her head and never made a wrong turn. Next came Ace and I, on the Road King. I kept a steady pace, just above the speed limit. Alice pinned herself to my rear wheel, staying a couple of seconds back and always visible in my mirrors. Magnus brought up the rear. Twice I saw him duck down side streets and circle back to make sure Novak and his boys were not tailing us.

We rode the reverse route that Winter Rose and I had taken yesterday. Once past Augusta, we skipped into South Carolina and followed the river up Route 81. Consciously or not, Winter Rose was riding close to me when we passed the spot where I'd ditched the van with the bodies of the rapists. Two sheriffs' cars blocked the entrance to the side road, strobes flashing blue and red in warning. One lane was closed and we all waited while an impatient deputy waved the southbound traffic by.

When a gap appeared in the traffic he held up a hand to halt the next car and motioned us forward. Winter Rose let her clutch out too quickly and stalled.

The deputy shouted, "Come on, come on!"

Winter Rose thumbed the starter, revved it once and tried again. This time she gave it too much gas and flashed by with the front wheel slightly off the ground. I eased past the startled deputy and gave him a shrug. Alice and Magnus followed. I could see in my mirror that the deputy was already busy waving more cars along.

The rest of the ride up to Cherokee was the kind motorcyclists pray for the night before a long trip, when all the planning is finished and the bike sits ready out in the driveway. With clear skies and clear roads, we rolled north past Anderson on the back roads, skirting west of Greenville and crossing into North Carolina on Route 178. We climbed County Road 215 until it put us on the Blue Ridge Parkway at that confusing little section where the northbound road is actually heading south and vice versa.

The temperature dropped as we climbed, dipping into the low fifties. We pulled off at the first lookout and dug out our warmest riding gear. All of us had ridden in the cold many times, so everyone was prepared. All the bikes were equipped with heated grips, except for Winter Rose's Ninja. She zipped quilted liners into the high tech two piece riding outfit she wore and protected her hands with gauntlet-style gloves. The rest of us added chaps to our leather jackets. Alice and I both carried heated jacket liners in our saddlebags.

"Ahh. That's cheating, isn't it?" Magnus said, as I plugged

mine into the little pigtail from the battery that was tie-wrapped to the frame behind my leg.

I grinned. "You'll be crying for one, ten miles from here."

"Hah!" he said. "Rangers weak. SEALS tough."

The parkway worked its magic, in spite of the dire circumstances of our ride north. For the next half hour we gave ourselves over to the soothing ballet of riding a motorcycle on an empty twisting road. Everything faded away except the next curve. The line between machine and rider blurred until the mechanics of riding seemed as natural as breathing. We leaned through the parkway's curves in an easy rhythm while the sun settled below the trees. Sky blue shifted to dark blue and orange, then purple and pink and finally inky black as our headlights guided us onto the Cherokee reservation. We left Magnus, Ace and Alice in the parking lot of the Inn of the Seven Clans where we had rooms for the night, then I followed Winter Rose to the medicine woman's place.

We doubled back on Route 441 for a few miles before turning onto a narrow road that climbed quickly up one of the foothills northwest of the casino. I don't know what I'd been expecting – a sweat lodge maybe or something with at least a hint of traditional Cherokee – but we pulled into the driveway of a little house that would have looked right at home in any small town in the country.

Pale yellow clapboard exterior, white window boxes with yellow daffodils and a pair of old-fashioned wooden gliders on a neat porch, lit by a trio of lamps spreading a welcoming light. A pair of cats, one an orange tabby and one as white as virgin snow, except for its black nose and green eyes, lounged tranquilly together on one of the gliders. As we mounted the steps, the cats jumped up and ducked through a pet door hinged to the bottom of the front door.

Alerted by the cats if not the sound of the motorcycles, the medicine woman opened the door before we had a chance to knock. Unlike her house, she fit my image of a Cherokee. According to Winter Rose she was pushing seventy, but her face defied age. She had smooth dusky skin, straight dark hair streaked with gray, and widely spaced eyes that radiated a quiet and comfortable confidence. Her only jewelry was a small ivory crescent moon suspended close to the base of her throat by a very thin gold chain. She was slim, about five-five or six. She wore a long skirt, a light blue blouse with long, loose sleeves and a padded vest with wooden buttons. Her clothes looked hand sewn, made from cotton or possibly a light, tightly woven wool. She glanced briefly at me, then stepped up to Winter Rose and took both of her hands in her own. She examined her silently for a moment, taking in the still healing split lip and the bruised jaw.

"Tsi lu gi, Winter Rose," she said. "I have missed you."

Still holding Winter Rose's hands, she looked over at me and said, "Welcome to you, too, Roman Keane."

She smiled at my surprise.

"You brought our Winter Rose home. And you saved her life. Of course I know you, Roman."

"How did you know about…?"

She smiled serenely and said, "Your faces tell me the story as clearly as the writing in a book, Roman. Do not worry, your secrets are safe with me."

I decided not to fight it. Something about the woman was irresistible anyway. Like sunset or rain. Inevitable, elemental; so you'd best go along.

"Thank you, ah… Medicine Woman."

She smiled at my awkwardness and put out a slender hand.

"I am Margaret Keystone," she said. "It's true, I am a medicine woman. *Didanawisgi* in our language. But you may call me Maggie."

She put an arm around Winter Rose's shoulders and pulled her toward the inside of the cottage.

"Come," she said, smiling over her shoulder to include me. "Both of you. We have much to talk about, but first… the Ancestors are anxious to greet Winter Rose."

She guided us down a short hallway, past a door leading to a tiny kitchen. We crossed into the living area, a surprisingly large room with bookcases built into three walls. A U-shaped couch filled the center of the room, looking toward the floor-to-ceiling windows that made up the fourth wall. One of the windows turned out to be a sliding door, which Maggie opened. We stepped out onto a wooden deck.

It was like walking off the planet and into space.

The night sky shimmered with stars. It blazed in an endless black panorama sparkling with a billion diamonds. I have seen incredible night skies in places around the world from Australia to Afghanistan, but never anything like this. All three of us stood silently, staring upward. Usually, the night sky looks two dimensional: like all the stars are tacked out there on a black curtain. But the more my eyes adjusted to the dark, the more stars I saw. Suddenly I could see forever.

"Whoa," Winter Rose said, grabbing the rail with both hands. I stepped forward and leaned against the rail, too. The stars looked so close, it seemed like you might be sucked out into the universe.

"Now Roman," Maggie said, "if you will please step back. Let Winter Rose stand alone before the Ancestors."

I moved back as requested and found seat on a plain wooden bench on the side of the deck. Winter Rose stood by herself, a dark silhouette against the brilliant stars.

"You remember the seven sacred directions, child?"

Against the night sky I could make out Winter Rose's head nodding.

"Yes," she said.

"Turn then and reintroduce yourself to the Ancestors. First face north," Maggie instructed.

I could see Winter Rose searching the sky. She was looking for the big dipper, I thought, but there were so many stars visible, it was difficult to spot at first. She must have picked it out about the same time I did because she followed the pointer stars Merak and Dubhe with her hand and found Polaris, the north star, hidden in plain sight among the countless other stars.

"Very good," Maggie said. "You tracked the Great Bear through the sky like the Cherokee hunters before you. That brought you to north, the way of peace and tranquility. That is where you must start your journey to find yourself again. Let go of your anger. Let go of your confusion. Let peace reign in your heart."

She stood motionless for a long minute. I don't know about Winter Rose, but I felt soothed by Maggie's words. The sheer immensity of the night sky that hovered over her mountains brought me an unexpected peace too. Tomorrow's possibilities seemed as limitless as the stars.

"Now face south my dear," Maggie said. "South is joy and happiness, laughter and fun. You cannot imagine it tonight, but you shall laugh again soon."

I'll look forward to that, I thought, even though it was difficult to imagine after seeing the look on Winter Rose's face when she first stepped out of that white van. Like black is the total absence of light, the look on her face at that moment had been the total absence of laughter.

"Now east, where the sun rises. A new day. A fresh start. Your rebirth."

I already liked this Cherokee notion of seven sacred directions. I wondered what Virgil would think if he was here tonight. He was more into sit-in-the-church religion than I was, but surely this experience would affect him too.

"West," Maggie said as Winter Rose dutifully rotated in that direction, "is where the spirits live, the sunset of life. In the west, your mother and father will welcome you back to their arms one day. They celebrate every day of your life, my child, and wait joyfully for you."

Winter Rose lifted her hands, as though she was a child about to be picked up by her father. She sobbed once and dropped to her knees. I leaned forward, ready to go to her, but Maggie stopped me with a hand on my shoulder.

"Let her be," she said quietly. "She mourns the loss of her parents, but she has always held her grief inside. She clutches it with such an iron fist that she has strangled her own heart. She must let go."

Winter Rose cried out, a gut-wrenching forlorn cry of infinite sadness that echoed into the vast blackness. She slowly keeled over, ending up on her hands and knees, head hanging down, shoulders heaving as her tears dripped on the wooden deck. Maggie waited in silence. I tried not to squirm, but Winter Rose's raw catharsis was like pulling emotional teeth with a rusty pair of vise grips. I stifled the urge to get up and go to her.

When Winter Rose's sobs tapered off, Maggie gently said, "Down is the direction of Mother Earth, who provides for us."

Winter Rose, her head already hanging down, simply nodded. She seemed exhausted. Maggie rose, crossed the deck to her and helped her stand.

"Put your hands on my shoulders, Winter Rose," she said. "We are nearly finished."

They stood face to face in the starlight, looking like mirror images of each other at different ages. It struck me suddenly that Winter Rose was going to be one of those rare people blessed with ageless beauty. I hoped she would find the serenity she'd need to enjoy it.

"Look up now, to the stars. The Great Spirit watches from the sky, waiting to see what you will do with the gift of life."

Maggie dropped her arms from Winter Rose's shoulders and stepped back.

"Now you must look inward, my child. At yourself. Only one person chooses what your life will be. You. What do you choose?"

Winter Rose tottered on her feet, like an exhausted soldier at the end of an all-night march. Maggie guided her over to the bench.

"Here, child," she said, peeling Winter Rose's motorcycle jacket off her shoulders. "Let's make you more comfortable."

Winter Rose shrugged the jacket off without protest and silently wrapped herself tightly in the blanket Maggie draped in its place. Maggie motioned me toward the sliding door.

When we were inside, she said, "Sheriff Silverwood would like to meet you, Roman Keane. Perhaps you would honor him with a visit while you are waiting for us?"

I looked briefly through the window at Winter Rose, who seemed content to stay alone with the medicine woman.

"Of course," I said.

Maggie gave me directions to the sheriff's office, then returned to the deck. She crossed over to Winter Rose and they sat arm-in-arm. As I left, both cats materialized from the darkness and took up positions on either side of the two women.

CHAPTER 27

THERE WAS MORE activity at the sheriff's office than I expected for this time of night, then I remembered it was Friday. It probably doesn't matter where you are in the world; Friday nights are a busy time for the police. Two black four-wheel drive Ford Explorers with light bars and tribal police markings left the parking lot as I rode in. Another deputy came out just as I approached the door. He politely held it open for me, then watched me with open curiosity as I entered.

Inside the small foyer, another deputy sat behind a bullet-proof window like a teller at a bank. He rose as soon as he saw me, looked me over with the same curiosity the other deputy had shown, then said hello courteously and invited me to follow him down a short hall. He stood aside, motioned me through the last open door on the right. The sheriff, who was sitting behind a polished wooden desk, closed the lid of his laptop as he rose to greet me. He was dressed in a neat black uniform, with captain's bars on the epaulettes. The metal nametag over his pocket said Silverwood. Age was beginning to thicken his waist, but a broad chest and big shoulders helped him carry it well. He had a striking, aquiline nose – the kind a Hollywood casting director would associate more with an Italian aristocrat than an Indian sheriff – and high cheekbones above a big slab of a jaw. His dark hair had receded all the way across the top of his head and he wore it rather long on the sides. His skin was like saddle leather, pummeled to a soft brown sheen by sun, wind and rain. He reached across the desk, wrapped my hand up in a hard, brief grip and pointed to one of the two chairs arranged in front of the desk. The deputy paused at the door.

"Close it, Max," the sheriff said. "And leave us alone for a bit, would you?"

He sat, carefully removed his reading glasses and leaned back with a creak of protest from his chair. He caught me looking at the carving that sat on the corner of his desk, a beautifully rendered Indian head with long flowing locks.

"The Wind Clan," he said, "a.k.a. Hair Hanging Down Clan." He rubbed the top of his head and grinned, revealing big, ultra-white teeth. "My clan, although you'd be excused for not guessing it."

"Sheriff," I said, "I'm here because – "

He held up a hand and said, "This is a small reservation, Master Sergeant Keane, and Winter Rose is, well, for lack of a better word, one of our celebrities. Your arrival was reported to me more than an hour ago. Maybe you noticed the unusual attention you received from my deputies as you entered. Naturally, I checked out the man who brought the prodigal daughter home."

"It's just plain Roman Keane, now sheriff. I retired yesterday. My friends, especially the well-informed ones, call me RK."

Another brief flash of the bright white teeth.

"Dwayne," he said, pointing a thick finger at himself. "Tell me, how did you get Winter Rose to come back to Cherokee? Never thought I'd see her again."

"No big effort on my part," I said. "She said she needed to see someone here."

"Oh?"

I hesitated. I didn't know how the medicine woman knew so much about Winter Rose's situation, but when she sent me to the sheriff, I figured that he had somehow learned what had happened and told her. Apparently, that wasn't the case. It left me mystified again about the medicine woman. And in the same quandary I faced with Magnus regarding Winter Rose's situation. What should I tell the sheriff? The answer, of course, was nothing. If Winter Rose wanted him to know, she'd tell him herself. But I sensed that something more was going on in Cherokee. That this man wasn't simply curious, but also had Winter Rose's best interests at heart. I decided to approach the problem from the flank rather than head on.

"Let me ask you something, Dwayne. We rode by some kind of accident or crime scene on the way up here from Savannah. On State Road 81. Know anything about it?"

"A burned out van with the three bodies inside? Those fool boys the papers called the Roaster Rapists? What about it?"

I shrugged.

"Just wondered what you knew about it."

He leaned forward and focused a steady look on me. The kind of look cops use when their interest is suddenly piqued.

"I know they found the bodies of three white boys from Huntsville who raped four women."

"They have evidence of the four rapes?" I asked.

He nodded.

"The FBI is turning Huntsville upside down. They discovered one of the idiots kept trophies at home. Jewelry, panties, that kind of thing. He also had a laptop with photos and videos showing all three of those boys, clear as can be."

A dark frown crossed his face like a storm cloud rolling over the mountains.

"I heard the video shows them laughing about it, RK. Laughing and joking about it. About raping four girls and taking their lives."

"So, no doubt about their guilt?"

"They're fried. So to speak. Fitting end, if you ask me."

"And does the FBI know who lit the match?"

I kept my expression carefully neutral as I asked that. The sheriff slowly sat up straight. I saw him make the connection to Winter Rose and myself. He locked eyes with me for a long second, then his face assumed exactly the same neutral look as mine.

"No," he said finally breaking eye contact. "And if you ask me, I don't think they'll ever know. That van burned so hot it almost melted through to China. Whole thing was one black blob no higher than a rezdog's butt. Only reason they know who those boys were is because they found their driver's licenses on the ground."

He gave me a microsecond of the tiniest smile.

"Lot of folks want to give the vigilante who torched that van a medal," he said. "Including me."

I started breathing again.

"How do they think this vigilante found the rapists?"

He shook his head.

"They think he might be related to one of the victims. That he tracked them down and finally found his opportunity. They're looking at all the relatives, but not very hard. It's as good an ending to a sad affair as we're likely to get. Nobody seems in the mood to push it any further. That what you wanted to know?"

I nodded.

"So," he said, "you brought Winter Rose to see Maggie."

I appreciated the deliberate change of direction.

"The medicine woman? Dida… huh, didana…"

"Didanawisgi," he said, smiling at my attempt at the Cherokee word. "Oh, yes. Margaret Keystone is the oldest of the Paint Clan. Our, ah, ranking medicine woman. Winter Rose is with her now?"

I nodded.

"Good, good," he said. "Excellent hands, she's in excellent hands." He leaned forward and propped his elbows on the desk. "And you, RK? What do you want?"

"Some background, maybe? I'm trying to help Winter Rose, but I'm working in the dark."

He nodded and pressed his lips together into a thin line. "She's our enigma girl, all right. What did she tell you about herself?"

"Just that her parents died when she was very young and she was raised by relatives."

He came as close as someone his size can to giggling, then said, "Not exactly loquacious, huh?" Then he said it again, "Not exactly loquacious." He looked at me quite seriously and said, "Thank you. Always wanted to use that word in a conversation."

He tapped a manila folder that sat on his desktop between the computer and the phone. It had the worn, frayed look of an old file that was still accessed frequently.

"Got some photos in here you might want to see. But first I want you to read something."

Without fully opening the folder, he slipped a document out, taking it off the top of the pile. It was a newspaper clipping, carefully cut and folded.

"This was written by Bernadette Dickerson. Bernie's Paint Clan, like Maggie, but she's not a medicine woman. Tried it for a bit, though. She was *tsila* for five years, an apprentice medicine woman. Finally decided writing was her calling, not healing. Anyway, she wrote this for the *Smokey Mountain Journal*, one of our local papers. She wrote it like a story, like a... um, what the hell's the word?"

He drummed the desk impatiently with his fingers, then gave it a mighty whack.

"Narrative! A modern Cherokee legend is what she called it. Reads just like a story, but she got the facts from reading reports and interviewing witnesses."

"Like a historical novel?" I said.

"Exactly!"

He held it out to me, said, "Go ahead, read it. Believe me, it'll answer a lot of questions."

I took the clipping from his hand, slipped on my own reading glasses and settled back in my chair. The piece had no photos, only text. It was titled "The Legend of Winter Rose."

She was born seven minutes after midnight on the winter solstice of 1977, on the cold bench seat of a '65 Ford pick-up in the worst snowstorm to hit North Carolina in fifty years. Twenty minutes before the birth her mother, Miranda Ridge, had awakened her husband with an urgent shake.

"Joshua!" she said. Pain and fear sharpened her voice, cutting Joshua out of his exhausted sleep like a knife.

"What? What's the matter?" he asked.

He reached out in the dark for the light and turned it on. When he saw Miranda in the yellow glow of the lamp, his tiredness vanished like smoke in the wind. Miranda's dark hair was matted to her forehead with sweat. Her wide eyes radiated alarm as urgently as the screaming siren of a fire truck.

"Now?" he said, already slipping out of bed. "The baby's coming now?"

Miranda – who was making explosive "he-he-hew! he-he-hew!" sounds that threatened to rip her diaphragm apart when she breathed – nodded her head emphatically.

"Yes! yes!" she said, when she managed to save enough air for speech.

"It's three weeks early!" Joshua said.

"I… he-he- hew… know… he-he-hew… Joshua."

"Sorry, sorry," he said. "I'll call Dr. Carson, tell him we're on the way to the hospital."

As he picked up the telephone on the nightstand, they locked eyes for an instant. Both were thinking of Dr. Carson's concerns about Miranda's pregnancy. After the second of her two previous miscarriages, he had strongly advised them not to try again. After a period of disappointment, their love for each other had buoyed them to a reluctant acceptance that they would have to adopt if they were going to be parents. Meanwhile they had taken precautions in bed.

But life finds a way. While they were still exploring the adoption option, Miranda had discovered she was pregnant again. Carefully following Dr. Carson's guidance, they had made it through the critical first trimester. After six months, hope had banished fear. Joy had crept cautiously into their lives again. Now this.

Joshua held the phone to his ear, then pushed the receiver button again. He jiggled it up and down. Nothing. He slammed it back into the cradle.

"The phone lines are down," he said, hurrying around to help Miranda off the bed. "We'll just go."

"But Dr. Carson-

"They have radios at the hospital. They can call the Tribal Police, send them over to Dr. Carson's house. He lives about a mile from the hospital, remember? He'll be there by the time they get you into the delivery room. Come on, now, here we go."

After he helped Miranda dress, Joshua threw on jeans, an old gray sweatshirt and his new coat, a red nylon parka stuffed with real goose down that Miranda had given him to celebrate our Cherokee National Holiday the previous September. She had ordered it by catalog from Patagonia in California. He had protested that it was too expensive, but she had explained calmly that the money wasn't from their regular meager budget. For three years she had saved all the cash she had made from selling dream catchers in the co-op craft store on the reservation. Hers were exquisite creations, combining the traditional dream catcher with the legendary white and gold Cherokee Rose that had comforted her ancestors during the brutal forced march

*from North Carolina to Oklahoma in 1838 – our ancestor's
Trail of Tears. She had cleared only a dollar for each one, but
tourists bought hers because they were small enough to hang
from the rear view mirrors of their cars. The coat those dollars
bought kept Joshua warmer than Patagonia had ever promised.*

*Nearly a foot of snow had already piled up on their truck,
turning it into a white blob in the driveway. Joshua hurriedly
cleared off the windshield and helped Miranda inside. Shifting
the truck into gear, he pulled onto the road.*

*A layer of ice beneath the unplowed snow made the going
treacherous, even with four-wheel drive. Joshua backed off every
time the truck skidded, but his wife's desperate pain urged him
to push the limits of his driving.*

*Distracted by Miranda's screams as another wave of severe con-
tractions hit, he missed a turn. Joshua hit the brakes too hard
and the truck skated sideways. It launched itself off the road
and plunged down a steep embankment, caroming off boulders
and tree trunks like a pinball. Near the bottom of the drop-off,
it slammed into a ledge of granite. The back of the truck rose
high in the air and it nearly flipped over before gravity pulled
it down, wedging it tightly between a tall pine and a rocky
outcropping that ran perpendicular to the ledge.*

*Thirty-six hours later, after Miranda missed a scheduled
appointment and Dr. Carson raised the alarm, rookie Cherokee
Police Deputy Dwayne Silverwood was searching the road for
some sign of the Ridge's pick-up.*

*His sharp eyes spotted a small nick in the bark of a pine just off
the shoulder. About the same height as the bumper of a truck.*

It looked fresh, too. Deputy Silverwood leaned across the seat and peered down the slope. Nothing but trees and snow. Deep snow. Might as well take a quick look, he thought. He stepped out into the cold, turned up his collar and pulled on his gloves. He walked slowly up the road, his boots scrunching noisily on the cold dry snow. He stopped and listened. Nothing. He was about to turn and head back to the warmth of the car when he heard a muffled cry. He climbed the mound of snow piled up on the roadside by the plows and listened. Except for the brief squawking of a raven perched high on a naked branch over his head, he heard only the sound of his own breathing. He inhaled a deep lungful of air and held his breath. Nothing disturbed the silence for twenty or thirty seconds, then suddenly the cry came again. High and thin, but definitely human. After calling for help on his walkie-talkie, he worked his way carefully down the snow-clogged ravine toward the sound. Both the truck and its path down the slope had been disguised by wind drift and by the sheer mass of snow deposited by the storm, but finally he found it.

He clambered up the rock that was jammed against the driver's door and used his gloved hand to brush away the snow on the window, but discovered the glass was glazed with ice. He whacked on the ice with the side of his fist, but still couldn't see inside.

He called out, "Mr. Ridge, Mr. Ridge! It's the Cherokee Police, Mr. Ridge!"

No answer.

His police academy advisor, who was so fond of saying,

"Think on your feet, cadet," would have been proud of Deputy Silverwood when he pulled the heavy Maglite flashlight from his belt and swung it at the glass. He would have wished, though, that the excited deputy had used the butt end instead of the lens, because the light shattered with the window. When his eyes adjusted to the dim light inside the cab, Deputy Silverwood could scarcely believe what he saw.

Joshua Ridge was behind the wheel. From the knees down he was a frozen, bloody mess. Both legs were badly broken, jagged white bone still poking through his ruined trousers. From the waist up he was naked. His skin, normally the ruddy reddish clay color of his clan, was stark white. Horrified, Deputy Silverwood stripped off his glove and touched Ridge's shoulder. It was as cold and hard as ice.

He sighed, his condensed breath drifting into the cab like a cloud. As he straightened, he heard a small sound. Not really a cry this time, but a tiny plaintive noise, like a puppy locked out on a porch. The deputy shuffled through the snow to the other side of the truck. Braced against the tree trunk, he scraped away more of the snow, to avoid showering the inside of the cab with snowflakes. This time he took more careful aim and used the back end of the Maglite. The safety glass fragmented as designed and Silverwood jumped back in shock.

Miranda Ridge was looking directly at him, a faint smile on her face, as though she knew he was coming and was glad to see him. Like her husband, the frigid temperature had frosted her to an eerie alabaster. Also like her husband, she was sitting in a pool of frozen blood, both legs broken in the crash. Her arms were forever circled around a large red bundle in her lap.

Looking closer, the deputy saw that the bundle was actually a down parka, which he figured belonged to Joshua Ridge, since Miranda was wearing a jacket of her own. The coat was folded around a gray sweatshirt, presumably also Joshua's.

Deputy Silverwood reached out, stopped himself and actually said, "Excuse me, ma'am." Then he carefully pulled aside the layered cloth. When he finally got it open, he was stunned to see an infant. The baby looked at him with large liquid eyes, irises flecked with gold. For years afterward, whenever he told the story, which was far more often than anyone who knew him would have preferred, he swore that little baby smiled at him just like her mother.

When two more deputies arrived, they managed to retrieve the baby, parka and all, by easing her out of her mother's arms and through the window opening.

Something small and light fell to the snow as the deputies turned from the truck to head up the hill. Deputy Silverwood reached down and retrieved it, a miniature dream catcher. Straightening up, he let it dangle from his finger for a moment, admiring the smooth white fur stitched to the frame and the fine craftsmanship.

"Here little one," he said, tucking it in a side pocket of the parka, "I've got a feeling your dreams are going to need all the magic they can get."

The senior deputies headed up the hill to their cruiser, leaving Deputy Silverwood behind to "stand guard." He spotted a yellow paper on the seat between the bodies of Joshua and Miranda. Curious, he pulled it out. The paper was a receipt from Monroe Muffler in Ashville, showing that the muffler had been replaced and new shoes installed on the brakes back in July of 1976. He turned it over, read the handwriting on the back. He quickly scanned it again to be sure he wasn't mistaken, then he called for the deputies to stop.

"Here," he said, holding up the receipt, "you'll want to take this along."

"What is it?" the older of the two deputies said, not wanting to risk climbing back down the slippery slope.

"It's a note from Mrs. Ridge," Deputy Silverwood said.

"Well, read it."

"OK, but I'm telling you, you'll want to take it with the baby."

Shooting the rookie a look of exasperation, the deputy said, "Let me be the judge of that, newbie, just read it."

"OK, OK. It says, 'Joshua died tonight. I cried until I heard his voice in the dark. He said, "Do not be sad, my love. Remember the Cherokee Rose. Even in the blackest hours, the Great Spirit sends a tiny ray of beauty to light the way. Take joy in the little one, she is our Winter Rose."'"

I held the clipping out to the sheriff, who accepted it with both hands, the way a curator in a museum would handle rare artifacts. He placed it on his desk.

"Tough thing for a rooky to experience," I said.

He looked over at me, sadness as heavy in his eyes as it must have been on that winter day.

"Yes, it was. I'll never forget one second of that day. And I can tell you that Bernie might have taken a little poetic license in her telling, but it happened pretty much as she wrote."

"You really break your flash on the window?"

He grinned, shook his head. Some of the darkness left his eyes. "Yeah. Dumb newbie."

He looked off into the distance over my head. I sat quiet for a moment, knowing he was back there on that frozen hillside again. He sniffed, focused on me again.

"Got a strong stomach? What am I saying? Course you do. But let me warn you, those photos are pretty grisly."

I held my hand out and he slipped the manila folder over to me. I flipped it open and leafed through the eight by tens stacked inside. He was right. What a way to die. Talk about sacrificing your life for another. Beneath the photos I found the original note written by Miranda on the back of the muffler receipt. I read it silently. In my peripheral vision I noticed the sheriff watching intently and I had the feeling that he was following along, reading from a memorized version of the note in his head.

I finishing reading, placed the note and photos back in the manila folder and handed it back.

"When I first met her," I said, "she told me her name was Winter Rose. Then she looked at me strangely and said she hadn't gone by that name in many years."

He sighed and said, "No, she hadn't. She was raised by Miranda's sister, Sarah, and Sarah's husband, Jacob. Jake already had three kids of his own when Sarah married him. They didn't have much money. Plus, Jake… well, Jake had a gambling problem. Wasn't the best situation."

"Abused?" I said, wondering how much Virgil and I had in common with her.

"No, no," he said, flashing his palms at me. "Not abused, at least not physically. Call it severely disillusioned. She hated her surrogate family and she hated the reservation. By the time she was thirteen, she had rejected everything Cherokee."

"The opposite of what would have happened if her parents were alive."

He stabbed his index finger at me again and exclaimed, "Exactly!"

"Speaking of her parents," I said. "That dream catcher her mother made for her? She got it back today."

"What?" the sheriff said. He cocked his head toward me. "No kidding?"

"No kidding," I said.

He rocked back in his chair, a bright look of pure wonder on his face.

"Winter Rose came in to the office one day," he said. "Long time ago. She was seven, I think. I was still a deputy. Happened to be on the desk."

He flashed that white grin.

"She wanted me to arrest her brother. Well, like I said, not her real brother – her cousin."

"She told me that he stole the dream catcher," I said.

"Yep. She walked here by herself to 'press charges.' "

He shook his head and laughed.

"Got to be close to four miles from her front door to here. She was dead serious. Kept her voice low and even, but drilled those dark eyes into me like lasers. I had to bite the inside of my cheek to keep from laughing while I took her statement. Typed it up and had her sign it. Her tongue stuck out the corner of her mouth while she concentrated on printing her name, Rose Ridge. She left off the 'Winter' part, but it was nice and neat, like they teach in the school. I found another deputy to relieve me on the desk and I drove her home in a cruiser. She made me light up the flashers. I showed her the button for the siren. She whacked it with the side of her fist and looked straight out the windshield, as serious as a state trooper on the way to a six-car pile-up. I bit the inside of my cheek so many times I damn near ate my own face from the inside out."

He chuckled over the memory, shaking his head.

"How did she come by that dream catcher again?" he asked.

"Turns out an old friend of mine had it since he was a kid. Winter Rose's cousin sold it to him on the street here in the reservation. He bought it for his sister, who died of leukemia."

I told him about finding the dream catcher in Ace's car which lead, in the way of policemen everywhere, to him extracting the whole story of Ace's sudden appearance at the G-String, the attempt to kill him later and our flight in search of the list and the man who calls himself the General.

"Incredible," he said. "You rescue Winter Rose and this fellow Ace Emory from dire trouble, both on the same day? And it turns out that he had Winter Rose's dream catcher all these years?"

He clapped his hands like a child watching a magic show.

"Don't you love it?" he said. "Like karma or something, huh?"

"It's a bit unusual, if it's actually the same dream catcher," I conceded.

He grinned and gave me a quick nod.

"If she says it's the same dream catcher, I don't doubt it, RK."

He snapped his fingers and said, "Hey, does Maggie know about this?"

I shrugged.

"Only if Winter Rose tells her," I said.

"She needs to know," he said. "Let's see if she answers the phone."

He picked up the phone on his desk, tapped a button for a line and quickly punched in a number. Apparently, Miss Keystone and Winter Rose were at some point where they could be interrupted because the sheriff said, "Hi Maggie, got a minute? OK, I'll make this real quick."

He gave her a condensed version of my condensed version of the Ace and Winter Rose saga. She asked a couple of questions, to which he said "yes" both times. Then he hung up and gave me a satisfied look.

"You think this wandering dream catcher connects Winter Rose and Ace in some way?" I said.

"Do you believe in destiny?" he asked. "That certain things are meant to happen?"

I shrugged.

"I believe we control our own lives – up to a point. You do everything you can to make things happen the way you want, but in the end… well, sometimes your best effort may not be enough."

"Other forces may be at work?" he suggested.

"Maybe," I said. "You decide what you want to do… where you want to go. You prepare yourself as well as you can. Then you hit the road. But don't be surprised when life throws a detour at you."

"Exactly, my friend! But consider this: maybe life is simply putting you back on course. Back where you were destined to go."

"So," I said, "you think the dream catcher was some kind of… of a karma catalyst to bring Ace and Winter Rose together?"

"Why not? That dream catcher journeyed from mother to daughter to a random stranger and back to the daughter. But think about it. Was Ace Emory really a random stranger?"

"The dream catcher was destiny at work?" I said.

Dwayne sighed. I'm sure the tone of my voice gave away my skepticism.

"OK," he said, "Maggie Keystone would have better words, but listen... no one lives completely alone. Our lives are interwoven with the lives of many others. I believe that dream catcher is like a thread, RK, a thread that ties Winter Rose to Ace."

"Winter Rose and Ace?" I said. "Together?"

I thought about it for a moment. She did watch over him at St. George's, but that was exactly what I would have expected from anyone with her training. I remembered the look on their faces when I opened the panel and helped them out of the hidey-hole under the altar. There was nothing remotely sexual about it. More like a couple of strangers who had survived the same train wreck. The incredible journey of Winter Rose's dream catcher seemed more like something for *Ripley's Believe It Or Not* than the hand of fate. I could guess where Virgil would stand on this: not the hand of fate, but the hand of God. I shook my head. Virgil and I were never going to agree on that one.

"When did Winter Rose finally leave the reservation?" I asked, to steer the conversation back to more practical ground.

"I don't have to think on that one much," he said. "She left the day she turned eighteen. Never heard another word from her. I kind of kept track, informal like. Knew she graduated from NC State, knew she earned a reserve commission in the Army. Not much after that."

I told him about seeing her in the flight suit and about her flying Apache gunships.

He raised both hands in the air, then put them on his head, like a kid hearing he won a trip to Disney World.

"Gunships!" he said. "Guess I shouldn't be surprised. She's

Wolf Clan, you know. The hunters. I'll bet she enjoyed the irony of flying an Army attack helicopter named after an Indian tribe."

He looked up toward the ceiling and grinned. Probably thinking about Winter Rose hovering in the air like a hawk about to strike. He chuckled, then seemed to remember I was there.

"Well!" he said, standing up. He came around the desk and opened the door for me.

"Tell Winter Rose I asked about her, would you RK? Maybe she could find the time to call me someday?"

"Of course."

He walked me down the hall and out past the duty desk to the parking lot. When he saw my bike resting on its side stand under the security lights, he gave a low whistle.

"That's yours? Nice, man, nice."

"Thanks, Sheriff," I said.

"Dwayne," he reminded me. He stepped closer and bent to examine my helmet, which I'd left hanging on the side mirror as usual.

"Very nice," he said. "May I?"

When I nodded he lifted it up and held it to the light. I have several helmets, but this was one of my favorites; an open face helmet, glossy black like the bike. A very realistic looking, slightly-oversized, brain was painted on it in exquisite detail. The illustration was the work of a woman I'd met in the New York Public Library one day many years ago. I had taken the train in from Baltimore to indulge my fascination with old maps in the Lionel Pincus and Princess Firyal map room. She'd taken the same train and ended up in the map room quite by chance while she waited for her attorneys to finalize her divorce. We had recognized each other from the train and struck up a whispered conversation. The next morning I was on the phone in her bedroom asking for a three-day extension to my leave.

On subsequent post-divorce visits to her estate on the Severn River above Annapolis, she has painted two more for me, one with a robot head full of gears and levers and one with a glowing white, clinically accurate skull. I haven't seen her for several years so husband number four must be a winner, but if there's a next time I might see if she'll paint a T-Rex on a full face helmet.

A deputy opened the door behind us, looked around and waved when he spotted Dwayne.

"Got to go," he said, carefully handing me the helmet. "Don't forget to remember me to Winter Rose. Anything I can do to help, you just call."

He handed me his card, shook my hand and squeezed my shoulder the way I imagine a father might. By the time I had buckled the helmet and started the Road King, he had disappeared into the station. I headed for the Inn of the Seven Clans.

CHAPTER 28

A TIRED LOOKING WAITRESS seated Magnus, Alice and me at a pleasant restaurant nearby called Maudie's Grill. She perked up when she recognized Magnus, who was not only memorable to females in general but also a generous tipper. He had eaten there earlier with Ace and Alice. At the moment Ace was asleep – probably the best thing for him – and Winter Rose was still with the medicine woman. Maggie hadn't mentioned dinner, but I was certain she wouldn't keep Winter Rose all this time and not feed her. After we ordered coffee all around and a grilled cheese for me, Alice said that she and Magnus had spent the last couple of hours doing research with her laptop.

"Looking for this so-called General, dontcha know?" Magnus said.

Alice gave a rapid little headshake of frustration.

"We discovered that high ranking officers are like any other CEOs – most are dedicated and honest, but a small percentage are thieves and scoundrels."

"Yah," Magnus said, "a small percent like she says, but you know how many damn generals we got in the US military?"

I hadn't thought about it. I raised an eyebrow and encouraged Magnus to answer his own question.

"Almost five hundred! Can you imagine all that gold braid in the same room?"

Alice and I both smiled, then she said, "And that's only the active duty number. The pool of possibles gets much larger if you include retirees."

We all digested that news while the waitress poured our coffee. When she had left with the pot, Alice said, "We found five generals that had recently been accused of crimes. The same stupid stuff some men get into when they're not properly supervised: spousal abuse, child pornography, embezzlement."

"Power, sex and money," I said.

"The story of the human race," Alice said with a sad smile.

"Tell me about the embezzler," I said.

"Old story now," Alice said, shaking her head. "From five years ago. Some retired two star named Deale landed a nice job with Aetna, then got caught siphoning off about a hundred grand. He used the one-of-the-little-people-under-me-did-it-without-my-knowledge defense. Most of the money mysteriously turned up later and Deale quietly left without any legal action by Aetna."

"A jerk," I said rubbing my tired eyes, "but small shit compared to murder and, like you say, old news."

Alice stifled a yawn behind a hand.

"Sorry," she said, "The others were jerks that ought to be locked up too, but small timers, relatively speaking."

I glanced at Magnus for his opinion. He had his chair tilted back, his back arched, his arms over his head and a monumental yawn threatening to dislocate his jaw. When he saw me looking at him, he shook it off without apology and let his chair down with a thump.

"I think this general we're looking for, he's too smart to be in the news, eh?

Alice nodded.

"He's right, RK. Our search was way too superficial. A good researcher could probably come up with a useful list, but it would take a couple of days at least."

"OK," I said, "on to Manassas."

"Manassas?" they both asked in unison.

It wasn't hard to figure where the RV with Ace's hidden envelope was headed. Back in Savannah, Betty Jo Bob had said the couple who owned the RV were going to ride in Rolling Thunder and stay at a farm. I thought it had to be the Greenville Farm Campground near Manassas, Virginia. I'd stayed at the Greenville Farm myself for Rolling Thunder about three years ago, when a group of us camped there before and after the ride. I generally ride by myself and stay in hotels, but a group camp-out has a lot to offer, especially when you're with a bunch of like-minded riders. I might have a different view of it if we had actually camped, with tents and sleeping bags and Coleman lanterns, but we all bunked down in a huge and luxurious RV owned by Vince and Sophie Linkmore, who had lumbered down in lush style from Harrisburg to ride their Honda Goldwing in Rolling Thunder. Eight of us had no problem finding a place to sleep in that leviathan, so we had a great time. As soon as I'd figured out that Ace's RV was probably headed for Greenville Farm, I'd called Vince to see if he was available. He said he and Sophie were up on Lake Erie, but they were looking for an excuse to leave. It was rainy up there on the lake and too damn windy. They could meet us in Virginia Saturday night. Five bunks? No problem. Don't worry about food, either, he said. He had a load of steaks in need of grilling before they freezer burned and a fridge full of beer that Sophie didn't want adding to his already considerable girth.

"Manassas, Virginia?" Alice asked. "I may not have your memory for maps built into my brain, but it seems to me that's a long day in the saddle."

"Eleven hours," I said. "But that's including a stop every hour or so."

I planned a route in my head to stay off the highways, initially heading east on Route 19 then working our way northeast. We'd ride a stretch of the Blue Ridge, and eventually take 221 up through Boone and cross into Virginia around Galax. From there we'd loop south of Roanoke and Lynchburg, ride through Appomattox and Culpepper, then shoot straight up Route 15 to the campground. Like Alice said, a long day, but not impossible for Ace if we gave him plenty of breaks. Too bad we didn't have time to tour. The Greenville Farm campground is only about seven miles from the Manassas National Battlefield Park, where my great, great, great grandfather Lawson Tidwell fought under Brigadier General Ambrose Wright in the Second Battle of Manassas. If we found the list without any problems, maybe I'd have a chance to go over to the battlefield on Sunday morning before Rolling Thunder.

My sandwich arrived and I wolfed it down while Magnus and Alice reviewed the route on a map.

"This is a serious ride," Alice said after she'd traced the roads all they way to DC. "Are you certain Ace is up for it? He's still pretty shaky."

"Pretty shaky?" Magnus said. "Yep, for sure. But he's doing better than a lot of guys would."

"Listen," I said, "Ace and Winter Rose are both doing much better than I expected. They'll be fine. We just have to start early and take it easy."

I pulled out my wallet and left enough money to cover the bill and a Magnus-sized tip.

"Now let's get some sleep. It's going to be a long day tomorrow."

CHAPTER 29

WE WHEELED QUIETLY out of the hotel parking lot before sunrise, with morning twilight just beginning to lighten the eastern horizon. The DC weather forecast called for a high of 75°, but the temperature was somewhere south of 50° in Cherokee, so I had the grip heaters on high.

Magnus rode point, the multiple taillights of his big Ultra easy to follow. I was next in line, with Ace on my passenger seat. Winter Rose stayed close behind me instead of zooming ahead as she had on the way up to Cherokee. She was even more quiet than usual. She hadn't said a thing to any of us about her session with the medicine woman, but it looked to me like some of Maggie's serenity had stayed with her. Alice brought up the rear, holding a good position about two seconds behind Winter Rose.

First light is always the best time to ride. Crisp morning air, fresh clothes, rested body, clear head, light traffic. In our case, no traffic. We had the road to ourselves and fell into a good rhythm. On this trip we didn't have a weak rider to coddle and, as long as Ace managed to stay aboard, I thought we could make good time. Winter Rose was riding like a pro. She looked so relaxed on that ratty looking Ninja rocket ship of hers that I suspected she'd ridden a lot of track days.

Magnus set a fast pace. We hammered along like a four bike train, using the full width of our lane. The Road King cut a smooth track across the pavement, deft and powerful. I gave myself over to that motorcycle magic. The world disappeared except for the bike and the road ahead. The knots in my neck and shoulders began to relax.

About an hour into the ride, with the sun just clearing the tree tops and a cool breeze building out of the northwest, a truck cut Magnus off.

CHAPTER 30

T HE TRUCK – a silver Ford F-150, not the black truck I'd been watching for – rolled up from the opposite direction. The driver suddenly jerked the wheel over, skidded across both lanes and rocked to a halt. Magnus's brake light flashed and the nose of his bike dipped under hard deceleration. I saw him shift his butt to the right as he struggled to get the heavy Harley stopped. He was headed straight for the right front wheel of the truck. I thought for sure he'd be thrown over the hood, but he swerved just enough to clear the front of the truck by an inch. He was a split second from a miraculous recovery when his wheels locked up in the loose swale on the edge of the road. The last I saw of him, he was standing up on the big Ultra with the front wheel crossed up like he was jumping a motocrosser. Then he disappeared into the brush.

Meanwhile I was hard on my own brakes. The Road King's forks compressed to the stops, even with the new progressive springs. Taken completely by surprise, Ace slammed into my back and pushed me up onto the gas tank. His left knee hit my left elbow, knocking my hand off the bars. The front end swerved and we almost went down, but I managed to grab the stalk for the rear view mirror and straighten the bike up. I shifted my hand back to the grip, pulled the clutch in and stopped about two feet from the truck.

Winter Rose glided up on my left. A second later, Alice pulled up on my right. Like Winter Rose, she had plenty of warning and stopped without fuss.

Two men climbed out of the cab of the truck. Manion and Bailey. Both carried the same MP-5 submachine guns with the fat silencers. They held their weapons as competently as before, not pointed directly at any of us, but ready to swing instantly into action if required. Neither man said a word. Bailey, who had been behind the wheel, stayed behind the mass of the engine and the hood. Manion, who was closest to me, partially sheltered himself with his open door. I turned my head and looked to the rear.

As I expected, the familiar black crew cab approached from behind us, moving deliberately but without haste. The driver didn't bother to turn sideways, but simply pulled up behind our bikes and stopped in the middle of the road. I shut off the Road King's engine and told Ace to get off. I kicked the side stand down, then I unbuckled my helmet and set it on its usual storage spot on the right hand mirror. I swung my leg over the saddle and turned to face the second truck.

Winter Rose held her front brake with two fingers, blipped the throttle with her wrist and spun her rear tire to swing the back of her bike around until she was sideways on the road. She looked from one truck to the other, then at Ace. I knew what she was thinking. Get him out of the kill zone. But this wasn't that kind of ambush. If it was, he'd already be dead. I waved away some of the rubber smoke and made a throat-cutting motion for her to kill her engine. She gave the throttle one more angry blip, then shut it off.

Alice dismounted too. She carried her Sig P229 in a standard issue clip-on belt holster that rode high on her right hip. I knew she was pretty fast with it in her everyday clothes, but now it was zipped away under her riding jacket and she wisely didn't even try to get it out.

Novak climbed out from behind the wheel of the crew cab and stood on the pavement. He was dressed in black jeans, a white shirt and a black leather jacket. He pointed toward the spot where Magnus had disappeared and said, "Go. Find your friend. I wait."

Alice and Winter Rose had taken positions on either side of Ace. I told them all to stay where they were and went to check on Magnus. I approached the edge of the road where he had disappeared and looked over the side.

At first it looked like he had just been swallowed up by the bushes. Then I spotted a bit of blue and chrome. The slope was steep here and Magnus must have literally flown off the road. I scrambled down and pushed my way through the foliage.

Magnus was on the ground, both legs trapped under the Harley. His back was braced against the hillside and he had his Wilson in a steady two-handed grip. When he saw it was me, he lowered the pistol.

"Come on down here, Roman," he said. "If it's not too much trouble. Cheese and fucking mice, these pipes are *hot*."

I grinned, knowing he wasn't hurt. He only let loose with his unique blend of profane Minnesotanese when he was seriously annoyed.

"Told you to wear real boots," I said. "Those walking shoes may be comfortable, but they don't help much in a crash."

I saw where I could lever the bike up with my legs and eased myself into position to lift it.

"I didn't crash, eh," Magnus said.

"Of course not," I said, digging my heels into the soft ground. "But it's a damn poor park job."

I braced my back under the point where the seat meets the tank and lifted with my legs.

"I got run off the road," Magnus said, scrambling up as the weight of the bike came off him. "It's different, dontcha know?"

He surveyed the damage to his beloved Ultra, which appeared to be limited to the clutch lever. It was broken off at the tip but otherwise functional. There was a crack down the center of the stubby windshield and some scratches to the paint. The massive Harley roll bars had done their job. But Magnus was furious. He still had the pistol in his hand and used it to point out the dings in the once flawless finish.

"Look at that! My poor Eloise," he said. "I'm gonna kill that bastard."

He started up the hill, but I caught him by the shoulder.

"Magnus!" I said.

He turned, saw me looking at him expectantly.

"This isn't about you or Eloise. It's about Ace. They're here for him. And the list."

"But… we don't have it."

"Not yet," I said. "Come on, let's see what else we can arrange."

"Well, OK, then."

Magnus holstered his gun and we clambered up the hill together.

CHAPTER 31

THE SCENE ON the road was unchanged. Ace stood by my Road King between Alice and Winter Rose. All of them were still sandwiched between the two pickups, held in place by the guns of Novak's men. I motioned Magnus behind the others, then I stepped up to face Novak. Up close he still smelled like an old ashtray. We looked each other over. I could see the bulge of a shoulder holster on the left side of his jacket, but he made no attempt to draw the pistol.

"It's your party," I said after a moment.

Novak reached out and opened the rear door of the crew cab with its darkly tinted windows. Virgil was inside. He was bent over with his head resting against the seat back in front of him. His arms were jammed awkwardly behind his back, and I could see the rope knotted tightly on his wrists.

Novak's man Cutcher sat on the other side of the seat, angled sideways so he could hold a gun to Virgil's head. It was a ridiculously big Smith and Wesson revolver with a six-inch barrel, the one Ace had told me about. Cutcher sneered at me, then twisted it viciously against Virgil's temple.

Virgil scowled in Novak's direction through the open door. Then he saw me and his eyes widened.

"Roman!" he shouted, rocking his upper body forward and trying to thrust himself out of the truck.

Cutcher snaked his free hand around Virgil's throat and yanked him back. At the same moment Novak slammed the door.

His voice was muffled inside the truck, but I heard Virgil yell, "Go Roman!" before Cutcher bounced the heavy barrel of the Smith and Wesson off the side of his head.

Leaving now was the last thing I'd do. What I'd seen when Virgil leaned out of the truck triggered a black rage in me. His left eye was swollen shut and his left ear was ripped. His white collar was missing and the thighs of his jeans were dark with blood that had dripped from his damaged face. Somebody was going to answer for that.

I spun toward Novak, intent on inflicting the same damage and more. But Manion stopped me by the simple expedient of firing a quick burst of three rounds into the dirt at my feet. The silencer reduced the weapon's discharge to a dull clatter, but the warning was unmistakable. I pulled up, breathing as hard as if I'd just sprinted fifty yards. My fingers tingled with excess adrenaline. I balled them into fists and squeezed them tight, aching to pummel Novak into a bloody heap. Manion watched me carefully through slit eyes. He raised the barrel of his MP-5 slightly and shook his head. I forced myself to relax. I flexed my fingers, let my hands fall to my sides.

"Just to let you know we are serious," Novak said when he had my attention again.

I clamped my jaw, fought to keep control.

I took a deep breath and said, "What do you want?"

"Simple," he said. "Give us list – we give you brother."

CHAPTER 32

"I CAN'T GIVE IT to you," I said. "I don't have it. None of us have it."

He shrugged.

"Get it," he said.

"The list is in Virginia," I said. "Near a place called Manassas."

He shrugged again.

"Get it," he said again. "Then give to me."

"Maybe I'm wrong about where it is now. I might not be able to find it."

He didn't shrug this time, but jerked a thumb over his shoulder at the pickup behind him.

"Your brother counts on you. Find list."

I glanced at the pickup where I knew Virgil sat tied up behind the dark glass.

"I'll have it by tomorrow morning," I said, hoping for Virgil's sake I could deliver on this promise.

"Good," he said, smiling for the first time. His teeth were as yellow as his fingers.

"How do I contact you?" I said. "When I have the list?"

He waved that thought away, like an insignificant problem.

"I find you here," he said. "I find you again."

"Maybe, maybe not," I said. "Tell you what. Go to Manassas. You can find the Manassas Battleground there easy enough. It's on all the maps. There's a famous place on the battleground called the Stone House. Right where 29 intersects with 234. It has a parking lot for visitors that's open all the time. Meet me there at first light tomorrow. We'll have it to ourselves. I'll have the list for you."

Novak looked over at Bailey, who nodded once. If he didn't know where it was already, he seemed confident he could find it. I knew Novak would like it: a public place that would be totally private at that early hour. The perfect spot for a risk-free exchange.

"All right," Novak said. "Bring the list." He stabbed a finger at Ace. "And that man."

Novak crooked the same finger at me, then walked back to the bed of the pickup. He opened the chrome metal toolbox that was bolted across the bed behind the cab, reached inside and came up with a coil of rope. It was an old length of half inch black nylon. Both ends were frayed and it was lumpy with old knots, the kind of rope you might find in half the pickups in America. He shoved it at my chest.

"For blue motorcycle," he said.

Then he climbed into the truck and pulled around our group standing in the middle of the road. The other two men piled into their truck, reversed to let him by, then followed. In thirty seconds we had the road to ourselves. I looked at my watch. The whole affair had taken eleven minutes. I wondered if Novak had more men closing the road off above and below the ambush point, or if he had just been lucky that no other vehicles had passed by. Either way, he had been way ahead of me.

Damn it! I was retired from the Army for less than forty-eight hours and already I had made mistakes I'd never made in combat. I had almost gotten Ace and Magnus killed, and Virgil had been kidnapped and savagely beaten. If I didn't get my shit together… well, after two decades in the Army I have few close friends and only one brother. I didn't want to lose any of them.

Winter Rose touched my arm.

"Your brother's alive, RK. That's the important thing."

"She's right," Alice said. "His face was bloody, but his voice was strong. I don't think he's hurt bad."

I didn't want to admit it, but I appreciated that fact that it was both of the women who found something positive to think about. I was still seething and Magnus looked like a thunderstorm just before it lets loose. Even Ace, physically shaky and working just to stay on his feet, looked mad. Alice and Winter Rose were right, though. Attitude is half the battle and anger never helps. Up to now I've been a step behind Novak at every turn. I needed to get in front of him. Setting up the next meeting on familiar terrain had been a good first step, and one that I'd arranged mostly out of reflex, but now I needed a bold move to take the initiative. Without, I reminded myself, getting Virgil killed.

I walked down the road a few paces to gather my thoughts. When I stopped being angry and started thinking rationally again, I quickly realized that Virgil wasn't likely to be mistreated further. This general, who ever he was, needed Virgil alive to trade for Ace and the list. And I needed this general to save Virgil and Ace.

From Alice's experience last night, I knew I wasn't going to come up with his name just surfing around the Internet. Mentally, I ran down the shortlist of generals I had met personally and came up absolutely blank. One or two had reputations as tough bastards, but all were honorable officers. There was a longer list of generals I knew *of* but hadn't actually met, but I was certain these were likewise above board.

I needed more information and that realization brought me back to Novak. If I could crack him, I'd find this general. With luck and some help, I could make that happen. I retrieved the card Sheriff Silverwood had given me from my pocket. He answered his cell phone almost immediately. I told him what had happened, then I told him what I wanted and why. There was a moment of silence when I'd finished.

Finally he said, "You took it literal-like when I said *anything you need*, huh?"

"It's a lot to ask, I know," I said.

There was another silent interval. Then a sigh.

"We got two," he said. "You can have them. You leave them at the scene of a crime though, and I'm out of a job. Take about one minute to track them back to the tribal police by the serial numbers and somebody would be knocking on my door about two minutes after that."

"Thanks Dwayne," I said. "You'll get them back soon."

"And quietly, huh?"

I promised no CNN or Fox News. I hung up and walked back along the road to join the others.

"Magnus," I said, "you mind riding back to Cherokee?"

Magnus shot me a puzzled look.

"Where we just been?" he asked.

"A sheriff named Silverwood is going to loan us some equipment."

"Some equipment, he says," Magnus said with satisfaction. "So, we have a plan then. What am I going to pick up?"

I told him. The puzzled look came back, but he said no problem. He could double back to the reservation, pick up the gear we needed from Sheriff Silverwood, then take the freeways north to make up time. He might even get to Manassas before us.

I handed him the rope.

"We can pull your Ultra out of the trees with my Road King."

He nodded miserably. "Poor Eloise! I hope she still runs."

CHAPTER 33

GREENVILLE FARM CAMPGROUND really is a farm. Newcomers might be put off by the genuine farm smell of the cattle barn near the entrance, but the camping area is set further back in a couple of hundred acres of woods and meadows, with a stream bubbling between placid fishing ponds. There is a swimming pool near the tent sites and the office, and as we idled down the narrow road I could see a neat row of RVs beyond it.

Vince and Sophie had already arrived. In spite of the situation, I was glad to see them again. They are a plump couple in their early seventies. Vince was a geologist in the oil industry until about twenty years ago, when he inherited thirty acres of land south of Lebanon, Pennsylvania. While he was poking around the rubble of the defunct iron mine that occupied a sizeable chunk of the property, Vince became convinced that, as he likes to say, "There's gold in them thar hills." Now he and Sophie live comfortably on the proceeds of a gold mining lease. They are so close in height, weight and appearance that people often mistake them for brother and sister. Cruising on their

Goldwing, dressed to ride in matching jackets and helmets, they look more like twins than Virgil and me.

Their RV sparkled in the late afternoon sun and they were relaxing in lounge chairs under a retractable awning that had been cranked out from the side of the massive vehicle. I was surprised to see that they had no trailer and the Goldwing was nowhere to be seen. They put their drinks aside when we rolled up and came over with glad cries.

"Roman!" Sophie said, giving me a wet kiss before I could even get my helmet off. I hugged her quickly then shook Vince's hand.

"No Wing?" I asked.

He gave me a chagrined look and a shrug.

"You'll have to ask Sophie about that," he said.

She put both hands on her hips and said, "Last September, Vince dropped it in the parking lot while I was climbing off the back. Nearly broke both our legs! Then he dropped it again all by himself, back in October. At an intersection on a hill, this time. I said two strikes and you're out, buster."

I raised my eyes and grinned at her bluster.

"It's three strikes and you're out, isn't it?"

"Not in my game it isn't!"

She waved a hand dramatically at the RV behind us. "If Vince gets hurt who's going to drive this barge and mix my martinis?"

"So the Wing is up in New Jersey now, being converted into a trike," Vince said, taking up the story. His eyes lit up, though, and I could tell he secretly liked the idea.

"Enough with the bikes and trikes already. You haven't introduced your friends, Roman," Sophie said. "I'm Sophie, dears."

After introductions all around, Sophie ushered Winter Rose and Alice into the RV, an arm around each of them.

"Come on, girls, I'm sure you're ready to freshen up after that ride."

As the door of the RV shut behind the three women, Magnus rode up. His bike was streaked with road grime and he had the dusty, tired look of a Pony Express rider. He had made up a lot of time on us by hitting the highways. Vince shook his hand and looked him up and down as I made the introductions.

"You, sir, look like a man who can use a drink. Can I pour you a cocktail?"

"A guy could use a cold drink, you bet," Magnus said. "Make that a beer, and you've got a friend for life."

Vince grinned, then reached into a nearby cooler and pulled a bottle out of the ice. He handed it to Magnus who had half of it down before he stopped to breathe.

Vince held up his martini glass.

"How about you gentlemen?"

"Sorry, Vince," I said. "Ace and I have got one more errand before it gets dark. Can we take a rain check?"

"Of course! Of course! Mr. Magnusson and I will carry on for a bit, then I'll start the dinner preparations."

I nodded. "We'll give you a hand when we get back."

He waved dismissively with one hand while he polished off the remains of his martini with the other.

"It's all under control," he said, setting down the glass. "Steaks, baked potatoes, corn on the cob. Sophie stocks this beast to feed an army." He shooed us away with his fingers. "Go. Go. Come back hungry."

I smiled my thanks and patted him on the shoulder. I glanced at Magnus, who raised his nearly empty bottle.

"I'll stay," he said, "in case there's more beer in that cooler, eh."

"Silverwood came through?" I asked.

Magnus nodded. "Latest thing. Fresh batteries, too."

"Good," I said. Then I set off with Ace to search for the RV.

We passed half a dozen vehicles without any sign of recognition, so I gave him a prod.

"Any of these rigs look familiar, Ace?" I asked.

He shook his head glumly.

"I'm sorry, RK. I just can't remember."

It didn't look good. I had pinned a lot on finding the RV where he'd hidden the envelope with the list here at Greenville Farms. It was foolish, but I had no contingency plan. If the RV wasn't here… well, there are times when you have to go with what you have.

We hiked on down the line, checking each vehicle. Nothing perked Ace's memory until we got to a Winnebago with a motorcycle trailer that was parked at the end of the line.

With a hopeful quaver in his voice, Ace said, "Maybe… maybe this one."

"Really, Ace? This could be it?"

We walked around the rig, trying to appear casual.

"I think it was older, like this. Not sleek like Vince and Sophie's."

But our hopes were dashed when we cleared the back of the rig. Ace stopped in his tracks. His face fell and he shook his head. He pointed at a pair of motorcycles perched on their center stands. One was a BMW adventure bike, a big R1200GS. The other was a smaller version of the same style motorcycle, a black and yellow F800GS. Neither one could be mistaken for the "chrome sculptures" Ace told me he remembered.

"Those definitely aren't the right bikes, RK."

I put a hand on his shoulder and gently moved him along the road.

"Don't sweat it Ace, there are more sites down in the woods. Let's check those out before we start to worry."

We passed one campsite after another, nestled in the trees. Most were tents, a couple were vans with tents attached, one was a pickup with a pop-top camper. Several sites had motorcycles parked next to the tents, but none had motorcycle trailers. Where the road turned back by a creek we found one RV, but it was a tiny rig based on a Toyota truck frame. We followed the return loop past the last remaining campsites and eventually came out by the main field where all the larger RVs were parked. I didn't say it out loud, but I was starting to get as worried as Ace.

"Let's check with the office," I said. "Maybe they haven't arrived yet."

We continued past Vince and Sophie's elaborate rig in tense silence. We passed the pool and trudged along the section of road between the cattle pens. Neither of us bothered to comment on the manure smell, but it didn't help our spirits any. When we rounded the house and turned toward the little office, we saw it.

"That's it! That's it!" Ace said.

I grabbed his shoulder just as he was about to break into a run.

"Take it easy, Ace," I said. "If it is the right RV, we need to retrieve that envelope casually – without attracting any notice. These are probably nice folks, but these days it seems like everyone wants to use their cell phone video cameras and be on the news."

"Right, right. Sorry, RK. I wasn't thinking."

It was an older Winnebago Brave, sun-faded but clean and well-maintained. An aluminum box on wheels compared to the Linkmore's lavish motorcoach, but a good choice for a family on a budget. A fifty-ish woman with platinum hair and wrap around sunglasses smiled and waved at us from the front passenger seat. Ace and I returned the wave and continued toward the rear of the vehicle. Without being too obvious, I peeked in the side window. Through open curtains I could see an empty dinette.

At the back of the rig we found the motorcycles that had caught Ace's eye back in Savannah. His and hers Harley Low Riders, strapped to an open grid trailer that was probably meant to haul riding mowers and other landscaping equipment. What this couple saved on the trailer and RV, they spent on chrome. Ace was right – the bikes looked like a pair of sculptures in silver. Everything from the hand controls to the engine cases appeared to have been dipped in chrome.

"Quick – show me where you stashed the envelope, Ace," I said.

He trotted around the bikes to the passenger's side and looked left and right along the flank of the RV. He scratched his head, looked again, shook his head and ran around to the driver side again. I glanced at the office. How long does it take to register? The driver would be coming out any second.

Ace waved frantically and stabbed a finger at the side of the RV. I slipped alongside him and took us both back a step so that we wouldn't be visible in the side mirrors.

"That's it, RK! I opened that little door and stuffed the envelope behind the propane tank."

"All right, Ace. Now go around to the window on the other side and tell that nice lady in the passenger seat that you think their bikes are show stoppers." I pushed him in the right direction. "If the husband comes out, keep him busy for a couple of minutes."

I waited until he cleared the front of the RV, then gave it another ten seconds before I crouched down and went to work on the access door. It was hinged at the front and fastened shut with two knurled knobs. The bottom knob turned easily, but the top one had a lock built into it. If it opened for Ace, it must have been unlocked, but it wasn't moving now.

The whole structure of the RV wasn't anything more than thin sheet aluminum. I could pop the door open with a decent sized flat tip screwdriver, but these folks were innocent couriers. Besides, something didn't seem right. If the door opened while the rig was parked in front of a BBQ joint for lunch, why was it locked now? Maybe the owner had left it open by mistake once, but corrected things later. I shook my head. It seemed unlikely that Ace just happened to luck out like that.

I looked forward along the side of the RV. About midway between the axles there was another small access door. I moved quietly up to it. This door was secured by a single knob on the bottom. I twisted it and swung the door up. Inside was a white propane tank. I reached over the top of the tank and felt around. My fingers found the envelope.

I lifted it out quickly and stared at it for a moment, relief flooding in. Then I slipped it under my shirt and tucked it into my waistband. I refastened the access panel and tried to look nonchalant as I walked around to the front of the RV.

Ace was standing with the driver, a rail thin guy with an enormous handlebar moustache and sun wrinkled face. Ace had apparently run dry on small talk and looked relieved to see me. I smiled and held out my hand.

"We were admiring your bikes," I said. "Looks like you could have your own show."

"Aw, ain't nothing but shiny stuff right out of the Harley catalog, but thank you, friend, for the compliment." He looked from me to Ace and back. "You folks riding in Rolling Thunder tomorrow?"

I nodded. "Yes, four of us will be doing our part."

He gave me a smile that crinkled his eyes. If you imagined a big Stetson to top off that handlebar moustache, and maybe squinted a bit, he looked just like Wyatt Earp.

"See you on the road, then," he said.

He turned and climbed into the RV. Ace and I stood until it rumbled away. When it was out of sight, I pulled the envelope out of my waistband and handed it to Ace. He fumbled the flap open and unfolded a sheaf of three pages. He scanned them quickly, then held the last page out to me.

"Here is where he wrote the names," he said.

I held the paper in the fading light and squinted to read the names. Brad Beardsley and Lincoln Price. Printed legibly, but quickly. Almost like signatures. I started to hand the sheet back to Ace, then something made me read the names again.

"What?" Ace said.

I stared at the names for another ten seconds, then folded the paper. "Not signatures," I said, mostly to myself. "Death sentences."

I handed it back to Ace, who placed it back in the envelope with the first two pages. He slipped it carefully into his pocket.

"All right!" I said. "We're halfway there."

Turns out we were halfway to someplace I never imagined.

CHAPTER 34

I CAN GRILL A good steak as long as it's fresh, but give me the best hunk of beef on the planet from the freezer and I'll turn it into a hockey puck. I just don't have the patience for proper thawing. Vince, on the other hand, has no such limitation. He served up the best steaks any of us could remember and we gorged ourselves by candlelight under the awning. I wondered what Virgil's captors gave him to eat and felt a bit guilty, but I shrugged away the thought. Nothing I could do but get him back as soon as possible.

After dinner, we declined another invitation for cocktails and I asked if we could use the RV for a strategy meeting. Sophie waved a dismissive hand and picked up her seemingly bottomless martini pitcher.

"You go right ahead, dear. Vince and I will park ourselves out here under the stars and sip a bit of pomegranate delight."

Vince looked like he'd rather sit inside with us and listen to the battle plan, but he eased himself into the chair next to Sophie's and said, "Let me know if you need anything."

After everyone had squeezed into the RV's little galley, I brought them up to speed.

"Remember when Novak opened up the tool box on the back of his pickup and gave us the rope?"

Nods all around, but then it was the sort of humiliation that you don't soon forget.

"When he had the lid up, I noticed a molded fiberglass case inside. A long, narrow case with five latches."

I looked at Magnus to see if that raised any flags with him.

After a couple of seconds, his chin came up. "Five latches, he says. On a fiberglass case." He snapped his fingers. "An M-24! A sniper rifle!"

I nodded.

"Exactly, a sniper rifle. Although I don't know how he got his hands on a weapon made for the military and the police."

Magnus snorted. "Remington sells 'em by the ton, eh? To any sniper wannabe."

"Not with a Savannah Police SWAT decal on the case," I said.

"There you go then," said Magnus with a shrug. "Probably the real McCoy."

Alice said, "So this Novak likes to shoot. That's no surprise, is it? He already shot up your place and that Manion creep let off a few rounds out on the road today. But do you really think he's planning another ambush?"

"Yes," I said. "I think this General is too cagey to let this situation go as far as an exchange of live hostages. I think he's planning to have Novak kill Ace, then exchange Virgil for the list. That way he gets everything he wants with much less risk. But this is our chance to turn the tables on him."

"Turn the tables?" Alice said.

I glanced at her and dipped my chin.

"He thinks he's setting us up, but instead we set him up."

I spread out the park service brochure I'd picked up from the rack in the campground office out on the table. It had a bird's eye view of the battleground, with the movements of the troops from both sides illustrated in red and blue. There wasn't much in the way of terrain features, but the existing roads and creeks were shown, along with the significant landmarks such as houses, bridges and cemeteries.

I had toured the Manassas Battlefield Park three years ago, walking the fields and trying to picture where my ancestor Lawson Caswell had fought, so the topography was on file in that mass of neurons between my ears. I pointed out the Stone House.

"This building is an old sandstone tavern built before the Civil War. It survived the clash of armies twice by sheltering wounded soldiers, at First Manassas in 1861 and Second Manassas in 1862."

I traced the roads intersecting next to the tavern.

"This is Route 29. It was called the Warrenton Pike back then. And this is Route 234 – the old Sudley-Manassas Road. The parking lot where I told Novak we'd meet is off this first road, Route 29."

I looked around the faces at the table.

"Novak won't choose a shooting position at the building. You can't see it on this map, but the tavern is enclosed by a zigzag split rail fence that offers no real cover. The building itself is too much in the open and too plainly visible from the road to offer good cover. Besides, the morning sun would be directly in the eyes of anyone watching the parking lot from the house."

I put the tip of my knife on the map and traced a line up from the tavern.

North of the tavern, the ground sloped gently upward

toward Buck Hill: an open, grassy area like much of the park. Behind the parking lot next to the tavern, a stream called Youngs Branch skirted the slope of Buck Hill, looping north before eventually turning east to mingle with the waters of Bull Run. The dense tree line between the stream and the base of Buck Hill would provide good concealment less than two hundred yards north of the parking lot – the perfect position for a rifleman.

With the point of my knife balanced on the eastern slope of Buck Hill, I said, "If Novak is planning another ambush, this is where he'll be."

"So, you've been planning this since we had that set-to with Novak back in the mountains," Magnus said. "That explains why you sent me back to Cherokee to borrow night vision goggles from Sheriff Silverwood. We're going to get there before him."

CHAPTER 35

AFTER OUR BRIEF war council, Alice motioned toward the front door of the RV.

"Let's take a walk," she said. She stood up and strode down the aisle, her rigid back and quick step clearly making it a command, not a request. I hurried after her, but didn't catch up until she stopped in the weak pool of light by a utility pole about thirty yards up the road.

"It's time to call in the cavalry, RK," she said, spinning to face me. "Let the FBI handle this. Kidnapping is what they do best."

I shook my head. "They'd never get a handle on this fast enough to save Virgil. And what about Ace?"

"What about him?" she asked.

"Say we call in the FBI. Fine, they're pros. They'll nail Novak no doubt about it. Maybe they'll even rescue Virgil. But they won't get the boss man. And if the boss man of this whole business isn't caught, who do you think they're going to crucify in his place?"

"Novak, of course. Don't tell me you'd lose any sleep over that." she said.

I shook my head, but kept silent.

After a few seconds of thought, she added, " And Ace."

"And Ace," I agreed. "If we're going to save both Virgil and Ace, we need the boss. The General, whoever he is."

"And Novak is the key to the General," she said.

I nodded.

"Novak and I need to have a quiet conversation."

Alice held my eyes briefly, but whatever she saw in them made her look away.

"That's going to be anything but a quiet conversation, RK," she said.

I shrugged.

"How it goes depends on him."

I dragged the edge of my boot across the ground and pointed down.

"You said there's a line you wouldn't cross – well, here's one for both of us. I have to cross it. I have to get Virgil back. I have to keep Ace alive and out of jail. I can't just dial 911 and hope for the best."

"So I twiddle my thumbs until you've saved the day?"

I shook my head.

"No, Alice, it's not like that at all. I didn't say it back in the RV, but I'm depending on you. Listen, this is still Secret Service territory, right? The whole identity and veteran's benefits theft thing, I mean?"

"Don't forget the murders. And Virgil's kidnapping."

"That just ups the ante, doesn't it?"

"Maybe, but– "

"So we need a headline hunter in the Secret Service. Someone high up enough to have the juice. But it must be someone who's willing to sit tight until we call, then jump in with both feet to wrap it up and take the credit. Know anyone like that?"

She put her head down and shifted her weight from one foot to the other. I kept my mouth shut and let her think it through. She walked off for a few minutes, then worked her way back.

Finally she said, "There's a guy named Ted Franklin. He's the Assistant Special Agent in Charge in the Washington field office. He's an obnoxious ass – I'm sure he pictures a young Tommy Lee Jones playing Special Agent Franklin in the movie about his life – but he knows his stuff."

"Is he ambitious enough to play along?"

She smiled.

"If it gets him promoted, he'll cuff his own mother."

"Call him," I said. "Tell him he'll be a hero with both the Treasury Department and the Veterans Administration. Interpol, too, if he delivers Novak to them. Get him primed, but make sure he'll wait for your word to go."

CHAPTER 36

AT 3:30 IN the morning, the roads were dark and quiet. Stars sparkled against a clear black sky as we pulled into a gravel parking area near a cluster of information signs put up by the park service just east of Youngs Branch. I was on the back of Alice's Softail. Winter Rose had piloted Magnus's Ultra with Magnus on the back, since her own bike had only a fiberglass cowling where the tiny rear seat had been. When she gave him the OK, Magnus levered himself off the back seat and stood up next to her.

"Not so bad for a sportbike squid," he said.

Winter Rose lifted her visor and regarded Magnus silently, like a cat. Then a tiny hint of a smile flitted across her lips.

"And your Harley's a nice bike," she said. "If you like trucks."

"Hey now," Magnus said. "Eloise is the sensitive type."

"Eloise?" Winter Rose said.

"Don't ask," Alice said. "He won't talk about Eloise."

"An old flame?" Winter Rose asked.

Alice grinned.

"From second grade, probably."

"Let's get moving," I said, opening the tour pack on the back of Magnus's Ultra. I retrieved a pair of the night vision goggles Magnus had stored there earlier, and stashed my helmet inside. Magnus reached in and picked up the rope Novak had given us and the other pair of goggles. He put his helmet next to mine and closed the lid.

"OK, let's go over it once more," I said.

"Winter Rose and I ride back to the campground," Alice said. "I'll take my bike, we'll put Ace on your Road King and Winter Rose will take the Ultra again. We time it so we get to the Stone House parking lot at dawn. Ace holds the manila envelope in his lap where anyone can see it. Then we wait."

I rubbed my face. If I was wrong about Novak's intentions, this could turn to shit in a second.

"Last chance to call for help, RK," Alice said.

I took a deep breath. Then I shook my head.

"My brother, my friend," I said. "My way."

Alice grinned.

"Knew that would be the answer, but I had to try. Let's make it work, then."

I put my hand around her shoulder, gave her a hug. When I let go, she surprised me by grabbing my neck and pulling me close. She kissed me once, hard and long on the lips, generating roughly the same heat as a blowtorch, then pushed me out to arm's length.

"Don't you dare get yourself killed, Roman Keane. Our time may come yet."

Then she fired up her bike, kicked it into gear and gunned it onto the road, leaving a long patch of rubber on the asphalt. Winter Rose gave me a slow appraising look, then flipped her visor down and rode off at a more leisurely pace.

"Wow," said Magnus, as silence and darkness reigned again in the night.

I scowled at him, hoping to discourage any further discussion. Against the black sky, his smile glowed like neon.

"What then?" he said. "All I said was wow."

"She's married," I said.

"So's her husband," he said. "What I hear is, it ain't stopping him."

"His wrong doesn't make it right – for her or for me."

"A guy's just saying…"

"Right. Let's go."

Magnus gave it one more grin, then draped the coiled rope over his shoulders like a bandolier. We lowered the goggles over our eyes and set off through the park. We slipped into the trees and headed west until we found Youngs Branch. Keeping the creek on our left, we double-timed quietly to the north, dark shadows invisible on a black battlefield.

Running with night vision goggles creates a curious sensation of disembodiment. You seem disconnected from your own feet. The ground is way down there and your head is way up here. You feel much taller than usual. Everything glows in a green haze. The goggles Sheriff Silverwood loaned us were late model technology – good gear, but still limited compared to normal daytime vision. It's like being trapped halfway between 2D and 3D. You feel like you're running on someone else's legs. You have to stay on your toes and let your knees absorb the unexpected shocks.

Tendrils of fog floated in thin blankets on the chilly night air. I paused for a moment and looked around. In the green cast of the goggles I imagined Rebel and Union soldiers clashing here, muskets in their hands and hearts in their mouths. The Union headquarters had been just over the crest of Buck Hill to our front and Longstreet's Corps had attacked from our left. My ancestor, Lawson Caswell, was a captain in the 3rd Georgia Infantry during that battle. For a moment I saw him in the strange tint of my goggles, running at the head of his company, mouth wide open and a terrifying rebel yell erupting from his lungs like a volcano. I squeezed my eyes shut and pictured Virgil in the back of Novak's pickup. Captain Caswell and his phantoms disappeared. The present flooded back. I picked out my path through the trees and moved out.

Moving fast and quiet, we covered about four hundred yards before we slowed to cross the creek. At that point it was a dribble that hardly wet our boots. Another two hundred yards from the creek, we started up the eastern slope of Buck Hill. The trees thinned out quickly, giving way to knee high grass that swished quietly beneath our boots. About half way up the slope of the hill, we crouched behind a fallen tree trunk. The parking lot was less than three hundred yards away. Fifty yards to our front a pair of fir trees perched together on the side of the slope. Nearer the creek, there was another fallen trunk like the one we sheltered behind. One of those two spots was where Novak would set up to fire.

At least that's the way I read it. But I worried that I was betting way too many lives on it. We settled in to wait.

Magnus saw Novak first. He touched my elbow and pointed to the west. Novak was alone, crossing the open field north of the Stone House. I could see the long barrel of a rifle jutting up next to his head. He must have been dropped off somewhere along Route 234 and was staying away from the trees, depending on darkness for concealment. With our night vision goggles, he might as well have strolled across the field at noon. He stopped behind the second of the two large fir trees, about half way down the slope. As we watched he slipped the rifle off his shoulder and knelt on the side of the trunk where the smaller trunk of another tree was jammed up against it. The position was a good choice, affording him concealment and a commanding field of fire from the parking lot all the way over to the Stone House.

He was about a hundred yards from us. I figured we had about an hour until sunrise, plenty of time to quietly work our way down to him. I motioned Magnus out to my left. With a nod, he slipped away. In forty-five minutes we had closed the distance to twenty yards. Magnus was about ten yards from me, crouched behind a small bush. Like me, he had taken off the night vision goggles and let them hang by the strap around his neck. We wouldn't need them again. The sun would be up soon, and the eastern horizon was already showing a lighter gray against the black. I gave Magnus another hand signal. We eased still closer.

Over Novak's shoulder, I saw Alice, Ace and Winter Rose arrive. They stopped as instructed in the parking area, and stayed on the bikes. Magnus's big Harley Ultra was easy to pick out, a blue locomotive leaning on its side stand. Winter Rose was a poor match for Magnus in height, but when she was seated on the bike it didn't seem so obvious. Ace was on my Road King, wearing my helmet with the brain painted on it. He had the envelope propped prominently on his thigh. Alice was beside him, on her Softail. We had to nail Novak before he realized Magnus and I weren't down there in the parking lot.

To get Virgil back alive, I needed Novak alive. Fortunately, I had the perfect weapon for the occasion – Magnus the Magnificent. We had decided how to work it last night, so all it took was a nod from me now. We both slipped the night vision goggles from around our necks and set them silently on the ground. I counted off with my fingers, three, two, one. On one, Magnus leaped to his feet, took one loping stride and launched himself into the air like Michael Jordan driving for a layup. He came down with one knee square in the middle of Novak's back and both forearms across his neck. Judging from the explosive "Oof!" that burst from Novak's throat, the impact was roughly the same as having a water buffalo dropped on you from an airplane.

I dived after Magnus and snatched the rifle away. Novak made one half-hearted attempt to keep his grip on it, but let it go when Magnus slammed his palms over both of Novak's ears simultaneously. When Novak lifted his hands to his head, Magnus grabbed his right arm and twisted it viciously high behind his back. Something tore loose with a grisly, grinding pop; his wrist or shoulder maybe. Magnus probably figured it was a little payback for the damage done to his bike. Novak gave a harsh moan, which Magnus stifled by shoving his head into the dirt.

I hefted the rifle Novak had been carrying. As I suspected, it was a military sniper rifle, one of the M24A2 rifles. I popped the magazine and cycled the bolt. A live shell ejected from the breach – Novak had been ready to shoot. I lifted the rifle. I've fired many rounds through one exactly like it, and this one came up to my shoulder with the familiarity of an old lover. I put my eye to the Leupold scope and Ace's face appeared as though he was standing twenty yards away, not two hundred. The shot was a piece of cake for the M24, but I wondered if Novak had the skill to take out multiple targets with a bolt-action rifle, even from this close range. I lowered the rifle, noting this particular weapon had the long suppressor threaded to the end of the barrel. I set the rifle aside and made a rolling motion to Magnus.

With as much tenderness as a dogcatcher would show a Pit Bull with rabies, Magnus turned Novak over. Straddling him like a wrestler, Magnus drew his pistol and rammed it into the soft skin under his jaw. He pushed until Novak's head was tilted back as far as it would go.

"Move, and I'll put two rounds into your brain lickety-split. Just you fuckin' bet," he said.

Novak didn't even attempt to nod. Magnus edged aside for me, keeping his pistol jammed under Novak's jaw.

I searched him quickly. I picked his glasses out of the grass and stuck them on his face. I wanted him to see everything that happened next very clearly.

He had a pistol in a shoulder harness, butt down under his left arm. I yanked it out. On the right side of the rig, where normally you'd carry a couple of spare magazines, he had a fat black silencer. I took that, too. No wallet, no keys. But he did have a cell phone in a case on his belt. I took it out and stuffed it in my pocket. I turned my attention back to the pistol. It was a compact semi-automatic of some make I'd never seen. Something from the Czech military, I guessed. I popped the magazine. Full load of 9mm semi-jacketed hollow points. The same type of round that had killed Dalbert. I shoved it back into the grip and jacked the slide back to load a round into the breech. I screwed the thick silencer onto the barrel.

I jammed the end of the silencer against his forehead, just above the frame of his glasses. He tried to pull back, but I pushed until his head hit the tree trunk with a hard thump. I ground the pistol against his skin, careful to hold it on one spot while I twisted it back and forth. I stepped back. Novak had exactly the same mark on his forehead as Dalbert's body back in Ace's office.

Blood seeped out in a neat red ring. I watched it drip into his eye. He screwed his eye shut, shook his head and blinked to clear his vision. When he looked up at me, I extended my arm and pointed the pistol, sighting down the barrel like I was aiming at the bloody round target on his forehead.

"Bet I can beat your best shot," I said.

He stared at me for about three breaths, then he grinned tightly.

"No," he said. "You... you are American soldier. It is, how do you say... below you?"

"Beneath me, you mean?"

I dipped the barrel and shot him in the left thigh, low and outside where there was little chance of hitting a major artery. The big silencer worked perfectly. The loudest sound from the pistol was the clack of the receiver jerking back and forth to chamber the next round. Novak's scream was another matter. While I waited for the stream of remarkably fluent cursing to taper off, I thought about being the first in my family in one hundred and fifty years to shoot someone on this historic field of battle. Eventually Novak ran out of steam and his ranting subsided to random obscenities muttered through clenched teeth.

"Big mistake, Novak," I said. "I'm not a soldier anymore, but I *am* still a brother."

I took aim at the circle on his forehead again. He clamped his jaw down, sucked air through gritted teeth.

"And I'll trade your life for my brother's – in a heartbeat."

If my eyes get intense when I'm pissed, they must have looked radioactive now. Novak had ignored them on the road yesterday, but whatever he saw in them this morning broke him. He slumped.

"The phone you took from my belt," he said. "You press '7.' It calls him. Only the General. He has your brother."

With my left hand I retrieved the phone from my pocket. It was one of the cheap folding Samsung phones that come with prepaid minutes. Untraceable most likely.

"What's his name?" I said, flipping it open.

"I don't know," he said.

I leaned over and touched the barrel to the raw spot on his forehead. He twisted backward like I'd pressed a hot branding iron against his skin.

"He is General! Only General! Always General!" he said. "I ask what is his name. He laughed to me. He told me I don't need to know his name."

I looked at Magnus. He shrugged.

"Only one way to find out."

I pushed the number 7 key, held it down long enough to activate the speed dial function. After two rings, someone picked up at the other end.

"Speak," a deep voice commanded.

"If my brother's not alive," I said, "you're dead."

There was silence for a long beat, then the voice said, "Put Novak on."

I passed the phone over. Novak listened for a minute. If it was possible, he looked even more miserable. He said yes twice, apparently in response to questions from his boss. At one point he looked from me to Magnus, then he said, "Keane and a big man. Another soldier, I think. No, not Emory." He listened again, nodded, then flipped the phone shut.

"He still has your brother – alive. Today is the motorcycle day? Motorcycle rally, yes? The Rolling Thunder? He says you must ride in it. As you go, look always to left. On side road you will see black truck with orange cloth wrapped around the side mirror. Pull over next to it. Give up list and the man Emory. Finish ride. If you do as instructed, you will find your brother near the Vietnam Wall."

Damn. This guy was cautious, I'd give him that. Clever, too.

I heard an engine start off to the west. The General warning Novak's men to leave the area, I guessed. Novak probably had them positioned to mop up after he finished with the rifle. The vehicle accelerated away hard and I knew they were gone.

I looked around the hillside, considering what to do next. Then I realized Novak might still provide some useful intel.

I squatted to get down to his level.

"How long have you been working for this general?"

Novak glared at me, lips squeezed into a tight white line. Magnus rapped him on the top of the head with the barrel of his Wilson.

"Speak up, eh?"

"Three… no four, years!" Novak said, covering his head with one hand and clenching his bleeding thigh with the other.

"You never met him, right? So how did he hire you?"

Novak looked cautiously up at Magnus, then to me.

"He pay my bail."

"Without meeting you?"

Novak nodded vigorously.

"Yes! Yes! Without giving name. How do you say it?"

"Anonymously?" I said.

"That! Yes, that!"

"Where was this?" I said.

"Savannah," Novak said. "I just come to Georgia. No money. I stole from students at ATM, but police catch me."

"You came from the Czech Republic," I said, remembering what Alice had discovered at her computer. "By way of Halifax."

Novak's eyes widened and he dipped his head in a quick nod.

"While I was in jail, I was scared police would find out I was wanted in old country. If they find out, they send me back and I am dead man. I think, any minute it will happen. Then someone pays my bail. Police give me big envelope with watch, wallet, phone. I hurry away. A mile walking, maybe more. Then phone rings." He pointed to the phone I still had in my hand. "That phone. Was not mine. Was in envelope. That is how I meet the General."

"And the rest of your crew?"

"I find them myself. Hire them with money General gives me."

I stood up. Alice's people could get a lot more out of him later, but I was out of questions for now. Whoever this general was, he covered his tracks well.

"What next, RK?" Magnus asked.

"I guess we ride," I said.

"And him?"

I checked the wound in his leg – a nice clean through-and-through that had already slowed to a moderate seep. If steady pressure was applied until help arrived, he'd live. Probably even walk around the prison yard without a limp.

"We use his belt to bind up that leg," I said. "Then tie him up with his own rope. We leave him here and let Alice's people round him up."

Magnus sat Novak up unceremoniously, by grabbing a handful of his hair and jerking his head upward.

"Rem'ember that blue motorcycle?" he said as he roughly stripped Novak's belt off. "My sweet Eloise?"

I stifled a smile and headed up the hill to retrieve the night vision goggles we had discarded earlier. Novak wouldn't die of the gunshot wound, but I was certain Magnus's knots were going to make his morning thoroughly miserable.

Magnus and I hiked down to the parking lot, where the others were waiting with the bikes. Compared to the long route we took through the woods in the dark, the straight line off the hill took only a few minutes.

I handed Novak's pistol to Alice, along with the bolt I'd removed from the sniper's rifle.

"Lock these in your saddlebag for now," I said. "The pistol is Novak's. I'm pretty sure ballistics will match it to a batch of unsolved murders, including Dalbert back in Ace's office in Savannah."

She gave me a brief silent look, then pulled her gloves back on. She walked to the back of her Softail and opened one of the saddlebags. She wrapped the pistol and bolt in a cloth she keeps handy for cleaning her windshield and shoved them down into the bag.

"I take it from the scream we heard that he didn't exactly give up voluntarily."

"You probably don't want to know the details," I said, raising an eyebrow.

"Probably not," she said.

"Maybe you could call Agent Franklin and tell him to collect Novak from the woods."

Her eyebrow lifted to match mine.

"Might take an hour or more," she said. "He'll still be there?"

"Ask him," I said, pointing at Magnus, who was stowing the goggles in his top case.

"You bet," Magnus said with a thin smile. "He'll still be there next week. So tell them to take their sweet time."

CHAPTER 37

BY 11 O'CLOCK the vast concrete basin of the main Pentagon parking lot was awash in gleaming chrome and polished paint. As the bikes rolled in, volunteers had parked them in dense, neat rows, packing the motorcycles in tightly but leaving walk-around room between the rows.

Riders and passengers sat patiently on their bikes or walked the rows talking quietly, making new friends and admiring the hardware. Some ate burgers or BBQ sandwiches purchased from vendors set up in tents along the outer edges of the lot. As we eased slowly by, I saw a small crowd gathered in front of a booth set up by the Veterans Administration. The entire back of the booth was taken up by a map of the US showing the locations of VA Medical Centers and clinics. Volunteers in red, white and blue vests were handing out brochures and talking with anyone who stopped by. Next to the booth was a large tent with a banner proclaiming "Free Ice Water Here," which I thought was a sensible precaution on the part of the organizers with the air temperature hovering unseasonably around 80°.

We were near the middle of the vast pack of machinery. For a while there was nothing to do but wait. And hope that

Virgil was OK. I sat astride the Road King, stretched across the tank with my elbows braced on the handlebars, and tried not to worry. The girls leaned against their saddles with their legs crossed out in front of them. Magnus announced suddenly that a guy's got to keep his strength up, and he hauled Ace off in search of sandwiches. They returned about twenty minutes later with a bag of foil-wrapped barbecue sandwiches and cold cans of coke. Both looked overly nonchalant, and Magnus passed out the food with more banter than usual. I wondered if they had been up to something more than buying food, but one bite of the surprisingly good sandwich diverted my attention. It wasn't Betty Jo Bob's, but it was damn good and I didn't realize I was so hungry.

When the food and drink was gone, I gathered up the trash and said I was going to stretch my legs. Winter Rose decided to join me, then Magnus stood up and said he wanted to take a look around too. Alice and Ace said they would stay with the bikes.

We sauntered along the rows of bikes, admiring the hardware and working our way toward the outer rim of the parking lot. As we passed the VA booth, one of the volunteers held out a slim booklet. I took it mostly out of politeness and stuffed it in my back pocket.

"Will you look at that then!" Magnus said, when we climbed the grassy slope leading up to Highway 27 and turned around for a better look at the mass of bikes. "Must be near a thousand tons of chrome out there."

"What do you think?" I said. "About three quarter Harleys and the rest a mix of every other brand?"

Magnus held a hand up to his forehead like a visor while he continued to scan the sea of machinery.

"Mostly Harleys," he agreed, "although any ride seems welcome."

Winter Rose nodded. "We walked by dozens of sportbikes on the way up here. Suzukis, Yamahas, Hondas – you name it."

"Lots of BMWs, too," I said. "Even a fair number of trikes. Shame that Vince and Sophie aren't here."

Magnus grinned.

"If I downed as many martinis as Sophie did yesterday," he said, "I wouldn't want to be within ten miles of this place when they fire those bikes up."

I smiled too.

"Yeah," I said. "I was glad they were both dead to the world when we left early this morning. I imagine they're still gonna be moving a bit slowly."

We sat on the grass for a few more minutes, soaking up the sun and watching the far side of the lot also fill with motorcycles. Even with the engines off it was an impressive display. Maybe the Pentagon tarmac was simply the most convenient staging area, but the sight of all those bikes parked around the iconic military headquarters like a huge chrome necklace was a powerful image.

"So, then. How we gonna handle the rest of this ride?" Magnus asked, bringing me back to reality.

"I want you and Winter Rose riding point together," I said. "The main route is closed to traffic, so they'll have to park that black pickup on a side street. Remember, Novak said to look left so that narrows it down some. Shouldn't be too hard to spot with an orange flag on it. I'll follow, with Ace on the back of my Road King. Alice will ride trail."

They both nodded.

"I want you to have plenty of time to position yourselves

before we get to that truck, so we'll stay well behind you – a couple of blocks anyway. When you see the truck, ride on past it and pull over. Then come back to the truck on foot."

"No problem," he said. "So now Winter Rose and I have our eyes on the truck. What next?"

"Without Novak, they're down to three men, not counting the General."

"Why leave him out?" Magnus said.

"He's always stayed in the background, hasn't he? I'm betting he's going to be directing the action from a distance today too. Especially here. Washington, DC, during Rolling Thunder? Too much risk."

Magnus nodded.

"OK, so three."

"At least one of the three will be guarding Virgil," I said. "They can't afford to let him escape now. So at most there's only going to be two men with that truck. I'm going to let them see Alice and myself with Ace. Get them focused on us."

"Then Winter Rose and I take them from behind?"

I nodded.

"You two move in quickly, as soon as they lock onto us. When they turn to you, we'll hammer them from our side."

Magnus looked doubtful.

"You better be quick then. Don't forget those MP-5s."

I rubbed a hand over my face and blew out a lungful of frustrated air. Magnus had put his finger right on the problem. The rumbling stream of motorcycles would easily mask the muted clatter of a silenced MP-5. Those boys could open up from behind the truck, take out Ace and a few more of us, and be gone in less than ten seconds. Spectators in the area probably wouldn't even realize something had happened. The General wouldn't get the list, but I feared that he might be willing to take that risk at this point, as long as Ace was out of the picture.

"You're right, Magnus. But Novak was their platoon sergeant, the guy who led them in the field. With him gone, I'm betting these guys don't react too well."

"Tin soldiers, eh?" he said, frowning.

I could tell he was thinking even a tin soldier could spray a lot of death at eight hundred rounds per minute. Any fool with a heavy finger could rip through a thirty round magazine in less than three seconds. Two or three heartbeats.

"It's desperate, I know," I said, "but this is our only chance to save Virgil and Ace. This General, whoever he is, will send Novak's guys out to get us. We've got to use them to get him."

CHAPTER 38

AT 12:00 SHARP, the riders at the front of the line started their engines. The rest of us cranked up too. Some of the bikes roared through loud pipes, some burbled more gently through stock mufflers, but the combined sound was incredible. It rippled in waves across the vast parking lot, building into a visceral crescendo that vibrated through your bones and shivered down your spine like the war cry of fifty thousand soldiers.

Someone at the front gave the sign, and the river of motorcycles flowed out of the lot. There was an elemental force to it, masses of solid metal melting into a liquid that seemed to have a life of its own. It reminded me of lava pouring from a volcano, glowing and irresistible.

By my watch, twelve minutes passed before the front of the line reached us. Magnus and Winter Rose looked over their shoulders at me one last time, then rolled out together. I pulled off to the left with Ace and Alice eased in behind me, allowing the rest of the bikes behind us to go on. After a brief wait, we eased forward too. A gap politely formed to let us rejoin the stream behind a pair of trikes and in front of a trio of custom choppers with wildly raked front forks.

The Rolling Thunder route would take us over the Memorial Bridge, east on Constitution, south on 3rd Street, then west along Independence. The ride officially ends in a lot south of the Lincoln Memorial, but before the day was out I knew bikes would be parked everywhere along the Mall. Speakers and bands were set to entertain later from a stage set up at the head of the Reflecting Pool, but the focus of the day would be on the Vietnam Memorial Wall, where dismounted bikers and visitors by the thousands would trace their fingers over the names of friends and family lost in the war.

The pace was stately, mostly second gear speed, as we followed the snaking line of bikes. Since the entire route had been cordoned off, we had the road to ourselves. Flags decorated every corner. Both sides of the street along the way were packed with spectators. Uniforms, and bits of uniforms, were frequently visible.

The line came to a halt as we approached the east end of the bridge, and I pulled up behind two trikes. Both of them were decorated for the occasion, flying the American flag on the right side and the black and white POW/MIA flag on the left. The one on the left had two bumper stickers plastered to the rear. One read "If you enjoy your freedom, thank a VET," and the other "Liberty is not free!". The other trike had two stickers, one that proclaimed "My daughter is in the US Army" and one from West Point, with the eagle and shield coat of arms. The older couple aboard were presumably the proud parents. On the sidewalk behind the trikes another VA booth had been set up, with the same big map that had been in the booth in the Pentagon lot.

The line of bikes moved again. Alice and I edged forward with them, bending around behind the Lincoln Memorial and heading toward Constitution Ave. As the VA booth slid out of my peripheral vision, an outrageous thought struck me like a thunderbolt.

I swerved out of line and hit the brakes hard enough to skid to a stop at the curb. The sudden stop caught Ace by surprise and the side of his helmet banged off mine with a hard clack. Two of the riders immediately behind me honked and shouted in protest, but nobody crashed and the rest of the motorcade growled on. Alice, also taken by surprise, somehow executed a tight U-turn in the narrow space between the stream of bikes and the curb. She rode back and stopped facing the opposite direction from me, close enough that our legs touched when she put her feet down. Magnus and Winter Rose must have seen the commotion in their mirrors because I saw them duck down a side street to double back.

I stood straddling the Road King and fished the booklet I'd gotten from the first booth out of my pocket. Ace wobbled on the back for a second, then sat quietly. I checked the listing of all VA medical centers and clinics in Georgia. My heart started pounding in my chest. I twisted around and asked Ace for the envelope with his list. He passed it up to me and I checked the last page.

I sank back on the seat and said, "Oh, fuck."

"What?" Alice asked simply. She knew from my face that something was seriously wrong.

Instead of answering her directly, I asked her if she could have Agent Franklin check some records. She killed her engine, pulled an oversized smart phone out of her windshield pouch.

She tucked her sunglasses away in its place and posed with her thumbs ready over the keys.

"What do you need?" she said.

I told her.

Her eyes widened.

"Seriously?"

I nodded.

"I know. It seems impossible, but it's the only thing that makes sense. Just check it out, OK?"

Alice was already tapping the keys at a speed that would have dislocated both my thumbs. She sent the request and we waited. The river of bikes rumbled steadily by. Sweat trickled down the inside of my helmet and irritated the powder burn on my forehead. Winter Rose and Magnus managed to loop back. They stopped alongside and looked at me expectantly. I was about to explain the situation when Franklin sent his answer. Alice scanned her screen, then held it up for me to see. I didn't want to believe the name on the message. But there it was.

Gilbert Rumsdale.

CHAPTER 39

ALICE ROTATED HER phone so that Magnus and Winter Rose could read the name on the screen.

"Your uncle?" Winter Rose said. The astonishment in her voice carried clearly over the collective growl of motorcycle exhaust pipes on the street behind us. "He's behind this?"

Magnus glanced off to our left front, toward Georgetown. He turned back to me with a scowl. "He has a place in DC," he said. "Not far from here, eh?"

I nodded, hardly trusting my voice.

Nobody else said anything either. Even the noise of the motorcycles seemed to fade away.

After a ten count Winter Rose said, "You're going in, aren't you?"

I nodded again. "I have to get Virgil back."

"What about the guys in the truck?" she asked.

"You and Magnus have to take them out."

"You don't want us with you?" Magnus said.

I reached over and placed my hand on Magnus's shoulder. "Nothing I'd like more, but I can't be worrying about my back."

Magnus glanced over at Winter Rose. She had that danger-ous glowing gold fleck look in her eyes again.

"OK then, you can count on us," Magnus said. They hit their starters and rode off.

I cranked the Road King up and slipped back into the stream of motorcycles, Ace still on the back. Alice bumped up on the curb, scattering a few startled spectators as she turned around quickly, and followed. Winter Rose and Magnus continued east on Constitution searching for the truck along the parade route, but Alice and I hooked a left on 21st Street.

After we left Rolling Thunder, the streets seemed nearly deserted. Near the Foggy Bottom metro station, we turned left on I Street and motored down the tree-lined lane, passing one townhouse after another until I found the right address.

It was painted pale yellow. Dark green shutters framed the windows. Flower boxes fastened to the wrought iron porch rail-ing sprouted red and purple petunias. It should have been a cheerful combination, but it filled me with dread.

Granite steps led up from the sidewalk to the polished oak main door. A smaller set of stone steps lead down to another door below street level. Cars were parked hood to trunk along the curb on both sides of the road, except for a space right in front of the townhouse. We pulled in and shut the bikes off.

I kicked the side stand down, parked my helmet over the mirror and looked around the neighborhood. An elderly couple walked by hand in hand, leading a little gray poodle on a red leash. A refrigerated delivery van, advertising Boar's Head deli meats, turned on the street from 26th Street and rattled off to the east. Nothing seemed out of place on the street.

Suddenly a man with a gun bolted out of the basement steps and across the sidewalk. It was Bailey, with an MP-5 in his hands and a toothpick in his mouth as usual. He shoved it against Ace's ribs, using his body to shield the weapon from the couple with the dog.

"Go ahead and dismount, Ace," I said.

When we were all standing, Bailey shifted his toothpick to the side of his mouth and said one word: "Inside."

I walked up the steps and opened the door. Last time I was here, the house seemed friendly and inviting. Now it radiated a dreadful déjà vu.

Bailey prodded me in the back with his gun. He pointed down the hall. I knew where he wanted me to go, but I was rooted in place like an ancient oak. I glanced back, toward the exit. Bailey jabbed me again, harder.

Screw it, I thought. Sometimes there are no choices. You just have to keep moving forward. I took a small step, then another. I opened the door and stepped inside.

The room I entered looked distressingly similar to my father's den in our old house in Savannah. It had the same kind of high ceiling and overly generous proportions that made you feel small, like you'd wandered into the house of a giant. Same staid library-style leather furniture, light brown this time, instead of burgundy. Virgil was tied up again, looking as battered and beaten as he had that grim day more than twenty years ago. A blindfold of black cloth was tied over his eyes. A hook-shaped cut sagged open on his cheek. Dried blood caked the side of his face and matted his long hair.

At least he was fully clothed this time. He was sitting in an overstuffed reading chair, his hands tied behind his back. His head was tilted uncomfortably, forced to the side by the long barrel of a .44 Smith and Wesson. Cutcher was pushing it against Virgil's temple again, with the same pleased smile on his face that he'd had in the truck back in North Carolina.

Uncle Gil stood in front of his desk, as my father had stood in front of his so long ago.

CHAPTER 40

UNCLE GIL CRADLED a shotgun casually in his arms. I recognized it with a flash of horror: the old Ithaca 12 gauge double barrel I'd used to kill my father. Uncle Gil had told me he had destroyed it, but this was definitely the same gun – I could see the distinctive v-shaped gash that marred the right side of the stock.

Bailey pushed Alice and Ace forward, lining them up with Alice on my left and Ace next to her. Gilbert motioned with the shotgun. Bailey nodded, then crossed the room and stood on the other side of Virgil's chair, adding his MP-5 to the firepower pointed at Virgil's head.

Two objects sat on the desk near Gilbert's left hand: his Patek Philippe pocket watch and a cell phone identical to the one I'd taken from Novak. He saw me glance at the cell phone. He gave a little resigned nod. I pulled Novak's phone out of my pocket. I pressed "7" and we all waited silently.

Then the phone vibrated against the smooth mahogany. We all watched it with a strange fascination, then Gilbert picked it up and turned it off. He sighed, shook his head, then motioned for Cutcher to remove Virgil's blindfold.

"Oh, right," Cutcher said. "Guess now it don't matter none, does it?" He jerked the cloth up and off.

Virgil blinked against the sudden light. He shook his head to clear his vision, then surveyed the room. When he came to Uncle Gil with the shotgun in his hands, his chin dropped and one unpriestly word escaped his lips.

"Shit!"

Gilbert set the phone back on the desk. He kept the shotgun ready, as though he was next up on the skeet range.

"How did you figure it out, Roman?" he said.

"I didn't. Not until it was too late, anyway."

"Even Novak didn't know who I was."

"No," I said. "He didn't give you away."

"What, then?" he demanded.

"Out there in Rolling Thunder it all finally clicked in my head, but actually it started back there in Savannah. Somebody knew too much right from the start. For instance, how did Novak show up so quickly after Ace arrived at the G-String? You were there. You saw Ace. Then you tipped Novak off."

He kept silent, so I continued.

"When Novak showed up, he searched Ace's car but he didn't search the G-String. He knew Ace didn't bring the list into the building. Because you told him."

He stayed expressionless, didn't deny it.

"Then there was the way Novak blasted away at the bottom bunk and split. He thought he killed Ace, but he only smashed some bathroom fixtures stored under a blanket. At the time all of us were amazed at Ace's luck. If Novak had turned the light on, he would have seen that it wasn't Ace in the bottom bunk. I missed the more important fact that Novak went straight for the storeroom. Why would he do that unless he knew Ace was there? How would he even know there was a bed in that little room? You told him. And you heard me tell the guys to put Ace in the bottom bunk. You didn't know we had to shift him to the top."

"The details," he said. "It's always in the details." Gilbert gave a little snort, a quick shake of the head. "Anything else?"

"After the attack at the G-String, Magnus said we were fortunate that your men aimed too high. It wasn't a mistake, was it? You told them to aim high. Plus, why outfit the MP-5s with silencers?"

Gilbert gave me a bleak smile.

"And?" he said.

"I think you needed Ace, but you didn't want to kill anyone else. So you sprayed the place with automatic fire, but kept it over our heads. Same rationale for the silencers – you wanted commotion, but not police."

"That's it?" he said.

I shook my head.

"It should have been enough to clue me in, but I still didn't have my brain in gear. I was blindsided by that ambush outside Cherokee. The location and the timing were damn near perfect. Novak knew right where we would be and when. How? You told him."

He acknowledged that bit of news with a nod.

"And then I kept trying to work out where somebody like Novak, a relative newcomer to this country, got all the weapons. Silenced MP-5s? A sniper rifle that belonged to the Savannah SWAT team? When everything else fell into place, I realized that a nationally ranked skeet shooter like yourself, with so many contacts in the police and government, would know where to get firepower like that."

I shook my head at my own denseness. I should have seen the pattern much sooner.

"But like I said, all of that fell into place later," I went on, "after two things hit me during the Rolling Thunder ride. The first came from seeing the map at the Veterans Administration booth over in the Pentagon parking lot. The back of the booth was a huge map of the US, with all the VA medical centers and clinics labeled on it. I looked at it while we were waiting for the ride to begin, then I saw it again as we exited the parking area. I remembered Ace said that somebody must have inside access to the VA records and it occurred to me that those clinics were all connected to the VA system. Stupidly, I still didn't figure it out. That finally came when we were already out on the street with the rest of the riders. I damn near caused a major pile-up of motorcycles when I pulled over and asked Special Agent Cushner to check the records for the hospital you own, United Mercies. In addition to the main hospital, it turns out you have six small satellite clinics around the state. The one in Macon is leased to the Veteran's Administration."

"And the second thing?" Gilbert asked.

"This," I said, holding out the list Ace had given me. "Something bothered me about the two names written on the bottom, Beardsley and Price. After I'd worked out the VA clinic connection, I realized what it was. See the way the letter "e" is finished off on the end of Price? It's subtle, but there's a distinctive little whip at the end." I looked up at Gilbert. "That's the way you sign your name. You wrote those two names."

Gilbert looked at me oddly, a strange cross between chagrin and pride.

"If anyone was ever going to figure it out, I thought it would be you, Roman."

"Why?" I asked.

"Because you are most like – "

"Not why me," I said, cutting him off. "Why… why this?" I swept a hand out to encompass all of us, Virgil with his battered face, the guns. "Why the fraud? And above all, why the murders? You're a successful businessman from an old family. You have money. You have prestige. How much more do you need?"

At first he didn't respond. Then he pointed the shotgun to the side and stepped close to me. His face was flushed, his lips a tight thin line. His eyes radiated a fury that I'd never seen before. He looked so angry, so close to losing control, I thought he might swing the butt of the shotgun at my head. I tensed, ready to move.

Instead, he took a deep breath and leaned even closer. When he spoke his voice was harsh and scratchy with anger.

"They killed me when they threw me out of West Point."

He stepped back a bit, and shook his head slowly, just a millimeter from side to side.

"The family money was long gone by then, thanks to my father and his brother."

He relaxed his jaw enough to give a little snort of disgust.

"Brainless bastards, both of them. By the time I was eighteen, there was no portfolio of stocks, no fat bank account. Nothing! The old house was mortgaged to the hilt. The IRS was hounding my father for a fortune in past taxes and penalties."

He raised his chin and looked around the room. He seemed to regain his self-control. He moved back to the desk and leveled the shotgun again.

"The Point was my last hope," he said. "As an Army officer, I would continue a long, illustrious line of military tradition. It was the path to restored honor for the Rumsdale family, to be readmitted to the inner circle. Loans would have been arranged, bargains struck."

He shook his head again.

"But the real cheater needed a scapegoat and he chose me. And the military morons running the place went along with him."

He hitched the shotgun up under his arm. He looked like he wanted to shoot somebody with it, maybe a lot of people.

"Back in Savannah, I was blacklisted. A lot of sins can be forgiven among the old bloodlines in that city. Adultery, assault, theft, even murder. As long as you're properly repentant, all may be forgiven. But not military dishonor. That stain is permanent."

He paused, eyes narrowed and chin set. Then he gave a little shake and went on.

"I swore I'd get even. I sold everything I could – furniture, jewelry, art – to raise some cash and started my real estate business. It was tough, but I made it."

Gilbert smiled, at least it might have been a smile. It came and went so quickly I wasn't absolutely sure.

"They came crawling back, offering their little honors. The Chamber of Commerce, the City Council, the Police Board. And of course the charities. I was everybody's favorite and I helped them all – hospitals, stray cats and dogs, orphans, you name it. I dipped my toes into politics and found I was exceptionally good at it. I started small in the Chatham County GOP and worked my way up over the years. By the time I was on the Executive Committee, there was talk of the governor's office. Serious talk."

Gilbert stopped abruptly. He turned his head to the side and made a spitting sound, as though something vile had risen in his throat and left a bitter taste on his tongue. He looked back at me.

"Then somebody remembered West Point."

Gilbert chuckled at the thought, if you can call a harsh, dry laugh totally devoid of humor a chuckle.

"Boy, did the air go out of that balloon! 'Sorry, Gil,' they said. 'We can spin away a lot of sins, but not that one. Too many untouchable issues attached to it, like honor, country and patriotism. We need people like you in the party, but public office just ain't gonna happen.'"

Another dry laugh rattled from his throat.

"West Point would just not go away. The consolation prize was a fast track on the Georgia GOP. Fun, but the behind the scenes stuff only goes so far. The *real* power, the *real* prestige is reserved for the man in the office and that door was slammed shut."

He sighed, probably imagining the rides he'd missed in the long gleaming limo, the legions of bowing and scurrying staff he never had, and the luxurious governor's mansion he never enjoyed.

"Then came the mortgage meltdown at the end of the Bush years. It hit me even harder than most. I was thirty days from absolute ruin when you provided my inspiration."

"Me?" I said. "No!"

"Oh, yes. I remember it perfectly. We were having lunch together when you told me about one of your friends who was having trouble getting his veteran's benefits. The whole plan fell into place in my head."

"What plan?" I said.

"You don't know the details – why should you, it was before you were even born – but the cadet who framed me for his cheating was named Martin Deale. That bastard retired after his twenty and is still alive."

"Deale!" I said, glancing quickly over at Alice. We had been on the right track, but we'd let it go. She shrugged and lifted her hands palms up in a "too late now" gesture. I turned back to Gilbert and said, "Deale used to work for Aetna."

"Ah, Roman," Gilbert said. "Always the quickest in the class. Yes, you're right. Brigadier General Martin Deale, US Army Retired, worked briefly for that insurance carrier. He is now a senior financial officer of the Veterans Benefits Administration. He's been in the branch they call the Compensation and Pension Service for the last three years."

"Novak said he only knew his boss as the General," I said. "That was you leaving a trail to Deale?"

"Nice touch, wasn't it? Deale still insists everyone call him General. That idiot even refers to himself as the General."

"You told me somebody named Martin was the agent for the Irish group that bought our old house on West Perry. Another pointer aimed at Martin Deale?"

He nodded without elaborating and I wondered briefly if somehow he'd taken advantage of Virgil and me in the sale of that house.

I said, "So you set up this whole scheme to discredit this guy Deale?"

"Discredit? No! Oh no, that wouldn't be near enough. Destroy! I meant to destroy him! And it was perfect. So much money, so little oversight. It was easy to steal, and even easier to point all the evidence right at Deale. Once I had the access, it was simply a matter of recruiting the right people to carry it out. Including your friend here, Mr. Emory."

"Fraud is one thing," I said, "but murder?"

Gilbert shrugged.

"The one led to the other. Deale would wiggle out of the fraudulent claims with a slap on the wrist, Roman. You knew he was hired by one of the big insurance companies after he retired, but did you know he left under a cloud of embezzlement accusations?"

I just nodded mutely.

"He paid back a bit over half of the money he stole, then Aetna let him go rather than air their dirty laundry in public. It made setting him up for fraud and identity theft easier, but white-collar crime like that wouldn't be enough. I wanted him to *burn*. For that you need murder."

What do you say to a staggering revelation like that?

"What happens now?" I asked. "Where can we possibly go from here?"

Now he smiled, a genuine smile that reminded me I had called him *Uncle Gil* nearly all my life.

"You let me slip away."

"What?!"

He shook his head.

"Martin Deale doesn't go down in flames," he said, "and that's a disappointment for sure. But this operation has netted plenty of money. I can just disappear." He nodded off to the side where Virgil was under the guns of his men. "I can even give the boys here enough cash to do the same."

"Why the hell would I...?"

He cut me off by raising the barrel of the shotgun.

"You recognize this shotgun?" he said.

I nodded cautiously. As if I could forget that shotgun.

"Well?" he said when I remained silent.

I shook my head, kept my lips clamped shut.

Gilbert gave a dry laugh.

"Always been stubborn as a mountain of granite," he said. "Both you and your brother. All right, I'll enlighten the rest of the folks here in the room."

He held the Ithaca up so everyone could see it.

"Roman thinks he blew his father's brains out with this shotgun."

I didn't turn my head, but I could hear Alice suck in her breath. Like everyone, she'd heard the stories about my father's death. The details varied, but in all of them he killed himself. Gilbert's cover up had held together all these years.

"I know what I did," I said.

He shook his head.

"You know you killed *somebody*," he said.

To Alice, he added, "He did it in self defense, of course."

To me he said, "You're just mistaken about who you killed."

Now it was my turn to shake my head.

I said, "There was no mistake. I killed my father, Randall Keane."

"You're half right," he said. "You killed a man named Randall Keane, but he wasn't your father."

"What?"

"Randall Keane was not your father," Gilbert said. "I am."

CHAPTER 41

I DIDN'T BELIEVE IT. Neither did anyone else in the room, judging by the stunned expressions. Virgil's mouth actually hung open.

"That's absurd! You're not even my real uncle, much less my father."

"I can prove I'm your father right now."

"Now? Here? How?"

"Smile."

I refused to give him the satisfaction. A stone bust had nothing on me.

He shrugged.

"OK, now's not the time for smiling. But when you smile, you've got a dimple in your cheek."

Keeping the shotgun on me with his right hand, he waved his left at Virgil, who had also clamped his jaw obstinately tight.

"So does Virgil. You have them on opposite sides, but you both have them."

"So?" I said, wondering what he was getting at.

"Randall Keane didn't have dimples. Neither did your mother."

I could only nod at that. It was true.

He gave a ghastly imitation of a smile and put his finger to his cheek.

"I have one on my left cheek!"

The light was dawning now. Dimples are inherited.

"You and Virgil were about a year old when your mother made the connection. She was horrified that someone would notice. Made me start growing a beard that same day. I've had it ever since."

From the chair, Virgil said, "If you're our father, why didn't you marry our mother?"

Gilbert kept his eyes and his gun on me as he answered, as though I'd asked the question instead of Virgil.

"We were all so young. Your mother. Me. Her fiancé."

"Fiancé?" Virgil said.

"Not the man you knew as your father," Gilbert said. "Another man. His name was John McDaniel."

Virgil and I looked at each other.

"I see you know the name," Gilbert said.

"We came across an old photo once, up in the attic," I said. "It was a picture of our mother with a man we'd never seen before. His name was written on the back, inside a heart. When we asked Mom, she snatched it out of Virgil's hand and said it was an old boyfriend from high school."

"Well, that part at least was the truth. The three of us, John, me and your mother were close all through high school. Grade school, too, for that matter."

He chuckled. "We were inseparable. Called ourselves the Three Musketeers. Your mother flirted with us both, but all three of us knew she'd marry John someday. Then the Army reached into our lives."

He grew serious again. "I won an appointment to West Point, but John was drafted. The day he left for Vietnam, he asked your mother to marry him. She said yes, of course. Six months later, I was thrown out for cheating. When I got home, your mother tried to raise my spirits. We had our own little party. We toasted the Three Musketeers. We drank – too much. The next thing we knew we were in bed together."

He puffed his cheeks, blew out a breath of air. "Never happened before or since. You can imagine your mother's reaction the next morning. A single, highly religious, high society woman sleeping with a disgraced ex-West Pointer? While she was engaged to an honorable soldier serving in Vietnam, no less? She was mortified. No, mortified isn't strong enough. She was beside herself. Throw-yourself-off-the-roof-disconsolate. I swore I'd never say a word. It would be like it never happened."

He seemed to look inward for a moment. He shook his head slowly.

"We were kidding ourselves. What's done is done. You can hide it, but you can't change it."

He took a deep breath and favored us with a manic smile.

"Meanwhile, my parents had called in every favor they had left in Savannah to try and bury the cheating scandal. An old friend of the family was taking his yacht around the world. They arranged for me to be a 'guest.' More like a crewmember it turned out. Anyway, I would have had to leave the planet to be more out of touch.

"Two days after I left, your mother learned that John had been killed in action. She was convinced he died at the exact hour we'd been in bed. Three weeks after she got the news about John's death, she learned that she was pregnant."

That explained a lot about my mother. It was easier now to

understand her extreme sense of guilt and her willingness to be "punished by God for my sins."

"The man you knew as your father, Randall Keane, was simply a convenient face saver."

He stole a look at Virgil, then came back to me. For a brief second he seemed like the man I'd always known as my uncle again – kind and concerned.

"I would have married her, you know. But I didn't even know she was pregnant until after you two were born."

In the silence that followed that proclamation, Virgil and I sought each other's eyes. Once more our world had been turned upside down. Our entire childhood had been one big lie, our adult lives launched from a lie. All those years struggling with a guilt that was not ours. What do you do when the foundation of your whole world is a fabrication?

Ace broke the spell, tottering on his feet, nearly losing his balance. He looked like exactly what he was: an alcoholic wishing he was within arm's reach of a fat tumbler filled with mind-numbing amber whiskey. His hands trembled like some- one suffering from a sudden onset of the DTs. He flexed his fingers, then tightened them into fists. Finally he gave up and stuffed both hands in his pockets. He clamped his eyes shut like he wished he could make the whole world disappear.

The two men standing over Virgil with their guns snickered as Ace wobbled. Gilbert cut them off with a quick hard glance, but couldn't hide his own smirk.

"He may not look it at the moment," he told us, "but Mr. Emory here is another of my little successes."

"Yeah," I said, "he told me you kept him from being charged with drunk driving or manslaughter after the accident that killed his wife."

"Did he tell you about the car?"

Ace's head came up, a startled look on his face. I sensed another bomb about to drop.

"What about the car?" I asked.

Gilbert waved the gun casually. "The police impounded it, but it was never examined. Somehow, it was released with two others to be auctioned off."

"You bought it?" I said.

"Me? Of course not. Emil Novak bought it. On my instructions, of course. I had him take it straight to the crusher."

Ace managed one word. "Why?"

"To hide the fact that the steering had been tampered with," Gilbert said. "Earlier on the day of the party Novak cut through most of the steering column. Every turn made it weaker and weaker. Eventually it simply broke and presto – instant accident."

"But why?" Ace said again.

"To eliminate your wife! I knew she was pressuring you to quit drinking, to get yourself rehabilitated and start over. But I was in too deep to let that happen. How do you think I stayed afloat when the real estate market went up in flames like the Hindenburg? Thanks to the cash you laundered, I grew while everyone else shrunk."

He shook his head, then he said, "You almost spoiled everything. You weren't even supposed to be in that car. I counted on you being drunk in your office or some bar as usual, but the fates were looking kindly on me. She was killed and you weren't even scratched."

A sob wracked Ace's thin body. He doubled over at the waist, like he'd been kicked in the stomach.

While attention was on Ace, Alice shifted her weight, but the telltale move wasn't lost on Gilbert. Her thumb had already released the snap on her holster when Gilbert stopped her by pivoting the Ithaca in my direction. The barrels pointed precisely at my eyes and twin black holes looked as large as howitzers.

"No, no, Agent Cushner. Not unless you want Roman to die exactly like his... well, let's just call the man his stepdad."

Her shoulders sagged. She dropped her arm away from her pistol.

"Don't worry, Al," I said. "Why should he kill us? He's got enough money to live like a king somewhere else. Someplace where he can't be extradited."

Gilbert nodded.

"He's right. Time for Plan B. These days the smart people go to the Philippines or the Maldives. Ten or twelve hours head start and I'm out of here. Free and clear. All I need is some help from my *son*."

He said "son" with a special emphasis, like I should forgive everything because that's what a son does for his father. I couldn't help but notice that the shotgun stayed locked on my face, though. Gilbert held it steady with both hands, watching me carefully over the tops of the barrels.

I took a deep breath, felt my heart slow to a steady ka-thump, ka-thump. The people in the room snapped into sharper focus; the walls receded. Time shifted into overdrive. I'd felt this way before, in the heat of a firefight or the moment before springing an ambush.

I looked over at Ace. He had straightened up and his breathing had steadied. His hands were still jammed in his pockets, but I saw him roll his shoulders fractionally to release the tension in his upper body. His eyes were open, small slits that didn't blink.

I slid my eyes in Virgil's direction, paused for a microsecond, then swiveled back to Gilbert.

He said, "Take that pistol out of Agent Cushner's holster. Slowly now, Roman. Left hand, two fingers only."

I reached out for Alice's gun. With my thumb and forefinger, I eased the Sig upward an inch.

"Easy…" Gilbert cautioned. "*Easy!*"

His voice drew my eyes his way for an instant, and I saw an infinite sadness in his eyes. I saw a man who knew he'd fucked up in the biggest way possible. I realized he must have known he had no options left as soon as I walked in the door. All that flashed between us in a microsecond, and I knew that Plan B wasn't life in exile with his stolen money. He had just made a full confession. He knew this was the end.

I saw his finger tighten on the trigger and the barrel swing toward Virgil. Gilbert didn't have the nerve to kill himself, but he knew I wouldn't let him kill Virgil.

I dropped my hand onto the Sig's grip, snatched it from Alice's holster and fired.

I hit Gilbert center of mass as he pulled his trigger. The shotgun jerked up with the impact of my bullet. The dense wad of pellets from the shotgun crunched into the ceiling with a tremendous bang, showering half the room with plaster dust. I pivoted toward Virgil, my heart sinking. I knew that no matter how fast I was, I was too late. Cutcher was going to kill Virgil with his Dirty Harry magnum. Bailey was going to mow the rest of us down with one lethal rip from the MP-5.

What happened in that instant amazed us all.

With a smooth, fluid motion, faster than the eye could follow, Ace whipped Magnus's little Colts out of his pants. Before he could possibly have aimed, almost before the barrels cleared his pockets, both pistols went off with a single sharp crack.

I looked across the room at Gilbert's two thugs. Each had a

small black hole precisely centered above his nose, in the exact middle of his forehead. Dead on their feet, they toppled into each other like felled trees and crashed to the carpet with a heavy thud.

Gilbert watched them go down. He shook his head side-to-side slowly, unable to believe the speed of it. He turned back to me. His mouth hung open. Even behind the beard I could see the color had drained from his face.

"That," I said to his stunned eyes, "is why we call him Ace."

He dropped the shotgun and clutched his chest with both hands. Bright red blood leaked through his fingers. He coughed lightly, a tiny spasm. More like a hiccup. The red trickle became a flood. He stared down at it, closed his fingers in a futile attempt to stem the tide. He staggered backward, bounced off his desk, dropped to his knees and pivoted onto his face. He hit the floor hard, rebounding with the careless finality of the dead.

My ears were ringing like fire alarms from the sudden gunfire, but Alice's voice, high and clear, penetrated the din.

"Holy crap!"

No one else said a word and no one moved. My legs felt like they had turned to stone. Even the air, tinged with the acrid tang of burned cordite, seemed heavy.

Then I felt Alice's hand on my shoulder. She reached across and gently retrieved her pistol. She thumbed the safety lever down to drop the hammer and slipped it back into her holster.

Ace clicked the safeties up on both pistols and offered them butt first to Alice.

"Magnus loaned me these before the ride this morning," he said. "Would you see that he gets them back?"

She took them carefully, a new look of respect on her face.

"I don't think that will be a problem, *Ace*," she said.

I crossed the room to Virgil, who was still sitting on the chair with his arms tied behind his back. I slipped the knife off my belt and sliced quickly through the ropes. He stood up and we hugged each other tightly.

CHAPTER 42

THE REST OF the day was the definition of tedium. Alice switched effortlessly to her official persona: Special Agent Cushner of the United States Secret Service. First she asked Ace to sit in the armchair on the far side of the desk, then she moved Virgil to the couch and let him lie down. After she had him as comfortable as possible, she called for paramedics. She wheeled the padded office chair behind Gilbert's desk over to the wall by the armoire and parked me in it. I noticed that she had neatly arranged it so that we were separated from each other and from the bodies, but we were all contained within her sight. Then she called Special Agent Franklin for the second time this morning.

He must have been sitting nearby waiting for her call, because he came striding through the door of Gilbert's townhouse in less than five minutes. He stopped for a moment just inside the study and stood with his feet spread and his hands on his hips. I couldn't decide if he was studying the scene or posing for a photo op. Alice stepped over and talked to him earnestly for a couple of minutes. Finally she pointed a hand in the direction of the chair where I had been quarantined. I stood as they approached and when he smiled genially and tried to crush my fingers with a hearty man-to-man handshake, I was ready for it.

Alice was right, he was already starring in his own movie. He had adopted that no-nonsense, mile-a-minute attitude that Tommy Lee Jones had portrayed so well in *The Fugitive*, but the act was almost comical in real life. I was glad he was here, though. I thanked him for responding so quickly.

"Just doing my job," he said, smiling modestly. Then he waved an arm over his head like a cavalry commander and unleashed a squad of agents and technicians.

They examined, marked, measured and photographed every detail from floor to ceiling. The DC police made a brief appearance in the form of two detectives and a uniformed officer, but then gratefully left the whole mess to the Secret Service.

Alice had disappeared moments after Franklin's grand entrance. When she returned about twenty minutes later, she told me that she had gone out with two agents supplied by Franklin to look for Magnus and Winter Rose. She said she found them sitting on the lowered tailgate of a black pickup with an orange T-shirt wrapped around the driver's side mirror, the same truck Novak had been driving with Virgil in the back yesterday. They had been talking about repainting Winter Rose's Ninja.

After Alice had introduced the agents with her, Magnus and Winter Rose slid off the tailgate and stepped aside to reveal the back of the pickup bed. Manion was lying there, hogtied. His nose was smashed flat and he appeared relieved to see Alice and the two agents. Apparently, he had tried to take Magnus hand-to-hand.

I grinned at the thought.

I said, "Manion might have had twenty or thirty pounds

advantage, but it was stupid of him to think he could take Magnus. Nobody's faster."

"He can ponder his mistake all the way to the emergency room," she said. "Speaking of which, Emil Novak was successfully treated for a gunshot wound to the leg and is in custody in the Reston Hospital out near Dulles airport. Seems he had a perforated eardrum, two broken ribs and a cracked sternum as well."

She arched an eyebrow at me.

Keeping my expression as deadpan as possible, I said, "It was dark out there in the woods, Alice. Maybe he ran into a tree and fell on a rock."

"Yeah, sure," she said. "An oak named Magnusson and a chunk of granite named Keane."

Fortunately for me, Franklin grabbed her elbow and started to pull her toward the other side of the room, so she quickly told me that Magnus and Winter Rose were outside and we could hook up later.

The paramedics wheeled an ambulance gurney into the room, zeroed in on Virgil without hesitation and measured his vitals. They jabbed a needle into the back of his hand, hooked him up to an IV bag and announced that they were transporting him to Georgetown University Hospital. They let me say good-bye. He said he felt like crap, but then he'd just been worked over physically and emotionally. I didn't want to delay his departure, so I just told him I'd call Doc Lukens and get him to run things at St. George's for a while. That got a weak smile and a grateful nod.

When Virgil was gone, I checked with Alice to make sure it was OK, then made the call to Doc Lukens. As usual, he agreed to help without the slightest hesitation. When I finished the call, a wave of exhaustion washed over me. I'd been up since three in the morning. Our counter-ambush in the woods at Manassas seemed like it happened a week ago. Even the incredible experience of riding in Rolling Thunder had faded into the distant past. Only the events in this room seemed real and all I wanted to do was put them out of my mind forever.

The bodies made that impossible. They had been left as they fell. I could at least partly ignore the two thugs that Ace had killed. They lay crumpled on the other side of the room behind the big chair Virgil had occupied. The remains of Gilbert Rumsdale were much closer to me. The crimson pool under his chest slowly spread another inch in diameter. He seemed to shrink inside his clothes as I watched. Old memories haunted me again. The spell was broken when a female medical examiner arrived with her assistant. She worked in silence until she turned over the bodies of the two gunmen who had been guarding Virgil. When she saw the identical bullet holes centered in their foreheads, she gave a low whistle and straightened up.

"Is this your work?" she asked, looking over at me.

I shook my head and pointed at Ace.

She followed the direction of my finger and seemed to notice him for the first time. He was easy to overlook – a skinny figure nearly swallowed up by the big easy chair where Alice had parked him, knees together and his hands tucked tightly under his armpits.

She turned back to me and asked, "He's one of the good guys, right?"

"Definitely," I said.

She winked at Ace and said, "Nice shooting, then."

Ace managed a wan smile.

The tech who had been videoing the proceedings mounted

his camera on a tripod and set it in front of my chair. When he gave them a nod, two agents brought wooden chairs in from the dining room and arranged them on either side of the camera. They introduced themselves as Special Agents Graham Connor and Stephen Jackson, passed me a cold can of Coke, then they took me through the whole story. It took about three hours, with frequent questions to clarify or amplify points as we went along. On the other side of the room, I could see two more agents quietly doing the same with Ace.

Alice, still in the Special Agent Cushner mode, waited until the agents were finished with their interview before she updated me on Virgil's condition. She said he was OK, but frowned when she said it.

"They said it's probably nothing to worry about, but he might be concussed. He might have some internal injuries, too. So they're going to do some tests. They'll keep him overnight."

She introduced me to two new pairs of agents, from the FBI and ATF. She asked me to summarize the whole story for them. I did, starting with Ace's sudden appearance at the G-String. Even pared to bare bones the story took twenty minutes, with the junior agents of each pair taking notes as I spoke. When I finished, the senior agents asked a few questions. They retired to separate corners, one for the FBI pair and one for the ATF, and conferred in hushed tones for a few minutes. Then they all shook hands with me, thanked me for my time and left.

After I sat back down Alice touched my shoulder, bent close to my ear and whispered, "Guarding their turf. But don't worry…"

She broke off when shouts suddenly erupted from the front of the house. She patted my hand to indicate I should stay where I was, then she hurried toward the commotion. Nearly fifteen minutes passed before she returned, obviously suppressing a smile.

She plopped back into the chair beside mine and said, "That was Brian Blount, a.k.a 'Bulldog.' Seems that Special Agent Blount spent all day chasing his stubby bulldog tail around Savannah yesterday and just got to the party here in DC. As you heard, he arrived in a state of high agitation, practically foaming at the mouth." She rolled her eyes theatrically to show what she thought of his antics. "Special Agent Franklin sent him scurrying off. Old Bulldog probably never thought he'd run into someone even more ambitious than himself. Like I was about to say, don't worry – this case is staying with us."

Alice left and I sat until Special Agent Connor escorted me to the half bath down the hall around six o'clock. When I finished, he was waiting in the hall with Magnus. He gave me that wide Magnusson grin and punched me on the shoulder hard enough to lift my heels off the ground.

"Glad to see you're alive, RK, but geez! First, I miss all the real action. Then, I have to sit on my ass outside all afternoon. But Alice's been a sweetheart, eh. She came out when they took Ace off to headquarters or wherever the hell they went. So she made them let Winter Rose go along."

He stopped talking to shake his head and snicker over the image.

"Told them Winter Rose was his sister – his only living relative, can you believe it? Ha! Like those two could be related. So the guy leading Ace gave Alice this you-better-be-kidding-me look, and she said, 'Step-sister, step-sister.'"

I asked him how it went out on the street and he told me Winter Rose had made the whole thing easy.

"She spotted the pickup two blocks away, RK, and sent me

around the block so I could come up from behind. So that's what I did, dontcha know. Then I don't know who was more surprised at what happened next, me or that Manion guy." He shook his head and gave us one of his biggest white grins. "Just as I round the last corner, Winter Rose comes tooling up fast. I mean fast, RK. Then she stands that gray rocket ship of hers on its nose. Balanced it up on the front wheel 'til she was nearly on his toes, then she finally lets the rear wheel come down. Easy like, though. Nice as you please, like she was riding through the park on Sunday. That Manion, he stood there with his mouth open until I tapped him on the shoulder." He shook his head again at the memory of it, then he said, "But that Winter Rose, eh? Woman can ride!"

Connor smiled the way everyone does the first time they hear Magnus unleash his Minnesota enthusiasm. He pointed us further down the hall, into the dining room, rather than back into the den. Like the rest of the townhouse, the dining room was high ceilinged and grand, with a massive mahogany table centered under a crystal and silver chandelier. A crowd of agents and techs sat around the table. Franklin motioned us inside.

"Consider this a tactical retreat from the living room while the coroner removes the bodies," Franklin said. "No sense blocking their way."

The look on Alice's face told me Franklin didn't want to watch the grisly process of peeling the bodies off the floor and stuffing them into body bags anymore than the rest of us did.

Alice, Magnus and I found places together at the far end of the table. After Magnus got his long legs adjusted under the table, he turned to me and said, "So then, RK. You mad about the guns?"

I shook my head.

"We were dead in there, Magnus. I was fast enough to nail Uncle – I mean Gilbert Rumsdale – but those two thugs of his had us cold with a .44 magnum and an MP-5 on full auto. Then Ace whipped your Colts out of his pockets like a magician."

I let a beat go by, then I said, "Besides, I was counting on it."

"What?"

I grinned.

"I knew you gave him the guns."

"What?"

I laughed.

"Back in the Pentagon parking lot – before the ride started, when you two came back with the sandwiches. You and Ace were like a couple of kids with a new secret. Afterwards Ace kept sticking his hands in his pockets to check on the guns. Hell, he almost fell off the back of the Road King once."

Magnus's mouth dropped open, then he threw his head back and let loose a single, loud, "Hah!" Then he clapped a big hand on my shoulder and said, "So anyway, when can I get them back?"

"You'll have to ask Special Agent Cushner," I said, pointing at Alice.

"They're evidence now, Magnus," she said, "but I'll get them back to you as soon as I can. Don't hold your breath, though. It's going to be a couple of months, at least."

"Thanks, Alice," Magnus said. "As long as you're looking out for them, I'm good. Got a couple of those new Smith and Wesson Bodyguard 380s back home, dontcha know. A guy could make do with them for now."

I said, "That Ithaca shotgun is actually mine – well, mine and Virgil's. Can I get it back?"

Alice looked at me in surprise.

"Of course, RK! Unless Rumsdale made a will that says otherwise, everything is yours – except any proceeds from his criminal activities. Family heirlooms will certainly go to you and Virgil. You two are his only sons, right?"

It hadn't occurred to me. Not for a second. But it did make me feel a little better about the Patek Philippe watch I had in my pocket. I'd palmed it after the shooting, when I crossed by Rumsdale's desk to cut Virgil loose. Nobody, including Alice, seemed to notice that it was missing. I had an idea about that watch, and I wanted to run it by Ace later.

Somebody opened the door and crooked a finger at Franklin. He conferred with them briefly, then announced that the bodies had been removed and the techs had packed up their recorders and camera. All the agents rose and pocketed their notebooks.

The wrap-up proceeded swiftly from that point, and by quarter after seven Alice, Magnus and I were standing in the hall, ready to go. One last pair of agents was checking the house room-by-room to make sure it was ready to be sealed.

"They took Rumsdale's computer and everything from his desk," Alice said. "Of course, they'll do the same with his office and his house in Georgia."

"Ace told me his laptop and cell phone are missing," I said. "They might turn up at Rumsdale's house too."

She nodded.

"I'll make sure they look for them."

"Alice," I said, "when – or maybe I should say, if – they find the money Rumsdale stole, where does it go?"

"Interesting question. Most of it, if I understand the whole scheme properly, was outright fraud. The money was stolen from the U.S. government based on invented claims. A smaller portion, belonging to the murdered veterans, would have been legitimately paid to them during their lives. Unfortunately their benefits terminated with their deaths, so even that money was fraudulently obtained."

She shrugged.

"The department attorneys will have to figure it out, but most likely any money recovered will either be added to the Secret Service budget or simply go back into the treasury."

She paused, then said, "I'm supposed to give both of you the 'keep your mouth shut' speech."

I glanced at Magnus.

"Don't worry," I said. "We know Ace's future is hanging in the balance. Neither of us is going to talk to anyone."

She looked carefully at each of us, then she nodded her head in satisfaction.

"All right. I'm going over to the field office, but you guys are free to go."

She stopped with one hand on the knob.

"I'll guide you. It's a media zoo out there. Special Agent Franklin's holding court."

She flashed a quick smile.

"Probably leaked the news himself. We've got vans from CNN, FOX and two local stations out in the street. The reporters are roaming around with their cameramen looking for anyone with a crumb of news who's willing to talk on camera. The whole area directly out front is packed with official vehicles, but I had our bikes moved to the alley before the news people showed up. I think we can get away clean. Ready?"

She pushed the door open and we piled out quickly.

CHAPTER 43

AFTER ALICE RODE off, I swung a leg over my Road King, but Magnus stood on the pavement morosely looking over the damage to his Ultra.

"Made up my mind, RK," he said. "I'm gonna sell her, eh. Fly home after this job."

"Sell Eloise? Really?"

He pursed his lips together and nodded seriously.

"Yep. She won't ever be the same."

Then he raised his eyebrows and lit up the evening sky with that big grin of his.

"Had my eye on a CVO Street Glide anyway. Bigger engine. Nice machine."

"Won't you feel bad about selling her?"

Magnus gave me the look one five-year-old kid gives another who just doesn't get it.

"She doesn't go away, RK. The new bike will be Eloise too, you bet."

"Eloise II? Like with Roman numerals?"

He shook his head.

"Not Eloise the second, just Eloise."

"Ah," I said, pretending complete denseness, "*Just Eloise.*"

"Scoff if you like," Magnus said.

I relented. "Are you ever going to tell me about Eloise?" I said.

Magnus turned his head to the skyline and looked off into infinity for a moment.

"Sure, RK," he said. "Someday."

"Look, how about letting Ace ride Eloise back to Savannah for you?"

"What? Why?"

"You'll get a better price at home, after you've fixed some of the easy stuff."

"Well, that's true…"

"And it gives you a chance to change your mind. Just in case."

"There's that," he agreed. He looked relieved that the decision to sell was no longer irrevocable. He mounted up and said, "So you think he can handle her then?"

I nodded.

"He's an experienced rider. Had a nice old Bonneville for years. Did all right with my Road King too, remember? Besides, Winter Rose will shepherd him along."

I could almost see the wheels turning as Magnus gave the notion some thought. Finally he gave an emphatic nod.

"That's sweet with me. Tell him OK," he said.

"Great. And listen, leave the night vision goggles in the tour pack. Ace and Winter Rose can drop them off in Cherokee on their way back to Savannah."

"No problem," he said, twisting the ignition switch. "You got a place to stay tonight? You can bunk down with me if you want. My client's got a huge suite reserved. Plenty of room."

"What's your client going to say?"

Magnus shrugged.

"She won't care, eh. Probably try to eat us both alive if you're still there when she arrives tomorrow night."

"What hotel?"

"Mayflower Renaissance. A guy could do worse."

I flashed him a thumbs up and hit the starter.

"You bet!" I said.

CHAPTER 44

A T HALF PAST eight the next morning, I stepped out of the elevator at the Secret Service field office on Connecticut Avenue wearing a visitor's badge the guard in the lobby had given me. I walked down the corridor to the left as instructed and spotted Alice at her loaner desk. She looked very official among the other Secret Service agents who worked their phones and keyboards with quiet intensity. She was wearing a cream skirt with a matching jacket over a pale green silk blouse that accented her red hair nicely. Sensible heels in matching green elevated her to the stratospheric altitude of five feet four. I wondered where the hell she had stashed that outfit on her Softail, then I remembered she and her husband have a place here in D.C. No doubt she has a closet full of business suits and high heels there as well as in her rented apartment in Savannah.

"Special Agent Cushner," I said, slipping into the empty chair at the side of her desk.

She looked up from the report she'd been reading intently and smiled.

"Mr. Keane," she said.

When she glanced quickly at the agent sitting within earshot at the next desk, I was glad I hadn't called her Alice, or worse yet, Big Al. She stuffed the report in a drawer and stood up.

"The conference room is open," she said. "Let's walk down the hall."

I followed her to a door marked, appropriately, "Conference Room 1". It was a small space, with eight black vinyl chairs crowded around a wood veneer table that looked like it had been ordered from the dining room section of the Ikea catalog. Alice took the chair at the head of the table closest to the door. I sat at the next one on the corner.

She gave me a wistful smile and said, "I've got good news and more good news – and bad news and more bad news."

I matched her smile and said, "Good news first."

She took a deep breath and said, "With Gilbert Rumsdale dead, Novak and Manion are climbing over each other to cooperate. As far as any criminal acts go, the consensus among our attorneys is that Ace was completely coerced. They're not particularly happy that he came to you instead of the police, but I'm pretty sure the department is going to offer him immunity in return for his testimony."

I thumped the table lightly with my fist. "That's great news!"

She held up a palm.

"It's not written in stone yet – there are a lot of details to work out – but the truth is the head of the Veteran's Administration is leaning on my chief to make this go away with minimum publicity."

She leaned back in her chair and gave a little unladylike snort.

"As if multiple murders of military veterans by a gang using confidential VA records could slide by in this town. And to make sure the media is whipped into a frenzy, the head of the whole shebang turns out to be a well-respected Savannah businessman and southern aristocrat who is shot to death in a swanky Georgetown row home by a decorated former Ranger."

I'd watched a few minutes of the news this morning, before I left the hotel.

"All the cable news stations had the bit in their teeth this morning," I said. "The usual breathless on-scene reporting on the sidewalk outside the townhouse. Not much substance this early in the game, but since when have they ever let that stop them?"

She shook her head.

"Don't worry," she said. "The frantic coverage won't make any difference. As long as Ace cooperates, the government will keep up their end of the bargain. It's going to be a mess, but nothing compared to the fiasco it would have been if he hadn't come to you."

"And of course he's cooperating, right?"

"Oh, yeah. No problem there. At the moment he's lodged in one of our… well, I guess under the present circumstances you'd call it a safe house. It's a condo three blocks from here. Normally it's used to house agents temporarily in D.C. for special events or training."

She smiled.

"It has three bedrooms. Ace is in one, another agent is in one, and guess who is in the third?"

"His self-appointed guardian, Winter Rose."

She nodded. "Winter Rose."

"I need to see both of them for a couple of minutes. Think you can arrange that?"

"Sure. You want to go over there from here? It's a five minute walk."

I nodded.

She picked up the phone and made a short call.

"All set. There's an agent named Connor baby-sitting them now. He says he knows you from yesterday."

I nodded again.

"I remember him."

I leaned back in my chair and stifled a yawn. I'd slept like the dead at the Mayflower after Magnus pressed one of the outrageously priced beers from the suite's mini-bar on me, but you don't recover from serious sleep deprivation in one night.

"So, what's the other good news?" I said, dropping my hand after I managed to get my mouth closed.

She looked chagrined.

"I'm up for a commendation, so it looks like I'm going to be officially out of the doghouse."

"Hey!" I said, coming alive again. "That *is* good news."

I reached across and pulled her close for a hug. She returned the squeeze briefly, then sat up straight again. She smiled, but the look in her eyes was misery.

"And the bad news?"

"I'm being re-assigned – back to DC."

"Oh." I gave her my best ironic grin. "Not all of us consider Savannah to be the doghouse."

She punched me on the shoulder, hard enough to leave a bruise. She didn't have Magnus's horsepower, but her technique was flawless.

"You know what I mean," she said.

I rubbed my arm and said, "OK, OK. That's the bad news, so what's the *more* bad news?"

"Dylan swears he wasn't messing around with blondie."

I didn't say anything. I didn't trust my voice. I tried not

to let my expression give my emotions away. I certainly wasn't entitled to any expectations. All she had said – back there on the Manassas Road – was our time might come yet. What did that mean really? One big "maybe someday" or "wouldn't it be great if?"" So I swallowed my disappointment. It went down like a handful of broken glass. I couldn't forget the way her high voltage kiss had sizzled all the way from my lips to my toes.

We struggled through an awkward moment of silence, then she hurried on to explain.

"Last night we talked for hours. And he convinced me. We decided to start over with a clear slate."

She reached out slowly and put her hand over mine on the table.

"If he's lying, I'll shoot him myself. But I think he's telling the truth. I have to try, RK."

I pulled one hand out and placed it over hers, so that I had her hand in both of mine.

"I know, Al. Follow your heart. Don't worry about me."

Tears welled up in her eyes and slipped down her cheeks. I leaned over and brushed them away, then straightened up.

"It's not like I'll never see you again. And who knows? Maybe someday…"

She smiled, but clamped her mouth shut. Her lower lip trembled and the tears threatened to return.

To change the subject, I said, "I'm going to offer Ace and Winter Rose jobs."

She raised her chin and forced a smile. "Really, RK? Both of them? That's wonderful."

I waved a dismissive hand.

"It won't be make-shift work for either of them. I already have a guy replacing windows and patching holes, but I'm going to rebuild the G-String. Bigger stage, more seating, a second floor for a new office. I hope those two will tackle the whole effort and then run it for me."

Alice smiled, then looked horrified as a thought occurred to her.

"You're not going to make the G-String into a real strip club, are you?"

I laughed.

"Naw. Same as before, just a place for friends to relax and enjoy some good music. I'm going to improve the acoustics, though, and install a better recording system. Word got out after *Blue Jeans and Black Leather* hit the charts and a couple of people have asked about using the G-String to work out some new material."

"Anybody I would recognize?"

I smiled and said, "You'll have to come and see for yourself."

"I will, Roman. Don't you doubt it." She touched my cheek and said, "I'm glad you're taking care of Ace. And Winter Rose, too. I like them both."

"Me, too. But like I said, it's not charity. Don't tell Ace, but I've got a notion that he will be the one using that new office space, not me. I'll probably use the same booth by the bar as my so-called office, but I'd like to see Ace back in the legitimate money managing business. Maybe I can talk him into running a genuine investment service for vets. It really is a good idea, especially for the younger ones. Hey, that reminds me. Would you do one more thing for Ace?"

"Sure," she said. "What is it?"

"After his wife was killed in the car crash and his life went to pieces, Ace lost track of his son, Brett. Would you try to locate him?"

She nodded. "Can you give me a starting point?"

"His full name is Brett Owen Emory. He graduated from the Motorcycle Mechanics Institute in Orlando about a year ago, then he disappeared. He's probably working as a mechanic somewhere, but according to Ace he was determined to cut off contact. He might be anywhere in the country."

"I'll find him," Alice said.

CHAPTER 45

OLLOWING ALICE'S DIRECTIONS, I found the safe house without difficulty. When I knocked on the door, Agent Connor opened it immediately. He gave me a friendly, "Hello," and a handshake, then stepped aside and pointed to the dining room, where Ace and Winter Rose sat eating cereal from plastic bowls.

"I'll be in the back, if you need me," Connor said, discreetly giving us some privacy. As he closed the door to his bedroom, I sat down facing Ace.

The change in him was miraculous. He was sitting up straight and the color was back in his face. Most of all, you could see it in his eyes. For the first time since he stumbled into the G-String, Ace held my gaze without flinching. He looked something like the old Ace again. I glanced at Winter Rose. There was a new calmness about her too.

"I hear they're going to give you a deal, Ace," I said.

His confident look buckled a bit and I realized he had a long way to go yet. Both of them did, I'm sure. Nobody jumps right back up from the kind of disasters they had experienced.

He reached across the table and grabbed my hand with both of his.

"Thanks to you, RK. And Special Agent Cushner. And Magnus." He glanced at Winter Rose and gave her a nod. "And Winter Rose, of course."

I pulled my hand back before he could kiss it.

"That's what friends are for, Ace."

He shook his head.

"It's more than that."

"Nonsense," I said, waving the thought away impatiently. "But, if you feel up to returning a favor, Magnus needs someone to ride his bike back down to Savannah."

"He'd trust me to ride his Harley? His Eloise?"

"Like I said, you'd be doing him the favor."

Ace looked at Winter Rose. I could see enthusiasm for the idea grow in their eyes.

"It would help if you stopped by the Cherokee reservation and returned the night vision goggles we borrowed from Sheriff Silverwood. And I think Silverwood would be very happy to see you, Winter Rose."

A brief smile flickered across her face.

"I should stop by," she said. "He has always looked out for me and I've been… well, I've been absolutely horrid at times."

"Make some time for Maggie Keystone, too. I'm sure she would be delighted to see both of you," I said.

I guessed that Winter Rose hadn't considered that Maggie Keystone would like to meet Ace. She looked surprised at first, but then gave me an emphatic nod.

"We will," she said.

"That's settled, then," I said. I told them the bike was at the Renaissance garage and that Magnus would leave the keys at the front desk. I made sure they knew Magnus was going to be tied up in DC for at least three weeks, so there was no hurry getting back to Savannah.

"Look," I said, "there's something I'd like you to give some thought to while you're riding south." I pointed from one to the other and said, "Both of you."

I told them about my plans for renovating and improving the G-String. I warned them that there was no charity involved, that I expected results. With no hesitation at all, both of them started nodding like bobble-head dolls. I gave Winter Rose my set of keys to the place and the phone number of the contractor I planned to use so they could get started without me.

"I know you don't want to hear how much we are in your debt," Winter Rose said, "but the simple truth is both of us owe you our lives."

She held up a hand to stave off my objection.

"But it's also true that being around you is exciting! It's what I've been missing since I left the Army, minus the military bullshit. No posing, no empty words. You cram each day full to the brim, but somehow it's not work. It's like… it's like a celebration. If I can have more of that, then I'll shovel coal in a dark basement for you."

I looked at Ace.

He simply nodded and said, "Count me in."

To make sure they knew I was serious, I shook hands with both of them. Then I slipped Gilbert Rumsdale's watch out of my pocket and laid it on the table between us.

"The man I used to think of as Uncle Gil was a big fan of John D. MacDonald. Had a collection of all his books in hard cover, many of them signed first editions. Either of you ever read MacDonald's *The Girl, the Gold Watch and Everything*?" I asked.

Ace cocked his head for a moment while he thought about the question. "MacDonald wrote the Travis McGee books, didn't he?" he said, "I've read a couple of those, but I don't remember that one."

"He wrote it before he started on McGee. Back in 1962, actually. It's an amusing story – almost science fiction, but not really."

I turned to my left and looked at Winter Rose.

"How about you, Winter Rose? Ever read it?"

She shook her head.

"Sorry, RK. I guess MacDonald was never on my reading list."

"You both might enjoy it," I said. I picked up the gold watch and idly twisted the winding knob. "I won't give the story away in case you want to read it later, but the main character, Kirby Winter, inherits a gold watch from his late uncle. Kirby discovers that stopping the watch stops time for everyone except the person holding the watch. His uncle used the watch to amass a fortune."blonde

I held the gold watch up with my left hand and let it dangle where all three of us could see it.

"Gilbert Rumsdale owned this watch for most of his life," I said. "From bust to boom."

"And the watch was the secret of his success?" Ace asked, looking even more puzzled now.

"In a way," I said. "Seeing the watch yesterday made me think of what you said back at St. George's, Ace."

"What I said? About what?"

"About tracing the money until you came to a dead end in the Caymans."

"Oh, right," Ace said. "I followed the trail right up to the last bank, but I didn't have the final account number."

I stopped the spin of the watch with my right hand. I opened the back and held it out to Ace.

"What's written on the inside of the case?" I asked.

Ace leaned forward and squinted.

"Made for Patrick S. Rumsdale, July 17, 1919, by Patek, Philippe & Co., Geneva, Switzerland. Number 175…"

Ace grabbed the watch out of my hands and angled it toward the window to get better light.

"Oh my God! The date, July 17, 1919 and the serial number 175046! It fits!"

He looked over at me with the same astonished expression on his face that I imagine was on Kirby Winter's face when he discovered that his uncle's watch would stop time.

"It fits, RK. Twelve digits: 171919175046. That's it! That's got to be the account number in the Cayman Islands."

"I thought it might be," I said. "So how do we find out for sure?"

"I just need a computer and access to the Internet," Ace said.

We all looked around. A Dell laptop was sitting on a card table in the living room.

"Agent Connor said we could use that computer if we wanted," Ace said. "They keep it here for visiting agents."

We moved our chairs over from the dining table and huddled around the computer.

Ace jumped on the Internet and started paging from DC to the Caribbean. While we waited, I passed the watch to Winter Rose. She examined it silently, then shook her head and smiled. She set it down on the table. Ace picked it up immediately. He checked the serial number to make sure he had it right, then entered it on the web page he had accessed. We all held our breath for the twenty seconds it took to verify.

Ace lifted his head suddenly.

"This can't be right!" he said, turning the screen so I could see it clearly.

I read the figure.

"Twenty-one million, six hundred and fifty-six thousand, three hundred and twenty-four dollars and..." he turned the computer back to himself, "fourteen cents."

He pushed himself back in his chair.

"He couldn't have accumulated more than nine million with this veterans scam, RK. Ten, tops."

I said, "I think he's been funneling money into that account for a long time. I think if Virgil and I take a closer look at the inheritance he managed for us until we came of age, we'll find out he siphoned some of that out too." I shrugged. "Other people's money too, but no way to account for any of it now. The early stuff was back in the prehistoric times of paper records and Rumsdale was extremely good at covering his tracks."

"Twenty-one and a half million," Ace said. "What happens to it now?"

I said, "Alice told me that if this money was ever recovered that one way or another it would go to the government. Poured back into the big pot."

Ace thought about it for a moment.

"I think she's right," he said. "It'll go into the general treasury fund. Too bad. Twenty-one million sounds like a lot, but it's parking lot change to the federal government."

I smiled. "I've got another idea," I said. "Find the website for the *Intrepid Fallen Heroes Fund*."

When he had it up, I said, "I've sent them some small

donations in the past, so I checked them out. They have an excellent rating."

"Intrepid Fallen Heroes?" Winter Rose said. "What do they do?"

"Well, up to 2005, they gave money directly to the spouses and children of soldiers killed in the line of duty. The government provides more benefits like that now, so Intrepid Fallen Heroes focused their efforts to rehab, especially for traumatic brain injuries. They put up two big facilities, one at Brooke Army Med Center in Texas and other at Walter Reed National Military Med Center in Maryland, and they're working on a series of satellite facilities as well. Damn near every dollar they get goes directly to help vets."

"So, are you suggesting what I think you're suggesting?" Ace said.

I nodded.

"Make an anonymous donation – a *big* anonymous donation."

Smiling widely, Ace tapped at the keyboard for a couple of minutes. He looked up.

"It's ready to go," he said. "Twenty-one million, six hundred and fifty-six thousand, three hundred and twenty-four dollars and fourteen cents. Untraceable and completely clean, so it won't raise red flags with any auditors." He pointed to the enter button and said, "Just touch this key."

I put my palms up and sat back.

"You send it, Ace."

He took a deep breath and pushed the button. The light in his eyes told me it was the first step on his journey back to life.

I picked up the gold watch and held it out to Ace. He shook his head and pushed it back to me.

"That watch is worth a lot of money, RK."

I turned his hand over, placed the watch on his palm and folded his fingers around it.

"You hang on to it. Maybe it will bring you luck."

Rising from her chair, Winter Rose said, "Luck? I don't think you believe in luck, RK."

I smiled.

"You're right. I believe we make our own luck." I kissed her on the cheek and whispered, "Most of the time."

Ace stood too and we all shook hands. I reminded them that there was no hurry about getting to Savannah and renovating the G-String, then left them together in the safe house.

CHAPTER 46

AFTER I LEFT Ace and Winter Rose, I called Georgetown University Hospital. I was put on hold three times, then a harried sounding woman told me Virgil had already been discharged. No, she didn't know where he'd gone, just that he'd asked for a cab. I stood on the sidewalk and thought for a minute. Then it came to me. I knew where to find him.

I climbed on the Road King and took K Street to 21st NW and rode it south. Some idiot with a cell phone to his ear banged a sudden left in front of me at G Street, but I was riding in full inner city defensive mode and managed not to T-bone his Taurus. I lucked into a parking spot half a block down from C Street. I crossed Constitution on foot and walked down the path to the Vietnam Veterans Memorial.

I stayed back on the grass and worked my way along the wall. I spotted Virgil near the apex. He had his left hand on the marble, as though he was communicating with the stone through his palm. I stepped over the chain and eased my way through the slowly moving line of visitors to stand beside him. When he saw my reflection in the polished stone he dropped his hand and turned my way.

"John McDaniel," Virgil said, nodding at the name etched into the wall.

"That old photo, right?" I said.

Virgil smiled.

"I knew you'd remember, too."

"It wasn't the greatest photo," I said, "but he was smiling and you could see his dimples."

"He was about our height."

"Built about the same, too."

"So, maybe."

"Not if Gilbert had the timing right," I said, "but I guess everything he ever said to us is suspect now, so… maybe."

"I wonder what kind of father John McDaniel would have been."

I traced the name with my own fingers. I remembered Sheriff Silverwood's theory about destiny and the way our lives are interwoven with the lives of others. I shook my head. Thank you for your bravery and sacrifice John McDaniel, I thought. I would like to have known you, maybe even called you "Dad." But life can change direction in a heartbeat and sometimes it screeches to a stop just as quick. Whoever's running the universe sent no dream catcher to bring you back to my mother.

"Come on, Virgil," I said. I turned him away from the wall and we worked our way through the crowd to find a spot on the grass overlooking the memorial.

After we sat I took a close look at him. His hair was clean and neatly combed, but his face was another story. Both lips were split and swollen and his bloodshot left eye barely managed to peek out from beneath a dark, puffy eyebrow that had been partly shaved and closed with three precise stitches. One ear was bandaged with gauze and white tape. Six more black stitches closed up the cut on his left cheekbone. I could see he was going to have a hook-shaped scar more suited to a boxer than a priest.

I slipped my arm around his shoulders.

"Shit, Virgil, I'm sorry."

"About this?" he said, pointing both index fingers at his face. He shook his head slowly, gently probed the corner of his mouth with his tongue.

"Don't worry about me. This will heal. How do *you* feel, Roman?" he said.

"How do *I* feel?"

"Yeah, you. You killed our father twice, you know."

"No," I said, shaking my head. "The first one doesn't count. He wasn't really our father."

"Still," he said, "We thought he was."

He had a point there.

"The truth?" I said.

He nodded and held my eyes to show he was serious. I hesitated. Virgil had agonized over the death of our first "father." I knew the fact that he was a drunken, violent wife beater and child abuser did little to relieve Virgil's feelings. I was glad I had been the one who pulled the trigger, not Virgil. It didn't keep me up nights at all. Neither would this.

"Virgil," I said, "you're going to think I'm making a joke, but I'm not."

He raised an enquiring eyebrow.

"So?"

"The second time was easier."

I didn't say it, but I was thinking Gilbert Rumsdale used me because he didn't have the guts to kill himself. "Suicide by Roman," instead of "suicide by cop." Virgil looked at me steadily without speaking. I knew the implications of Rumsdale's death had already occurred to him too.

He closed his eyes, brought his hands together and tucked his chin against his thumbs. When he finally opened his eyes, he said, "I've prayed for you many times over the years, Roman."

I nodded. Way back then, the man we knew as our father would have killed us if I hadn't killed him. That simple fact satisfied me, but that wasn't enough for Virgil. It was irrational, but "Thou Shalt Not Kill" had been stamped in black and white on his young brain and the tragedy would give him no peace as an adult. I often wondered why we had such different beliefs. We had been dipped in the same vat of religious dye as kids, but Virgil had been colored by it much more than I.

"So senseless!" he said. "All that pain Mom put herself through."

"Not to mention the pain she let us in for," I said.

"All for one mistake."

"Two, if you count us both."

"Can't you be serious for one minute, Roman?"

"I'm just trying to help you move on, Virgil. You're the twin with the tendency to over-think stuff. Me? I feel… unburdened. I – we – carried the weight of our parents' mistakes a long, long way for nothing. No sense fretting over it now. Let's dump it and enjoy walking with a lighter step."

He touched his fingertips to the stiff white collar around his neck.

"Maybe you're right. I'll try not to *over-think* as you put it, but… well, it's going to take some time to clear my head."

"Clear your head of guilt you shouldn't have in the first place? Remember that religions of the world T-shirt I gave you as a joke years ago? What did it say about Catholics? If shit happens I deserve it?"

He laughed.

"Yeah, maybe you're right. Come on, let's go."

Virgil swayed when he stood up. I grabbed his elbow, but he shook me off.

"Stood up too fast, that's all. I'm fine."

I kept my hand out, ready to hold him up. He pushed it gently away.

"Really. I'm fine."

I locked eyes with him and he looked back steadily. I thought I saw a lightness deep inside that I hadn't seen since we were very young. It gave me hope that maybe he really would be able to jettison some of the burden he'd been carrying for more than two decades.

We made our way back to Constitution. A mild breeze blew clusters of soft white clouds across the eastern horizon. Overhead and to the west, the sky was a crisp blue. Yesterday's unseasonable heat had abated and the temperature was a more typical 70°.

I waved a hand toward the Road King.

"I can give you a ride back to Savannah if you want, Virgil. Magnus has a spare helmet we could borrow."

Virgil put out a hand as if to hold the bike at bay and actually took a small step back.

"Thanks," he said, "but I have a flight in... ," he checked his watch, "two and a half hours."

"Ride to the airport?" I said.

"Taxi," he said, indicating the line of three cabs waiting by the curb.

"You need money?" I asked.

He shook his head.

"Amazingly enough, I still have my wallet. I've got some cash, a credit card. I'm fine, Roman, really."

He walked across the road with me and watched as I slipped on my leather jacket, then my helmet and gloves. I twisted the ignition and flipped the run switch, then hit the starter. The Road King rumbled to life between my legs and idled with that classic Harley lumpy cadence.

When I looked up, Virgil bent down and lightly touched his forehead to my helmet.

"Eye to eye," he said.

"Heart to heart," I said.

"Brothers forever," we said together.

Virgil straightened up. He waved for a cab.

"What are you going to do, Roman?" he asked, as the first taxi pulled out of line and glided toward us.

I smiled and kicked the Road King into gear.

"I'm gonna do what clears *my* head," I said. "I'm just gonna ride."

I let the clutch out and headed west.

ACKNOWLEDGEMENTS

Heartfelt thanks to Kathleen Harrigan for her constant support and advice, to Gary T. Mitchell for his encyclopedic firearms expertise (any mistakes in that regard are mine alone) and to Maureen Broderick, Betty Broderick and Michael Edwards whose enthusiastic endorsements of Roman Keane and his friends helped me keep moving ahead.

Cover Art by Damonza
Editing by Bubblecow
Author Photo by Michael Edwards

Made in the USA
San Bernardino, CA
22 December 2019